The Detonation Series! – Book 1

# FIFTY

Eldon H. Kellogg

ISBN: 9781983026423

Chapter 1

"O divine art of subtlety and secrecy! Through you we learn to be invisible, through you inaudible; and hence, we can hold the enemy's fate in our hands."

Sun Tzu (~520 BC)


Yan Longwei sat alone in his darkened living room and played the VHS tape over and over. Each time, the grainy black and white film showed an aerial view of the Japanese city. Each time, a bright flash was followed by a billowing cloud reaching for the heavens like an angry, glowing fist. His wife and daughter were asleep, unaware that he was haunted by this scene of tens of thousands of deaths.

"Millions would die; not thousands, but I have no choice. I have a duty to my country," he told himself, as he ran the tape back, and played it once more.

As the Hiroshima weapon detonated, he glanced at his watch. It was 1 AM and time to leave.


San Francisco, California, USA
Pier 19
July 10, 1992, 0120 hours PST


"It never rains this time of year. Why tonight?" Longwei said, as he drove his truck behind Warehouse 4.

Sleep had eluded him for two days. The fact that the summons had come, after all these years, had left him stunned and afraid.

"I am Chinese. I have an assignment. I must do my duty to the Motherland," Longwei said aloud, as the warehouse door lifted, and he backed his truck into the dry loading bay.

As the door lowered shut, he placed the truck into park and set the brake. His hands were shaking so hard that he almost dropped the ancient bronze coin as he pulled it from his shirt pocket. He had possessed this coin for 12 years. It had become an afterthought, until two days ago.

He heard a tapping noise, glanced to his left, and saw the muzzle of an AK-47 pressed against the glass. He smiled, bowed several times, and cranked down the window.

"The sun always rises on the Chinese empire," Longwei said, as he presented the coin to the man holding the AK-47.

The man took the coin, and handed it to another man standing behind him.

The tall man stepped into Longwei's view while he studied the coin and asked, "And where is the Chinese Empire?"

"Everywhere," Longwei answered.

"Stay in the truck. I'll let you know when the loading is complete," the other man ordered.

Longwei nodded and bowed several more times.

"We trust this shipment to him? He looks like he's ready to piss himself," Cheng Li said, as the two men walked away.

"He will be escorted. Just follow the plan. Give him the coin back. It is his to keep until the package has been installed. To do otherwise would be bad luck. When all is complete you are to retrieve the coin. It must be sent back to its owner," Lung Shen said, as he handed the coin to Cheng Li.

Longwei kept his head down, staring at his shaking hands.

"*Just get through tonight. Everything will get back to normal after this. This is just a precaution to protect our country. I must do my duty,*" Longwei told himself, as he felt the truck sag as a great weight was added to the back.

"*They will help me unload the package, make sure it is stored properly and then leave. Nothing will ever happen . . . nothing, and I will have fulfilled my duty to my homeland,*" Longwei thought, as he heard the rear door slam shut.

4

He jumped when Cheng Li appeared at his window.

"Follow the plan Yan Longwei. That is all you have to do. Drive back to your restaurant. My men are in the back. They will secure the package and build the wall. Then they will disappear, and you will go back to cooking and raising your family," Cheng Li said, as he handed the coin back to Longwei.

Longwei bowed several more times as he took the coin, and went to return it to his shirt pocket. He missed, the coin bounced off his thigh, and landed at his feet. As he reached for it, his seat belt jerked him upright. He jumped as the warehouse door rose letting in the sound and the smell of the rain.

"On your way now and drive carefully. It's still raining," Cheng Li cautioned, as he banged on the driver's door of the truck.

Longwei bowed, cranked up the window, and started the truck. As he put it into gear, it lurched forward and stalled. He glanced at the man with the AK-47 who was shaking his head. Longwei took a deep breath as he restarted the truck. Then he shifted the truck into first, and let up on the clutch. He shifted into second as the truck cleared the warehouse entrance, and turned on his headlights and wipers.

"That is the best China has; a restaurant owner?" Cheng Li asked, as the truck disappeared into the heavy rain.

"That's the beauty of it, my friend. Who would ever suspect a little xiaoqiang like that of hiding a nuclear weapon in the shed behind his restaurant," Lung Shen said, as the warehouse door slammed shut.

Longwei drove through the abandoned streets near the port. His restaurant was only three miles away, but the trip seemed to take an eternity.

"Why is every light red? It's the middle of the night, every light should be green," Longwei said, as he left Pier 19, and turned left on Embarcadero.

He stalled the truck again, and began cursing in Chinese as he restarted the truck. His heart was beating so hard that he could feel the pounding in his chest.

"Left on Washington, left on Drumm, right on California, and head for the restaurant," Longwei said, as the wipers tried to keep the downpour off the windshield.

"Four red lights in a row! Deep breath, Longwei, deep breath, almost home," he said, as he turned left on 9th Avenue.

5

The driveway that led to his brick storage building was narrow. The only illumination was from a street light twenty yards down the street.

"I've backed down this alley a thousand times. I can do this in my sleep," Longwei said, as he passed the driveway, and swung the rear end into the narrow opening between buildings.

"That's it, careful. If I hit Mrs. Kau's house she'll wake up, and be in the road with an umbrella cursing at me," Longwei said, as he lined up the truck and checked both mirrors.

"I can't see a thing," he muttered, as he glanced out both side windows.

"Relax, it's centered," he said, as he began backing down the alley.

"Fifty feet, stop, get out and check, then open the doors and back in five feet. You've rehearsed this. Just do it," Longwei told himself, as he squeezed the large panel truck between the buildings.

"That should do it," he said, as he set the parking brake and leapt from the truck.

He didn't notice the small bronze coin fall from the truck, bounce once, and settle against the brick wall of the back of his restaurant. Removing the padlock from the doors, he swung them both open, climbed back into the truck, and backed it five feet into the building.

He raised the rear gate on the truck, and found a pistol staring him in the face.

"We are here. Everything is ready," Longwei said, as he bowed several times.

"Forklift?" the fat man asked.

"Back there, under the tarp. The key is in the ignition," Longwei answered, as he backed away.

The man gestured to two other men, and they headed for the forklift.

"This will do," the fat man said, as he walked around the building.

"Brick, no windows, just this one door," the fat man observed, as he walked over to two cubes of cinderblocks, bags of mortar mix, a large tub with jugs of water standing beside it, and tools lying beside them.

The sound of the forklift cranking up reverberated inside the building as others removed the tarp from the package still resting inside the bed of the truck.

"Bring the forklift, now" the fat man ordered.

"Gently, gently, get the forks under the pallet. All the way in, then up, be careful it's heavy," he directed, as the forks slid under the steel pallet.

"Up, up, now be careful as you back up," the fat man said, as he backed away from the package.

Longwei stood outside in the rain. Thunder and lightning tore through the heavens above him as the package slid from the bed of his truck. The package was encased inside a wooden crate, a crate that would live in his dreams for the remainder of his life.

"Place it against the back wall. You two start mixing the mortar, quickly now," the fat man told two of his crew, as they crouched in the back of the truck.

An hour later it was over. Longwei's storage building was now six feet shorter on the inside than it had been. The shelving that had been moved away from the old wall was now reinstalled against the new wall.

"Good, the shelving completely covers the wall. Now hurry, and reload the shelves, and be careful not to bang the new wall. The mortar hasn't set up yet," the fat man said, as he directed the other workers.

"Longwei, come here," the fat man ordered, as he gestured for Longwei to come in out of the rain.

"Longwei, you have done well. You have proven your loyalty to the Party and the Motherland. Go dry off, and go back to cooking dim sum. Have a good life," the fat man said, as he exchanged bows with the sodden Longwei.

Longwei bowed once more, and noticed that his hands had stopped shaking. He felt relieved that it was over. After all these years of waiting for this night, it was over.

"One more thing, Longwei, give me the bronze coin. It must be returned to its owner," the fat man said.

Longwei began to search his pockets, but couldn't find the coin.

"I think I've lost it," Longwei replied, as he ran over to his truck, and began searching for the coin.

A minute later he was dragged from the truck, and thrown to the ground in front of the fat man. He could hear two men rummaging through the cab of the truck as they looked for the coin.

"Longwei, if the coin is lost, it reflects on me. I will be punished for this failure," the fat man said, and kicked Longwei in the ribs.

He was kicking him again when the two men exited the truck and shook their heads. The fat man grabbed Longwei by the front of his sodden shirt and dragged him to his feet.

"When I was younger I had a violent temper. My mother used to say, ' If you are patient in one moment of anger, you will escape a hundred days of sorrow.' So I will not kill you for your stupidity, Longwei. We will depart as comrades. Keep the silence, and do not disappoint the Motherland," the fat man said, as he released Longwei, and bowed ever so slightly.

.    .    .    .

Unknown to all, a young pair of eyes peered out through the blinds in the upstairs bathroom on the back of the restaurant. Lihwa was his daughter and only child. At ten years old, she had sharp eyes and a sharper mind.

# Chapter 2

"The skillful leader subdues the enemy's troops without any fighting; he captures their cities without laying siege to them; he overthrows their kingdom without lengthy operations in the field."

Sun Tzu (~520 BC)

Beijing, China
22 Base Headquarters
100 meters below the Beijing Botanical Gardens
October 1, 2013, 0730 hours CT-China Time

Lieutenant General Kung Yusheng sat behind a battered oak desk. The previous owner had been Japanese Lieutenant General Masaharu Homma of the Imperial Japanese Army. The initial owner had been General Douglas MacArthur. MacArthur had used the desk prior to his evacuation from Corregidor on 12 March 1942. Homma had taken the desk as a souvenir. His family had kept it after his execution by the Americans in 1946. His connection to the Bataan Death March had left the Americans in a less than forgiving mood. Lieutenant General Kung had purchased the desk at auction in 1982.

"Comrade Lieutenant General, we have received a package from the United States. It has the number 42 on the back," Colonel Peng Zihao, said with a slight bow as he stood in the doorway of Lieutenant General Kung's office.

Kung unlocked a drawer on the left side of the desk and removed a small metal box. It was an old tin of Edgeworth sliced pipe tobacco from 1941. It had come with the desk. He set the tin on the desk and gestured for Colonel Peng to enter the room.

Peng entered and shut the door. Despite all their precautions they knew that one word heard by the wrong set of ears would be their undoing. He placed the small package in the center of the desk and stepped back.

"Fourth one this year, Comrade Lieutenant General. The Americans are becoming more cautious, but the southern border and ports are still open," Peng said.

He was nervous, despite the many years that he had worked as Lieutenant General Kung's aide.

"Yes, the Americans have a saying about closing the barn doors after the horses have already fled," Kung replied, as he removed a cotton cloth and an old steel pocket knife from the pen drawer of the desk. The blade was engraved with an Iron Cross.

He examined the markings on the package, and then began to slice through the layers of wrapping paper. Setting these aside he found a small wooden box sealed with a dark red wax. Hand carved into the wax was the Chinese character for 'sun'.

"Beautiful wood, a claro walnut burl from Oregon or northern California," Kung observed, while cutting through the wax seal using the antique German army knife.

The knife had belonged to General Erwin Rommel in 1942 while campaigning in North Africa. Kung wiped the blade, folded it, and placed the blade and cloth back inside the desk.

"The significance of this moment is never lost on me, Peng. It never gets old," Kung said, as he stared at the two boxes sitting before him on the battered surface of the desk.

He carefully lifted the top from the tin box and set it aside. Next he lifted the top from the walnut box.

"Exquisite wood and the craftsman had enough sense not to ruin it by carving the surface. Chinese craftsmen seem compelled to carve every surface they touch," Kung said, as he studied the beautiful grain and satin finish.

Setting the top aside, he picked up the box and glanced at the item inside.

"I remember this one, Emperor Wen, 175 BC. The condition is remarkable, near mint considering the age of the coin. Both the square hole and the edge are rimmed, very rare indeed," Kung said, as he removed the ancient bronze coin from the box.

"Over 2100 years old, my friend. This coin was cast soon after China first became a unified country. Perhaps we will cast a coin when we have unified the world," Lieutenant General Kung said, as he studied the ban liang coin.

"Burn the walnut box and the wrappings. There must be no trace, no record, as usual," Kung ordered, as he continued to study the coin.

"Of course, General," Peng replied, as he bowed, and retrieved the box and wrappings.

"Don't forget the wax," Kung added, as he brushed the wax toward the front of the desk.

"Yes, General," Peng said, as he removed every trace of the package, box and wax from the desk.

With another bow he left the room and Lieutenant General Kung with his thoughts.

"One more coin," Kung mused, as he gently placed the coin on top of the growing pile in the Edgeworth tin box.

"I was a young man when we started this. So much risk the first time. I really thought the Americans would catch us and that would be the end of it. Now . . . 42 . . . we are almost there. A few more critical placements and we will have them. It becomes more difficult with the passing of each year. The Americans are wary, but they can't stop the flow of our goods into their country. They can't even stop the flow of illegal people into their country," Kung said, while lifting the lid of the tin box and staring at the faded inscription on the inside. Then he read it aloud.

"Save this tin. It has many handy uses. Larus and Brothers Company Inc., Richmond, Virginia, U.S.A.," Kung said, and smiled at the irony.

Chapter 3

"To secure ourselves against defeat lies in our own hands, but the opportunity of defeating the enemy is provided by the enemy himself."

Sun Tzu (~520 BC)

Manassas, Virginia, USA
Mission Center for Weapons and Counterproliferation
Central Intelligence Agency
November 8, 2016, 0945 hours EST

"Good morning, Amanda! Did you go vote this morning? Wow, based on your work area it looks like you've settled in to stay," Markus said, as he leaned around the corner of Amanda Langford's cubicle.

"Well, a few plants and a few pictures cuts down on the industrial look. I'm surprised the Agency still uses cubicles. The concept is a little outdated and no, I'm going to go vote tonight after work," Amanda replied, as she crawled out from under her desk.

"Second day on the job and already cracking on the Agency," Markus quipped, as he stepped into the cubicle and helped Amanda off the floor.

"It's not that! I just expected everything to be the best and latest tech. Nothing's wireless. I still haven't figured out where all the cables go," Amanda said, as she brushed off her slacks.

"If that's what you were looking for you should have hired on at Apple or Google. The Agency is 'old school' and that goes for most of the resources too," Markus said, as he lowered his voice and looked around.

"But trust me, the tech's here. It's just not available to everyone," Markus said, as he handed Amanda a multi-plug outlet strip.

"I've been looking for one of those. I was going to go out and buy one on the way home," Amanda remarked, as she snatched the multi-plug out of Markus' hand.

"Yeah, tech support holds on to these things like they were gold plated. The guy beside me moved out and his wound up in one of my drawers somehow," Markus said, as Amanda ducked back under her desk.

"Looks like you're still busy. I'll catch you later," Markus said, as he admired the view of Amanda working under her desk.

"Good morning, Markus. Based on the fact that you're not in your cubicle am I to understand that the two projects that you're working on are nearing completion?" Janet Davidson asked, as she walked up to Markus and looked into Amanda's cubicle.

"Umm . . . no, Ms. Davidson, at least the end of next week. I was going to duck out and vote and then get back to work," Markus replied, as he smiled and quickly backed away.

"Vote on your own time, Markus. I want those reports completed by the end of this week. Is that understood?" Ms. Davidson said.

"Markus, you don't happen to have another spare power . . ." Amanda began, as she reappeared from under her desk.

"Oh, Ms. Davidson, I was just hooking up . . . some equipment," Amanda said, as she stood up.

"Ms. . . . . Langford. I'm glad to see that you finally showed up for work. I was beginning to wonder if you had decided to take another position," Janet said, as she read Amanda's ID badge.

"Sorry, ma'am, but I believe I mentioned that it would be six weeks before I could start when you interviewed me," Amanda said.

"I vaguely remember the interview. By the way, we do have tech support personnel that work for the agency. They actually prefer to set up everything themselves. They keep a list of all devices hooked into our systems," Janet said, as she stared down at the diminutive young woman in front of her.

Janet Davidson was from Wisconsin and a retired Marine Corps Lieutenant Colonel. At six-foot-two and 170 pounds, there were few people in the Mission Center for Weapons and Counterproliferation (MCWC) that she didn't intimidate.

"Yes, ma'am, I know that, but they couldn't get to me until tomorrow and I didn't want to sit around and twiddle my thumbs until then," Amanda said, immediately regretting the tone of her voice.

"First of all I'm not in the Marines anymore. You may address me as Ms. Davidson or Assistant Director Davidson, but not 'ma'am'. Is that understood?" Janet said, as she leaned over the five-foot-three Amanda.

"Sorry, it's just a sign of respect we use for our elders back home," Amanda said, and forced herself to not look down at her feet.

"When I was a . . . younger woman . . . I was a Marine. I thought that I had left behind the days of dealing with young girls that still had the smell of the farm on them," Janet said, as she locked eyes with the young woman.

"Ms. Davidson or Assistant Director Davidson, I may have grown up on a farm in North Carolina, Page Farms outside Raleigh in fact. We grew strawberries, blueberries and pumpkins, but I graduated first in my class at Broughton High School, the highest rated high school in the state. I had to get up every morning at 4AM to catch a bus into the city, and had a perfect attendance record. I graduated Magna Cum Laude from North Carolina State University with a BS in Nuclear Engineering and a BA in International Studies. I speak Mandarin, Korean and Japanese and will complete my Masters from George Washington in Modern Chinese Military History next year with a specialty in their Nuclear Weapons Programs. So I am not fresh from the farm!" Amanda said, and began wondering how long it would take her to get another job.

"Good! You may look like a puppy, but you don't roll over like one," Janet replied, and smiled.

"After you finish hooking up all your equipment call IT and tell them I said you need Level 3 access immediately. While you're waiting, read this file. It's in Chinese. The last page contains a file name and location that you'll need Level 3 to read. Come to my office on the 9th floor tomorrow morning at 0800. I want a detailed analysis of what you think. Any questions? Good, I'll see you tomorrow morning," Janet ordered, as she turned and walked away.

Amanda stared at the woman's broad shoulders as she walked away and took a deep breath. She glanced at the folder in her hand and threw it on her desk, then dropped onto her knees and crawled back under her desk.

"First things first," Amanda said, as she began plugging things into the multi-plug.

. . . .

"So what do you think, Janet?" Caleb McElroy asked, as he stared out the ninth floor window.

"If I didn't think she was the right person then I wouldn't have hired her, but we'll find out for sure tomorrow morning," Janet said, as she stood beside the CIA Director of the Mission Center for Weapons and Counterproliferation.

"I really hope you're wrong about this. I really fucking hope you're wrong," Caleb said, as he sipped on his glass of 10-year-old Laphroaig scotch whiskey.

. . . .

It was 4AM. Amanda had been staring at her dual screens and the file alternately for over twenty minutes. Her mind whirled as she continued to run the data back and forth in her mind.

"This can't be right. Why would she give this to me? This is some kind of a test to see if I'll draw the wrong conclusions. She wants to see if I'm just a redneck country girl who'll follow the wrong lead. It has to be. It just has to be," Amanda said, as she massaged her temples.

"It's way too much material and there are other things, other pieces that scare the shit out of me. This can't be real. It has to be a test," Amanda said, as she laid her head on her desk and fell asleep.

Chapter 4

"Do you want to know who you are? Don't ask. Act! Action
will delineate and define you."

Thomas Jefferson

Manassas, Virginia, USA
Mission Center for Weapons and Counterproliferation
Central Intelligence Agency
November 9, 2016, 0759 hours EST

"Interesting, she never left the building last night. Well, at least
she's dedicated," Janet said, as she studied the building's security
access files on her phone.

"Like most of our work the information is open to
interpretation. My opinion is still North Korea. I never have bought
into the Abdul Qadeer Khan story. I think that was just a cover for the
Chinese providing the North Koreans with nuclear material," Caleb
said, as he stood at Janet's office window on the ninth floor.

"Now how is it that you have a better view than I do, and I'm
your boss?" Caleb asked, as he took another sip from his morning
coffee.

"First come, first served. I moved in before you did. Plus, I
stay on your good side so you haven't thrown me out yet," Janet
replied, as she reviewed the files she had given Amanda the day
before.

"Do you ever put that thing down? Sometimes I think you're a
20- something in disguise," Caleb said, as he glanced over Janet's
shoulder.

"Either keep up with the tech or the '20-something' will wind
up as your boss. Sometimes it scares me how much information I can
access on this thing," Janet said, as she heard a knock on the door.

"0800, right on time. Now we'll see how she functions without
a lot of sleep. Come in," Janet said.

Junior Analyst Amanda Langford opened the door and stepped into the room. She had expected to see Assistant Director Davidson, but was surprised to see their boss, Caleb McElroy, Director of the MCWC, sitting across from her.

"*A bit disheveled, bags under her eyes and an odd look on her face. She's afraid of something,*" Janet thought, as Amanda pulled a laptop from her shoulder bag.

"Good morning, Ms. Langford. Director McElroy and I have discussed the file I gave you, and he's interested to see what conclusions you have come to. Please, have a seat and proceed," Janet said.

Amanda could feel her hands shaking as she nodded and hooked her laptop into the display link built into the table. She wasn't sure if it was fear or the three cups of coffee that she had had in the last hour.

"Good morning Director McElroy, Assistant Director Davidson. At your request I have reviewed the file that you gave me yesterday. As you know it deals with the production of weapons grade U-235 and Pu-239 by the People's Republic of China from 1964 to 2010. Due to the extreme secrecy of the Chinese in this matter it has always been extremely difficult to accurately estimate the total amount of fissile material that they have produced over this extended time period," Amanda began, and felt herself begin to calm down as the presentation continued.

.    .    .    .

Five minutes into the presentation Amanda glanced up and saw that Director McElroy had turned in his chair and was staring out the window. Assistant Director Davidson was drumming the table with her fingers. The look on her face had only one interpretation . . . disappointment. Amanda knew that she had one minute to impress this pair or she would be forever relegated to grunt work within the Agency.

"I can continue to bore you with the history of Site 22 and PLA Missile Forces, but your time is far more valuable than mine so I'll jump to my conclusions," Amanda said, and felt her heart pounding in her chest, as she abandoned her carefully constructed presentation.

"There seems to be a substantial amount of highly enriched uranium (HEU) missing from known Chinese inventories," Amanda said, as she laid her career on the table.

Director McElroy spun his chair back to the table and asked, "And what is your basis for that conclusion?"

"Our previous estimates of their historical production capacity are underestimated by at least six percent. That's assuming they don't have production sites that we haven't discovered," Amanda said.

"And your basis for the six percent?" Assistant Director Davidson asked.

"The Heping gaseous diffusion plant is supposed to have shut down in October of 1987. Our records of the site's energy usage agree with that timeline. However, the power plant that provided energy to the site did not decrease output for an additional two and a half years. Where did the energy go? I suspect that the site had additional production capacity that international observers weren't aware of," Amanda said.

"Some would say that the additional material wound up in North Korea and is the source for their material," McElroy said.

"Director, all nuclear detonations have a unique signature that betrays the point of manufacture of the nuclear material. The North Korean detonations have been a mixture of domestic material and Chinese. Based on the estimated yields of the North Korean detonations and the typical isotopic fingerprints of the Heping product, the excess material from Heping has been diverted to other uses. It didn't wind up in North Korea," Amanda said.

"Based on your estimates, how much weapons grade HEU are we talking about?" Assistant Director Davidson asked.

"Approximately a ton . . . more or less," Amanda said.

"Our estimate for their total national production from all their gaseous diffusion plants has always been around sixteen tons. Now you're suggesting that there may be a missing ton of weapons grade HEU?" Director McElroy asked.

"Yes Director, that's my best estimate," Amanda said, as she wiped her sweaty palms together.

"How many devices could they make with that amount of material?" Director McElroy asked.

"It would depend on the size of the devices and when they were manufactured. Older nuclear devices used more HEU to make them work due to the lack of sophistication of the overall design of the weapon. Over the decades the devices have become more and more efficient. Meaning, they need less material to get the same or greater yield. So depending on the desired yield, somewhere between twenty and sixty devices" Amanda said.

Director McElroy stood, walked over to a side table and refreshed his coffee. He then walked over to the window and began staring outside.

"I think we're finished here, Amanda. I trust you haven't discussed this information with anyone else?" Janet asked.

"No ma'am . . . Assistant Director Davidson, I haven't discussed this with anyone else," Amanda said, as she shutdown her laptop and prepared to leave.

"Excellent work, Ms. Langford. We'll be in touch," Director McElroy said, as he returned to the window.

"Thank you, Sir," Amanda said, as she nodded to the Assistant Director and left the room.

"I can't believe none of our analysts looked at energy usage," McElroy said, as the door closed.

"They all did. They didn't look at energy usage after Heping shut down. I didn't catch it either, and I spent a month looking at their procurement and processing system from ore to final product. Based on other indications that have popped up over the years, we both knew something wasn't right. With this piece of data . . . we may have twenty to sixty devices unaccounted for," Janet said, as she took off her glasses and began massaging her temples.

"So . . . if we have twenty to sixty devices unaccounted for . . . where are they?" McElroy said.

"And that, Sir, is the hundred thousand dollar question," Janet said, as she walked around her boss, and stood beside him at the window.

# Chapter 5

"Security against defeat implies defensive tactics; ability to defeat the enemy means taking the offensive."

Sun Tzu (~520 BC)

San Francisco, California, USA
Fire Station 31
March 11, 2017, 2030 hours PST


Jamar swore that his head had just touched the pillow when the alarm bell went off.

"Shit! Not again. That's the third alarm this shift. If I catch one of these damn kids tripping fire alarms I'm going to wrap them in an empty hose and then pressurize it," Jamar said, as he jumped into his fireman's boots, stood up, and slipped the pants suspenders over his shoulders.

"The anaconda! I like it!" Heather said, as she ran past him and headed for the fire pole.

"Girl's fast, you gotta give her that," Tom said, still rubbing sleep from his eyes and sitting on the edge of his cot.

"And you better get your old ass moving or Chief Moore will have you polishing the drive train on No. 2 again," Jamar said, as he trotted over to the pole.

"Right behind you," Tom replied, as he worked the kinks out of his neck while stepping into his boots.

"Come on, Tom! Moore's already yelling," Jamar said, as he slid down the pole.

Tom Jackson sighed as he pulled up his pants, secured the suspenders, and strolled over to the fire pole. He'd been a professional fire fighter for 24 years. He'd been a veteran when the chief was a rookie, and his attitude showed his disdain for his co-workers.

"Come on Chief, you know this is another false alarm. We haven't had a building fire in over two months," Tom said, as he slid into the front seat of No. 2 beside Chief Walter Moore.

"Tell that to the owner of Good Luck Dim Sum. His business was burning down while we sat waiting on you for over two minutes. I'm writing this one up Tom. Your shit's starting to wear thin and the union won't protect you forever," Walter said, as he turned on the siren and pulled out of Station 31.

"That place is over on Clement, four blocks away. We'll be there in three minutes," Tom said, as he reached inside his jacket pockets and removed his gloves.

"I'll stop at the corner outside of See's Candies. The hydrant's there. You and Jamar off load hose, and hook into the hydrant. It's about two hundred feet to the store front. The report said it's a kitchen fire that's gotten out of control. If we don't get this quick the whole block will go and we'll go from a one alarm to a three alarm real quick," Walter ordered, as he headed up 12<sup>th</sup> Street and turned right onto Clement.

"Hoses? That's a rookie's job. Heather should be doing that," Tom said.

"The rookie was the first one on the engine. You were last. Just hook up the fucking hose and do as you're told," Walter said, as they sped down Clement.

Smoke was obscuring their vision as they pulled up in front of See's and began offloading equipment.

.   .   .   .

"I told you this was going to be good. Here comes the fire department," Angela Chin, field reporter for KPIX5 said, as she slapped the arm of her cameraman, Alton Stopen.

"Chill, girl, I'm filming the fire. We'll need some lead in footage," Alton said, as he slowly panned across the block by the Chinese restaurant.

"I heard this come up on the police scanner and I just had a feeling," Angela said, as she positioned herself between the camera and the fire down the street.

"Alton, you ready? Please tell me you're ready. This backdrop is great," Angela said, as she checked the fall of her hair and practiced her award winning smile.

"On you girl, we're live in 3 . . . 2 . . . 1, go," Alton said.

"This is Angela Chin, with KPIX5 Alive, live from a massive fire on Clement Street. It would seem that a local restaurant is experiencing a catastrophic fire that may threaten the entire neighborhood," Angela said, as a fire truck screeched to a halt right beside her.

.  .  .  .

"Heather and I are going inside to check it out. You and Jamar gear up and then run the hose outside the building and wait on overwatch," Walter yelled as he slipped on his Scott Pack.

Heather stood beside him already dressed for a live entry into the fire area. She carried a large fire extinguisher in one hand and a large Streamlight Vulcan flashlight in the other.

"Okay, check me out," Walter asked, as he finished tightening his helmet.

"Forgot to turn on your Life Flasher," Heather said, as she pressed the on button of the safety device hanging from the web gear of Walter's Scott Pack.

The Life Flasher gave off a constant bright strobe that was visible even in dense smoke. It allowed fire fighters to find each other if they became separated in a burning building.

Walter glanced up the street and saw Jamar connecting the hose to the hydrant. Tom wasn't wearing his Scott Pack and his helmet was lying on the ground beside him.

.  .  .  .

"Jesus, lady! Get the hell out of the way. You're standing beside the fire hydrant, Jamar yelled, as he shoved the reporter aside.

"Hey, asshole, I'm live here. First amendment rights. The people have a right to know what's going on," Angela said, as she regained her balance.

"They got a right not to burn to death too," Jamar Stevens said, as he began spinning the plug out of the fire hydrant.

"Alton, move on the other side of the fire truck. We'll film from the middle of the street. It'll be a better angle," Angela said, as she flipped off Jamar and began moving around the back of the fire truck.

"Much better angle, more dramatic. We're live in 3 . . . 2 . . . 1, live," Alton said.

"This is Angela Chin, with KPIX5 Alive, live from a massive fire on Clement Street. It would seem that a local restaurant is experiencing a catastrophic fire that may threaten the entire neighborhood," Angela said, as he began to stroll down the street towards the fire.

"As you can see SFPD has arrived on scene along with the brave men and women fire fighters from Fire Station 31," Angela said, as she glanced at the markings on the fire truck.

"It looks like two of the fire fighters are preparing to enter the burning building, while the other two are running a hose in support," Angela said, while stepping closer to the front of the building.

.  .  .  .

Walter and Heather were heading for the front door when a police officer ran up to them and shouted in Walter's ear.

"One of the worker's from the restaurant says the owner is still in there. He's an old man in his 60's," the officer said.

"How about the rest of the family?" Walter asked.

"Two grown children live with the old man. His wife's deceased. More family live six blocks north. We sent the two young adults there. They didn't want to leave, but we escorted them out," the officer replied.

"We'll find the father. Clear the buildings on this block and keep everyone back and call for more fire support. We're going to need more help to keep this from spreading to adjacent buildings," Walter yelled, as Heather opened the front door.

As Heather held the door Walter installed a door wedge. The narrow restaurant was already filled with white smoke and visibility was only five feet.

Jamar and Tom ran up dragging the charged hose. Tom still wasn't dressed and his helmet lay up the street by the hydrant.

After signaling for Heather to wait, Walter grabbed Tom by his coat and jerked his face towards him.

"What happened to you? You used to be a great firefighter. Now you're just a liability. Union or no union I'm going to run you out of this department. Get your shit together," Walter said, as he pushed Tom away.

"Jamar, you're the nozzle man. Tom's your back up," Walter ordered, as he turned, picked up the second fire extinguisher, and gestured for Heather to head into the building.

Tom was left staring at their backs as they disappeared into the billowing smoke.

Jamar jerked on his arm and said, "You're helmet's back at the hydrant."

Tom glanced up the street, saw the helmet, and shook his head as he began jogging up the street. The wail of sirens increased as more police arrived on site and began clearing out people on both sides of the block. He knew that more fire support wouldn't be far behind.

. . . .

Walter rested his left hand on Heather's Scott Pack as they worked their way into the restaurant. He knew that the kitchen would be in the back. If they were lucky this was no more than a grease fire that had gotten out of control.

. . . .

"Angela, you're getting too close. If there's a blowout we've got a problem," Alton said, over their private comm link.

"As you can see the two fire fighters are entering the building with the woman taking the lead position," Angela said, as she stepped a few feet closer.

Angela Chin was fifteen feet from the front of the restaurant when the explosion shattered the front window. She and Alton were caught up in the blast and pelted with fragments of glass. KPIX5 Alive went to a scene of feet running by through shattered glass and smoldering fragments of wood. The station cut to a commercial.

. . . .

The sudden explosion threw Walter and Heather onto their backs. Heather lay sprawled across his legs as his eyes opened up. Walter was staring up at a rollover walking across the ceiling. He had seen them before and it was like the fire had become a living thing. For a second he was mesmerized until Heather began to groan.

Walter pulled his legs from under Heather and began to stand up. It was like rising up into an oven. He dropped to his knees, then grabbed Heather by the harness on her Scott Pack and began dragging her back toward the entrance. Wooden tables around them burst into flame as the temperature in the building reached the ignition point. Walter grimaced as he tried to use his right arm to move debris out of his way. From his training he knew that the shoulder was dislocated, or something was torn or broken inside.

"Crap, we're in the shits," Walter groaned, as the heat intensified.

He glanced up and the fire seemed to be smiling at him as tendrils of fire began to descend towards them. He began to pull Heather again while using his head and shoulder to move flaming debris out of his way.

Walter smiled as he suddenly felt a cone of water cascade across his body. He looked up and the flames seemed to scream at him as they were forced to retreat. He blinked and the flames were replaced by Tom's eyes staring down at him through the faceplate of his Scott mask. Jamar crouched at his shoulder as he played the cone shaped spray of water across the interior of the narrow building.

The second explosion knocked them all back to the ground. Jamar's hand had slammed the bale on the nozzle forward and shut off the flow of water. Once again Walter found himself flat on his back. The rollover had intensified and the fire racing across the ceiling wasn't smiling at him anymore. It was screaming in rage. The fire thrust downward at his face only to be beaten back again by a wall of water. This time Tom held the nozzle and the lifesaving cone of protective water.

"Find the old man. He might still be alive back there," Walter yelled, as he shifted his weight and began to drag Heather toward the exit.

"You're fucking crazy! He's gotta be dead," Tom said, as he narrowed the cone and beat the rollover back towards the kitchen.

"Find the old man, asshole! It's what we do," Walter yelled, as Jamar reached past him and dragged the unconscious form of Heather over his legs.

Tom crouched over the trio and maintained a shield of protective water as Jamar dragged Heather and Walter out of the inferno.

Glancing back, Tom saw Jamar remove both injured fire fighters from the entrance and began to stalk the inferno that blazed to his front.

"Fuck you demon! I know your weakness . . . water. Without the heat you're just an illusion. I've seen you before. So has Walter, but I'm not afraid of you," Tom screamed, as he checked the remaining pressure on his breathing air.

"Sixty percent, bitch, you're mine if all you've got is a couple of propane tanks," Tom said, as he began stepping forward while maintaining the cone of protective water that filled the narrow building.

Flames filled the cone, desperately trying to reach him. He smiled as he sensed the weakness of this fire borne demon.

"You can't pass the water. Dead or alive I'll find the old man and you can't stop me," Tom said, as he reached the area of the kitchen.

Tom glanced over the smoldering counter and then glanced behind him to verify that the fire had not reignited behind him. He knew that other firefighters would have arrived on scene by now and would be throwing water into the upper stories of the restaurant.

The fire began to weaken. Tom knew from experience that he needed to vent the building and allow the smoke to dissipate from the building. He kicked open the back door and smiled as the smoke began to billow out through the exit.

"No heat, no fire," Tom said, as he turned, narrowed the hose stream, and began to hose down the interior of the restaurant.

"Now where's the old man?" Tom asked, as he shut down the stream and began to look around the inside of the building.

Glancing backward he saw two other firefighters hosing down the interior of the restaurant from the front doorway. They waved and gave him a thumbs up. Turning, he stepped out the back door and saw that the fire had spread to a large storage shed behind the restaurant. The old man was standing on the roof with a garden hose as the building began to burn around him.

"Shit, you have to be kidding me," Tom said, as he pulled back on the yoke and continued to drag the last length of his hose outside the building.

Most of the roof of the long shed behind the restaurant was ablaze. Tom tried to pull more hose clear, but knew that was it. All he could do was try to keep the old man from being cooked alive.

A series of explosions shook the shed causing the roof to blow out and the wall near Tom began to collapse. Tom shut the bale on the nozzle and ducked back into the restaurant as a cloud of smoke and burning debris knocked him to the ground.

"Third frigging time. You'd think this was a war zone," Tom said, as he pushed himself to his feet.

The fire still smoldered, but the blast had removed the roof and most of the combustible material from the building. Tom picked up the hose and began soaking the material that still burned while he looked around for the old man's body. He had a memory, a fleeting image burned into his mind's eye, of the old man being hurled straight up into the air.

"Tom, glad to see you in one piece," Heather said, as she slapped Tom on the shoulder.

"Here, I brought a spare bottle," Heather said, as she began securing Tom's almost expended one.

Only then did he notice the alarm ringing in his ears as the bottle neared empty.

"I'm glad to see you standing. I was afraid you were messed up bad," Tom said.

"Just knocked me out. The EMTs said I was okay," Heather replied.

"All the explosions . . . my ears are ringing so bad I couldn't hear the alarm," Tom said.

"Hold your breath. I'm changing the bottle," Heather directed, as she slid the old bottle free, inserted the new one and hooked it up.

"You're good," Heather said, and slapped him on the shoulder.

"Have you seen the missing man?" Heather asked.

"He was on the roof. The fire in the shed pretty much blew itself out. Let's go look for him," Tom replied, as he began walking toward the ruined shed.

The long left wall of the shed had collapsed during the series of explosions. The shingled roof had disintegrated leaving three walls intact. As they passed the back wall they saw a large wooden crate sitting in the middle of a back room. The old man lay beside the box partially buried in smoldering debris. They ran over and began pulling the material off him. To their surprise the old man's eyes opened and he began pointing at the box.

"He zha dan . . . qu pao kai, paobu" the old man said, shuddered once and closed his eyes.

"Is he still alive?" Heather asked.

Tom pulled off his gloves and checked the man's pulse. He pulled back the man's charred shirt and saw a long metal splinter protruding from his sternum.

"Must have nicked his heart. He bled out quick. Probably for the best, he's all busted up and burned over most of his body," Tom said, as he stood up and glanced over at the crate.

The top of the crate had been shattered by the roof and cinder block walls flying around. Tom took a small flashlight from his pocket and looked inside the box. Later he would be asked why he had bothered to look inside the box. He never could give an adequate answer.

"Forget the box, Tom. We've got to notify the police and let them know we've got a casualty back here," Heather said, as she tried to pull Tom away from the broken crate.

"We'll have to tell them about more than that," Tom said, as he continued to stare inside the crate.

· · · ·

Tom had walked back through the ravaged restaurant, formerly known as Good Luck Dim Sum. Heather had remained to watch over the old man's remains. He had told her to not touch the crate and not allow anyone else near it. When he reached the front he found Jamar waiting for him.

"Hey Tom, nice work in there, brother. That second explosion knocked me for a loop," Jamar said, as he and Tom fist bumped.

"Is the Chief okay?" Tom asked, as he looked around for the police.

"He's a little busted up. The EMT's hauled him away a few minutes ago. They told him he had a fractured collar bone, a busted shoulder and some other stuff. He wanted to stay, but those boys don't take a whole lot of crap," Jamar replied.

"I need a cop. They're never around when you need one," Tom said, as he began looking around the street.

"Hey man, Walter was shocked when he came to and I told him about all you had done inside," Jamar said, and began to laugh.

"I think he was pissed. He said he wouldn't be able to fire your ass now," Jamar said, and clapped Tom on the shoulder.

"Yeah, nice to know you're appreciated. Listen Jamar, Heather is out back behind the building. I left her on overwatch with the hose. We found the owner. He didn't make it. When we found him he said something like, 'poo boo'. You've got a Chinese girlfriend. Got any idea what that means?" Tom asked, as he gestured to a cop who was walking by.

"You mean 'paobu'. Jingfei told me that when her father caught me in her room one evening when we first started dating. It means run, like get the hell out," Jamar said, and laughed at the memory.

"Officer, we need some help out back. We found the owner. He's dead. Also we need Hazmat and EOD, ASAP," Tom said, as a police officer walked up.

"I'll call for a wagon. What about hazmat and EOD? You got more propane out back?" the officer said.

"Not exactly, and you might want to start clearing this area out," Tom said.

"What? Like a couple of more blocks?" the officer asked.

"No . . . like the whole damn city," Tom said.

Chapter 6

"But this momentous question, like a fire bell in the night,
awakened, and filled me with terror."

Thomas Jefferson

Manassas, Virginia, USA
Mission Center for Weapons and Counterproliferation
Central Intelligence Agency
March 12, 2017, 0530 hours EST

"That's not possible. Where the hell did it come from?"
Director Caleb McElroy asked, as he was briefed on the incoming
report forwarded from the San Francisco office of Homeland Security.

"The investigation is still in progress. We aren't even sure if the
device is stable. It was damaged in the fire," Assistant Director Janet
Davidson replied.

"Who knows about this?" McElroy asked.

"The usual, the President, the JCS, CIA, Homeland, the FBI
and a few personnel from the scene," Janet said.

"Have the knowledgeable personnel at the scene been secured?
If this hits the press the country is going to go into a panic. All
knowledgeable personnel have to be secured or have the highest
security level. This has to stay under wraps until we know what is
going on." Caleb said.

"Evidently the device was found by a firefighter after they
responded to a fire in the Good Luck Dim Sum Chinese restaurant on
736 Clement Street in San Francisco. He had hazmat training in 2002
in Albuquerque, New Mexico, at the Nuclear Hazards Training
Course. They showed them models of old devices as part of the
training. That's how he knew what he was looking at," Janet said.

"Homeland secured the site. Said it was a chemical hazard. All
personnel involved in the incident have been secured and quarantined
due to possible chemical exposure. I guess that's the best cover they

could come up with on short notice. They haven't moved the device yet. Weapons experts are enroute. That's about all we know," Janet said.

"Where the hell did it come from? How the hell did it get into the country? A Chinese restaurant . . . the implication of that scares the shit out of me," Caleb said, as he stood and walked over to his window.

"Any guidance from above? I guess Homeland has the lead," Caleb asked.

"I think everyone is trying to digest the implications and waiting for more information," Janet said.

"Remember our discussion with Amanda about missing material? I never heard any more about that," Caleb said.

"She said it kept dead ending. Did you ever push it upstairs?" Janet asked.

"No, I wanted more definitive information. Tell Ms. Langford that I want her to collate all her data on her theory and be prepared to present it later today. Go get her up to speed on this mess in San Francisco. I've got a painful phone call to make," Caleb said, as he let out a deep sigh and removed his cell phone from his coat pocket and began dialing.

"Director Maddox, it's Caleb . . . reference the incident in San Francisco . . . I may have some pertinent information . . ."

Chapter 7

"There is no bigger task than protecting the homeland of our country"

George W. Bush

Washington, DC, USA
The White House
Presidential Quarters
March 12, 2017, 0545 hours EST

"I know it's early, Jamila, but get in there and wake him up. You have to get him out of bed now. Either you do it, or I'll barge in on him and the Missus, and she won't be happy about that," said Roger Yost, White House Chief of Staff.

"You wait here, Mr. Yost. I've worked for them for seventeen years. I'll wake him up," Jamila Andrada replied, as she pushed Yost's hand away from the door to the president's bedroom.

After knocking on the door three times, Jamila cracked the door open and said, "Mr. President, you need to get up. Mr. Yost is here, and he says it's very important."

Hearing nothing she opened the door a little further and peeked inside. Both occupants were still sound asleep.

"Listen, you have got to get him up . . . now," Roger said, in a loud whisper, as he began to push against the bedroom door, only to be met with an open fist jab in the center of his chest.

"Ow . . . was that necessary?" Roger asked, as he backed up and began massaging his chest.

"Muay Thai. My Father was a Master. I think of myself as their last line of defense," Jamila said, as she pointed at Yost and pointed at the floor.

"Okay . . . I'll stay right here," Yost said, as he held his hands up in surrender.

Jamila stared at Yost once more and then slid quietly into the bedroom.

"Mr. President, I apologize, but you have to get up now. Mr. Yost says it's very, very important," Jamila said, as she began to shake the president's shoulder.

"Yost? What the hell's he want this early?" President Konrad Miller asked; as he cracked one eye open.

"Can't you just hit him a few times and make him go away?" the President asked.

"I tried that, Sir. He still won't go away," Jamila replied.

"Tell him to wait in the sitting area outside, order some coffee, and tell him I'll be there in five minutes," the President said, while sliding out of bed.

"Yes, Mr. President," Jamila, said, as she turned and left the bedroom.

"Well where is he? This can't wait," Yost said, as soon as Jamila left the bedroom and shut the door.

"You go sit over there. He'll be out in five minutes . . . and don't even think about touching that door. I'm ordering coffee," Jamila ordered, and pointed at the 18$^{th}$ century padded chairs that sat by the window in the sitting room.

"Make yourself useful and move that small table over to the chairs," Jamila said, as she walked off to order the coffee.

"Well, if I didn't know who had seniority around here I do now," Yost said, as he rubbed his chest again, and walked over to move the small table.

The Chief of Staff had just moved the table and sat down when the door to the president's bedroom door opened.

"Good morning, Mr. President. I'm sorry for the intrusion, but this is critical," Yost said, as he stood up.

"Sit down, Roger. I know you wouldn't risk Jamila's wrath without a good reason," President Miller said, as he sat down.

"So just how bad is this piece of news?" the President asked.

"Mr. President, a hidden nuclear device has been discovered in San Francisco," Yost replied.

"Do you mean a dirty bomb?" the President asked.

"No Sir, a fission device. Homeland estimates the yield at somewhere between 20 and 40 kilotons," Yost said, as Jamila entered the room bearing a tray with two cups and a small kettle.

As she set down the service and poured two cups, the President said, "Thank you, Jamila. That will be all."

After she left the President sipped on his coffee and asked, "What all do we know?"

"There was a fire at a Chinese restaurant last night about 8:30 PM their time. The fire spread to an adjacent building behind the restaurant. The fire was out by about 10 PM. The owner died in the fire. Evidently a fire fighter saw something suspicious in the building in the back and reported it to the local police. They contacted their EOD people and they reported a possible nuclear device. Local DHS confirmed their suspicion. Homeland took over the scene and secured the whole area," Yost said.

"Evacuations?" the President asked, as he sipped his coffee and stared out the window.

"Five block radius. They're using a possible chemical hazard as a cover story," Yost said.

"Good. Now the big question . . . does the media know about this?" the President asked, as he drained his coffee, and began refilling the cup.

"No, Sir. They're just reporting a fire with possible chemical material involvement. The only problem is that media was on the scene outside the restaurant. There were some explosions, propane tanks, some reporter and her cameraman were injured and taken to a local hospital. Homeland is rounding up all local personnel that might know the truth and placing them in holding. The family has also been held for questioning," Yost replied.

"How many people are in the area?" the President asked.

"Almost 900,000 in San Francisco and another 400,000 in Oakland, right across the bay," Yost said.

"I trust that we have our best and brightest working on this bomb?" the President asked.

"Yes, Mr. President. This is Priority One across all the appropriate federal agencies," Yost said.

"This, young man, is a pretty crappy way to start the day. How the hell did a nuke wind up in a Chinese restaurant in San Francisco? For the time being this has to be kept secret, and I mean secret. I don't want Congress to hear about this or they'll leak it to the press for sure. Make sure this stays 'need to know', the President said.

"What time is it?" the President asked, as he killed his second cup of coffee and poured a third.

"It's 0602, Sir," Yost said, as he checked his cell phone.

"At 0900 I want the entire cabinet in the Situation Room downstairs. If they aren't available by then, I want them on a secure link. Cancel my appointments for the remainder of the day. Give the press some lame excuse that will keep them off my back for 24 hours. I'll want updates every hour on what is going on in San Francisco," the President ordered.

"Did I forget anything?" the President asked, as he stared into the rapidly draining cup.

"No Sir, I think that will get things started. Anything else, Sir?" Yost asked, as he got up to leave.

"Yeah, if you bump into Jamila, ask her to have breakfast for two up here in thirty minutes . . . the usual," the President said.

"Will do, Sir," Yost said, as he left and shut the door behind him.

"I've got to talk to Marie, get a shower, get dressed, and get composed. This is going to be a rough one," the President said, as he drained the third cup and walked back towards the bedroom.

Chapter 8

"Making no mistakes is what establishes the certainty of
victory, for it means conquering an enemy that is already defeated."

Sun Tzu (~520 BC)

Beijing, China
22 Base Headquarters
100 meters below the Beijing Botanical Gardens
March 12, 2017, 1745 hours CT

Lieutenant General Kung Yusheng studied the penjing
carefully. The next cut was crucial and was long overdue. He had been
indecisive for over three days. The indecisiveness bothered him more
than how to trim the ancient plant.

"Lieutenant General Kung, my apology, but there is a matter of
serious import that we must discuss," Colonel Peng, said from the
doorway.

"This penjing is a cutting from the Sandai-Shogun-No Matsu in
Japan. It is over 200 years old. The Japanese call them bonsai. The
Japanese are so proud of their culture despite the fact that most of it
has been stolen from China. When their protectors are brought low the
Japanese will cease to exist as a nation. They will find that China has a
very long memory," Lieutenant General Kung said, as he gently
placed the tiny shears beside the penjing and turned around.

"Now, what is this matter that had to break my focus?" Kung
asked.

"There was a fire in a Chinese restaurant in San Francisco,"
Colonel Peng said, as he shut the door to Kung's office behind him.

Kung reached into a small pocket that had had added to his
uniform pants and removed an old pocket watch. It had belonged to
George Herman Ruth and commemorated the 1923 World Series
victory.

"I lose track of the time down here," Kung said, as he opened the case on the watch that was shaped like a baseball diamond.

"Good, it's still light out. We will go upstairs and go for a walk in the garden," General Kung said, as he replaced the watch, grabbed his hat and coat, and walked towards a blank wall on the right side of his office.

Andy Warhol's portrait of Chairman Mao hung on the wall mounted in an ancient carved frame replaced during renovations to the Imperial Palace. He touched sensors on either side of the frame and a door opened in the wall to his right. The private elevator led to the surface inside the tomb of Liang Qichao, whose writings had inspired Mao. As the elevator surfaced, and the doors slid back, Colonel Peng stepped out and lowered a small screen mounted in the small anteroom outside the elevator.

"The way is clear, General," Colonel Peng said, as he pulled a lever which open a small door on the outer wall of the tomb.

As they exited the tomb, General Kung breathed deeply and sighed.

"Jasmin, such a beautiful scent. An early spring means a lucky year. Now Colonel, tell me about our problem. I want all the detail that you have," General Kung said, as he began walking down the gravel path beside the tomb.

"There was a fire at the location of the Number 1 device. The caretaker was killed. The Americans have cordoned off a kilometer wide radius around the restaurant. They have told the local media that it's a toxic chemical concern. Our agents within the US have said that the incident has risen to the topmost levels of government including their various spy agencies," Colonel Peng said.

"Irony . . . the only coin that was never returned was the first one. We have been lucky for many years, my friend. We must assume that our deception may be nearing its end. What is the status of the final device?" General Kung asked, as he bent down and plucked a blossom from a wild flower beside the path.

"It is due in New Orleans on the 18th. Then it will travel by rail across the southern US. It will arrive in Alexandria, Virginia on the 22nd," Colonel Peng said.

"Ten megatons! We may have need of it sooner than later," General Kung said, as he sniffed the flower, then crushed it in his fist and threw it away.

"Use every resource. Find out what the Americans are doing, what they know or what they think they know. I want names and profiles, how they think, their professional experience, party affiliation, family, everything you can find. If they can definitely link Number One to us then they will discretely contact our government. If they publically announce that a nuclear device has been smuggled into their country their people will panic. The global markets will crash. They will not risk that. It may be time to reveal ourselves to the Central Committee. They will not be happy with us, Colonel Peng, not happy at all," General Kung said, as he slapped his thigh and began laughing.

Chapter 9

"Experience teaches us that it is much easier to prevent an enemy from posting themselves than it is to dislodge them after they have got possession."

George Washington

San Francisco, California, USA
Department of Homeland Security
450 Golden Gate Avenue
March 12, 2017, 1930 hours PST

Room 817

"Interesting file, Mr. Jackson. Twenty four years with the SFFD and still a line fire fighter. According to this you were once on the fast track. Sounds like a lack of ambition or work ethic," said Investigator Akeem Williams, steeling himself to discredit a brave man.

"You offering me a job? If the money's good I might just take it," Tom said.

He'd been awake for twenty seven hours and wasn't in the mood to be messed with.

"No, Mr. Jackson, I'm not offering you a job. I just want to figure out why you're such a loser," Akeem said, as he leaned across the table.

"Am I under arrest? If not, I'd like to go," Tom said, as he stood up.

"You are considered a person of interest in a case that has the attention of DHS. Now sit down . . . please," Akeem said.

"Oh, you mean the nuclear bomb behind the Chinese place? Yeah, that might be of interest to D . . . H . . . S, I suppose," Tom said, as he sat back down and crossed his arms.

"Any chance I could get some food? I'm starving," Tom asked.

"Now what makes you think that you saw a nuclear device" Akeem asked.

"Why are we going over the same questions over and over? Do you want me to change my story? Do you want me to say that I didn't see shit in that shed behind the restaurant?" Tom asked.

His lack of self-control had cost Tom over the years, and he could tell that he was rapidly losing what little control he had left, but he couldn't help himself. It was like he was having an out of body experience and watching some fool provoked into doing something that he really didn't want to do.

"Are you looking for your fifteen minutes of fame? Is that it? Talk to the media, make the rounds of the talk shows, and collect a few grand for telling an elaborate story, and scare the shit out of half the country? Is that it, Mr. Jackson," Akeem asked, as his voice rose in a threatening manner.

"How about you go fuck yourself. Either charge me with a crime, read me my rights, or let me go," Tom said, as he stood up and yelled across the table.

"You are not going anywhere, Mr. Jackson. Now have a seat and we'll start again," Akeem said.

. . . .

Room 822

"So . . . let's talk again about the Chinese that the restaurant owner supposedly spoke right before you and your partner let him die of his injuries," Investigator Louise Chou said.

"What? He had a piece of metal in his chest. I don't know why he wasn't dead when we found him. We didn't do anything wrong. He was burnt and busted up. Tom tried to help him, but when he ripped open his shirt we saw the spike. He died right then," Heather said, as she continued to pace behind the small table.

"I repeat . . . what did the man say?" Louise asked.

"Listen lady, I don't speak Chinese. It sounded like 'pow boo' and then something like 'heziedan' or something," Heather said, as she ran her fingers through her hair.

They had been taken from the scene by police, and she was still wearing her fire pants and boots. She smelled, was exhausted and hadn't eaten in twelve hours. This had turned into the worst night of her life.

. . . .

## Room 836

"Come on, this is bullshit. You're holding me against my will. This isn't Alabama. This is San Fran fuckin' Cisco. You can't be treating me like this," Jamar said, as he began heading for the door.

"Mr. Stevens, if you open that door you are going to find three large men. They will bring you back into the room and secure you in that chair, and they won't be nice about it. I would strongly suggest that you sit back down and we continue our discussion," Investigator Aniyah Jones advised.

"Sistah, you'd use three white boys to do your dirt work?" Jamar asked, while sliding into a chair beside Investigator Jones.

"Actually, one is black, one is white, and the other is Hispanic. They are all big, and they all work for me. So please sit down, over there, Mr. Stevens," Aniyah said, as she removed his hand from her arm.

"Diverse organization, I like that. Now why can't I leave?" Jamar said, as he returned to his chair and sat down.

"We'll go over this again. What did you see behind the restaurant and what did you hear?" Aniyah asked.

"I didn't see shit and I didn't hear shit. Ask my partners. They were behind the restaurant. I never went back there," Jamar said.

"What did they tell you they saw back there?" Aniyah asked.

"Some dead Chinese dude and he was rambling on about something right before he died," Jamar said.

"What did he say?" Aniyah asked.

"I don't know. I wasn't there. Ask them what he said," Jamar replied.

"Did they tell you what he said?" Aniyah asked.

"Yeah, but they don't speak Chinese so it's probably bullshit," Jamar said.

"What did they say he said?" Aniyah asked again.

"Look, I'm not a native. My girlfriend has taught me enough so I won't say something bad in front of her parents, but that's all," Jamar said.

"One last time . . ." Aniyah said.

"Okay, but it didn't make any sense. As best as I can tell, and this is a guess, the old man told Tom to 'paobu, qu pao kai'. That means 'run, go run away'.

"Was that all?" Aniyah asked.

"One other thing, but this makes even less sense. I think the old man was crazy and dying," Jamar said.

"What else did he say?" Aniyah asked.

Jamar rubbed his eyes and said, "He added something like, 'he zha dan'. Which makes no sense at all."

"Are you sure that's what he said?" Aniyah asked, as she sat up straight in her chair.

"Yeah, 'run, go run away, nuclear bomb'. Ain't that some shit? Like I said, the old man was crazy, or maybe I just misheard what Tom said," Jamar said, as he leaned back in his chair.

.   .   .   .

March 13, 2017, 0130 hours
Room 801

"The family, the three firefighters, two police, two media, and two police EOD . . . is there anyone else?" Senior Investigator Dimitri Atkins asked, to the assembled agents.

"No, and the first responders are the only ones who saw anything or had direct contact with people that did," said Akeem, as he sat at the table with the other three agents that had been interrogating the first responders for hours.

"How about the fourth fire fighter, Chief Moore?" Aniyah asked.

"He was injured early on. By the time two of his people reached the shed he was on his way to St. Mary's Medical Center. Dislocated shoulder and a broken collar bone. He's clear. The same blast that got him, took out the two media types," Dimitri said.

"And the media?" Aniyah asked.

"The woman and her cameraman were standing near the front window when the first blast happened. She got messed up pretty bad. Concussion, glass fragments and burns. The last I heard she was still in surgery. The camera man was lucky. He was standing ten feet behind her. She shielded a lot of the blast. He still got some burns and a few fragments, but he'll be fine. He regained consciousness on the way to the hospital. The woman is iffy," Dimitri said, as he read from his notes.

"But they don't know anything?" Louise asked.

"They were both taken out of action by the initial explosion and removed from the scene. There's no way they could know anything about the device," Dimitri said.

"The two street cops are also clear. They think it's a case of toxic chemicals from a restaurant fire. The two EOD boys know everything. They've been trained in recognition and handling of radioactive materials to include dirty bombs and fissionable devices. They've both been briefed by DHS and the FBI. They won't be a problem. Which leads us back to our three fire fighters. What did you three get from the interrogations?" Dimitri asked.

"The first guy that recognized the weapon, Tom Jackson, knows exactly what he saw. He's 42 years old, volatile, and has an attitude. His record shows that he's smart, brave, and has little tolerance for bureaucratic bullshit. That's why he's still behind a hose. He's exactly the type that would leave here and go straight to the press," Akeem said.

"He would want the glory?" Dimitri asked.

"No, it would be to give us the finger. He's got authority issues," Akeem said, and laughed.

"The woman?" Dimitri asked.

"Heather Moore is Chief Walter Moore's niece. She's 21 years old, high school graduate, and went into firefighting upon graduation. She finished third in her class out of 63. There were only two other women in the class, so she must be pretty damn good at her job. She was with Tom Jackson when they found Mr. Yan and the device. She's pretty spooked, but she's smart enough to know that she's involved in something that's way above her head," Louise Chou said.

"Will she be a problem?" Dimitri asked.

"She's scared, tired, and just wants to go home. I think she'd like to just forget this whole event ever happened," Louise said.

"So we debrief her, caution her, mildly threaten her and let her go?" Aniyah asked.

"In my opinion . . . yes, she'll keep her mouth shut," Louise said.

"Screw the 'mildly'. Tell her that if she talks, she'll spend the rest of her life in a maximum security prison," Dimitri said.

"I can do that," Louise said.

"And the third guy?" Dimitri asked, as he turned toward Aniyah.

"Jamar Stevens, age 27, minor record as a juvee: shoplifting, possession of pot. Got religion and straightened himself out in his late teens. He's been with the SFFD for seven years, clean record, good firefighter. He has a Chinese girlfriend, and speaks some Chinese. He never saw the device, but he's the one that translated what the other two heard from the dying man," Aniyah said, as she referred to her notes.

"People, my inclinations are to lock up any civilian that knows anything about this event. The President has not declared a national emergency . . . yet, but he will. It's just a matter of time," Dimitri said.

"Boss . . . 48 hours, that's it in California. We have to charge them or release them. So what do we charge them with?" Louise asked.

"Move them down to Minus 3. Keep them separate. Let them clean up and feed them. For now we'll use the 48 hours. I'll talk to the Attorney General. We have to get the device moved and secured before we release these people. If there's no device, they can talk to the press all they want. They'll have no proof," Dimitri said.

"Now, one more thing, what about the family? They've had a nuke in their backyard for years, maybe decades, and I find it hard to believe that the old man was the only one that knew what was there," Dimitri said.

"The old man's children are downstairs on the 7th floor. The two oldest sons are married. The two daughters and the youngest son are still single. The two oldest sons have wives and eight children between them. The spouses and kids are with Child Welfare off site. We'll talk to them, but it will be a more subtle evaluation of what they know," said Irene Cochran.

"Oh, one other thing, the oldest daughter is a lawyer with some big shot firm downtown. That may be a problem," Irene said.

"Listen up! The children of Mr. Yan may be the key to this entire investigation. One or more of these adults may know what has been hidden behind the restaurant. We need to know where it came from, how it got there, when it got there, and if they have any contacts outside or inside the US," Dimitri said.

.　.　.　.

## Room 701

"They force us to come with them, question us all separately, and won't let us go. Lihwa, you're a lawyer. Why are they holding us? How can they hold us? Our father is dead and our restaurant . . . our family center . . . is gone. What is going on?" Deshi, the oldest son at 26, asked.

Lihwa set her cell phone on the table and sighed. She had been trying to contact her boss, but there was no signal.

"I was up for a senior position in the firm, and now this happens," Lihwa, the eldest daughter at 37, said.

"Father is dead and all you care about is your promotion. You are the eldest daughter, the eldest child, and all you care about is yourself," Chuntao, the youngest daughter at 17, said as she reached across the table and tried to snatch Lihwa's cell phone.

"Chuntao, no! Father would not have us turn on each other. We are family. We will protect each other no matter the cost," Deshi said, as he grabbed his younger sister's arm.

"Chuntao, you lazy egg. This is your fault and you try to blame me. This was a grease fire. You never clean up properly," Lihwa yelled.

"Father would be ashamed of both of you. Deshi is right. We stick together no matter what," Lei said, the third oldest son at 19.

"Father's dead and you're calm as always . . . Mister Ice Water," Chuntao said, and stared at her older sibling.

"Why are we here? This has nothing to do with Father's death or the fire. When they questioned me they kept asking about the shed out back," Jianguo said, the second oldest son at 23.

"Same here, they kept asking about the shed. I don't get it either," Deshi said.

"I've been thinking about this since they picked us up. I think I know or have an idea," Lihwa said, as she reached into her purse and removed a small silk sleeve.

"When I was a little girl, before any of you were born, something strange happened. It was the middle of the night and I got up to use the bathroom. I heard some noise out back and peeked out the bathroom window. Father was with some men unloading a big wooden box from a truck, and placing it in the storage shed. Father did something to make the men angry. They threw him to the ground and began to beat him. I was very scared. Father got up, talked to the men some more, and they left. I watched for a while, until father went back in the house. Then got sleepy and went back to bed. The next morning I snuck into the shed to look for the box, but the box was gone. Something didn't look right and then I noticed some mortar on the ground near the doors. It would still break up, like it hadn't quite set up yet. It was then that I noticed that the room seemed smaller. A new wall had been installed inside the shed during the night. I knew that the box was behind the wall," Lihwa said.

"You never told us this story. Are you sure it wasn't just a dream?" Deshi asked.

"I asked Father about the box later that morning and he got very angry. He said it was none of my business, and made me swear to never tell anyone about the box, even Mother. This is the first time I've ever told anyone. To tell you the truth, I'd forgotten about the whole thing," Lihwa said.

"Why would he put a box behind a wall? That makes no sense," Jianguo asked.

"Our restaurant burns down and now we're held by Homeland Security. This is all about that box. One other thing, late the next day, when father and mother were in the restaurant, I went out back to play and found this," Lihwa said, as she reached into her purse and pulled out a small bronze Chinese coin.

"I used to keep it under my bed in a small box filled with my favorite things," Lihwa said, as she starred at the coin and rubbed its ancient surface.

"When I left home for college I took this coin with me. During my junior year I did some research on the coin. It's a relic from the age of Emperor Wen, over 2100 years ago. The condition is quite extraordinary. This coin is why Father received a beating those many years ago. It was supposed to be returned to someone after the box was delivered," Lihwa said.

"Now you're guessing," Deshi said.

"No, I heard the man yelling at father while he kicked him. It was about the coin," Lihwa said.

"Did you tell Homeland this story and about the coin?" Deshi asked.

"No, the coin is family business. Besides, they have the box. I don't want to bring any disgrace on the family. We are nothing to them, but whatever was inside that box was something that they were very interested in," Lihwa said.

"The box, the coin, none of this makes any sense," Lei said.

"I don't claim to understand any of this. All I know is that Father is dead. The restaurant that he and Mother spent most of their lives working in so we would have a good life in America is gone. The only thing we have left is each other," Lihwa said, as she walked over to her little sister, kissed her on the cheek and hugged her tightly.

"Lihwa, you're the lawyer. You have connections outside the community. You have to find out what's going on," Deshi said, as the other siblings nodded in agreement.

"I will preserve the family honor so father and mother can rest in peace," Lihwa said, as she stood, and bowed to her brothers and sister.

Chapter 10

"Simplicity is the ultimate sophistication"

Leonardo da Vinci

San Francisco, California, USA
Site of the restaurant fire
736 Clement Street
March 12, 2017, 2030 hours PST


"Well at least they're through removing the restaurant, or what was left of it. It's hard to think with that much noise," Alan Parkins said.

"I was worried more about the vibration. As far as I can tell this thing has three safeties. At least one has lifted, maybe two. If two have lifted, and with the age of this device, moving this thing is really dicey," Nathan O'Malley said, as he adjusted the lighting system above his head.

The shed and the restaurant no longer existed. Both buildings had been demolished, and the debris hauled away. They had been removed to make room for a boom crane and truck. The device stood inside a temporary enclosure still sitting in the cradle built into the storage crate that had been its home for so many years.

The flap to the tent lifted and a red haired woman walked up to the two DHS nuclear weapon specialists.

"Kate Williams, National Nuclear Security Administration, Accident Response Group," Kate said, as she nodded to the pair, and began studying the device.

"Damn, an old gun type device. From the size of it probably 90 to a 100 pounds of HEU. That would produce a yield of around 30-40 kilotons. No fins, but you can see where they were cut off with a torch. Not the neatest work I've ever seen. This is a repurposed antique from a stockpile," Kate said, as she smiled at both men.

"Have you disarmed it yet?" Kate asked, as she patted the outer casing.

"Jesus, lady! This thing has three safeties. One was damaged in the fire and released. The second one has heat damage and I'm not sure how long it will hold. That leaves one frigging safety that's stable. As old as this thing is I don't know if it's really stable or not," Alan said, as he stepped between Kate and the device.

"Young man this is a Chinese Type 6 device dating from the early 70's. It was designed to be dropped from a bomber. I've disassembled two of these, and it's not that difficult. There's a port on the side that gives you access to the gun tube. Cut a slot in the tube, slip a plate in there, and you prevent criticality and a nuclear detonation," Kate said.

"Yeah, well, look on the bottom near the front of the cradle that this 'antique' sits on and tell me what you see," Nathan said, as he stood beside Alan.

"Step aside boys, and let an expert through," Kate said, as she separated the men and knelt beside the device.

Removing a mag light from her satchel she began studying the underside of the device.

"Ohhhh . . . now that's interesting. That looks like an anti-tampering device. It's newer than the bomb, but still analog. I bet it dates from the 80s. That releases all the safeties. I wonder if it triggers the device?" Kate said, as she regained her feet.

"This job just went from ho-hum to interesting," Kate said, as she smiled at both men.

"Oh, it gets better. Go check out the other side," Alan said, as he gestured in a less than friendly manner.

Kate walked around the device and stared at the package that had been welded onto the side of the bomb.

She knelt down, studied it for a minute and said, "That's a transmitter and it's active. What the hell?"

"Wow, something our senior citizen hasn't seen before," Nathan said.

"Careful, kid, I have a son your age and he's a Navy Seal. He doesn't take kindly to people bad mouthing his mother," Kate said, as she sighed and stood up.

"So . . . we have a repurposed nuclear device that has had an anti-tampering device installed, and an active transmitter. To me that implies that someone doesn't want it messed with, and wants to be able to set the device off on command," Kate said.

"That's pretty much the same conclusion that we came to," Alan said.

"Which leaves us with a series of problems. First, we have to stabilize the device prior to moving it; second, we have to figure out how to remove the anti-tampering device, and third, we have to figure out what to do with the transmitter," Kate said.

"Not necessarily in that order," Alan said.

"Agreed! Personally, I'm worried about the transmitter. What if there's a link between the anti-tampering device and the transmitter?" Nathan asked.

"What do you mean?" Kate asked.

"We kill the anti-tampering device and the transmitter sends a signal to whoever owns this thing and they send back a signal and . . . boom, San Francisco disappears, before we can neutralize the bomb," Nathan said.

"Well, we weren't sure where the device originated. Obviously the choices are limited, but why are you so sure that it's Chinese?" Alan asked.

"All of the Chinese bombs like this were made in Harbin over an eight year period starting in 1968. Back then everything was hand welded by specialist welders. They were able to produce consistent results with no flaws. At that time in China that was fairly rare. If you know what to look for, welders leave a signature. It's the same way that specialists can detect a forger of a great artist. The artist leaves a signature in his brush strokes. A welder is no different. I recognize this welder. I've seen his signature, his welds, on other devices. His name was Lung Guowei. He dies in '94, as I remember," Kate said.

"You're kidding us, right?" Nathan asked, sure that this woman was pulling his leg.

"Nathan O'Mally, 27, second in your class at MIT. You love chai tea and Taco Bell. I don't get that at all. You have a three year old Pug named Jack Bauer. Your mother's name is Irene. Your father's name is also Nathan. You and your older sister don't get along. Do you want me to go on? I have a form of hyperthymesia, and it leaves me cranky, which some people would call 'bitchy'. Basically, once I learn something I don't forget it," Kate said.

"Damn!" Alan said.

"Back to the device . . . chicken or the egg . . . anti-tampering or the transmitter?" Kate asked.

"Anti-tampering, but we need to be able to see inside. There could be leads on the inside of the casing. They'll be attached to all existing ports. If we cut a new access port and cut one of the leads we're screwed," Nathan said.

Kate took her phone out of her satchel, punched a few numbers, and said, "Jim, when are you getting here? We need the fluoroscope now! Thirty? Okay, we'll be waiting."

"Portable fluoroscope with a remote digital screen. The software will make a composite and give us a 3-D image of the internals," Kate said, in answer to the quizzical looks the other two were giving her.

"Like I said, not the first nukes I've had to dissect," Kate said.

"I thought we were supposed to be the experts," Nathan said, as he nudged Alan in the arm.

"We have a place east of here. The van will have a lot of specialized equipment we'll need. He'll also be bringing the rest of my team. Normally I'd run off any bystanders, but you two look like you might be trainable," Kate said.

"Lady, we're DHS, National Technical Nuclear Forensics Center. Nobody runs us off," Alan said.

"Listen boys, technically we're part of DOE, but we're not. I report directly to the President, not one of his flunkies. Don't push your luck. Like I said, you can stay," Kate replied, as she backed away from the device.

"Now what?" Nathan asked, as he glanced over at Alan and shrugged.

"Now be quiet while I think, and clean up your equipment. The fluoroscope is bulky. It'll need an eight foot space around the device. I'm studying the schematics of this class of weapon in my head," Kate said, as she crossed her arms and closed her eyes.

.  .  .  .

March 13, 2017, 0105 hours

"Jesus, Jim, three plus hours to set up. When we train it takes 45 minutes," Kate said, as she continued pacing.

"Yeah, 45 minutes on level concrete. We're in somebody's backyard. The fluoroscope weighs 3245 lbs. It has a small foot print which means it will sink into this soil. I don't normally stock 2 by 12 lumber in the truck and Lowe's isn't open at midnight," Jim Padenko said, as he placed a small level on the fluoroscope.

"Security procured this lumber from some construction site nearby. Half this shit's bowed. Crap! It's still not level. I think the lumber is still settling into the dirt," Jim said.

"Jim, we've got to be out of here by sunrise. Homeland says they can't hold the family or first responders later than 0800. Some of them may go to the media. The device has to be stable and gone in less than seven hours," Kate said.

"If this fluoroscope is as good as you say it is, just get a shot. At least we'll have something to look at," Alan said, while he was rummaging through NNSA equipment boxes.

"Please don't mess with our equipment. I have everything in a certain location for a reason," Jim said, as he shut the lid on the tool box Alan was poking around in.

"He's right, Jim. You've got five minutes to get the scope as level as possible. Then we're going to take one rotation and see what we've got going on inside the device," Kate ordered, as she slapped Alan on the shoulder.

"I knew it was a good idea keeping you guys around," Kate said, as she looked at Alan and Nathan.

"Five minutes? No, the image will distorted," Jim said.

"Five minutes! Then start the sequence. That'll take fifteen minutes. When it's done we'll have something to look at. Maybe we'll get lucky," Kate said.

"Please don't say that. You know how I feel about luck," Jim said, as he tapped his head with a closed fist.

"Highly superstitious," Kate said to Alan, as she nodded in Jim's direction.

For the next five minutes wedges were inserted, soil was compacted and Jim cursed a lot while checking to see if the fluoroscope was level. Most expletives were sent in Kate's direction.

"Alan, go tell security to verify no personnel are in these adjoining buildings," Kate said.

"I'm familiar with most fluoroscopy equipment available, but I've never seen a unit like this. Where did you get it?" Nathan asked.

"Custom made to Jim's specs. There are only three in the world. We keep one on each coast, and use one for training. I'd like to tell you who made it, but then I'd have to shoot you," Kate replied, while grinning broadly at Nathan.

"The rotating arm and x-ray source have an adjustable diameter. The x-ray generator is very potent. That's why I have to verify no one is within 100 feet prior to taking a shot," Kate said.

"What if this thing has a radiation sensor set above the background emissions of the bomb? It reaches a certain point and then . . . boom," Nathan asked.

"Then that would be something new that I've never seen, and there will be a big smoking hole in the middle of San Francisco," Kate replied, as she turned and stared at Nathan.

"I do like the way you think, Nathan. I might have to try to hire you away from DHS when this is over," Kate said.

"Three minutes, Jim, tick, tock. You're not getting paid by the hour. This job has a fixed fee," Kate said, as she turned and walked away with Nathan as Jim began glaring at her.

"Relax, Nathan, I'm not distracting him. He thrives under this kind of pressure. It helps him focus. With no pressure he has a tendency to drift," Kate said.

"Well, time for us to clear out. Jim and the rest of the crew will be along directly," Kate said, as she began walking toward the void that used to be the Good Luck Dim Sum Restaurant on 736 Clement Street.

.   .   .   .

March 13, 2017, 0330 hours

"Tell me you see a solution," Kate said, as she and Jim stared at the combined results of three radiographs of the Chinese nuclear weapon.

53

"The bastards installed a lattice work of wires on the inside of the casing. The lattice is connected to the anti-tampering sensor. The question is . . . if you break one of these wires does the sensor detonate the bomb or send a signal via the transmitter that the weapon is being tampered with?" Jim said, as he rubbed his eyes. He felt like he hadn't blinked in over an hour.

"Well, would you want us to know that you had snuck a nuclear device into our country, or would you rather just blow it up and kill a million Americans which would trigger World War 3?" Kate asked.

"What's the distance between the wires?" Adam asked, as he looked over their shoulders.

"Two centimeters, less than an inch," Jim said.

"Nathan, come here. We need to talk," Alan said, as he grabbed Nathan's arm and the two walked away from the device.

"And that is the next generation," Jim said, as he shook his head and returned to the screen.

"Don't underestimate those two. Just because they haven't lived long enough to see dinosaurs roam the earth doesn't mean they're stupid," Kate said.

"Speak for yourself. I'm the younger of this arrangement," Jim said.

"Six months, big deal. Women live longer anyway," Kate said.

"And whose fault is that?" Jim asked, as he poked Kate in the arm.

"We've got it. Or rather Nathan figured it out. Use diamond bits and drill a half inch hole between the wires. Those wires look pretty thin, so go nice and slow and you won't heat them to the point that they'll lose a signal. That puts us inside," Alan said, as he and Nathan exchanged a high five.

"We normally cut the gun tube and then install a steel plate to block the HEU from shooting to the other end and creating a critical mass. We'd have to use a long drill bit to penetrate the gun tube, and then install a steel rod to block the HEU," Jim said, as he looked up at the two DHS specialists with something approaching admiration.

"Better yet, North Carolina State has developed a material using magnesium which is light like aluminum, but as strong as titanium alloys. This material has the highest strength-to-weight ratio known to mankind," Alan said.

"Great! Got a three foot long, half inch rod in your back pocket?" Jim asked, as Kate chuckled and patted him on the shoulder.

"Boys, sometimes you have to make do with what you have on hand. Don't feel bad. The basic idea is brilliant. We'll be out of here in time for breakfast," Kate said, as she stood up and stretched the kinks out of her back.

. . . .

March 13, 2017, 0530 hours

"Here's the problem, we've got both holes drilled, but we're having a problem inserting the rod into the second hole in the Gun Tube," Jim said.

"Gentlemen, the sun will be up in 45 minutes. We have to be packed up and gone by then. I would think that you three men could figure out how to insert a rod . . . never mind. You've got five minutes. Figure it out," Kate said, as she turned and walked away.

Alan started laughing as he said, "You know, she's got a point."

"Just shut up. Let me try it again," Nathan said, as he grabbed the half inch steel rod from Jim.

"Relax, kid. Close your eyes and just slide it all the way in," Jim said, then started to laugh, stood up and walked away.

"Give me the damn rod," Kate said, as she walked up, knelt down, inserted the steel rod in the outer hole and thrust it in. The end cap welded on the back of the rod bottomed out against the outer casing of the bomb with a metallic click.

"And that, gentlemen, is how you insert a rod into a hole. Why did I hire these men?" Kate asked herself, as she stood up and walked away.

All three men burst out laughing as Jim motioned for one of his crew to weld the end cap onto the outer casing of the bomb.

"Get that crane in here. I want to be on the road in 20," Kate yelled, as she signaled to the crane operator.

Chapter 11

"Don't be afraid to see what you see."

Ronald Reagan

Washington, DC, USA
The White House
The Oval Office
March 13, 2017, 0900 hours EST

"Mr. President, we need to talk," National Security Advisor Clarisse Beaumont said.

"Clarisse, I have a scheduled meeting with the California Chamber of Commerce in seven minutes. Can it wait?" the President of the United States of America asked, from behind his desk in the Oval Office.

"I'm afraid it can't, Sir. This is of national importance," Clarisse said.

That had become their code for 'the bomb'.

The president opened a channel to his Communications Director and said, "Jamera, please inform the delegation from California that our meeting will be delayed for a few minutes."

"Yes, Mr. President, I'll let them know," Jamera Stone said.

"All right, Clarisse, what's new?" the President asked.

"They did it, Sir! They disarmed the bomb about thirty minutes ago," Clarisse said.

"Have they moved it yet?" the President asked, as he closed his eyes and smiled.

"It's in transit as we speak, Mr. President. They're taking it to one of our bases in Nevada," Clarisse said.

"Good! Remember, we have to keep the press away from this story. I don't care how pissed they get. The cover story has to remain secure until we know what's going on. If you have to hold people against their will, so be it. I can't tell the American people what I don't know. Contain this. We need more information. We need to know how this thing got in the country and how long it's been here. I need answers before we go public, if we ever go public. Is that understood, Clarisse?" the President said.

"We'll contain the situation, Mr. President. At this point the press still thinks this is a minor chemical hazard concern," Clarisse said.

"And Clarisse, I expect regular updates on this matter," the President said, as his National Security Advisor nodded and left the Oval Office.

The President looked down at his hands and noticed that they were shaking. He took a deep breath and said, "Damn, I may have to go to decaf."

Chapter 12

"If the freedom of speech is taken away, then dumb and silent we may be led, like sheep to the slaughter."

George Washington

San Francisco, California, USA
Department of Homeland Security
450 Golden Gate Avenue
March 13, 2017, 0830 hours PST
Room 801

"Here's the info. We can let them all go," Lead Investigator Dimitri Atkins said, as he looked across the table at his three agents.

"All of them?" Louise Chou asked.

"Yeah, even my guy, the ticking time bomb. He can't prove shit. When the media looks into his record, they'll come to the logical conclusion that he's just a trouble maker and blow him off," Dimitri said.

"Well, it's been a long night. Let's go put on happy faces, apologize for the inconvenience, and let them all get on with their lives," Aniyah Jones said, as she stood up and stretched.

.   .   .   .

"After all that crap they just let us go with a smile and an apology. I don't get it," Heather said, as they stepped into the elevator on the 8th Floor of DHS headquarters in San Francisco.

"They had no reason to hold us. They had to let us go," Jamar said, as the elevator door shut.

"Bullshit! They held us long enough to clean the site. I'll guarantee you that the nuclear bomb is gone," Tom said, as he pressed the Ground Floor button.

"Hey, let's go to the restaurant and see what's left. I hope somebody in the department picked up all our equipment. Then we can go visit Walter," Heather said.

"Walter's fine. My ass just wants to go to bed . . . for about a week," Jamar said.

"At least they cleaned our dress out gear. It hasn't smelled this good since it was new," Heather said, as she set her fireman's boots on the floor, and slung her heavy coat and pants over her back.

"Screw the equipment. I want to see the site again," Tom said, as the elevator opened on the 7th Floor.

When the door opened, five people stood and stared at the three fire fighters and their gear.

"We'll get the next one," Lihwa said.

"No. You were at the fire . . . at the restaurant," Deshi said, as he stopped the elevator door from closing.

"Yeah, are you the family . . . of the old man?" Tom asked, as he began backing up to make room in the elevator.

"Yes, the 'old man' was our Father. His name was Yan Longwei. Show some respect!" Jianguo said, as he glared at Tom.

"I'm sorry. I didn't know his name. I was with him when he died," Tom said, as everyone packed into the elevator.

"I was with him, too. We tried to save him," Heather said, feeling awkward in the close confines of the elevator.

"We have not even been able to identify the body. No arrangements have been made. We don't even know if we have a home to go back to," Lei said.

"I apologize for our rudeness," Lihwa said, and bowed toward the three fire fighters, as she introduced herself and her four siblings.

When the door opened, and all eight walked out, Heather said, "We were going to catch a bus and get off at the restaurant. Our station is only a few blocks away . . . if you don't mind us going there."

"We would prefer some privacy, some time to mourn," Lihwa said.

"What did our father say? Did he say anything before he died?" Deshi asked.

Tom, Heather and Jamar all stared at each other not knowing what or how much to say.

"We talked to him. It was behind the restaurant. He was trying to put out the fire in the storage building. The . . . roof . . . it collapsed while he was standing on it. We pulled him out, but he was so badly hurt . . ." Heather said, as tears welled up in her eyes.

"They have kept us here for two days. We don't even know where his body is," Lihwa said, as she stopped and stood in front of Heather.

Heather nodded as tears began to spill down her cheeks.

"I'm so sorry we couldn't save him," Heather said, as she dropped her boots and gear and hugged Lihwa.

Both women began crying as they hugged each other. The family began hugging as Tom and Jamar stood awkwardly, mumbling their condolences, not quite knowing what to do or say.

"They held us too . . . for the last two days. They kept asking us questions about the fire and what we saw . . . over and over. It was like they wanted us to change our story about what we saw, and what your Father said to us," Tom said.

Deshi stepped up and grabbed Tom by the arm, and said, "They did the same to us. They separated us, and kept asking the same questions over and over. They wanted to know everything about our family. When our parents came here, who we knew, did we still have relatives in China? Lihwa is a lawyer. I think we should sue them for harassment . . . or something."

"Jianguo, call a taxi. We need to get away from this place," Lihwa said, as she released Heather, and smiled at her.

"That's not a bad idea. Beats taking the bus," Jamar said.

"You got your wallet on you?" Tom asked.

"Crap!" Jamar said.

"I've got us covered," Heather said, as she pulled a soiled twenty dollar bill out of her t-shirt pocket.

"Hey, a girl never knows when she might need a little cash," Heather said, as she unfolded the bill.

"I still want to know what our father said," Lihwa said, as Jianguo stepped into the street to wave down a taxi.

"Look, I don't speak Chinese. Jamar has a Chinese girlfriend. He understands some. I just repeated what I heard to him. Your father was really hurt. What he said didn't make a lot of sense," Tom said, as he gestured toward Jamar.

"What did he say?" Lihwa asked, as she looked at Jamar.

"He just told us to run away, that's all. The rest was just gibberish. I'm sorry there wasn't more," Tom said, as he stared at Jamar who nodded in agreement.

Lihwa's shoulders sagged as she nodded and said," Thank you for trying to help him. I still don't understand why they held us for so long.

"Lihwa, come on! We have a taxi. Let's go!" Chuntao said, while sliding into the back seat of the taxi.

As they drove off, Jamar said, "Good move. They didn't need to hear the last part. We'd probably wind up back in this damn building."

"Yeah, but I still want to go back to the restaurant and look around," Tom said, as he began looking for a taxi.

.    .    .    .

736 Clement Street
0915 hours PST

Youngest daughter Chuntao began weeping as the taxi pulled up at 736 Clement Street. What had been the Good Luck Dim Sum Restaurant, and the home that all five of them had grown up in, was now a vacant lot.

Oldest son, Deshi, began swearing in a combination of Chinese and English as he stepped out of the taxi. The sidewalk had been swept clean of debris. The only signs that something had happened were the deep parallel scratch marks left by a heavy tracked vehicle.

"It's gone. Everything's gone. We have nothing," Jianguo said, as he dropped to his knees, and began rocking back and forth.

"The fire destroyed us and the government has removed us from the face of the earth," Eldest daughter, Lihwa said, as she reached into her purse for her cell phone.

"So what are you doing? Checking on your job promotion?" Chuntao asked, but received only a withering glare from her older sister.

"I'm calling the Richmond Police Station, and hold that taxi. They're only two blocks from here and we need answers," Lihwa said.

.  .  .  .

450 6<sup>th</sup> Avenue
SFPD Richmond Station
0930 hours PST

"I want to know where our father's body is. I want to know who tore down our home, our restaurant. I need answers, or my next stop is KPIX 5, and you can answer these same questions live on TV," Lihwa said, as she glared at the desk sergeant inside the police station.

"Listen lady, I'm real sorry about your father and your restaurant. I used to eat there a couple of times a week. He seemed like a good man, but this whole thing went way above my pay grade. I'll get the Lieutenant. She can give you all the details that we have," Sergeant Ruiz said, as he picked up the phone.

"Lieutenant . . . the Yan family is out front. They have a lot of questions. It might be better if they heard it from a person of authority," Sergeant Ruiz said, then pulled the phone away from his ear and smiled as he got her response.

"Lieutenant Baker will be right out. Go down that hall to the first room on the right, and you can have some privacy while you talk," Sergeant Ruiz said, as he pointed down the hall to his right.

The room contained an old wooden table and six chairs. The wall was decorated with standard scenes of San Francisco. Six large florescent lights mounted in the ceiling cast a harsh white glare over everything. The family settled into the chairs, leaving the chair nearest the door open for the Lieutenant.

Lieutenant Casandra Baker stopped at the front desk to glare at Sergeant Ruiz.

He just shrugged and smiled as he said, "Room One, LT."

She pointed at him, and made a fist, then took a deep breath, and headed for the waiting room. She opened the door and smiled as she entered. No one smiled in return.

"I'm Lieutenant Casandra Baker. I'm the SFPD Public Liaison Officer for Richmond Station. First, I would like to express the condolences of . . ." she began.

"Where is our father? Why was our restaurant and home leveled? Did anyone think to try and retrieve our father's personal effects from the home on the second floor?" Lihwa said, as she rose to her feet.

"As I was saying, I'm very sorry about your father's death. Due to the nature of his demise an autopsy was performed the morning after the incident. He was then taken to the Cathay Mortuary Wah Sang. It was our understanding that the specifics of a Chinese funeral ceremony would be met best at that location. They were instructed to prepare his remains, and await further instruction from the family," Lieutenant Baker said, as she handed a business card from the mortuary to Deshi.

Chuntao burst into tears, and hugged Lei who was sitting beside her. Being the youngest siblings by several years, they were very close.

"Good! They have an excellent reputation within the Chinese community. Now, why was our home leveled and cleaned away?" Deshi asked, as he tucked the card into his wallet.

Lieutenant Baker paused, and then opened the case folder that sat on the table before her.

"Look . . . what we thought was just a standard restaurant fire quickly changed when the fire fighters came across some type of . . . chemical hazard behind the restaurant. They notified us. We notified our Hazmat personnel, and they suggested that we notify Homeland Security. Once that happened things started to change quickly. The firefighters had put out the fire, but Homeland ordered us out of the area. We secured a perimeter ten blocks out, and had to evacuate all personnel from that area. That's when they had us locate all individuals who lived at the location, were immediate family, or had participated in the containment of the fire. After that, only Homeland, and some requested specialists, were allowed inside the perimeter for the last two days. By the time the perimeter was lifted, and we got back into the area, the building was gone. I have no idea what happened to any of the contents of the restaurant or your living quarters above. I'm sorry, but that's all I know," Lieutenant Baker said, as she closed the folder.

"Why? Why would they do this? I don't understand?" Deshi asked.

"You would have to contact DHS. They have a local office in San Francisco," Lieutenant Baker replied.

"That's where we've been for the last two days. They separated us, grilled us, and kept us against our will for two days. They just released us this morning," Deshi said, as he slapped the table.

"I understand your frustration, Sir, but I . . ." Lieutenant Baker began.

"Thank you, Lieutenant. I think we'll be leaving," Lihwa said, as she stood up.

"But we just got here!" Deshi said, as he grabbed Lihwa's arm.

"Deshi, they don't know anything, or they won't say. First things first. Father needs to be honored and put to rest. Everything else will wait," Lihwa said, as she pulled her arm free, and started for the door.

"Thank you, Lieutenant. We're leaving," Lihwa said, as she signaled the others to get up, and headed for the door.

As they stood on the sidewalk outside the one story brick building Deshi said, "I don't understand. They told us nothing. We still don't know why we were treated like this."

"Deshi, they are low level workers in the system. They just do what they're told. I will find out what happened, but not today. Father comes first. Deshi, you are eldest son. It will be expected that you contact the mortuary to finalize the arrangements. Make sure they recommend a reputable feng shui master. The most fortuitous date and time of the ceremony will be recommended by him. Father wanted to be buried beside Mother. He bought another plot in the Chinese Cemetery in Daly City," Lihwa said, as she began making assignments for her siblings.

"Jianguo, you will begin contacting all our relatives and friends. They will want to know when the visitation and funeral are scheduled. Coordinate with Deshi. Lei, you and Chuntao only own the clothes on your back. Go down to Ross and do some shopping. I have an account there. You can stay at my apartment for the time being until things settle down," Lihwa said.

"Why are you giving orders?" Chuntao said.

"Because I am eldest, and I'm the only one that is thinking straight," Lihwa said.

"It's almost 10. We will meet at my apartment at 3 o'clock and see where we are. Any questions?" Lihwa asked.

"And where will you be? You gave us all the work," Deshi asked.

"I'm going to go talk to the fire fighters. The police don't know anything. Homeland won't tell us anything. The fire fighters know something else. I'm a lawyer. I can tell when someone's holding back information. Now get going. I'll see you at 3," Lihwa said, as she turned, and began walking south down 6th Street.

"*I need to clear my head and think. They said they were from the 31st. I think that fire station is over on 12th Street. It's the only station in the area. The walk will do me good,*" Lihwa thought, as she increased her stride.

"This is no different than preparing for trial. The crate and the coin are linked. They may even belong to the same person, but what was in the crate? I think that tall fireman knows. He had the look of a defendant telling half-truths. What was he hiding from us," Lihwa asked herself, as she crossed onto Anza Street and began walking west.

"What was so important that father would risk his life to protect it? This makes no sense. I will find out what's going on no matter what it costs," Lihwa said, as her will to see this through hardened.

Chapter 13

"Truth will ultimately prevail where there is pains to bring it to light."

George Washington

San Francisco, California, USA
Fire Station 31
Chief Walter Moore's Office
March 13, 2017, 1030 hours PST

"Look, Chief, I'm not the one with his arm in a sling. I don't need the time off," Tom said, as he began pacing in front of Chief Moore's desk.

"Too bad, Tom! District says the three of you all get two weeks off . . . paid. What's the problem? It's free money. Go get drunk for two weeks. Go for a drive up the coast. Do whatever the hell you want, but I don't want to see your face around here for the next two weeks. It's out of my hands, so beat it!" Chief Moore said, as he could see that Tom still wanted to argue.

"Heather and Jamar left an hour ago. She's going to visit her sister in San Diego. Jamar and his girlfriend are going to Vegas. Go relax for two weeks," Chief Moore said, as he pointed at the door to his office.

"Admit it. You'll miss me," Tom said, as he turned for the door.

"Like a boil on my butt," Chief Moore said, as Tom left his office.

"So now what?" Tom said to himself, as he was half way down the old wrought iron staircase from the second floor.

"So now you and I talk," Lihwa said, from the bottom of the open staircase.

"Ms. Yan? I didn't expect to see you again," Tom said, as he left the stairwell and shook her hand.

"Again, I'm sorry about your father. I hope everything is working out," Tom said.

"My name is Lihwa. Things are progressing. Have you been over to the restaurant?" Lihwa asked.

"Not yet. I was going over there now. The Department is making me take two weeks off for some reason, so I've got some time on my hands," Tom said, as they walked out through one of the open barn doors of the firehouse.

"There's nothing there. Homeland razed the place and scraped it clean, including the shed in the back," Lihwa said, as she studied Tom's face for a reaction.

"Damn! That doesn't surprise me though," Tom said.

"What didn't you tell us this morning? What really went on behind the restaurant? What did my Father really say to you? What was inside the crate?" Lihwa asked.

"I didn't say anything to you about a crate. How do you know about that? You should work for Homeland. You're pretty good at this grilling thing. All you need is a bright light and some thumb screws," Tom said, as he began walking down the street.

"Listen, Mr. Jackson, I've been a lawyer for over ten years. I work for Morrison & Foerster. They're a big firm, and they don't hire slackers. Apple is one of our clients. I know when somebody is holding back," Lihwa said, as she grabbed Tom's arm and forced him to stop walking.

"Listen . . . Lihwa, unless you want to spend some more time in that Homeland building being asked the same question over and over, you need to let this drop and get on with your life," Tom said, as he gently removed her hand and began walking down the street again.

"I don't scare easy and I want to know what happened," Lihwa said, as she began walking after Tom.

"No you don't, or you'll just bring more trouble down on your family. I'm surprised they let us go, especially me. I don't know if I want to push my luck any further," Tom lied, knowing that he would find out what was going on. He just didn't want to drag anyone else down with him.

"With or without out you, I will find out what happened. I have my own theory, but it doesn't make any sense," Lihwa said.

Tom stopped walking and turned around.

"And what theory might that be?" Tom asked.

Lihwa told him the story of the night the men visited her father. When she mentioned the crate Tom's jaw dropped.

"Holy crap! You know when it came into the country," Tom said.

"When what came into the country? Tell me what happened behind the restaurant," Lihwa demanded.

"Oh man, oh man," Tom said, as he began rubbing his face, and stared at the woman standing in front of him.

"You know, you're very pretty when you're angry," Tom said.

"Tom . . . please . . . what happened?" Lihwa asked.

Tom stopped and stared at her. He knew that this was one of those forks in the road that you walked up to only a few times in your life. If he told her what he knew than he would be forcing her down the path he had already chosen to follow.

"Listen . . . Lihwa . . . I'm a loner. I have my own ways and they suit me just fine. Trust me. You don't want to go down this road with me. Go back to your family and rebuild your lives together. You're lucky. You have people that care about you. I'm just a bull in a china shop," Tom said, as he began to turn away.

"My father's dead. Everything he worked for has been destroyed. I have to know why? None of this makes any sense. I'm a very good lawyer. I'm very good at figuring things out, and this makes no sense. The fire I understand. His death I understand, mostly, but why this heavy handed involvement by Homeland Security. That I don't understand," Lihwa said, as she grabbed Tom again and kept him from walking away from her.

"My car's parked down the street. We need to go somewhere and talk. The restaurant can wait. It's probably best we don't go there together anyway. Someone may be watching," Tom said, as he turned, and headed off down the street at a rapid pace.

At six-foot-three, Tom had a long stride, and Lihwa had to jog to keep up.

"How far is your car? I'm still dressed in heels," Lihwa said.

"Just around the corner," Tom said, as they turned left on Geary Street.

He slowed down another hundred yards up the street and pointed ahead.

"Isn't she a beauty!" Tom said, as he pointed at an old '67 Camaro RS.

"That thing is your car? It's a beater," Lihwa said.

"Sweetness didn't like my first wife. She tried to kill her twice. You notice that I still have the car, so be careful what you say about her. She's very sensitive," Tom said, as he unlocked the car door with his key.

Sliding in the driver's seat, he slid over and pulled up the door lock on the passenger side.

"Get in. We'll go for a spin and talk," Tom said, as he started the engine.

Lihwa opened the door, which creaked, and reluctantly got in after Tom threw some old In-N-Out burger bags into the back seat.

"There's only one In-N-Out in San Francisco. I can't believe you drive all the way up to North Beach for this. If I'm going to have a burger I'd rather eat at Jack-In-The-Box and they're right here on Geary," Lihwa said, as she wrinkled up her nose as Tom threw another burger bag into the back seat.

"Please! Square burgers? Woman, you have no shame," Tom said, as he cracked open his window.

"Best to roll down your window about half an inch. I have an exhaust leak, and that keeps the carbon monoxide levels bearable," Tom said, as he released the emergency brake and reached up on the steering column to put the car in gear.

"I thought the city paid fire fighters better than this," Lihwa said, as she tried repeatedly to get the seat belt to release so she could pull it across her lap.

"Hey, once I get Sweetness fixed up she'll be worth a fortune. Hold on to the belt until I get up to about 35. When I tap the brakes at that speed the solenoid will release the belt lock and you can pull it free," Tom said.

"Any more trade secrets?" Lihwa asked.

"Yeah, lock your door with the button. I can't do it from here. Sweetness is pure old school. I just wish she was a manual instead of a three speed automatic. Try the belt now," Tom said, as he hit the brakes.

"Where are we going?" Lihwa asked, while securing the seat belt and the door lock.

"Well, I was going to suggest something to eat, but since you're a burger snob, how about chicken?" Tom said.

"Krispy Krunchy Chicken or nothing," Lihwa said, as she felt herself start to relax for the first time in days.

It felt so good that it made her feel guilty, but at least she felt like she was starting to make some progress in solving the mystery of the coin, the crate and Homeland Security.

"Way over in Bayview-Hunters Point? Good, that will give us some time to talk. I'll just get on the 101 and head south. That'll get us close," Tom said, as he headed East on Geary.

"So what did my Father say behind the restaurant?" Lihwa asked.

"Sorry, Sweetness can't abide serious shit while she's on the road. If the chicken's good you'll get your answer then," Tom said, as he reached between the seats, retrieved a cassette tape and popped it into the player built into the dash.

.   .   .   .

San Francisco, California, USA
Krispy Krunchy Chicken
4517 3rd Street
March 13, 2017, 1150 hours PST

"Okay, so the chicken's awesome. I guess I owe you some answers," Tom said, as he finished the last of twenty buffalo wings.

"What I can't believe, is that you ate twenty wings. A two piece combo and I'm stuffed," Lihwa, said as she wiped off her hands.

"That was just a snack. I'll be hungry in three hours," Tom said, as he tried to discretely belch.

"We used to have an all-you-can-eat buffet on Thursdays. My father would have cringed to see you walk in the front door . . ." Lihwa began, then turned away and stared out the window in silence.

"Yeah, when I was young I used to look for places like that," Tom said, then just let the silence have its moment.

"I'll dump the trash," Tom said, as he opened the door and took advantage of the opportunity to empty all the trash from his car into a nearby can.

"I'm all right. I think you owe me a story," Lihwa said, as Tom got back in the car, started it up, and began to drive away.

"Heron's Head Park is right down the road. We'll walk and talk," Tom said, as they turned right on Evans and headed for the Park.

.  .  .  .

San Francisco, California, USA
Heron's Head Park
Jennings Street
March 13, 2017, 1230 hours PST


"Yeah, it's not much to look at, but my ex and I used to take Alex here before he died," Tom said, as they began to walk along a path toward the water.

"I'm so sorry. What happened?" Lihwa asked.

"Leukemia . . . he was 3 years old when he died. We tried to keep it together, but it didn't work out. Sharon moved back to Michigan. We haven't talked in ten years. I think she remarried, but I'm not sure," Tom said, as he picked up a small stone and threw it into the India Basin.

"Anyway, like you said, I owe you the whole story," Tom said, and proceeded to tell Lihwa everything that happened the night of the fire.

She listened without interruption. They walked back and forth in the small park until she sat down on a concrete bench and reached into her purse.

"I've been playing back the night the men came and placed the crate in our shed over and over. And now you say that the crate that sat behind our restaurant for over 20 years was an atomic bomb?" Lihwa said, as she sighed, and showed Tom the ancient Chinese coin that she had removed from her purse.

"This coin is in near mint condition, which is amazing since it's over 2100 years old. From the research I've done this coin shouldn't exist. I had it appraised by a specialist in New York several years ago. At first he thought it was a fake. The condition was too good. Then he offered me $30,000 cash on the spot. He said it had to be part of a buried hoard from a mint that had been destroyed or burned down or something," Lihwa said, as she handed Tom the coin.

"My father emigrated from China when I was 2 years old. I have no memory of China. Father always said that we were very poor when we came here, but he bought the building, and installed the restaurant 6 months after we arrived. When I was young, I never gave that a second thought. When I got older, and learned how things worked in this country, I asked him once about how he was able to do that. He told me I was a rude girl, and should be more grateful, and to not question my elders about such things," Lihwa said, as her voice began to crack.

"My God . . . my father was an agent for Communist China. I'm the daughter of a traitor . . . a terrorist," Lihwa said, as tears began streaming down her face.

Tom sat beside her on the bench not knowing quite what to do. Her small frame began shaking as she cried, and leaned against his right side. He reached around with his right arm and gently hugged her as her sobs became more intense.

"I've already decided that I'm going to conduct my own investigation into this shit. The government will do their thing and then bury it. If I had any sense I'd just leave it alone, but I've been told more than once that I don't have any sense. So, there you go," Tom said, and knew that he was rambling.

"What do you think is going on?" Lihwa asked, between sobs.

"I've been thinking about this for the last two days. Why would the Peoples Republic of China smuggle one nuclear weapon into the US of A? If they hit us with one nuke it would just piss us off. It would be like a hornet sting. We'd figure out who did it and clean them off the map. It would get ugly and millions would die, but it would be a no brainer. It would just happen. So, if that made no sense then what would be the alternative?" Tom said, as he hugged Lihwa closer after she sobbed again.

"More nukes?" Lihwa asked, as she reached into her purse for some tissues.

"That's what I figure, and I'm going to find another one. Who knows, if there are enough inside the country the bastards in the government might just surrender to save their own asses. They keep their positions in a puppet government and the rest of us are screwed," Tom said.

"You sound like a conspiracy nut to me," Lihwa said, as she blew her nose.

"Yeah, but I'm the conspiracy nut who found a nuke behind a Chinese restaurant in San Francisco," Tom said.

"I'm coming with you. I have to prevent my father's sins from harming more people, and you're right, the government will protect themselves first. We have to protect the people," Lihwa said, as she began to cry again.

"Like I said . . . no serious shit while riding in Sweetness," Tom quietly said, as he stared off into the bay, and pulled the sobbing woman closer.

. . . .

"It's 2PM and I have to be somewhere at 3," Lihwa said, while she and Tom were walking back to the Camaro.

"I'll drive you there. I'll ask Sweetness for a special dispensation so we can talk about serious shit during the drive," Tom said.

"She would do that?" Lihwa asked.

"That's why I call her Sweetness. She has a good heart," Tom said.

"Where are we going?" Lihwa asked.

"I thought you had a meeting or something," Tom said.

"I meant, where do we look for another bomb?" Lihwa asked.

"Well, I figure Homeland will check every Chinese restaurant in San Francisco first. Then they'll probably go to LA, San Diego, basically the whole state of California. If I was planting bombs back 25 years ago I'd have spread them out to lessen the chance of more than one being found. If we stick to the west coast, that leaves us with Oregon and Washington. If you look at population centers and military bases, then Washington wins that battle. You've got Seattle and nuke sub bases in the northwest part of the state. That's where I'd go first to look," Tom said, as he unlocked the passenger door, and held it open for Lihwa.

"So when will you be ready to leave?" Tom asked, as he got in and shut the door.

"My father's funeral comes first. It will probably be on the 18th. That would be a lucky day. You and your two friends are invited, just don't wear black. I'll send you the details. Two or three days for mourning and family matters . . . I'll take some vacation . . . we can leave on the 22nd," Lihwa said, while looking at the calendar on her cell phone.

"Agreed! We head to Seattle on a nuke hunt on the 22nd. Send me your address and I'll pick you up," Tom said, as they headed down Cargo Way.

# Chapter 14

"Appear at points which the enemy has neglected to defend; then march swiftly to places where you are not expected."

Sun Tzu (~520 BC)

New Orleans, Louisiana, USA
Albo Street Wharf
On the Mississippi River
March 14, 2017, 0845 EST

The huge diesel engine seemed almost diminutive when hanging in midair above the deck of the *Global Sun*, flagship of Seaward Shipping. At 108 tons it was far from diminutive.

The crane at the Alabo Street Wharf in New Orleans was rated at 120 tons, but to Gong Aiguo, the crane seemed far more ancient and spindly than the crane that had loaded the diesel engine on to the *Global Sun* in Shanghai.

"Relax, kid, I know what I'm doing," the crane operator said, as he eased the load from the ship and swung the heavy cargo towards the waiting rail car.

They stood on the dock beside the ship. The grizzled crane operator had his remote control hooked to a handrail as he deftly manipulated the heavy load. Aiguo stared at the man's hardhat, worn backwards for some reason, and the many decorations that were attached to the hat.

"*The American flag I understand. Many of them are still patriotic, but the other flag, red with white stars in a diagonal cross, what does that mean? A skull with crossed bones, a shrimp, and who are the Saints?*" Aiguo asked himself.

"We'll have this baby off loaded and secure within two hours. Americans know how to do things right," the old crane operator said.

"Thank you, I appreciate your efforts," Aiguo said, and knew that his English sounded too stilted, especially in this part of the United States.

"Where you headed with this thing?' the crane operator asked, as the crane continued its slow progression across the cloudless sky.

"Alexandria, Virginia, a factory along the Potomac. From where this will be sitting you'll be able to spit and hit the White House," Aiguo said, proud that he had chosen the correct amount of local dialect.

"Never been to Washington. Maybe when I retire, the missus and I will take a drive up that way," the crane operator said, as he turned and faced the waiting flatbed railcar.

"Kind of odd you escorting this diesel engine that far. Normally, things like this just pass along with the paperwork," the crane operator said, as he began to lower the diesel toward the railcar.

"We're a new company. This is our first big US deal. My boss wants to make sure that there are no mishaps along the way," Aiguo said, tension in his voice as the diesel engine swung in the stiff morning breeze.

"Relax, son, I been doing this a long time. The man on the tag line will straighten her out and we'll be down in less than ten minutes; and son, loosen that death grip on the handrail. I think you're starting to twist the metal," the crane operator said, and laughed at his own joke.

Aiguo wondered how much the stupid American would laugh if he knew what was inside the converted diesel engine.

"Your shipping manifest showed Norfolk Southern the whole way. That'll speed things up. Every time you transfer to another system it slows things down. You'll be taking a scenic tour of the Deep South. Good thing it's March. If it was July that would be a long haul. No air conditioning in that caboose you'll be riding in," the crane operator said, as the load straightened over the flat bed.

.   .   .   .

Albo Street Wharf
March 14, 2017, 1100 EST

As the train began to pull away from the wharf, Aiguo checked his watch. The diesel was landed on the railcar flatbed, secured, and covered. The crane operator had said two hours, and he had been correct. Breathing a sigh of relief, Aiguo looked around at the train car they called a 'caboose'. It had been arranged just for him so he could escort the package to Virginia.

"Very limited resources: a small refrigerator, microwave, bottled water and a pull down bed, but I've had far worse," Aiguo said, as he remembered his PLA training in the Taihang Mountains in the middle of winter.

"I am Special Forces. I can do anything," Aiguo said, as he dropped to the floor and began his standard routine of 100 pushups, every three hours.

His mind drifted back as his body responded. His acceptance into the Shenyang Military Region Special Forces Unit, known as the "Siberian Tigers", had been the proudest day in his life. His transfer six months later to Project 22 had been disheartening. He felt he had become nothing more than a security guard.

"Yet here I am, three years later riding a train in the United States. This mission may determine the fate of our struggle against the decadent forces of the US. Thanks to General Kung, I am a very lucky man," Aiguo said to himself, as he jumped to his feet.

"*Three days, then a long plane ride. This is like a vacation, but one with great responsibility,*" he reminded himself, as he checked his watch and began to inspect the contents of his new rolling home.

.   .   .   .

Meridian, Mississippi
March 14, 2017, 2000 EST

Aiguo stood on the back porch of the caboose enjoying the cool air as the sun set behind the trees to his right. He had occupied his day by studying the terrain as the train made its way slowly north and east.

"*I expected to see a land of riches, but these people are as poor as the peasants in China that flee into our cities looking for work,*"

Aiguo thought, as he passed a group of black children playing in a stream beside the railroad tracks.

They waved at the strange looking man in the faded red caboose as it streamed by while they splashed through the muddy red water. Aiguo waved and smiled back. He wasn't sure why. He glanced at the homes behind them, as the lights inside were turned on to chase away the darkness. Most were small, with faded, peeling paint.

Fifteen minutes later the train slowed. A sign by the tracks said, "Welcome to Meridian, Mississippi'. The train stopped at a station. A man walked up below him and said, "You can get off and stretch your legs, or have something to eat if you want, but we'll be leaving in 45 minutes. They have some coffee inside the station."

"Coffee . . . Americans are addicted to coffee," Aiguo said, as he remembered more of his training on American culture, and climbed down from the caboose.

It was a Tuesday evening, and a faint glow remained in the evening sky as Aiguo walked into the building. It had a freshly painted sign that said 'Union Station'. He could smell the strange aroma of brewing coffee as he approached the counter at one end of the station. The interior of the building was in keeping with the exterior, all brick and stucco. The building still had the look of fresh construction, all shiny and new, in contrast with the houses that he had passed earlier.

Drawn by the smell of the coffee, Aiguo walked up to the counter while reaching into his pocket for his wallet.

"Please, coffee and a sandwich," Aiguo said, as he pointed at a wrapped ham, cheese and lettuce sandwich sitting inside the glass display.

"What size coffee?" the tall black woman asked from behind the counter.

"Large, please," Aiguo said, as he restrained himself from bowing politely.

"Cream and sugar are over on the table," the woman said, as he turned to pour the coffee.

Aiguo remembered that Americans put all manner of additional items in their coffee, as he said, "Yes, please."

The woman turned, and stared at him, as she placed the coffee on the top of the counter and reached for a sandwich.

"Honey, I can tell you're not from around here. So what brings you to Meridian? No passenger trains due this time of night," the woman said, as she placed the sandwich on a tray and added a bag of chips.

"I'm . . . just escorting some freight. Nothing important, just company business," Aiguo said, remembering that he had been instructed to minimize contact with the local inhabitants unless absolutely necessary.

"Honey, the chips come with the sandwich. That'll be $6.50," she said, as she saw Aiguo staring at the chips.

She placed all the items on a small plastic tray as she said, "I'll bet you're from China. I was watching a Bruce Lee movie last night after I got off. You're the first Chinese person I've ever seen live," she said, as she grinned and took the $5 and two $1's that Aiguo handed her.

"Here's your change. There's mustard and mayo over on that table beside  the cream and sugar," she said, as she handed him two quarters.

Aiguo looked at the image of the man on the quarters and recognized the face from his training.

"George Washington," Aiguo muttered, then placed the coins in his pocket.

"Yeah, another old, dead, white man. They need to put a sister on that coin," she said, and then burst out laughing at the thought of that happening.

"Don't mind me, son. Just go enjoy your food," she said, while wiping off the counter.

Aiguo added cream and sugar to the coffee after finding the bitter taste disagreeable. The sandwich was bland, but the mustard helped. The creamy dressing that the woman had called mayo was too sweet.

"No wonder Americans are so fat. Everything they eat has sugar," Aiguo said, as he pushed aside the honey, barbecue chips.

"I never thought I'd want a meal of Type 09 combat rations," Aiguo said, as he stood up, belched, and felt his stomach rumble.

"Honey, put your trash over in the bin and give me the tray," the woman said, as she pointed at a trash can beside a brick pillar.

Aiguo did as he was asked, and walked out of the building, and checked his watch.

"Another 15 minutes. A walk might help my stomach," Aiguo said, and decided that he would never drink coffee again.

As he walked around the front of the building he noticed a small wooden horse standing in the grass.

"I've seen these before. What are they called?" he said, as he walked up to the brightly painted prancing horse with a steel pole penetrating its back.

"A merry-go-round, I think," he said, as he touched the smooth surface of the horse's face.

Aiguo smiled, and thought of his little brother, and how much he would like this little horse.

"*I am losing focus. These people are the enemy. I am not here to make friends or experience their culture. They are decadent and corrupt. Their people are slaves to capitalism. I am here to help free them from their past,*" Aiguo thought, as he turned, and walked back toward the train.

"Hey, honey, I got you something for the road. I could tell that meal didn't sit real well, so I fixed you some green tea. My momma always said that a little green tea would fix an upset stomach," the tall black woman said, as she walked up to him and handed him a large styrofoam cup with a plastic lid.

"No, don't bother with that. It's on the house," she said, as Aiguo was reaching for his wallet.

"I hope you have a good trip," she said, as she smiled, and walked back into the station.

Aiguo sniffed the tea and then sipped it. It was delicious. He looked up, intending to thank her, but she was already gone. He glanced at his watch and was surprised that the train was due to leave in five minutes.

As he climbed onto the back of the caboose he glanced at the station and saw the woman cleaning his table. The train lurched as they began to depart, rapidly gaining speed as he left Meridian, Mississippi for the last time.

. . . .

Every day was the same. Endless forests and fields laced with pockets of humanity scattered in little towns. The buildings were either red brick or white wooden structures that looked like they came from an American movie set. He had expected some suppressed hostility. He had been taught that most Americans hated Chinese and viewed them as the enemy. What he found was just the opposite. He was stared at as a curiosity, but he was always treated with polite respect.

.  .  .  .

"Another day, another station, at least it breaks the monotony," Aiguo said, as the train lurched to a halt.

"Ten minutes, mister. We're just letting a passenger train go by. Don't be wandering off," the engineer said, as he came running up to the caboose, turned and then went running back towards the engine.

Aiguo stepped down from the caboose and began walking beside the train. "*Ten minutes is better than nothing*," he said to himself.

Twenty yards down the walkway, Aiguo noticed a young boy sitting on a bench just staring at the train. He was going to walk by until he noticed that the boy was Asian, possibly Chinese. He also noticed that the boy was crying.

"*None of my business; just keep on walking*," he told himself, but found that he couldn't take his eyes off the boy.

"Ni ku shenme? (Why are you crying?)" Aiguo asked, in Mandarin.

The boy was startled to hear Chinese and answered in English, "None of your business," and looked at his hands that were folded in his lap.

"Where are your parents? Are you waiting for them to come in on a train?" Aiguo asked in English.

My mom thinks I'm in school, but I come here sometimes instead," the boy said.

"What is your name?" Aiguo asked.

"Albert Wong?" the boy said.

"Albert, an American name," Aiguo said.

"I'm an American. I was born here, but you're not an American are you?" Albert asked, as Aiguo sat down beside him.

"No, I'm Chinese, from Shanxi Province . . . but I live in Taiwan now. I'm a citizen of Taiwan now," Aiguo lied, as he realized that he had made a mistake and got up to leave.

"My father was from China. I think he grew up in Fujian Province. His father and mother immigrated here when he was little. He said that China was not where he wanted to raise a family. He wanted to be free," Albert said.

"Where is your father now?' Aiguo asked, as he sat back down, glanced at his watch and saw he only had five minutes to get back on the train.

"He's dead. He was a helicopter pilot in the Army. He died in Afghanistan," Albert said, as he pulled his father's dog tags out from under his shirt.

"He got a Silver Star for rescuing a lot of wounded men. They said he went back four times for the wounded. He didn't come back from the fifth trip," Albert said, as he looked over at Aiguo, and tears began to stream down his face.

"It sounds like he was a very brave man. You should be proud to be his son," Aiguo said, as he comforted the child of an enemy soldier.

"We used to come here. He liked the sound and rumble of the trains, and the way they smelled. When I come here I pretend he's sitting beside me, just where you are," Albert said, as he lowered his head, and began to quietly weep.

"Albert Wong, listen to me. You come from strong people. Your father was a brave man and would want his son to honor his memory by growing into a brave man too. Do not be a disobedient son and cause your mother worry. Always take care of your mother and honor your father's memory. That is what Chinese do, and I suppose that Americans are the same, in their own way," Aiguo said, as the train started to move.

"This is my train, and I must get on, or I will be the one in trouble," Aiguo said, as he bowed to the boy, and began running for the end of the caboose.

As he caught the train and climbed the stairs onto the balcony at the end of the caboose, he turned, and was just able to catch a glimpse of the little Chinese-American boy sitting on the bench. The boy waved, then rose, and turned away as he left.

"*I should have followed my instructions and never left the train. They are becoming something other than my enemies*," Aiguo thought, as he opened the door to the caboose, entered, and dropped to the floor for a hundred pushups.

Chapter 15

"I was bold in the pursuit of knowledge, never fearing to follow truth and reason to whatever results they led."

Thomas Jefferson

Manassas, Virginia, USA
Mission Center for Weapons and Counterproliferation
Office of Amanda Langford
March 16, 2017 0345 hours EST

Amanda had not left the building in three days. Her hair was becoming greasy, and the stubble on her legs was becoming a distraction. The perfume in her purse was the only thing that kept her new office from smelling like a locker room.

"Every time I think I'm there it slips through my hands," Amanda said, as she leaned on her desk with her head in her hands.

She knew that she was exhausted, but she was too stubborn to admit defeat. Looking to her left, she stared at the wall full of yellow stickies. Each had a piece of data pertaining to the mystery nuke found in San Francisco.

"This has to be part of the missing nuclear material. It has to be the Chinese. But why would they do this? Or did someone steal a device from them? I just need more data?" she said, as she slid her keyboard aside, and laid her head on the desk.

"Just a couple of minutes," she said, as her eyes closed, and her conscious mind slipped into blessed oblivion.

. . . .

Three hours later the rising sun began to creep across her desk. When the glare reached her eyes, she moaned and reached for non-existent sheets. She desperately wanted to roll over and go back to sleep. The impact with the floor shocked her awake.

"Crap, that's it. I've got to go home, get cleaned up and get some food. The state I'm in right now makes me useless," Amanda said, as she used her desk to drag herself upright.

As she lifted her swivel chair off the floor, and slipped it under her desk, she glanced at the wall full of notes once more.

"Restaurant . . . Chinese restaurants . . . 20 to 60 missing devices . . . in Chinese restaurants . . . oh my God," Amanda said, as she pulled her chair out, sat down, and pulled the keyboard towards her.

"Okay, Google . . . how many Chinese restaurants in the USA?" she said, as she keyed in the request.

"Crap . . . 41,000 . . . plus. If I'm right, it's a needle in a haystack, says the country girl that looks and smells like she spent the night sleeping with the cows," Amanda said, as she leaned back in her chair, and stared at the wall full of data once again.

"I need more data . . . more proof. Without more links this is just a guess. They'll laugh at my theory. They won't search 41,000 Chinese restaurants unless I have more proof. The media would go nuts and the ACLU would go berserk. They'll start talking about Japanese internment camps," she said, as she logged off her computer and stood up.

"Okay . . . home, shower, food, sleep, and then right back here," she said, as she reached into her purse, spritzed herself one last time, and headed out the door.

# Chapter 16

"Disciplined and calm, to await the appearance of disorder and hubbub amongst the enemy:—this is the art of retaining self-possession."

Sun Tzu (~520 BC)

Baoji, China
22 Base Headquarters
Office of Base Commander, General Wu Fuxi
March 17, 2017, 0900 hours CT

"So, I'm to understand that Lieutenant General Kung wants a meeting with the entire Central Military Commission including the General Secretary. Has he lost his mind? I'd probably lose my position if I was stupid enough to forward his request. They would question my judgment, let alone his. Tell him the answer is no. It's out of the question?" General Wu said, as his adjutant fidgeted in front of his desk.

"Comrade General, apologies, but he told me that you would refuse his request. He told me to tell you that he would go over your head and request a meeting directly with his uncle," the adjutant said, as he bowed repeatedly.

"General Fan? The commanding general of the PLA? He has lost his mind. Why would he play that card? What's so damn important? Get him on the phone. I want to talk to him now, General Wu, said.

"Again, Comrade General, apologies, but General Kung said that you would get angry and would want to talk to him. He said to tell you that the matter had to be discussed with him . . . face to face," the adjutant said, and waited for the explosion.

General Wu felt his face redden as he pounded his desk. He stood, pounded it again, and then began cursing.

"Get that bastard on the phone and tell him to come to my office. Tell him that it is a direct order. If he doesn't come, then I'll have him arrested," General Wu yelled.

"Apologies, Comrade General, but General Kung is outside. He ordered me not to tell you he was here until you wanted to see him . . . personally," the adjutant said, and began wondering where the coldest PLA military base was located.

"Bastard! Send General Kung in," General Wu said, as his mood shifted from anger to reluctant admiration.

"At once, Comrade General!" the adjutant said, as he rushed to leave.

The door reopened, and General Kung stood in the doorway. Despite his age he was still as trim as the day he joined the PLA. His uniform was tailored and impeccable. The pants had been modified, against army regulations, to contain a certain pocket watch. His chest displayed no less than seventeen medals, six more than General Wu, a discrepancy that General Wu attributed to Kung's relation to General Fan.

"Close the door behind you. Subordinates shouldn't see generals yelling at each other," General Wu said, as he remained seated behind his carved rosewood desk.

"Now, now, general, we haven't seen each other in quite a while. I was just having a little fun. I've come a long way to talk to you," General Kung said, as he closed the door, and walked up to the front of General Wu's desk.

"I'm up for retirement in six months when I turn 67. You are trying to drive me to a stroke or a firing squad. I want to retire to Lake Taihu. I've bought land there. I love to fish, and I want to walk the hills while I still can," General Wu said.

"Based on your waist line you better retire sooner than later, my friend, or you will have to pick very low hills," General Kung said, as he looked at Wu and patted his stomach.

"Very funny, and I know how you work. Don't think that this friendly banter fools me. What are you up to? Why do you want to talk to your uncle or worse, the Central Military Commission?" General Wu said.

"I can't tell you, but it is very important, or I wouldn't be bothering you. I must be heard, but I will follow the chain of command," General Kung said.

"Yusheng, what did you do, lose one of our nuclear warheads?" General Wu said, and then felt his heart shudder when General Kung didn't smile at his joke.

General Wu took off his glasses, and began rubbing his face before he said, "Wenling tried to get me to retire last year. I should have listened to her. What have you done, Yusheng?"

"I must talk to the CMC and the General Secretary . . . and soon. This will not wait. It would be best if you forwarded the request through channels with your recommendation for approval," General Kung said, as he picked up an ornate jade vase from General Wu's desk.

"Do you know what you have here?" General Kung asked, as he turned the vase over, and studied the markings on the bottom.

"My wife bought it at an antique market in Beijing. She paid 1500¥ for that thing. I almost wrung her neck. Do you want to buy it? You can have it for 2000," General Wu said.

General Kung began laughing as he gently set the pure white jade vase back on the desk.

"Fuxi, old friend, when you go home tonight kiss your wife like you haven't kissed her in years. Give her a neck massage, a foot massage, and run her a hot bath. This white jade vase is from the Qianlong or perhaps the Jiaqing period. It is worth at least 500,000¥, possibly more," General Kung said, and began laughing.

"Now you're just messing with me again," General Wu said, as he stared at the vase that had been sitting on his desk for over two years.

"Of course I am, but it is a nice vase. I'll give you 1800¥ for it," General Kung said, as he crossed his arms, and stared down at his old friend.

"Ahh . . . you never change. Even when we were young lieutenants you were always sly. I always take things at face value. With you, a face is worth everything or nothing. What am I to believe?" General Wu said.

"If you forward my request the vase is worth 500,000¥. If you don't, you can pack it in a box, and take it with you when you retire," General Kung said.

"Now you are offering me a bribe. You think like a Japanese, or worse, an American. Everything has a price. I do not have a price. I cannot be bribed," General Wu said, as he thumped his desk.

"Careful, you might break the vase, and it is worth 500,000¥, but not from my pocket," General Kung said.

General Wu began to reach for the vase, but was now afraid to touch it.

"All right . . . I'll forward your request to Second Artillery. If General Wei sees fit it will be forwarded to your uncle . . . General Fan. Good luck getting past General Wei. He's a southerner, and his father was a Long March veteran. He will have little tolerance for your ways," General Wu said, as he gently picked up the vase, and placed it inside the lower left drawer of his desk.

"Everyone's father claimed to be a Long March veteran. Thank you, General Wu. You don't know it now, but you have performed a great service for the People of China," General Kung said, as he snapped to attention and, saluted General Wu.

"I'll forward the request within the hour. Now go away and let me do some honest work," General Wu said, as he saluted while still sitting at his desk.

Chapter 17

"Knowledge of the enemy's dispositions can only be obtained
from other men."

Sun Tzu (~520 BC)

Manassas, Virginia, USA
Mission Center for Weapons and Counterproliferation
Amanda Langford's Office
March 18, 2017, 1045 hours EST

"Young lady, I think you need to go back to your
apartment, and get some more sleep. If you think I'm going to
bring your theory to the Director based on what you've shown me
so far, you're mistaken," Assistant Director Janet Davidson said, as
she stared at the hundreds of sticky notes that covered two walls in
Amanda Langford's office.

Amanda was becoming frustrated; this discussion had been
going on for over thirty minutes. She knew that she had to find
another line of reasoning to convince her boss that she was right.

"Okay, why would the Chinese smuggle a single nuclear
weapon into the United States? What would that accomplish?"
Amanda said, as she began to pace in front of the sticky notes.

"It could start World War 3, but we haven't gotten there
yet," Janet said.

"So why take the risk over one device? It doesn't make any
sense," Amanda said, realizing that she was just traveling down the
same logic path, and based on the look on the Assistant Director's
face, she was running out of time.

"Our borders have been wide open for decades. The
Chinese know this. They play the long game. They're patient.
Pardon me for stereotyping, but it's their nature. They know that
they will never match up with us militarily. So what do they do?

They look for an edge. Look at this," Amanda said, as she handed a photo to Janet.

"On the outside wall of the library of the PLA's Command Academy they have one of Sun Tzu's sayings, ' *Use the normal Force to engage; use the extraordinary to win.'* That's what this is. This is unconventional warfare . . . a type of Trojan Horse," Amanda said, and saw that she had the Assistant Director's attention again.

"Next to Mao, Sun Tzu is regarded as the most significant thinker and strategist in their entire history. They even teach his sayings to common soldiers and sailors. Ms. Davidson, we've been had. This device we found in San Francisco, by blind luck, is an antique. It may have been sitting there for decades. We have no idea how many more devices have been smuggled into this country or where they are," Amanda said, then stopped, and took a deep breath, when she heard herself shouting.

"Ms. Davidson, normally I'm a very calm person. I don't get rattled very easily, but I'm scared. We have a gun pressed against our head, and we don't even know it," Amanda said, as her eyes began to well up.

"Amanda, anyone that's ever been in combat, and says they weren't scared, is a damn liar or crazy. I used to get this . . . feeling, before we started an operation. Logically, I knew that it was my adrenal gland starting to trickle. I've got that same feeling right now. You've convinced me. I'll arrange a meeting with Director McElroy, in his office. I think he's available this afternoon. Make sure you're ready," Janet said, as she turned, and walked out of Amanda's office.

. . . .

Director McElroy's Office
March 18, 2017, 1430 hours

"Sir, I appreciate you sparing the time to listen to my theory," Amanda said, as she finished her presentation to Director Caleb McElroy.

"Assistant Director Davidson had already filled me in on your theory. I have a great deal of respect for her opinion, but I wanted to hear it directly from you. So let's assume that you're correct. The People's Republic of China has a clandestine program for inserting nuclear weapons into the United States of America that has been going on for decades. What's their play?" Director McElroy asked.

"Sir, I have a minor in Asian History. I also read and speak Mandarin, Japanese and Korean. The Chinese want to dominate Asia first. Then they want the entire planet. They literally consider themselves as the 'Central Country'. We are in their way. Mao was once asked his opinion of another World War, this time with the West. His answer was, ' Don't make a fuss about a world war. At most, people die . . . half the population wiped out. This happened quite a few times in Chinese history. It's best if half the population is left, next best one-third...'," Amanda said, and began staring at her hands.

"You don't really think that they would detonate a number of nuclear weapons on our soil do you? That's preposterous! Our response would annihilate them," Director McElroy said.

"Who would give the orders to the sub commanders to launch their missiles if everything was gone?" Amanda asked, still staring at her hands.

"They would have to go after our command and control centers, military bases . . . that would take dozens of weapons," Director McElroy said.

"Yes, Sir . . . it would," Amanda said, as she raised her eyes, and stared into Director McElroy's.

"She can be unnervingly convincing. The whole thing starts to make a perverse kind of sense. If I was the Chinese I'd wait until everything was in place, and then arrange for a private meeting with the President. Then I'd tell him what I had done, and where he could find one of the devices. Things would progress from there," Assistant Director Davidson said.

"Blackmail! They could target our population centers and threaten to kill hundreds of millions," Director McElroy said.

"No Sir! That would go against the teachings of Sun Tzu. He said, ' In the practical art of war, the best thing of all is to take the enemy's country whole and intact; to shatter and destroy it is not so good.' They don't want to destroy us. They want to subjugate us. If we fall, the world falls. We will become the People's Republic of America," Amanda said.

"Agent Langford, if it wasn't for the device in San Francisco I'd fire you right now. It sounds like you're writing a Tom Clancy novel," Director McElroy said, as he stared at both women.

"If it wasn't for San Francisco, I would have fired her, and we wouldn't be having this conversation," Assistant Director Davidson said, as she nodded at Amanda, and gave her a thumbs up.

"I still think that the whole premise is shaky, but keep pursuing this. Keep me informed on what else you find. Right now this is still just a theory with a lot of circumstantial evidence," Director McElroy said, indicating that the meeting was at an end.

When both women had left the office, Director McElroy removed his glasses and began rubbing his temples. He had always had a problem with migraines, and he knew instinctively that they were going to be worse for quite some time.

Removing a key that was magnetically secured below the pen drawer of his desk, he took the key and unlocked the lower right drawer. He then reached in the drawer, and pulled a second key that was magnetically attached to the shelf between the lower and middle drawers. The second key had a thumb print identifier. Pressing his thumb against the identifier he walked over to a portrait of the President, and swung the portrait to the left, revealing a small safe. Using the key, he opened the safe, and retrieved a cell phone.

Pressing an eleven digit code he waited for a beep and said, "Fifty has been compromised," hung up, and returned the phone to the safe.

Returning to his desk he replaced the keys, and began to massage his temples

"If this comes out, ten million dollars won't help me. They'll hunt me down wherever I go. How can I stop this? That little bitch is like a pit bull," Caleb said, as he reached inside a drawer for his migraine pills.

Chapter 18

"Be courteous to all, but intimate with few, and let those few
be well tried before you take them into your confidence."

George Washington

San Francisco, California, USA
Green Street Mortuary
649 Green Street
March 18, 2017, 1018 hours PST

The funeral started precisely at 1018. The feng shui master,
Mr. Yee, had chosen the date and time as being the most auspicious
available. The open casket was mounted on a platform at the far end of
the chapel. Over fifty large flower arrangements were placed in the
area. Tables contained offerings and gifts for the deceased.

"You have done well, Deshi. Father would be pleased.
Everything is proper and quite beautiful," Lihwa said.

She, and her brothers and sister, sat on the front row of pews.
All were dressed in black. They were the only mourners dressed in
black, as was appropriate for a traditional Chinese funeral.

"The blanketing ceremony went well last night. Thirty nine
blankets were perfect. Though, Mrs. Tao was upset when we declined
her blanket. It would have ruined a perfect number, so I think she
understood," Deshi said.

"So many offerings. Father was respected and liked in the
community," Lei said, as he studied the various items that would be
burned at the burial site.

"Yes, he had many friends," Deshi said, as she fought back the
urge to start screaming, and tell her siblings what their father had
really been up to for so many years.

"Why did you invite the lao mei to father's funeral? It's not
right," Chuntao said, as she leaned against her older sister, and glanced
toward the back of the chapel.

"Don't complain! At least they didn't wear black," Jianguo said, as he poked his younger sister.

"I told them to wear something bright or it would be considered a great insult. They found it strange that only the immediate family can wear black. Now, all of you be quiet," Lihwa whispered, as she fought to remember the father that she had loved so deeply, but had not really known at all.

. . . .

"I know, but I still feel weird wearing a white dress to a funeral," Heather said, as she pulled the short skirt as far down as she could.

"You think that's weird? If one of the unmarried sons had died they wouldn't have a service. They'd just stick him in the ground," Jamar said.

"What? That's bull. Nobody would do that for a dead child," Heather whispered.

"I'm telling you that's what Jingfei told me. The young don't get any respect. I don't think their relatives are supposed to even cry. Like I said, they just stick them in the ground and move on," Jamar said.

"I just don't believe it. No one would treat a child like that," Heather said.

"Listen white bread, not everybody's culture is the same as yours," Jamar said, and had to stifle a laugh as Heather looked at him and flipped him off.

"You two behave," Tom said, as an elderly Chinese lady turned around and glared at the three of them.

. . . .

The brass band outside began playing traditional Chinese funeral music as the casket left the funeral home. The Longwei family exited first, and stood at the exit handing out red and white envelopes. The red envelopes held money. The white envelopes held a quarter and a piece of candy. The envelopes were presented with two hands and a bow.

The three firefighters were walking down the street to Tom's car as Heather said, "Money? I just got paid ten bucks for going to a funeral. What's in the white one?"

"Candy, to take the bitterness of a sad day out of your mouth. The quarter is to spend on something today. It's for good luck," Jamar said, as he popped the hard candy into his mouth, then pocketed the ten and the quarter.

"Looks like the band is heading off down the street. What now?" Heather asked, as they reached Tom's car which had been washed and waxed for the occasion.

"Lihwa said the band will lead the procession for nine blocks. When they drop off, the caravan will pick up the 101, then the 280, and head toward the Tung Sen Cemetery down in Daly City," Tom said.

"Lihwa . . . sounds like somebody else is getting a Chinese girlfriend," Jamar said, as he winked at Heather and nodded toward Tom.

"Nothing like that, we're just friends. We've just talked about some things. She's easy to talk to," Tom said, as he opened the door, and got behind the wheel of the Camaro.

"And easy to look at, plus she's a lawyer and is probably loaded. Things are looking up. About time you started looking for another woman," Jamar said, as he slapped Tom on his right shoulder while sitting in the back seat.

Heather had refused to crawl into the back seat while wearing a short dress.

"We're just friends, like I said. That's it," Tom said, as they pulled in at the back of the line of vehicles following the hearse.

"Yeah, guys always say that. 'I just want to be friends.' Then their hands start to wander," Heather said, while pulling down her short dress once again.

"So when's the burial supposed to start?" Heather asked.

"Lihwa said the ceremony starts at 1303. The internment at 1333 . . . precisely . . . something about lucky numbers," Tom said, as they progressed down Green street.

"Yeah, the Chinese are big time superstitious. We've got things like knocking on wood and the number thirteen, but they . . ." Jamar began.

"I don't step on cracks in sidewalks, and I haven't washed the heavy wool socks I wear in my fireman's boots in months," Heather said.

"I have a lucky Joe Montana jersey that I wear when watching the '9ers," Tom said, as they all began to laugh at each other.

"Hey, Jamar, why didn't you bring Jingfei?" Heather asked.

"I got the invitation, and asked her if she would come with me, but she said no. If you're not family, and not invited, it's considered rude to just show up," Jamar said.

"I'll be glad when this is over," Heather said.

"Yeah, Jingfei and I are driving out to Vegas tonight. Seven days on the strip! I'll be so broke when I get back," Jamar said, and laughed in anticipation..

"Yep, as soon as this is over I'm packing up and driving down to my sister's place in San Diego. Maybe I'll find a cute sailor when we go to the beach," Heather said.

"How about you, Tom? You got anything planned?" Jamar asked.

"I think I'm going to take a drive up the coast. I haven't been up to Vancouver in years. Sharon and I used to go there," Tom said.

"My man, I thought you were past that. She's moved on. You gotta let it go, or you'll be stuck in the past for the rest of your life," Jamar said.

"Yeah, I know. I just like the drive, and it's really pretty up there. Just a few places I want to go one more time," Tom said, as he popped a cassette tape into the player and turned it up.

.  .  .  .

Daly, California, USA
Tung Sen Cemetery
1333

The three firefighters stood at the back of the crowd of mourners that had come to the cemetery to pay their respects to Yan Longwei. Four red barrels surrounded the burial site.

"What's with the trash barrels?" Heather whispered, as the funeral director's assistants began burning all the offerings that had been presented at the funeral parlor.

"The smoke from the gifts mean they pass on with the deceased," Jamar said.

As the burial ceremony concluded, four men came and prepared to lower the casket into the ground. As they picked up the ropes, all the Chinese mourners turned their backs on the casket.

"Jeez, what's with this?" Heather said, as Tom grabbed her arm and turned her around.

"Bad luck to see the dead lowered into the ground," Jamal said, as he fiddled with the quarter in his pocket and began thinking about slot machines in Vegas.

. . . .

Tung Sen Cemetery
1410

"I thank you all for coming. The family appreciates the show of respect," Deshi said, as he bowed toward the fire fighters, turned and walked away.

Lihwa walked up and hugged Heather, then bowed to Tom and Jamar.

"Tomorrow at 10?" Tom quietly asked, as he stepped forward and shook her hand.

Lihwa nodded, then turned, and walked back to her family.

Tom smiled, placed his hands in his pockets, and slowly began walking back toward his car.

"Man . . . I'm impressed, confirming a date at a funeral. There's hope for you yet," Jamar said, as he nudged Tom in the right shoulder.

"It's not a date. We're going on a research mission up the coast," Tom said.

"First time I've ever heard it called that," Heather said, while nudging Tom in the other shoulder.

"Let's get back in the car. Then I'll fill you in on what's going on," Tom said, as they continued walking toward the parking lot.

Chapter 19

"A kingdom that has once been destroyed can never come again into being; nor can the dead ever be brought back to life."

Sun Tzu (~520BC)

Alexandria, Virginia, USA
The Torpedo Factory Art Center
105 North Union Street
March 18, 2017, 2300 hours EST

Chinese Special Forces Operative Gong Aiguo stood in the background as the diesel engine was off loaded from the extended flatbed trailer. It was bitterly cold, but he was used to far greater hardships than chilly weather. The train had arrived at the station at 4PM, but they had to wait for rush hour traffic to die down before going any further. The trip from the Amtrak Station had started at 8PM.

"Mr. Gong, it is quite exquisite, and quite the beast. It is exactly what I was hoping for. I just can't thank your government enough," Markus Candee, said, as he pumped Aiguo's hand.

"The Republic of China and the people of Taiwan are proud that this symbol of industrialization has been accepted as a token of our appreciation for the support your government has shown us over the years," Aiguo said, as he repeated the speech he had been given and memorized.

"Yes, yes, quite the beast. It's intended to become a symbol of free speech and solidarity. Ordinary people will be able to write whatever they want on it. We plan to have an annual painting by school children from all over the area. We'll erect scaffolding and ladders. It will be quite safe, but so very exciting. It will become a constantly changing piece of modern art. I couldn't be more pleased. I really can't thank you enough," Markus said, as he continued to shake Aiguo's hand.

As Aiguo pulled his hand free, welders were already moving into position to secure the 'art object' to the steel lattice work that would become its base.

"It's going to be marvelous. The bottom of the diesel engine will be seven feet off the ground. It will seem to float in the center of the stone courtyard where it will be on permanent display," Markus said, as he gestured grandly with his right hand.

"It took forever to get permission from the city to raze the old building behind the art center and allow us to install this beautiful stone plaza," Markus said, as he shielded his eyes from the glare of the welders.

"The location is beautiful. The Potomac River is close. It looks like fifty yards or less. Does it ever flood?" Aiguo asked.

"Actually . . . yes, but it's a rarity. That's one reason we mounted the object on such a tall framework. And the base, it goes down fifteen feet, reinforced steel and concrete. National endowment for the Arts paid for that, thank God. I was at wits end. The last thing we would want is for it to be damaged or washed away. That would be a disaster," Markus said, as he dismissed the very thought with a wave of his hand.

"Yes, if it fell over that would be a problem," Aiguo said, as he wondered if that would impact the functionality of the device.

"The welders will be at this for hours. It's late, but I'd be glad to take you somewhere to eat. At least it will get us out of this ghastly weather, and it's supposed to get worse. I know several fine restaurants that are open until one," Markus said.

"Thank you, but no. I appreciate the offer, but I have made prior arrangements. I have relatives in the area. They will be coming by to pick me up as soon as I give them a call," Aiguo said, as he removed his cell phone from his jacket pocket.

He glanced once at the terrible object that he had escorted across the world, nodded in mock respect to the effete American, and turned away from his great task.

"It's over and the mission is a success. So why do I feel . . . ashamed? This is war. I did this for the Motherland . . . for China.

America is the enemy, so why do I feel like this?" Aiguo asked himself.

Agitated, he placed his cell phone back in his coat pocket, and began walking north up North Union Street. Winding his way across Old Alexandria he would pause and stare in various shop windows. Most were darkened, but a few were still lit, as if the owners didn't care that few shoppers would be driving or walking by this late in the evening.

"Stout brick buildings and these strange stone roads, made from river rock, as if they were built hundreds of years ago. These people have a pride in their past just as we do," Aiguo said, as he stopped, closed his eyes, and took a deep breath of the frigid air.

When he opened his eyes all he saw was debris and swirling ash. The fine brick buildings were gone. The sky was the color of raw beef. The smell of death caused him to choke, as if he was breathing in the souls of the dead.

"Duty . . . duty is all that matters," he told himself, as he shut his eyes, and thought of his childhood home.

When he opened his eyes he was staring at the brick wall of a house, and sensed that the night was growing colder. Scattered snow flakes drifted before his eyes, held aloft by an increasing breeze. Yet still, he kept walking. Turning left, then right, he followed each road steadily northward until he came to a broad road labeled North Washington Street. Turning right, he began to follow the road as it headed north. There was almost no traffic as he walked along the side of the road. Soon the name of the road changed and became the George Washington Parkway.

"He was their Mao, their warrior liberator and first leader," Aiguo said, as he paused, and read the name of the road, illuminated by a nearby street light.

He checked his watch, and saw that over an hour had passed. He knew from experience that hypothermia was starting to set in. He wasn't dressed for this weather. If he didn't find shelter soon he was in trouble.

"What am I thinking? I have lost track of my mission," he told himself, as he remembered the faces of the Americans that he had met in the last four days.

"They are not what I expected. They are all so different, like Chinese. Many different accents and races . . . why do we have to kill them? They only want to get on with their lives and live in peace. What have I done?" he asked himself, as he noticed that the snow drifts were now past his ankles and his feet were getting numb.

"Ahh, America is fighting me. She seeks to punish the invader. Are we so very different?" he asked himself, as he passed a road labeled Marina Drive.

He pulled his cell phone from his jacket. His frozen fingers began to tremble as he tried to remember the number of his contact. His mind blurred as he found himself walking along the Potomac River when a large passenger jet soared past his right shoulder. The airport was huge and so brightly lit that he couldn't believe that he hadn't noticed it before.

"On the Potomac . . . Reagan . . . the destroyer of the Soviet Union . . . his airport," Aiguo said, as he rubbed his hands together.

The phone had disappeared.

The late winter's snow was thickening. His breath frosted in front of his face, blown by the steady wind from the north. He stopped and glanced to his front. Past the airport an obelisk appeared in the distance, barely visible through the thickening snowfall.

"Washington's Monument . . . the great warrior had this city named after him . . . the capital city of this great nation. Even Mao has not had so many edifices erected in his honor. They loved this man who created this place. Why am I here? What have I done?" Aiguo asked himself, as he dropped to his knees.

"Duty . . . the Motherland . . . demands all . . . no matter the cost," Aiguo said, as he fell prostrate under the overpass on South Smith Boulevard.

# Chapter 20

"The clever combatant imposes his will on the enemy, but does not allow the enemy's will to be imposed on him."

Sun Tzu (~520 BC)

Alexandria, Virginia, USA
Arlington County EMS
Ambulance 17
March 19, 2017, 0115 EST


The clatter of the snow chains could still be heard over the blare of the siren as the ambulance turned left onto Seminary Road, and headed for the Emergency Room Entrance at the Inova Alexandria Hospital.

"Damn snow! I almost wound up in a ditch on that last turn," Tyronne said, as they turned on North Howard Street.

"Just get us there in one piece. I got him out of his wet clothes, and bundled him up with blankets and hot packs. He doesn't look like a homeless guy. That was a nice jacket, but not for walking around in a blizzard," Jasmine Caster said, as she monitored the patient's pulse and blood pressure.

"His wallet says his name is Gong Aiguo. What the hell kind of name is that? Sounds like a disease," Malcom said, as he tried to verify the patient's ID.

"Oh, he's Chinese. Here's a company ID . . . in Taiwan . . . looks like they sell heavy equipment . . . and here's his passport. He must have been in town on business, and decided to go for a walk during the worst blizzard we've had in the last ten years," Malcom said, and started laughing.

"Malcom you're an asshole. Just do your job. This guy's lucky somebody drove by and saw him lying by the road. I'll tell you one thing, this guy is fit. He's cut like Bruce Lee, no fat at all," Jasmine said, as she adjusted the oxygen mask on Aiguo.

"No insulation, unlike Tyronne, he's built for 40 below," Malcom said.

"Jasmine's right. You are an asshole," Tyronne said in response, as all three started laughing.

"ER's waiting on us. One minute, get ready to transfer," Jasmine said, as they pulled under the cover of the Emergency Room carport.

Two orderlies and a nurse were waiting as they parked the ambulance, and jumped out the back doors.

Tyrone and Malcom began to pull the gurney out of the ambulance as Jasmine began transferring information to the hospital staff.

"Patient's unresponsive, but stable. Blood pressure is 110 over 70. Pulse is 55. He has the usual frostbite problems on fingers, toes, nose and ears. No other obvious injuries," Jasmine said, to the nurse as part of her patient turnover.

"Malcom, get his personal effects," Jasmine said, as she pointed into the back of the ambulance.

Malcom nodded as he jumped into the back and handed out the bag.

"He's Chinese. Looks like he's from Taiwan, based on his ID. I didn't find a record of his blood type," Jasmine said, as the hospital staff began to roll Aiguo away.

"Malcom, get our gurney back. They'll transfer him onto one of theirs inside," Jasmine said.

"How come I have to do everything?" Malcom said, as he looked at Tyrone.

"Because you're an asshole!" Jasmine and Tyrone both said together, and burst out laughing.

"And hurry up! We've got another call," Jasmine said, as Malcom followed their gurney into the hospital ER.

.   .   .   .

Inova Alexandria Hospital
Emergency Room
4300 Seminary Road

"Transfer him into one of our beds and start warming him up. Also, get a core temperature. Start IV fluids, blood work, complete surface exam," head nurse Donna Bradley said, to two other nurses.

"So what have we got, Donna?" Doctor Edward Moore asked, as he walked up to the scene.

"Asian male, mid to late twenties, unconscious, suffering from hypothermia, some signs of frost bite. Blood pressure is 110 over 70. Pulse is 55. We're focusing on basic work up and keeping him warm," Donna said.

"That all sounds good. I think I'll take a look at him while your nurses are working on him," Doctor Moore said, as he turned and began following the gurney.

The Emergency Room at Inova Alexandria Hospital contained 32 bays. First Lieutenant Gong Aiguo, late of the Siberian Tigers, was placed in Bay Number 4. That would not have been his choice.

"Keep his IV going. Make sure that the saline is body temperature. That's critical," Doctor Moore said, as Aiguo was wheeled into Bay 4.

"Bring warm blankets and get ready to verify his blood type. Keep monitoring his vitals while I perform an examination," Doctor Moore said, as the two nurses began their tasks.

Doctor Edward Moore had been through two patient law suits in the last five years. Having lost one of them, he now carried a tape recorder with him and turned it on every time he had interactions with a new patient.

"March 19th, 2013, 0130, patient was brought to the Emergency Room by ambulance suffering from hypothermia. Patient is a male, approximately 25 years old, Asian descent, excellent physical condition. He is presently unconscious, but in stable condition," Doctor Moore said, as he continued his examination.

"Nurse, what's his core temperature?" Doctor Moore asked.

"93 degrees, Doctor," Nurse Ashton Riley answered.

"Get the warm saline now. We're not going to wait," Doctor Moore said, as he turned the patient on his side.

"That's an odd tattoo. Where have I seen that before," Doctor Moore said, as he stared at the tattoo on Aiguo's upper right arm.

On the upper right arm were four Chinese characters. Below them was the head of a tiger. Below that was a dagger with lightning bolts over the blade. Doctor Moore jumped at the sound of instruments and a metal tray hitting the concrete floor.

"Nurse, what is the problem?" Doctor Moore asked, as he turned and saw one of the young nurses backed against the wall.

"Meifeng, What happened? Are you all right?" Nurse Bradley asked, as she walked over to the startled woman.

"The tattoo . . . he is a very dangerous man. Why is he here?" Meifeng asked, as she began to back out of the bay.

"Meifeng! Get a hold of yourself. This man is injured and we are nurses. We live to help the sick and injured," Nurse Bradley said, as she grabbed Meifeng's arm.

"You don't understand. He will kill us. That's what they do. He's Chinese Special Forces, like a Navy Seal . . . a Siberian Tiger from Shenyang. Why is he here?" Meifeng replied, as she tried to pull away from Nurse Bradley.

"That's where I've seen that logo. Nurse . . . Thompson?" Doctor Moore said, as he glanced from Meifeng's name badge to Nurse Bradley.

"She's married to an army officer. He works at the Pentagon," Nurse Bradley said.

"Nurse Thompson, what do the characters above the Tiger say?" Doctor Moore asked.

"It's from General Yue Fei . . . Southern Song Dynasty in the 12th century. His mother tattooed it on his back when he was a young soldier. She was angry with him for leaving the army and tattooed this on his back. It says 'Loyalty to the Nation'," Meifeng said.

"When I was on active duty a few years ago I was stationed with the First Special Forces Battalion in Okinawa. I went to a briefing on Chinese Special Forces, and I remember that logo. This is bizarre. What is a Chinese Special Forces operative doing in Alexandria during a blizzard?" Doctor Moore said.

"Nurse Thompson, he's not going to hurt anyone, I promise you. Nurse Bradley, please continue treating the patient," Doctor Moore said, as he looked at Meifeng and tried to smile reassuringly.

. . . .

Inova Alexandria Hospital
Security Office
March 19, 2017, 0215 EST


"Look Doc, I understand your concern, but Alexandria PD has their hands full now. Unless this guy's getting violent, I'm not calling them. This storm was supposed to be a nothing, just a few inches, and it's over a foot. Now the Weather Channel says it will get over two feet before it's done," Sergeant Ben Carson said, from behind his desk, as he reluctantly pushed a double cheeseburger to the side.

"There are only two of us here on nights, and I've got Sharon sleeping in a storage room. We're all going to be stuck here for a while. Now if you want, I can place a restraint on this guy. That will keep him from bolting if he wakes up," Sergeant Carson said, as he began rummaging around in a desk drawer looking for restraints.

"I'll have to look back in our storage area. We haven't had any convicts or crazies here in months. When I find some, I'll come back to the ER," Sergeant Carson said.


. . . .


The Pentagon
Sublevel 3
Room C26
March 19, 2017, 0230 EST


"Meifeng, calm down! My Chinese isn't that good to begin with. When you get excited you start talking in Wu. Mandarin or English, my sweet, please," Major Anthony Thompson said on his cell phone, from the Peoples Liberation Army Analysis Office in the Pentagon.

"Listen Tony, there is a Chinese agent in the hospital. He came in an ambulance less than an hour ago," Meifeng said, as she paced inside the nurses break room near the ER.

"Sweet, you've been reading too many spy novels. What makes you think this guy is a Chinese agent?" Anthony asked.

"He has a tattoo on his arm, that's why," Meifeng said.

"Yeah, and I have a tattoo on my arm. Does that make me a Chinese agent?" Anthony said, as he laughed and shook his head.

"It's a Chinese Special Forces tattoo, a tiger with a dagger and lightning. Above that is a tattoo of General Yue Fei's famous quote, 'Loyalty to the Nation', and don't you dare make fun of me," Meifeng said.

"A tiger and a dagger? Are you sure?" Anthony said, as he opened a database on Chinese Special Forces units.

"Damn! The Siberian Tigers!" Anthony said, as he sat up and started writing notes on a pad.

"Meifeng, take a picture of the tattoo with your phone and send it to me. Guys like this don't leave mainland China unless they're on a mission," Anthony said.

Anthony received the image two minutes later.

"Damn, she's right. Why the hell is this guy here?" Anthony asked himself, as he considered his options.

Calling Meifeng he said, "Meifeng, you may be right. Is this guy secured?"

"The on duty Doc used to be assigned to Special Forces in Asia. I told him about my suspicions, and he had this guy secured to the gurney by security. Then I called you," Meifeng said.

"You did the right thing. Let security know that DOD security will be there as soon as possible. You stay away from him. Do you understand me?" Anthony said.

"Tony, I understand. I know what this man is. If he wakes up I may just leave the hospital," Meifeng said.

"Don't go out in the cold in your condition, babe. This is a bad night. Just keep safe," Anthony said, as he kissed the phone and hung up.

"When in doubt move it up. If you get information that's too hot to handle, let your boss decide," he told himself, as he dialed up his chain of command, remembering his training from years earlier.

"General Stoner, Major Thompson here, I have received some information that I think you might want to know about," Anthony said.

"So what have you got, Major? I was just about ready to have my mid-shift meal," General Stoner said, while stirring warmed up pasta and Alfredo sauce.

"Sir, my wife just called from Inova Alexandria Hospital in Alexandria. She's a nurse there. They just received a patient in the ER that I believe to be a member of the Siberian Tigers, a PLA Special Forces unit," Major Thompson said.

There was a pause before General Stoner said, "What leads you to this conclusion, Major?"

"Sir, my wife took a picture of a tattoo on his right shoulder. I'm forwarding the pic to your cell phone at this time," Major Thompson said.

.   .   .   .

Inova Alexandria Hospital
Emergency Room
Bay 4
March 19, 2017, 0240 EST

Aiguo awoke as if from a deep sleep. He had been dreaming of when he was a little boy fishing on the Songhua River. The sun was so very bright and his grandfather had been laughing. When he opened his eyes it was still bright. He squinted as he recognized fluorescent lights in the ceiling above him.

"Where am I? What happened?" Aiguo asked in Chinese, as he tried to shield his eyes with his right hand.

He yanked his hands as his mind snapped into wakefulness. He remembered where he was and what his mission had been.

"Where am I? Why have you tied me up? I am a business man from Taiwan. What is going on?" he asked in English, as he continued to struggle against his bonds.

"Mister Gong, my name is Nurse Bradley. You're in the Emergency Room at Inova Alexandria Hospital. You were brought in by ambulance about an hour ago. You're suffering from hypothermia," Nurse Bradley said.

"Why do you have me tied up? My government will hear of this indignity," Aiguo said, as he yanked against his restraints.

"You were thrashing around so we secured you for your own protection. I'll see if I can find the security guard so he can release you," Nurse Bradley said, as she turned and hurried away.

Stopping at the nurse's station she called security while motioning to Meifeng and Ashton that the Chinese patient was awake.

"I stalled him, but we need security back here now," Nurse Bradley whispered, while holding the phone to her ear.

"Meifeng, go find Doctor Moore," Nurse Bradley said.

Meifeng nodded, and pulled out her cell phone as she ran off.

"Sergeant Carson, he's awake. I told him that you're the only one that can remove his restraints," Nurse Bradley said.

"No, I don't want them removed. Are you crazy? This man may be dangerous. I want Security here, and that's you. So get your ass down here now," Nurse Bradley said.

"Idiot! I think he's scared to come down here," Nurse Bradley said, as she hung up the phone.

"Ashton, prep an injection of Lorazepam, 10 mg equivalent and hurry," Nurse Bradley said, as she began slowly walking back towards Bay 4.

As she pulled the curtain aside she was startled to see that the patient had kicked his blankets aside, and was trying to loosen his restraints with the toes on his right foot.

"Mr. Gong, please stop that! I've contacted security. He'll be here in a few minutes," Nurse Bradley said, as she rushed into Bay 4, and tried to pull Aiguo's foot away from the restraints.

"Release me immediately or there will be problems," Aiguo demanded.

"Mr. Gong, please, let me replace the blankets. You're still recovering from hypothermia," Nurse Bradley said, as she bent over and picked up the discarded sheet and blankets.

"Donna, I have his injection," Nurse Riley said, as she pulled back the curtains on Bay 4.

Aiguo's right leg whipped up and hit Nurse Bradley just under her left ear. She dropped like a stone. Nurse Riley screamed as she jumped forward, grabbed Aiguo's right foot and jabbed the hypodermic into his calf. The heel of his left foot landed between her eyes hurling her backwards into the hall where she lay unconscious.

Aiguo began cursing in Chinese as he worked a big toe under the edge of the buckle and pried one end of the strap loose. He ignored the sound of screaming and pounding footsteps as he loosened the restraint on his left arm and yanked it free.

"Do not move or I will shoot!" Sergeant Carson yelled, as he rounded the corner of Bay 4 and pulled his 9mm Glock free of its holster.

Aiguo spun from the bed and onto the floor still attached to the bed by his left arm. Ducking beside the bed, he released the brake with his foot, braced his legs, and shoved the bed toward the startled officer. The first shot went over his head as the corner of the bed struck Sergeant Carson in the left thigh and knocked him off his feet.

Aiguo loosened the last restraint and flipped the bed over on the struggling security guard. Two quick punches and the guard lay still. It was then that he looked up and saw Doctor Moore standing at the end of the hall with Meifeng beside him.

Dressed only in a hospital gown, Aiguo swept up the 9mm and pointed it at the pair.

"Drop the phone!" Aiguo yelled, as he began walking up the hall.

Meifeng had the phone at her right ear as she said, "Tony . . . he's free."

Aiguo shot them both in the chest.

The ER was silent. There were no other patients or staff in the area. Aiguo knew what he had to do as he walked up to the unconscious guard and shot him in the head. He hesitated as he approached the two nurses.

"Loyalty to the nation!" he said, as he slapped the tattoo on his right shoulder and shot the two nurses.

As his adrenalin rush began to lessen, he began to feel the effect of whatever they had injected him with.

"This is no different than training. Extreme fatigue can be conquered by strength of will," he said, as he walked back to the doctor, and began searching through his pockets.

"Good, no more walking tonight," he said, as he removed a set of keys for a Lexus.

"I have been foolish and forgotten who I am. Now I have to disappear," Aiguo said, as he began looking for his clothes.

# Chapter 21

"Hence to fight and conquer in all your battles is not supreme excellence; supreme excellence consists in breaking the enemy's resistance without fighting."

Sun Tzu (~520 BC)

Beijing, China
Central Military Commission Headquarters
August 1st Building
Office of General Fan Shibo
March 20, 2017, 0900 CT

"Uncle, I am so pleased that you agreed to see me," Lieutenant General Kung said, as he stood at attention before the desk of General Fan Shibo, Vice Chairman of the Central Military Commission of the Peoples Liberation Army.

General Fan said nothing as he left the younger general standing at attention before his desk. He signed two documents, and glanced at his nephew once, before he placed the documents in a folder. After placing them in his 'Out' box, he rose from his chair, and stared out his window on the tenth floor of the August 1st building.

"My sister has not heard from you in over a year. Why do you disrespect your mother?" General Fan asked, his back still turned to Lieutenant General Kung.

"Work has been very pressing, uncle. The Party and the nation come before family," Kung answered, letting a slight edge come into the tone of his answer.

"Yes, they do. So what has brought you all the way to Beijing to stand in front of my desk, nephew?" General Fan said, as he turned around and smiled.

"I am glad to see you smile, uncle. I hope that when I leave you are still smiling," General Kung said, while still remaining at rigid attention.

"At ease, nephew. Unless you have lost one of the Motherland's precious nuclear weapons, you will leave with our friendship intact," General Fan said, as he rounded his desk and hugged his nephew.

"Now that we have played our games of position, what has really brought you here?" General Fen asked, as he backed up and inspected his nephew.

"You seem to have found the fountain of youth. I don't think you've aged in ten years. I need to find you a more stressful position," General Fan said, as he motioned towards a pair of ornately carved Chinese chairs that were positioned by a table at another window.

"I will order some tea and we will talk, but I must insist that you visit your mother while you're here. Otherwise, I'll be the one in trouble if she hears that you were in the area and didn't visit," General Fan said, as he sat and pressed a buzzer on the edge of the table.

"I appreciate the tea, uncle, but I do have something serious to discuss with you while I'm here," General Kung said, as he slowly sat at the other chair.

General Fan rested his elbows on the table, and stared at his nephew before saying, "I hope you haven't done something stupid. My sister would never forgive me if I had her favorite son shot."

"Hopefully it won't come to that, uncle," General Kung said, as the door opened.

"Chuntao, some tea, please," General Fan said, to the young female Lieutenant, who nodded and left.

General Kung glanced at the young Lieutenant as she left, and then at his uncle.

"What? She is extremely competent," General Fan said, as he held up his hands in defense.

"I'm sure she is, uncle," General Kung said, and smiled.

"Pleasantries are over General Kung. Why are you here?" General Fan said, as he shifted the intensity of the conversation.

General Kung slowly took a deep breath, and then began.

"Nine days ago there was a fire in San Francisco. It was in a small Dim Sum restaurant operated by an agent of mine. The fire unfortunately spread to a shed behind the restaurant," General Kung began, and felt his mouth dry up despite the hundred times that he had rehearsed this conversation in his mind over the last few days.

"So the Americans have discovered an agent of yours in San Francisco. Nephew, what am I going to do with you? It's a minor thing. We trade the man for something the Americans want. That's how things work," General Fan said, then paused at the look on his nephew's face.

"The agent was killed in the fire. The American's found . . . a nuclear device that has been hidden in the man's shed since . . . 1992," General Kung said, as he waited for the explosion.

General Fan said nothing as he stared at his nephew in disbelief. He clasped both hands together to keep them from visibly shaking. He stood up, never taking his eyes off his nephew, and walked toward the window behind his desk.

"It seems that my sister is going to be very unhappy with me. Please explain to me why I shouldn't have you publically shot," General Fan said, as he faced the window with his hands clenched behind his back.

"Well, I knew it would eventually come to this. Either I will be a hero of the state or a traitor," General Kung said, as he stood up, walked around the desk, and stood beside his uncle.

"General, I have your tea," the Lieutenant said, as she opened the door.

"Have you forgotten how to knock? Put the tea on the table and get out," General Fan shouted.

After the door shut, General Kung said, "Uncle, before you have me arrested and shot, perhaps you would let me tell you the whole story over some tea."

His uncle's head turned and looked at Kung as if he had lost his mind. Kung returned to the table and poured the tea.

"Please, uncle, if you decide to have me shot, this will be the last time we have tea," General Kung said.

"I always knew that you were too young for that much responsibility," General Fan said, as he turned and faced his nephew.

"Please, uncle. Let me tell you a story. Perhaps, in five hundred years, it will be known as the story of General Kung and his famous uncle General Fan, and how they defeated the hated Americans without firing a shot," General Kung said, as he finished pouring the tea, and gestured for his uncle to have a seat.

"You graduated so early, first in your class at the academy. You were first in everything. I was told you have an IQ equivalent to Einstein. How could you have been so foolish as to plant a nuclear weapon on American soil? It is an act of war," General Fan said, as he stared at his tea.

"Uncle, if I had only planted one seed in the garden then I would be a fool," General Kung said, as he sipped his tea.

General Fan sat upright as he stared at his nephew.

"I'm actually afraid to ask," General Fan said, as he felt his hands begin to shake again, and placed them below the edge of the table.

"Uncle, let me start at the beginning. During the First Gulf War I remember being stunned at the audacity and technical prowess that the Americans displayed as they invaded Kuwait and forced the Iraqis out of the country. Their use of combined arms tactics did not surprise me, but their use of advance technology was amazing. It was so far past anything that we were capable of that I had a feeling of total helplessness," General Kung said.

"We all felt that way. It was frightening, but we have come a long way since then. We are much closer. Soon we will surpass their capabilities," General Fan said.

"Perhaps we will, Uncle. But I think we are only close to matching what they could do twenty years ago. They are playing poker, and keep their hand very close to their chest. They will always be ahead of us," General Kung said.

"What of it? Our economy is strong. We are slowly expanding our influence across the globe. Their culture is corrupt. In the end they will self-destruct," General Fan said.

"Again, perhaps they will, but I doubt it. Now, I have taken the unknowns out of the equation. As the Americans would say . . . I have them by the balls," General Kung said, as he smiled and sipped his tea.

"You are insane. You see yourself as one of the great warlords of old," General Fan said, as he imagined himself standing beside his nephew and facing a firing squad.

"Uncle, as of two days ago I accomplished the goal that I set out to achieve many years ago. I have now planted fifty . . . well . . . make that forty nine . . . nuclear weapons inside the United States of America. The last one was a 10-megaton device. It is seven miles from the White House," General Kung said, as he grinned at his uncle.

The room was silent for several minutes. General Fan kept staring at his nephew and then looking away as thoughts raced through his mind. He gulped his tea and then began pacing the room. He would pause, stare at his nephew once again, and then resume pacing.

"How do you control them? How are they protected? Can you detonate them remotely, or do your agents have to set off each one? How do you . . ." General Fan began, and then stopped as his nephew began to laugh.

"Please tell me that you aren't insane," General Fan pleaded.

"No uncle, I'm not insane, and we do have them by the balls! They just don't know it yet," General Kung said, as he grabbed his uncle by the shoulders and smiled.

"The Chairman . . . he has to be briefed as soon as possible. He may still have us both shot," General Fan said, as his mind began to whirl with the strategic possibilities this could present.

"So arrange a meeting. I have all the details right here. I could do a Power Point presentation for the Central Committee," General Kung said, as he laughed, reached into his uniform jacket, and removed a thumb drive.

"I am 72 years old. I fought against the Americans in Korea when I was 16. That cost me three toes to frostbite. I thought that after surviving that horror that I would never be shocked or surprised again. Until today . . . I have been right. You are serious? This isn't some kind of insane joke is it?" General Fan asked, as he sat at the table once again and stared up at his nephew.

"No uncle . . . it's not a joke. It is the most serious event that has happened this century . . . so far," General Kung said, as he sat down and poured some more tea.

# Chapter 22

"Political power grows out of the barrel of a gun."

Mao Zedong

Alexandria, Virginia, USA
Parking Lot of the Inova Alexandria Hospital
March 20, 2017, 0200 hours EST


Aiguo stood shivering in the snow outside the Lexus SUV. His face, fingers and toes were still burning from mild frostbite despite the treatment in the hospital's emergency room.

"The door has no place for a key," he said, while staring at the key ring he had taken from the doctor.

"It's keyless . . . all of it. It's all electronic," he said, as he pressed the symbol for an open padlock.

When the door popped open he jumped in, shut the door, and tossed the guard's pistol on the seat beside him.

"Keyless . . . it will have a button somewhere to start the car," he said, as he bent past the steering wheel, and began searching for a starter button.

"There," he said, as he pressed a large button labeled 'Engine Start/Stop', and was relieved when the engine roared into life.

He felt for the pedals, but could barely touch them, and began cursing in Chinese about long-legged Americans. He reached under the seat, but did not find a bar or lever to pull the seat forward.

"Damn, it's all buttons. Nothing is manual," Aiguo said, as he began looking for a symbol of a seat.

Seeing nothing, he started feeling the edges of the seat, and found a series of buttons on the left side. After several failures, the seat began to slide forward until he could feel the gas and brake pedals.

After finding the wipers and the lights, Aiguo put the all-wheel drive Lexus into reverse, and began to slowly back out of the parking spot. Despite the deep snow the vehicle backed up without a problem. When he pulled forward he began looking for an exit while ignoring the gentle pinging of the seat belt alarm.

"Think Aiguo . . . remember your training . . . two safe houses in the area, primary and a backup. Get there and send the distress signal. Comrades will come and get you out of the country. The mission was a success. The hospital was just an unfortunate event. I left no witnesses behind. Never leave a witness that can identify you. That's what you were taught," he said, as he pulled up to the exit from the hospital parking lot.

"Which way? It makes no difference, just leave, find some place to stop and think," he said, as he turned left onto North Howard Street.

He stopped at a tee intersection. The street sign was barely visible in the falling snow. After turning right, he saw a sign for the Fort Howard Museum.

"I need some place quiet, with no people," he said, as he turned left onto the park's access road.

After pulling behind a two story wooden building Aiguo put the car into park, turned off the lights, and closed his eyes.

"If I sleep they will find me. Just relax and remember the maps of this area. Where were the safe houses?" Aiguo asked himself, as he began to recall the maps of this area of the United States.

"Dozens of safe houses scattered across this country. Two are in this area," he said, as he breathed deeply and focused.

"An apartment . . . 101 North Ripley Street, Apartment 204. I will say, 'Patriot in need', he will say, 'The inn is open'," Aiguo said, as he began studying the dash.

"This screen in the dash is like a computer screen. It will have maps . . . this says destination . . . how do you? Ah, this button moves to the various items on the screen. Now the address," he said, as he entered in the apartment address.

"Beautiful technology for the rich and powerful. I doubt if the masses have access to this," Aiguo said, as he backed the Lexus up, and began following the instructions from the navigation system.

The only vehicles he saw during his journey were snow plows and an occasional emergency vehicle.

.   .   .   .

Aiguo drove past the apartment, and then left the Lexus behind a McDonald's two blocks away. The short walk through the snow back to the apartment was far more painful than he had expected.

"No pain, no fear, show only strength. You are a Siberian Tiger," he told himself, as he trudged up the stairs to the second floor apartment.

After verifying the apartment number he rang the doorbell three times, waited ten seconds, and then rang it two more times. Ninety seconds later he repeated the sequence. Ninety seconds later he repeated it again, until he heard the door unlock.

A chain still crossed the opening. No face was visible, but a voice asked, "Who are you? What do you want this time of night?"

"Patriot in need," Aiguo said.

"What did you say," a startled voice replied.

"Patriot in need," Aiguo repeated.

"The inn . . . the inn is open," the voice replied, as the chain was removed and the door opened.

"Get in, quickly," the man said, as Aiguo stepped past him into the apartment.

The man closed the door, then turned and bowed several times before saying, "I have to admit this is a bit of a shock. I've been here for over three years, and have never received a message, let alone a visitor."

"Well, you have a visitor now. Are you alone?" Aiguo asked.

"Yes, a two bedroom apartment, but no one else is here but me. My apologies, my name is Lu Deming. It is an honor to serve you. Would you like some tea?" Deming asked, as he bowed once more

"Yes, some tea and some food. Then I will need access to a cell phone or computer," Aiguo said, as he looked around the apartment.

"Certainly, I have a PC in the second bedroom down the hall. The facilities are on the right," Deming said, as he headed for the kitchen.

"I need to send a message. Does the PC have a password?" Aiguo asked.

"Yes, 'Redskins'. It is the name of a local sports team," Deming said, as he started filling the tea kettle.

Aiguo steeled himself to the pain as he walked down the hall, entered the second bedroom, and turned on the light. The bed was plush and began to call him as he sat in front of the computer and turned it on.

"First things first," he said, as he entered the password, wincing at the pain in his fingertips.

After entering the web site of a furniture manufacturer in Shanghai, he clicked on a link to an interior decorator in Paris. Once there he clicked on another link, this one to a carpet manufacturer in London. This gave him access to a back door messaging system that only became visible if the links were opened in a certain sequence from specific websites.

A plain text box appeared and requested a password. A timer started counting down from 20 . . .

Aiguo entered, 'SIBERIANTiger001717a', and pressed enter. The clock froze, then disappeared, and the text box became live. A second clock began counting down from 30 . . .

Aiguo entered, 'ST1717a requires exit from loc 1 task comp' and pressed enter. The clock stopped, and the screen went blank, as the computer automatically rebooted.

"I have your tea, if you are ready," Deming said, from the doorway.

Aiguo nodded and stood up. His toes began throbbing as he walked out of the bedroom.

"I have minor frostbite on my fingers and toes. They have been treated, but I will need some ointment and aloe if you have any," Aiguo said, as he sat at the small table beside the kitchen.

"Of course, and you look like you could use some fresh clothes. We look like the same size," Deming said, as he placed a bowl of three warmed rice balls and vegetables beside the tea in front of Aiguo and headed for his bedroom.

Aiguo sipped the green tea, relishing the flavor and warmth as he swirled it around in his mouth. He picked up a rice ball with his chopsticks, dipped it in the vegetable sauce, and popped the whole thing in his mouth. He was trained to withstand deprivation, but he felt as if he hadn't eaten in a week. As his mind focused on the flavor of the rice and sauce, he could feel his body start to shut down.

"I've done all I can do. I must sleep," Aiguo said, as he finished the meal and stood up.

"I have turned down your bed, and placed fresh clothes on the chair. I have some fresh aloe and some Vaseline. I can treat your injuries if you wish," Deming said.

"No, I think I will sleep first. Thank you for your kindness," Aiguo said, as he entered the bedroom and shut the door.

He removed his light jacket, and then the pistol that he had tucked behind his belt in the small of his back. He sat down and began to remove his shoes, almost screaming as he pulled the socks from his frostbit toes. He knew that when he woke he would have trouble walking. He placed the pistol under his pillow, and then lay down on the soft mattress. Too tired to get out of his clothes, he immediately fell into a deep sleep.

A few minutes later, Deming cracked the door, and peaked in the second bedroom. The strange visitor had fallen asleep. He could see that the toes on Aiguo's bare feet were blistered, but not black.

"He will lose the skin, but at least the toes will heal. I'll give him some pain killers when he wakes up," Deming said, as he turned off the light and shut the door.

.   .   .   .

101 North Ripley Street
Apartment 204
March 20, 2017, 0730 hours

Deming felt as if he had just fallen asleep when the doorbell rang again. It was the same sequence as before; three rings, count to ten, two rings, ninety seconds later, repeat. He stumbled out of bed, and turned on the hall light as he left his bedroom.

"Another agent? I might as well set up a B&B," he said, as he passed the second bedroom, noticing that the door was still shut.

"*He won't be awake for hours. I may have to give up my bed if this one is in as bad shape as the first,*" Deming thought, as he cracked opened the door. The chain was still in place.

When the passwords were exchanged, Deming removed the chain, and swung the door open.

"Welcome, please come . . ." Deming began, until he saw the barrel of the small caliber pistol pointed at his head.

The silenced shot made little sound, and the man grasped Deming by the shirt as he fell backwards. The gunman lowered him to the floor, then turned and closed the door. He smiled at the stunned look on Deming's face. The small hole in the center of his forehead had bled very little.

The gunman raised the pistol in a two-handed grip, and began to methodically inspect the apartment, searching for his primary target. The living room, the kitchen, and then he turned down the hall and paused.

"*Three doors, two are open, and one is closed. Bedrooms on either side, bathroom at the end,*" the gunman thought, as he began a slow approach down the hall.

The first bedroom door was swung wide into the room. The rumpled bed told him that the greeter at the door had been sleeping there. A quick glance around the room, and he turned back to the hall.

He stopped outside the second bedroom door and paused, listening. After a moment he tried the door with his left hand, and found that it was unlocked. He nudged the door open and peered into the room. The occupant in the bed was buried under the covers and still asleep. The only light was from the ceiling light in the hallway.

The gunman took one step into the room and leveled his pistol at the head under the covers, and began to squeeze the trigger. He was thrown against the door frame as a bullet entered his right temple, fired from the figure crouching behind a dresser to his right. He slumped to the floor, his brain matter spread from the doorway to the bedroom wall on his left.

Aiguo rose and stepped from the shadows. He rolled the man over, kicked the gun from his hand, and looked at the man's face.

"*Chinese? They sent someone after me. Why?*" Aiguo thought, as he bent and searched the man for identity or any other clue.

After checking the apartment and finding Deming, he ran back to the second bedroom and put on his shoes. He barely felt the pain in his feet as he removed the man's wallet and car keys.

"*Coat, gloves and a hat,*" he thought, as he rushed into Deming's room, and began rummaging through his closet.

After putting on warmer clothes, he rushed into the hall, and saw a bottle of Tylenol sitting on the kitchen counter. Stuffing the bottle into his coat pocket, he looked around once more, grabbed a bottle of water, and went to the front door. He slowly opened the door. Hearing nothing, he left the apartment, shut the door, and rapidly descended the stairs into the parking lot.

It was still cold, but not as bitter as the night before. The sky was the texture of dirty cotton. The air had that feel that told you that more snow was on the way.

He saw only one car with no snow on the windows, and pressed the lock button on the key bob. The lights flashed and Aiguo knew that he had an escape vehicle.

"*The police will have found the bodies in the emergency room by now. They will be looking for the doctor's car. I can't use that one again,*" Aiguo thought, as he opened the door on the old Toyota Camry and slid into the driver's seat and started the car.

"Now where do I go? I'm expendable now. The second safe house won't be safe either. As soon as . . ." Aiguo said, as he reached into his new coat pocket, and pulled out the wallet of the assassin.

". . . Wan Guotin doesn't call in with a mission status, they'll have someone come over and check the apartment. Then they'll start hunting for me again," Aiguo said, as he put the car in gear, and pulled out of the apartment parking lot. He glanced at his watch. It was 0800 and he was on the run again, with nowhere to go.

. . . .

Regal Cinemas Kingstowne 16 & RPX
5910 Kingstowne Center
March 20, 2017, 1000 hours EST

Aiguo had parked in the open outside the Regal Cinema. He had been trained that hiding in the open was always a good tactic, unless you were found. He had parked at a distance until he saw two of the staff arrive early, and enter the movie theatre in their uniforms. He pulled up beside their parked cars, tucked his weapon beside the seat, within easy reach, and took out Deming's phone.

"Who can I trust?" he asked himself, as he turned on the cell phone.

"Grandfather . . . Grandfather Peng . . . he helped me get into the Siberian Tigers. He can tell them that I'm not a traitor," Aiguo said, as he struggled to remember his grandfather's cell number in China.

"It was a simple code . . . a word, a phrase," Aiguo said, as he smacked himself in the head in frustration.

He opened the glove box, found a pencil, and began writing the sequence to phone China on a scrap of paper.

"First, exit the USA, '011', then China, '086', now his code for his cell number. He told me that if I was ever in serious trouble to call him, but only if I was in serious trouble," Aiguo said, as he remembered his grandfather's smiling face.

He knew from when he was little, that his grandfather was a hero of the people. As a young boy he had fought at the side of Chairman Mao, or so the family story went. Aiguo knew his grandfather as the kind old man that took him fishing when he was a young, and then, as the respected officer that had helped his career in the PLA.

"Now, Grandfather, help me remember your simple code," Aiguo said, while closing his eyes, and remembered a day, not that long ago, when he had visited his grandfather in Beijing.

"The gardens . . . he always wanted to meet in the gardens. You would have thought that he worked there and tended the plants.

"You told me, 'If you want to access me, call ACCESPEN. It stands for 'access Peng'. You're a Siberian Tiger now. You should be able to remember this code,' and then you laughed, and slapped me on the back," Aiguo said, as his eyes popped open, and he began writing down the simple code of the English alphabet.

"A is 1, B is 2 . . ." Aiguo said, as he wrote down the 26 letters and corresponding numbers.

"Now I just have to work through the sequence. That's it . . . 011-86-133-5191-6514," Aiguo said, as he stared at the numbers and the code sequence.

He glanced at his watch, and was figuring out what time it was in China, when someone tapped on his window. He looked to his left and saw a policeman bundled up against the cold. He had been tapping on his car window with a nightstick.

Aiguo lowered the window and smiled.

"Officer, what brings you out on this chilly morning?" Aiguo asked, as he slowly placed his right hand above the pistol hidden below the right of his seat.

"We're just checking on people after the snow last night. We already found two people dead. They got stuck and decided to wait it out. That's always a bad call," the officer said, as his eyes inspected the inside of Aiguo's car.

"So what are you doing here?" the officer asked, as he leaned against the lowered window and sniffed.

"I'm just waiting for the 11 o'clock showing of Kong, Skull Island. I'm always up for an action flick. Plus, the power is out in my apartment," Aiguo said, as he smiled and gestured towards the theatre marquee.

"Yeah, it's pretty good. I took the kids last weekend. They loved it. Be careful driving today, and remember that the bridges will freeze over for sure, even if we don't get any more snow," the officer said, as he turned away.

"Thanks, I appreciate your concern. Have a good day and stay warm," Aiguo said, as the officer walked back to his cruiser and drove away.

"Looks like I'm going to a movie at 11. If I drive off he might get suspicious and call in my plate. I know he wrote it down," Aiguo said, as he started tapping in the sequence of his grandfather's cell phone.

"Sorry, Grandfather, it's 11PM there, but this is definitely an emergency," Aiguo said, as the phone began to ring.

Chapter 23

"If a secret piece of news is divulged by a spy before the time is ripe, he must be put to death together with the man to whom the secret was told."

Sun Tzu (~520 BC)

Beijing, China
The hills above the Xiangshan Residential District
Residence of Colonel Peng
March 20, 2017, 2300 CT

The phone continued to buzz as Colonel Peng Zihao, rolled over, and stared at the phone in the dim light of his bedroom. At 80 years old he was far past the mandatory retirement age of 60 for officers of his rank in the PLA. Only the direct intervention of General Kung had allowed him to serve for so long.

"Kung . . . why do you always call when I'm asleep," Peng said, as he reached for the phone.

He stared at the incoming call number and sat up in bed.

"*It's not the General. Who else has this number?*" he thought, as he answered the call.

"Yes, who is this?" Peng asked.

"Grandfather! It's Aiguo, your grandson. I apologize for disturbing you so late in the evening, but I need your help. The item was successfully delivered, but I had some complications after the mission," Aiguo said, and paused, waiting for his grandfather's reaction.

Peng slid out of bed and into his slippers. He walked to a window and cranked it open. The cold air shocked him further awake.

"I know of your problems, nephew. Five dead bodies are more than a complication," Peng said, as he stared into the forest surrounding his small house.

He could smell the scent of the evergreens as he remembered Aiguo as a small boy, and then the pride he had felt as his nephew had grown into a man and become a Siberian Tiger.

"I know Grandfather. I have not performed as well as I should have. I became injured, and was taken to the hospital. I didn't leave behind any witnesses. No one can identify me," Aiguo said, as he began to sense his grandfather distancing himself.

"Aiguo, one of the nurses took a picture of your tattoo. She sent it to her husband who works in the Pentagon. This has become very messy, and General Kung is very displeased," Peng said.

"Grandfather, I will do anything to make this right. One of our agents tried to kill me this morning, so there are further bodies. I am sorry, but he left me no choice. The safe house in the area is now gone. I don't have anywhere to go," Aiguo said.

Peng sighed as he thought about his only surviving sister, and her pride in her only son. Both he and his sister had been born long before the 'one child' policy had been enacted in 1979, but time had taken its toll on both of their families. Aiguo was the only surviving male.

"There is one final task for you to accomplish. An American agent of ours has become frightened. He is preparing to flee the country. This must not be allowed to happen. He lives in the area you're in. He is a rich man with a large house. He lives alone, so you'll be able to hide there while I try to come up with a permanent solution," Peng said.

"Thank you, Grandfather. I am very grateful to have this opportunity to redeem myself," Aiguo replied.

"I will text you his name and address," Peng said, as he opened a bureau drawer, and removed another cell phone.

After texting the information to Aiguo's phone, Peng turned off the phone, and placed it back in the bureau.

"Did you receive the text?" Peng asked, into the other cell phone.

"Yes, and I will not fail, Grandfather. I knew you would be able to help," Aiguo said.

"Do not call again, Aiguo. I will destroy this phone. If I need to contact you I will call the cell you are using now," Peng said, and terminated the call.

*"Kung is right. Everything we have worked for is at risk. If they capture Aiguo, and find the device in Alexandria, then we are lost. We will both be tried and executed by the Party. They probably will just skip the trial and have us shot. The Americans might decide to preemptively attack us. This could destroy all the progress we have made as Chinese in the last 70 years. I have to tell General Kung . . . poor Aiguo,"* Peng thought, as he stared at his cell phone and then picked it up.

Chapter 24

"In any moment of decision, the best thing you can do is the right thing, the next best thing is the wrong thing, and the worst thing you can do is nothing."

Theodore Roosevelt

Manassas, Virginia, USA
Counterproliferation Division of the National Clandestine Service
Assistant Director Janet Davidson's Office
March 20, 2017, 1015 hours EST

Janet Davidson had always had an open door policy, even when she was in the Marine's. She had occasionally regretted that policy. This was one of those times, as she heard a knock on her open door, and looked up to see an anxious Amanda Langford standing outside.

"Come in, Amanda. At least you don't look like you've been pulling another all-nighter, so it can't be too important," Janet said, as she sipped from her third cup of coffee that morning.

"Yes ma'am . . . Ms. Davidson," Amanda said, as she walked into the room and set a document in front of her boss.

"And this is?" Janet asked, as she picked up the document.

"There were a series of murders at the Inova Alexandria Hospital in Alexandria yesterday morning. A doctor, a security guard, and three nurses, were all shot and killed during the blizzard," Amanda said.

"Yes, it was on the news when I got up this morning. The police thought it might have been some homeless guy looking for drugs," Janet said.

"That's what they told the media. I have a connection in the Pentagon that says there is more to it than that. One of the victims was married to a Major Anthony Thompson who was working at the Pentagon that night. He works in the Peoples Liberation Army Analysis Office. His wife called him at 0230 and told him they had a Chinese agent in the ER," Amanda said.

"What was her proof?" Janet said, as she began reading the document.

"Look on the second page. She took a photo of a tattoo on the man's right shoulder and sent it to her husband. This guy was Chinese Special Forces, a unit called the Siberian Tigers. The report says they're comparable to our Navy Seals," Amanda said.

"What are these characters above the tiger?" Janet asked.

"Literally, it means 'Loyalty to the Nation'. It's based on a story about a Chinese general named Yue Fei from the early 1100's. The question is . . . what is a Chinese Special Forces operative doing in Alexandria, Virginia?" Amanda said.

"A bomb on one coast and a special forces operator on the other. I think your project just expanded, Ms. Langford. It's too coincidental. We started with missing HEU. Then we find a nuclear device in San Francisco. Now we have this guy in Alexandria. You get back to work. Find out if the police have a picture of this guy. Find out what he was doing in this area. I'll get Director McElroy up to speed on this," Janet said.

"Yes ma'am," Amanda said, as she hurried from the room.

"Again with the 'ma'am'. I'll never break her of that habit," Janet said, as she shrugged and twisted her head to get the tension out of her neck.

. . . .

Director Caleb McElroy's Office
March 20, 2017, 1030 hours EST

"I don't believe you're saying this," Janet said, as she stood before Director McElroy's desk.

"This is all crap, circumstantial evidence based on the fantasies of a 20-something. Why have you bought into this absurd theory? Now she's seeing boogeymen pop up on the east coast. I will not bring this up to the Director of the CIA. Now get out and come back when you have something more concrete," Director McElroy said, as he gestured for Assistant Director Davidson to leave his office.

"What's going on, Caleb? Our work is always based on circumstantial evidence. We find the dots and connect them. We need to push this up," Janet said, as she refused to leave.

"Assistant Director . . . go do your damn job . . . come back when you have some actual evidence," Director McElroy said, as he pointed towards his door.

Janet bit back a reply as she stared down at her boss. She nodded, turned, and left the room.

As the door slammed, Caleb McElroy placed one elbow on his desk and began massaging his temples.

.  .  .  .

Assistant Director Janet Davidson's Office
March 20, 2017, 1115 hours EST

"So is he acting on the intel? Do I need to present the data to him? I can be ready in half an hour," Amanda said.

"He thinks the intel is circumstantial and not worth pushing up to the Director. He said . . ." Janet began.

"What! Is he crazy? That tattoo alone . . ." Amanda began, before Assistant Director Davidson slammed her hand on the desk.

"Agent! You do not interrupt me. Now close the damn door!" Janet said, as she stood up and glared at Amanda.

"The door!" Janet repeated, and took a deep breath as Amanda turned toward the door and hurriedly closed it.

"Now listen to me, Agent Langford. You will continue your pursuit of evidence to support your theory. You will keep me informed of your progress. When I think that you have acquired enough data to support your theory, then . . . and only then, will we return to Director McElroy's office. Is that understood?" Janet said, as she walked around her desk and stood staring down at Amanda.

"I bet you were a damn good Drill Sergeant," Amanda said, as she stood her ground.

"The Army has Drill Sergeants. I'm a Marine. The Marines have Drill Instructors . . . big difference," Janet said, in her best Drill Instructor growl.

"Amanda, you're headed down the right trail. Keep looking," Janet said, in a softer tone.

"I'll keep looking," Amanda said, as she took one step back, felt for the door handle, and backed out of the room.

.  .  .  .

Analyst Amanda Langford's Office
March 20, 2017, 1140 hours EST

"Detective Morehead, my name is Amanda Langford. I work for the Central Intelligence Agency. I understand that you're in charge of the investigation into the five murders at Inova Alexandria Hospital. I have a few questions that I'd like to ask," Amanda said, over her cell phone.

"Lady, you reporters are all the same, and I don't have time for this crap. Put me down for a big, No Comment!" Detective Morehead said, and hung up the phone.

Amanda immediately dialed him back and said, "Detective Morehead, I really work for the CIA in Manassas and I . . ." only to hear the phone go dead again.

"Well, it looks like it's time for a road trip," Amanda said, as she logged out of the office, added in a trip to the Alexandria City Police Department, and logged off her computer.

.  .  .  .

Alexandria, Virginia, USA
Alexandria City Police Department
3600 Wheeler Avenue
March 20, 2017, 1400 hours EST

"Nice look, a fortress surrounded by steel reinforced concrete pillars," Amanda said, as she parked her car, got out, and started walking toward the main entrance of the Alexandria City Police Department.

"It will be interesting to see if I still get the 'go away little girl' response after he sees my credentials," Amanda said, as she strode up to the front door and yanked it open.

Twenty feet inside the entrance all personnel had to go through a metal detector and have all hand held items x-rayed. Amanda would have been shocked if that hadn't been the case. After processing through the detectors, she hung her CIA identification around her neck, and began heading for the information desk.

She walked up to the counter and was confronted with a bored looking Sergeant playing a game on his cell phone. He looked up at her, and then resumed playing his game.

"Just give me a minute to finish this level. I've been working on this all day," the Sergeant said, as his game play continued.

"Sergeant . . . Quinn, I'm Agent Amanda Langford with the Central Intelligence Agency. I'm looking for Detective Morehead," Amanda said, as politely as she possibly could.

"CIA? Yeah well, I don't work for the feds. I'll be right with you," Sergeant Quinn said, as he looked at her ID and went back to his game.

"Really? How would you like to meet some friends of mine in another federal agency? They call themselves the IRS, and if I suggest you as a possible person of interest, I'm absolutely sure that they would be glad to pay you a visit," Amanda said, as the volume of her voice peaked.

"Morehead? Yeah, he's in. Criminal Investigations is on the third floor, Room 312," Sergeant Quinn said, as he leaned back in his chair, and pointed towards the elevator.

"Thank you for your assistance, Sergeant," Amanda said, as she turned away.

"*That worked pretty well. I need to make some friends in the IRS,*" she thought, as the elevator doors opened.

.   .   .   .

"Come in!" Detective Angelo Morehead yelled, as he looked up from behind a pile of video tapes and files piled on his desk.

"Your office looks worse than mine," Amanda said, as she walked into the office and stuck her hand over the pile of tapes.

"Agent Amanda Langford, Central Intelligence Agency. I called earlier in the day. You hung up on me," Amanda said, as her hand was swallowed by the massive hand of Detective Morehead.

He began laughing as he stood up. Amanda was stunned at the size of the huge man and a booming voice that matched his size. He was stylishly dressed in gray slacks with a blue and white pinstriped shirt. The tie was black and matched the tone of his skin. The revolver in his shoulder holster was so large it looked like a movie prop.

"My pleasure! Well, sorry about that . . . I guess you aren't a reporter," Angelo said, as he stared at her CIA identification.

"So, Ms. Langford, what can I do for you?" Angelo said, as he released her hand and stepped around the desk.

The office was so small, and so filled with files and paraphernalia, that there was no way for her to step away from the man.

"Let me clear the chair off," he said, while grabbing a huge stack of files, and cramming them against the side of his desk.

"As you can see I'm a little behind. I'll repeat, what can I do for you?"

"The murders at Inova Alexandria Hospital . . . I need all the information that you have on the case," Amanda said.

"That's fascinating. The CIA wants info on a few murders at a hospital in Alexandria, Virginia. Might I ask why?" Angelo said, as he threw his gum in the trash can and opened a fresh stick.

"Nicorette, I'm trying to quit smoking," he said, as he slid the stick into his mouth.

"I'm not at liberty to discuss that. The only thing I can say is that the CIA would appreciate your cooperation in this matter," Amanda said, then flinched as the man burst out laughing.

"I'm afraid that would take a court order. First, the Alexandria City PD has jurisdiction over this case. Second, the FBI has shown no interest in this case what so ever. Third, I don't like people stepping on my toes. I have size eighteen feet and very big toes," he said, as he went back to his chair and sat down.

Amanda stared at the man as he sat smacking his gum, and waiting for her next move. It dawned on her then that they were now playing a game of chess.

"So, did you play ball in the pros?" Amanda asked, as she pushed her pawn forward, and took out her cell phone to check for any messages.

"Three seasons with the Wizards. Then I tore up my Achilles tendon. No jump, no hoops. I always wanted to be a cop. So after I had surgery and healed up, I applied down here. That was over ten years ago," Angelo said, as another pawn moved forward in their ongoing mental game.

"That must have been rough," Amanda said.

"I got over it. I saved enough money for a house, married my sweetheart from college, and moved into the suburbs. Three kids later, and here I am, a 6'10" 320 pound bad ass detective. Now, Agent Langford, if you want something, give me something. I can keep my mouth shut," Angelo said, as his knight moved into the center of the board.

"Our interest is in the perpetrator. My understanding is that he was from Taiwan," Amanda said, as she countered knight for knight.

"That's what his passport and company ID said, but we have our doubts about that," he said, as he spit out the gum again, and reached for another stick.

"Based on what?" Amanda asked.

"You know about the tattoo?" Angelo asked, as the smacking continued, bishop takes knight.

"Chinese Special Forces," she replied, queen takes bishop.

"Now we're getting somewhere. You have done a little homework. We were stonewalled by the Pentagon when we tried to interview the husband of one of the dead nurses. They gave me the standard line of bull about national security," Angelo said.

"It wasn't a line of bull, trust me," Amanda said, king castled.

"Okay . . . I'll trust you . . . a little. What do you know about this?" Angelo asked, as he handed Amanda a small manila envelope.

She looked inside and carefully slid a coin out of the envelope and into the palm of her hand.

"It's a ban liang bronze coin, from the Warring States period . . . around 220 BC, or would be if it wasn't a reproduction. A coin from over 2000 years ago doesn't look like this. This coin is near mint. It has to be a fake. Is this evidence?" Amanda asked, as she turned the coin over and inspected the obverse side.

"It was recovered from the locker in the ER where they stored his clothes and stuff. Must have dropped out of his pocket," Angelo replied, as Amanda took out her cell phone and took pictures of both sides of the coin.

"I'll do some research and let you know what I find," Amanda said, as she returned the coin to the envelope and handed it to Angelo.

"Okay, my turn . . . we have video of the emergency room. We have the murder on security tape right here," he said, as he patted the pile of tapes sitting on his desk, and his queen slid into battle.

"It took me a while to sort through all this crap and put the useful part on a DVD. Would you like to see it?" he asked, and watched closely for her reaction.

"That might be helpful. Have you identified him?" she asked.

"No, but I'd be willing to bet my pension that the CIA could. I bet you have a lot better facial recognition software than we have," he said, as he smiled across at the young woman.

"So what would it take for me to get a copy of that DVD?" she asked, prepared to sacrifice a rook to protect the king.

"Well . . . now you're asking me to let go of evidence without a court order. Why would I do that?" he asked, as the noose around her king tightened.

"*He wants more. How much do I dare tell him?*" Amanda asked herself.

"I think he's connected to an ongoing investigation on the west coast," Amanda replied, wondering if she'd said too much, but at least her king was safe.

"West Coast? Funny thing . . . you know where I went to college? USF, the University of San Francisco. I still have a lot of friends out there. My mother still lives out there. We talk every week.

I tried to get her to move in with us, but she won't leave the neighborhood, too any memories," he said, as he leaned over his desk, and stared at Amanda, queen takes rook.

"She lives in The Inner Richmond, on 7th Avenue. She was forced to evacuate for a few days less than two weeks ago, something about a chemical hazard. At least that was the story they gave people," he said, and just let the words settle, like a cloud.

"I really can't go into any details on that incident," Amanda said, as she felt her queen being threatened.

"Ahh . . . you know about the . . . incident, but can't talk about it," he said, and the room grew quiet as the end game began.

"Yeah, I still got a lot of good friends back in San Francisco. Some of them are cops, detectives like me. They told me how the 'chemical incident' was handled. Homeland was on it like stink on shit. Cops were ordered to set up a perimeter, and then weren't allowed with ten blocks. Lots of big and specialized looking equipment went in and out. They even saw a big package exit the area on a flat bed, all covered up so you couldn't tell what it was. Anyone seen taking pictures was immediately jumped by feds and detained. I bet they'd be interested to hear from me that I got a visit from a CIA lady asking about a Chinese Special Forces guy killing a bunch of people in Alexandria a few days after a Chinese restaurant burns down in San Francisco, and half the federal agencies in the country take over part of their city. What do you think, Agent Langford?" he asked, as her queen fell over and her king was one move from mate.

"I'll be back with a court order, and I would suggest that you keep your theories to yourself," Amanda said, as she stood up and headed for the door, having conceded the game.

"Agent Langford, you'll need this," Detective Morehead said, as he pulled a boxed DVD out of his drawer, and tossed it across the room.

"And like I said, I know how to keep my mouth shut," he said, as she caught the disk and smiled, knowing that the game was a draw.

. . . .

She found him sitting alone, in the cold, outside the Crystal City Sports Pub. The sitting area belonged to the Andalusia Hookah Lounge next door, but the place was closed. The sun had been down for over two hours, and the air was heavy and stiff with the feel of another late season snow. One pitcher sat empty, the second was half empty as he sloshed beer into his glass. She recognized his handsome face, but he was unshaven, and very drunk.

"Major Thompson? My name is Amanda Langford. I'm so very sorry for your loss, but I need to ask you a few questions," Amanda said, as she slid into the chair opposite the man.

She was bundled up in a long red coat, with only her face showing. He sat wearing a light blue windbreaker.

"Who the hell are you, and what do you want?" he asked, as he set the pitcher down, and began studying the foam in his glass.

"I hate to bother you, but I really don't have a choice," she said, as she pulled her ID out of her purse and handed it to him.

He stared at it, then tossed it back to her.

"So . . . now the CIA wants some information. Let me guess? Why did this Siberian Tiger kill your wife? You know what . . . she was scared shitless. She wanted to leave the hospital in the middle of a blizzard. Seven months pregnant, and she wanted to leave the hospital and flee, because she was so scared of this guy," he said, as his voice cracked, with the sound of his wife's fear ringing in his ears.

"I met her in Hong Kong, during a liaison mission. She grew up in Huludao, northeast of Beijing. The Siberian Tigers are based and recruited from up there. She was scared and I let her die. What kind of a man lets his wife get murdered?" he asked, while he stared at Amanda with the blank look of a broken man.

"I told her to stay there and everything would be fine. I feel like I killed her myself. I don't know what to do. I only know that the best part of me just died. No! . . . She was fucking murdered!" he screamed, as he hurled the glass out into the street where it shattered.

The snow had started to fall, as if a switch had been flipped. The flakes were big, the kind of snow that would pile up fast.

"Just leave me alone," he said, as he laid his head on his arms and wept.

Amanda glanced to her left, and could see a waitress standing inside the door to the pub, too scared to come back outside. Amanda held up her hand and gestured to her, as if to say things were under control.

"Major, you need to go home. Let me call you a cab. You'll freeze out here," Amanda said, as she laid a hand on his arm.

He sat bolt upright, stared at her and said, "I use to have a home. I used to have a wife, but that's all gone. Did you know she was pregnant? It was a little boy. I was going to have a son. I'm a West Point graduate, Iraq veteran, beautiful wife. I was up for lieutenant colonel, first one in my class. I would have been the first one in my class. I had it made. I was living the American dream and . . . now everything's gone. I'm just a drunk sitting outside a pub in the freezing cold," he said, and screamed in rage at the night, as the uncaring snow continued to fall.

"*What would Janet say to him? Would she jerk a knot him? Maybe . . . probably . . .*" Amanda thought, as she fought the urge to get up and run away from this frightening man.

"So, Major . . . is this what West Point taught you? Is this what the Army has trained you to be? You get ambushed by the enemy, so you turn tail and run?" Amanda said, and tried not to flinch, as he turned a withering glare on her, and balled up his fists.

"*Stare him down. Don't be afraid. He won't hit a woman . . . I hope,*" Amanda thought, as she stared back, and didn't move.

"It doesn't matter anymore?" he mumbled, as he unclenched his fists, and started drinking from the pitcher.

"Major, it's the only thing that matters. That's why I'm here, to find the man that murdered your wife, and help you get revenge," Amanda said, desperate for a way to reach him.

He put the pitcher down, and took a deep breath. He blew it up at the sky, and smiled at the thick fog, mixing with the flakes, until it dissipated in the light breeze.

"If he was here right now, I wouldn't ask him a thing. I'd just beat him to death," he said, as he pounded the table so hard that the pitcher jumped.

"I understand that, but I think he's attached to something bigger," Amanda said.

"Like what?" he said, as he began sloshing the beer around inside the pitcher until some spilled onto the table.

"Why was a Chinese Special Forces operator walking around in Alexandria, Virginia? What was his mission? Because I don't think he was here on vacation," Amanda said, as she reached out, and slowly slid the pitcher out of Anthony's hands.

"Siberian Tiger . . . their version of a Seal, but their special ops are different than ours . . . like a bunch of damn warlords with specialized troops. They . . . they just copy what we do, and twist it to fit their culture. I know all about the bastards," Major Anthony Thompson said, as he straightened his back, and slowly rose from the grave he had been digging.

"So what questions do you have?" Anthony said, as he rubbed the stubble on his face and scratched his head.

"Why don't we go inside and get some coffee. I'm freezing," Amanda said.

"Yeah . . . I need to use the head anyway. Coffee sounds good," Anthony said, as he lifted the pitcher, and threw the beer over the adjacent restaurant fence.

He slammed the pitcher onto the table as he staggered to his feet, and said, "Yeah . . . revenge! That's worth living for."

Chapter 25

"Man and woman have each of them qualities and tempers in
which the other is deficient, and which in union contribute to the
common felicity."

Benjamin Franklin

Near Rock Point Beach, California, USA
US Highway 1, the Coast Highway
March 20, 2017, 1245 PST

"I can't believe you want to take US 1 all the way up the coast?
Why don't we just get on Interstate 5? It would be a lot faster," Lihwa
said, as she studied the route on her cell phone.

"Yeah, faster, stressful, and boring. Look at the ocean. Look at
the hills. Isn't it beautiful?" Tom said, as they passed Rock Point
Beach.

"Look, Tom, I know this is a trip down memory lane for you,
but we're not just taking a cruise up the coast. I have to know what my
father was involved in. Believe me, I'd like to just turn my back on the
whole thing, but I can't. It would haunt me for the rest of my life. I
need answers, and a slow cruise up the coast doesn't fit into that
agenda," Lihwa said, as she turned and stared at Tom.

"This is what I love about Sweetness. She's comfortable, easy
to drive, just made for cruising . . . and . . . before you start giving me
a hard time, I know why were on the road," Tom said, as he could
sense Lihwa start to fume.

"I just thought we could use this time to get to know each other
a little better. Look around you. This is what California is about. The
big cities are just that . . . big cities. The only difference between one
and the next is the number of trees and the weather. Lots of roads, lots
of people, lots of pollution . . . it all sucks. Driving up this little two
lane road sends me back to when I was a boy. Besides, in a year this

could all be gone, and we could be dead," Tom said, as he rolled down the window, and rested his arm on the door.

A mile up the road they turned left onto Duncan's Landing Overlook. As they pulled over beside a small rock outcropping on the right, Tom parked the car, and slowly got out.

"I'll be back in a minute," Tom said, as he leaned back into the window.

Rounding the front of the car, he climbed up the rough stone surface. Yellow wild flowers, their faces turned toward the sun, were scatted throughout the small hill.

Lihwa rolled down her window, and sighed as the coastal breeze swept through the old car. She glanced at her cell phone, set the music alarm for ten minutes and closed her eyes.

The Slants, 'Level Up', jarred her awake, as she fumbled to turn down the volume.

"Wow, that was a quick 10," she said, as she glanced up the hill, and saw Tom sitting on top, just staring out at the ocean.

"Jeez, at this rate we'll never make it to Oregon tonight," Lihwa said, as she got out of the car, and slammed the door.

"Come on, Tom. It's time to go. Let's go," she yelled, but he didn't move.

"Crap!" she said, as she began to climb up the rocks.

When she reached the top, she nudged Tom in the shoulder and said, "I know you don't want to go, but it's already 1:30. It'll be dark in four hours."

She looked down, and saw that he was holding a small piece of clear plastic the size of a credit card. Inside was a small yellow flower. The same size and color as the flowers she had trampled on her way up the hill.

"The last time we were here I made Sharon a necklace by linking together the flower stems. Alex liked it so much he pitched a fit until I made him another one. After he died, and she left me, I found this in the back of a chest of drawers. His name was on it in her handwriting. I've kept it in my wallet ever since," Tom said, as he kissed the memento, and placed it back in his wallet.

"We used to picnic right here, right on this spot. I can see him scampering across the rocks like a mountain goat with Sharon chasing after him, afraid that he would fall and get hurt," Tom said, as he got up and brushed off his pants.

"God, it still hurts!" Tom said, as he glanced out at the ocean.

He didn't pull away when he felt Lihwa's small hand entwine in his. When he started to sob, she placed her arm around his waist and leaned her head against his shoulder. The sound of the breeze, and the surf below them, blended with the shared misery felt by two wounded souls.

. . . .

Near Leggett, California, USA
US Highway 1, the Coast Highway
March 20, 2017, 1445 PST

"I hate to say this, but I'm starving," Lihwa said, as she started to look for restaurants on her cell phone.

"Don't bother. We'll reach Leggett in about 15 minutes. There's a nice little restaurant in Leggett called the Rising Sun Café. It's not a One Star Michelin place, but it's cheap, and the food is good. I love the plantains. You'll want a salad," Tom said, as he popped out one cassette tape and inserted another.

"You're kidding me, the Beatles?" Lihwa said, as 'A Hard Day's Night' burst from the speakers.

"It's a classic. What's wrong with you?" Tom said, as he turned and looked at Lihwa as if she had just shot him.

"Are you sure you're only 42? You're like some guy who was born in the 50's and grew up in the 60's. Your tastes are just weird," Lihwa said.

"I prefer to think of myself as 'retro', thank you very much, which happens to be quite stylish these days," Tom said, as he pretended to be in a huff, but couldn't stop from laughing.

"So what's our plan?" Lihwa asked.

"We'll go to Seattle and start checking out Chinese restaurants. I think they'll go after the civilian population. It'll be blackmail pure and simple. That's what I'd do," Tom said, shifting gears as quickly as Lihwa had.

"That's because you're not Chinese. They will want the infrastructure intact: all the cities, power plants, dams, roads, railroads, everything. To do that, they have to take out the military," Lihwa said.

"But that's the way our military fights. They try to minimize the civilian casualties," Tom said.

"I've got news for you. The Chinese don't give a damn about non-Chinese. We . . . are the people of the 'Central Country'. Their objective is to make this a Chinese planet," Lihwa said.

"Whoa . . . you sound like that nut job, Alex Jones. You must have been reading some of his stuff on Infowars. Girl, that's some crazy shit. I bet you vote Republican," Tom said, as he turned off Highway 1 onto 271 and headed towards the Rising Sun Café.

"You ever read Sun Tzu's The Art of War?" Lihwa asked.

"I don't read Chinese," Tom said.

"The Art of War is over 2500 years old. It's been translated into more languages than the Bible. It's still studied today," Lihwa said, as they pulled into the parking lot of the Rising Sun Café.

"Well, Miss 'Art of War'; we have one example of what they would do. That example says 'restaurant'," Tom said.

"Yes, but I still think they'll go after the military. It's what Sun Tzu would do," Lihwa said.

Tom started laughing and then said, "WWSTD?"

"What?" Lihwa said.

"What Would Sun Tzu Do? Don't you remember the period a few years ago where people were saying WWJD? What Would Jesus Do? It was on t-shirts and bumper stickers all over the place," Tom asked.

"I'm driving up the coast with a crazy man," Lihwa said, as she shook her head, and returned to studying her phone.

"Okay, so we agree to disagree, now what?" Tom said, as he stopped the car and turned off the engine.

"We get up there and do both. We'll see who's right," Lihwa said, as she stuck out her hand to make the bet official.

"So when I win, what do I get?" Tom asked with a wicked smile, and held onto Lihwa's hand.

"You get another handshake," Lihwa said, as she jerked her hand free and Tom began to laugh.

"We'll start with your idea. I'll start cataloguing Chinese restaurants in the Seattle area. Then I'll start looking near military bases in Washington State. If I know you, you'll need two hands to eat," Lihwa said, as they both got out of the car.


.  .  .  .

"You didn't tell me it was Caribbean," Lihwa said, leaned back in the passenger seat of the Camaro and groaned.

"Yeah, you can hurt yourself in there. The portions are huge and not for the faint of heart," Tom said, as he hooked up his seat belt and started the car.

"I'll apologize in advance if I get a little gassy. Spicy food does that to me," Tom said, as they pulled out of the parking lot.

"Oh gross! We're don't even know each other that well yet. You're supposed to still be in the 'hide all your faults from her stage'," Lihwa said, as she rolled her window down a couple of inches.

"You said 'yet'. That means you want to get to know me better?" Tom said, as he pulled into the Patriot gasoline station just up the street.

Lihwa just rolled her eyes, and started studying the Chinese restaurant list that she had saved on her phone.

"I'll be right back," Tom said, as he got out of the car.

"Sweetness was really thirsty. I'm going to have to pay more attention to the mileage," Tom said, as he got back in the car.

"Mileage? The gas gauge doesn't work?" Lihwa asked, as she looked up from her phone.

"Naw, it hasn't worked for years. I just keep track of the mileage. 250 miles and I fill up. Usually I have a quarter of a tank left, but she was on fumes," Tom said, as he zeroed the trip odometer.

"It's 4 o'clock. I say we drive until 10, and then find some place to stop," Tom said, as he pulled out of the gas station.

"Fine with me as long as you don't fall asleep," Lihwa said, as she scrolled down her list of restaurants.

"So what did you find?" Tom asked, as he turned right onto US 1, then left onto US 101, and headed north.

"Basically it's a mess. There are 32 Asian restaurants in or around Seattle. I excluded non-Chinese and chain restaurants, and got the list down to 17. Then I researched which ones had been there the longest or had been recently sold, that kind of thing. That got the list down to 12. Then I started looking at location. If you want to take out the population you would need to be near the largest grouping of people or west of there so the fallout would kill them," Lihwa said, as she reached into the back seat and opened up her back pack.

"I shared the files with my IPad. Google Maps is a lot easier to see on a large screen," she said, as she turned on the IPad and began scrolling through screens.

"So what are you looking for?" Tom asked.

"Restaurants like ours. It won't be in a strip mall. It will need an outbuilding or someplace that you could lock the bomb up for decades. It can't be in the food storage areas of the restaurant. They get checked by food inspectors at least once per year," Lihwa said, as she began zooming in at various locations and checking the satellite view.

"How about military bases? Have you started looking near those yet?" Tom asked.

"Separate file, now be quiet and let me focus," Lihwa said, as Tom drove up the Redwood Highway, passing through an endless valley of towering evergreens.

Florence, Oregon, USA
US Highway 101
March 20, 2017, 2230 PST


"I think I fell asleep," Lihwa said, as she sat up, yawned, and stretched.

"That was about an hour ago," Tom said, as he popped a cassette into the player.

"Where are we?" Lihwa asked, as she rubbed her face, and reached into the back seat for a bottle of water.

"About ten miles from Florence, Oregon. We'll find some place to stop there," Tom said.

"I'll find us a place," Lihwa said, as she picked up her cell phone.

"Did you know that you snore?" Tom asked.

"Do not," Lihwa, said, as she began scrolling through prospective motels.

"Like a truck driver, or a logger with a chain saw. I'm not sure which. Plus, you're really cute when you sleep," Tom said, as he glanced over at her.

"The Lighthouse Inn, cheap without being a dump. Go over the bridge and it's two blocks down on the left. Eighty four bucks a night will work just fine," Lihwa said, as she turned off her phone.

"You sure it's not a dump? I thought lawyers made lots of money," Tom said, as Simon and Garfunkel sang the opening lyrics to 'America'.

"I started working in the restaurant when I was 8. I worked there seven days a week at least ten hours per day. When I went away to college I got a part time job so I could afford to buy some decent clothes so I wouldn't be laughed at. I'm not some silver spoon girl whose daddy made a fortune in real estate in Shanghai, and sent his darling little girl to Stanford with a new Mercedes. I don't waste money," Lihwa said.

"Hey . . . sorry I hit a nerve. Nice to know that you won't be high maintenance," Tom said, and then winced as he heard his own words.

"Mr. Jackson, I will never be a 'kept woman'. If I ever decide to have a long term relationship with a man, it will be as his equal or not at all," Lihwa said, as the chill air outside seemed to penetrate the inside of the car.

They checked in separately, and didn't exchange a word for the rest of the evening.

# Chapter 26

"Have inward spies. Make use of officials of the enemy."

Sun Tzu (~520 BC)

Beijing, China
Beijing Botanical Gardens
100 meters above 22 Base Headquarters
March 21, 2017, 0630 hours CT

"Well, Peng, it's been 24 hours. So the good news is that I haven't been arrested yet. That means that the Chairman is getting opinions before he acts. The more time that passes the better our chances, I would think," General Kung said, as he and Colonel Peng walked beside the upper part of the lake inside the Beijing Botanical gardens.

It was early morning and a chill was still in the air. The time for frost had passed, and General Kung found these early morning walks stimulating.

"You're assuming that General Fan forwarded the information that you gave him," Colonel Peng said, regretting that he had not worn his gloves.

"Oh, he'd never sit on something like this. The information is incendiary. If he delayed, it might look like he was in on the plan. My uncle won't take that chance. If this goes poorly, heads will roll . . . literally," General Kung said, as he made a slicing motion across his throat and smiled.

"If not for the bad news from Alexandria I would be quite pleased with how things are progressing. Five dead and a photo of a Special Forces tattoo have left a very messy trail. I doubt if our friend at the Counterproliferation Division can hold back an inquiry for very long. He has been useful, but I despise traitors. As I told you days ago, I think the time for removing that source of a potential problem has come. The only good news is that the device in Alexandria has been installed, and is still unknown to the Americans," General Kung said, with a sigh.

"Two exposures in less than a month. All these years and never a failure. Now, when we are so very close to the end game, this has to happen. I wonder if our intelligence services have picked up on the deaths in Alexandria?" General Kung said, as they continued their slow walk around the lake.

"Colonel, this special forces operative must be found and terminated. He has shown an inability to function under pressure. If the Americans captured him it would be over. They would force him to disclose the location of the device, and that cannot happen. Understood?" General Kung said.

"General, as you know, we do not assign agents to specific tasks within the United States. We leave that to their leaders that are loyal to you. We assign the task and they decide the best personnel to accomplish the assigned task," Peng began, aware that he was now starting down a very precarious path.

"Yes, Peng, get to the point. It's not like you to be so circumspect," General Kung said, as he stopped on the bridge that spanned the upper lake within the gardens.

"The agent in Alexandria called me at 2300 last night," Peng said.

Kung said nothing. He just turned and stared at Colonel Peng.

"General Kung . . . the agent is my only grandson. He has my private cell number. He called asking for guidance. His own people have already tried to have him killed. He admitted that there were complications with the mission, but that the device was delivered successfully," Peng began, as he rested his hands on the bridge railing, and looked down into the still waters of the lake.

"Peng, you know my policy on failures and loose ends. Your grandson failed when he was captured and killed five people while escaping. They photographed his Siberian Tiger tattoo. He might as well have stood on top of the White House and started waving the Chinese flag and said, 'I am a Chinese agent. Come question me and learn my secrets,' Kung said, as he joined Peng at the bridge railing.

"I knew you would react this way. I was just hoping that you could see a way for him to survive this. As you know, his father, my only son, Major Peng Tengfei, died while flying an experimental fighter aircraft. Aiguo was his only son. There are no other males in my family, only daughters. If he dies, then my line dies with me," Peng said, as he turned and looked into the stern eyes of his friend and commanding officer.

The pair said nothing as Kung turned away and stared into the distance.

"Where is the boy now?" Kung asked, as he sighed.

"I have sent him to the house of the American traitor, the head of the CIA Weapons Mission Center. The one you have said was now expendable. I found out this morning that we have been tracking his internet activity and he is preparing to flee. He has removed most of the cash from his checking account and has purchased a one-way plane ticket to San Paulo under another identity. Aiguo needs a place to hide for a while, and we need to permanently remove this man from your service," Peng said.

"So, you wish to protect your grandson, and give him a mission to restore my faith in him?" General Kung said.

"Yes, General, that was my hope," Peng said.

"Zihao, we have been friends for a very long time. I stood beside you at your son's funeral, but this puts all of our work at risk. We have had a device discovered in San Francisco. If one is found across the river from the White House, and it is a device of very considerable magnitude, then we are undone. The Americans will have us, and by us, I mean China, by the throat. I haven't even briefed the Chairman on our plan yet. If our secrecy disappears there will be no mercy from him or the Party. They will have us killed, and all the members of our organization killed. They might even extend that decision out to all our families. Do you want me to risk all these lives, and all our work, for your grandson?" General Kung asked.

"I know all this, Yusheng. I was only hoping . . ." Peng began.

"I understand what your intent was, but my answer is no. You know what has to be done. If your grandson accomplishes his new mission, then I will see to it that his name is honored within the Siberian Tigers. It would be best if he took his own life in a manner that left him impossible to identify. I am sorry, Zihao, but that is my final decision," General Kung said.

Colonel Peng snapped to attention and bowed. He felt every day of his eighty plus years as General Kung nodded, and turned away, continuing his morning walk around the lake.

Peng stared at the back of his commanding officer, and knew that he would not be invited on another of these morning walks. He also knew that the time for his retirement had arrived.

Chapter 27

"The quality of decision is like the well-timed swoop of a falcon which enables it to strike and destroy its victim."

Sun Tzu (~520 BC)

McLean, Virginia, USA
Williamsburg Middle School
March 22, 2017, 0230 hours EST

Aiguo sat in the cold, darkened car behind the Williamsburg Middle School, and read the text message from Uncle Peng for the tenth time. The shock of the message had worn off, and his mood was swinging between anger, depression and resignation.

"I have accomplished the mission. How can he abandon me like this? No, I'm a Special Forces operative, a member of the Siberian Tigers. I have new orders, and must obey these new directives. I am duty bound. I have no choice," Aiguo said aloud, as he stared out the window into the cold darkness of his certain fate.

Aiguo had driven past the house of the American traitor twice earlier in the evening. The lights had been on and the man could be seen walking through the house. Aiguo had been hopeful then. It seemed that there was still a way out of his dilemma. Now he knew that this mission would be his final one. He glanced at the time on his cell phone and started the car.

"0230 . . . it's time," Aiguo said, as he started the engine, and let it warm for a few moments.

He pulled out of the school parking lot, and turned left on North Harrison Street. The roads had been plowed during the day, but the snow had resumed soon after sunset. Now there was an additional six inches of fresh snow coating the roads, and there was no other traffic as he wound his way towards his target.

"The snow and the cold . . . they have been my undoing. Civilian clothes, no insulation, how could I have been so stupid? It was the little boy, I think. The little boy whose father had died in a war so far from home," Aiguo told himself, as he continued down North Harrison before turning right on 36th Street North.

"I let the little boy inside my mind. He weakened me, and I became soft for just long enough to forget my mission and my training. I relaxed after the delivery, and now I will not have a son to mourn my passing," Aiguo said, as the slow swoosh of the wipers clearing the snow from his windshield counted down the minutes left in his life.

Aiguo pulled over into another lot on his right, parked the car, and turned off the engine. He pulled his cell phone from a coat pocket, stared at it, and began to caress its surface.

*"I shouldn't call her. It would be better if I just disappeared,"* he told himself, as his fingers began to tap out her cell number with a will of their own.

"Hello," she said, as Aiguo paused, knowing that he should disconnect the call.

"Meili . . . it's Aiguo," he said, as he closed his eyes, and imagined her beautiful face.

"Aiguo, where are you? It's been weeks. I've been so worried," Meili said.

"You know how it is. They send me somewhere, and I can't talk about it," Aiguo said, as he relished every spoken syllable and the silken texture of her voice.

"But you call me now, and you sound strange to me. Is everything all right? Are you on your way home?" Meili asked.

"Meili, I called to tell you how much I love you, and to tell you how much I want to be your husband," Aiguo said, as he fought back the tears.

"Aiguo, this isn't like you. What's wrong? Are you hurt?" Meili asked.

"No, I'm safe, but I may not make it back to you. I think this will be my last mission," Aiguo said, and regretted having made the call as she started to cry.

"Meili . . . just listen to me. I don't have long. I wanted many years and children with you, but it's not meant to be," Aiguo said, as he hardened himself to the sound of her anguish.

"I won't tell you to forget me. I hope that you never do, but I want you to promise me that you will go on . . . for me. I want you to live a long life, and have many children. When they are grown, and understand such things, tell them about a young man that you knew once. Tell them that he loved you more than anything else in the world. Tell them that he died for China," Aiguo said, until the sound of her crying broke his heart, and began to break his resolve.

"Aiguo . . . no, " he heard her say, as he disconnected the call and wept.


. . . .


McLean, Virginia, USA
2000 Rockingham Street
March 22, 2017, 0310 hours EST


Aiguo turned off the lights as he neared the intersection of North Kensington and Rockingham Street. His target was on a small rise on the far left corner. It was an odd house, very different from any home he'd seen in America. It looked like a series of overlapping blocks turned at an angle. Large windows covered most of the outer surface. There was a lower driveway that led to a garage built into the bottom of the house, and an upper drive that led to the left side of the house and the main entrance. He paused at the intersection, and then turned left, drove uphill, and pulled into the upper driveway. He stopped by a large clay pot at the end of the driveway, and silenced the engine.

The house was dark. After waiting a few minutes, he got out of the car, and closed the door with a gentle click. He felt his right coat pocket to verify the presence of the 9mm semiautomatic that he had taken from the security guard. His left coat pocket held the small caliber pistol, with the silencer still attached, that he had taken from the assassin.

Aiguo removed the small pistol from his pocket, and held it in his right hand as he approached the side of the house. To his left was a six foot plank wall with a hidden entrance leading behind the house. He stepped through the entrance, and glanced at a headless stone angel, playing on a mandolin. The wooden wall continued on his left, enclosing a narrow courtyard that ran the length of the house.

Aiguo paused for a moment to listen. A faint hum as the wind stirred the naked branches in the trees above him, was the only sound that he heard. The foot deep snow crunched with every footstep as he approached the first of two glass doors that led to the interior of the house.

"*I've seen no security cameras, no sensors. Why would a man like this be so careless, so defenseless?*" Aiguo thought, as peered into the interior shadows of the house.

He froze as a shadow inside the house glided across the wooden floor. A baleful face appeared a foot inside the multipaned glass door.

"*Damn, a wolf hound,*" Aiguo thought, as he stared unmoving, face to face with this huge guard dog.

The dog's jaws opened like a steel trap revealing its large canines. The dog was silent, but the look in his eyes seemed to dare Aiguo to try to enter his domain.

"*He's trained not to bark. That means he's a killer,*" Aiguo thought, as he slowly raised the assassin's Kel-Tec .22 Magnum until the sights formed a line from his right eye to a point between the dog's eyes.

The crack of the glass was the loudest sound as the silenced hollow-point bullet penetrated the glass and the dog's brain at nearly the same instant. The dog dropped like a stone. Aiguo broke the glass pane nearest the door lock, opened the door, and slid in past the still form of the wolfhound. After closing the door he knelt, and listened for footsteps, or the glimmer of lights being turned on. There was no change inside the house.

"*Uncle Peng would want me to kill him now, and then burn down the house, with me in it,*" Aiguo thought; as he stood, and began clearing the ground floor, room by room.

He found one set of stairs that led downward. He assumed that they led to the garage, but also found another bedroom and separate bath, along with a well-stocked wine cellar. Once he had verified that the lower level was empty, he doubled back, and began to climb to the second floor, placing each step carefully, while he covered the floor above with the pistol.

At the top of the stairs the hall led left and right to different bedrooms. Aiguo turned left as he remembered a large balcony attached to the far right side of the house. He stepped down the darkened hallway, placing each foot toe to heel, listening for the slightest sound of movement in the room ahead of him. The bedroom door was swung open. Two pieces of luggage stood against the right side of the wall outside the room.

"*A trip you won't be making, my friend*," Aiguo thought, as he crossed the threshold, and entered the bedroom.

The man's head was visible above the covers. He was curled up on his right side in a fetal position.

"*One quick shot and it will all be over*," Aiguo thought, as he stepped within three feet of the bed, and lowered the pistol to within a foot of the man's temple.

He glanced down in the near darkness, and saw the faint glimmer of what he instinctively knew were plane tickets. A desperate plan began to quickly evolve in his mind.

"*I can steal his identity and fly out alone. He's CIA. They never search him when he travels. They probably look at the photo ID, and let him go without a question. But the name, the face?*" Aiguo thought, as he stood above the man weighing his existence with a fingertip on a trigger.

Aiguo looked around the room, and saw a wallet, cell phone, watch and ID piled together on a dresser. Slowly stepping backwards, while keeping the weapon pointed at the man's head, he stopped by the dresser and picked up the ID.

"*Top Secret Clearance, of course . . . very difficult to forge, possibly DNA encrypted, but all I have to do is flash it by a security guard at an airport. I can cut in my photo*," Aiguo thought, as he imagined smuggling Meili out of China and starting a new life in South America.

"I will complete the mission, Uncle Peng, but I will complete it my way," Aiguo said aloud, as he flipped on the lights in the bedroom.

# Chapter 28

"One frequently only finds out how really beautiful a woman is, until after considerable acquaintance with her."

Mark Twain

Olympia, Washington, USA
US Interstate 5
March 22, 2017, 0830 PST

"Look . . . I've apologized at least 10 times. I'm sorry if I stepped on your feminist toes," Tom said, then instantly regretted how he had phrased that.

"So, I don't get all cozy with you and that makes me a feminist?" Lihwa asked, as she sipped her coffee.

"What? Where did that come from? I make a little friendly banter and you get all huffy," Tom said, as they sped down Interstate 5. The speed limit was 75, but Tom was pushing 90 as his blood pressure increased.

"I know your type. You prefer docile women. You probably think I'd be 'cute' with bound feet," Lihwa said, as she ramped up her sarcasm.

"Whatever the hell 'bound feet' are," Tom said, then suddenly grew quiet.

"Typical American! You have no knowledge of other cultures," Lihwa said, as she began to list his various deficiencies.

When he no longer replied, she said, "What? Can't take it?"

"Sharon wasn't docile. She was a world class athlete. I mean she participated in Iron Man triathlon events. That's how we met. The Fire Department was providing support during the Escape from Alcatraz Triathlon in '04. I was covering a bad turn on a downhill portion of the bike race. She crashed, and skinned up her right leg really bad. I was cleaning and bandaging her leg while she was hopping around changing a flat tire. That's how we met," Tom said.

"Tom, I'm sorry. Sometimes I don't know when to shut up," Lihwa said.

"Sharon was small like you, and she had a fiery temper. When she was pregnant I told her she was starting to get fat. She gave me a black eye for that one. She apologized for days. That was the only time she ever hit me," Tom said, as he slowed down to the speed limit.

"Tom, I'm sorry. I do like you, but we need to focus on this. Besides, I'm not a very nice person. That's what makes me a good lawyer, the mean streak," Lihwa said, as while swallowing her guilt along with her coffee.

"Like I said, I'm used to it. So let's focus, like you said. Where are we going?" Tom asked.

"I spent most of the night on Google Maps studying satellite images. There were only two places that fit all the parameters. It had to be a Chinese restaurant, with long term stability, and a storage building outside the main restaurant. So it's either the Magic Dragon or the Gim Wah Restaurant. Your pick," Lihwa said, as she glanced over at Tom.

"Tom, I'm sorry for being so uptight," Lihwa said.

."I wish I had a tape of 'Puff the Magic Dragon'. I'd pop that in right now," Tom said.

"Puff the what? Where do you find these songs?" Lihwa said, as she playfully smacked Tom on the arm.

"Peter, Paul and Mary," Tom said, and then began to sing.

"Puff the magic dragon lived by the sea and frolicked in the autumn mist in a land called Honalee . . . Hey, that could become our song," Tom began, then laughed as Lihwa groaned.

"I figure another 45 minutes to Seattle. Which restaurant do we get to first?" Tom asked.

"You'll have to teach me the lyrics. Let's try the Magic Dragon. Take I-5 into Seattle and get off on West Mercer. Take Mercer to Elliott . . . why don't you have a Garmin? I bet you still have road maps in here," Lihwa said, as she opened the glove box.

She held up a hand full of maps as if she had just found another nuclear weapon.

"What? Like you're shocked? Maps come in handy, and they don't run out of power," Tom said.

Lihwa shook her head as she stuffed the maps back in the glove box, saying, "You just drive. I'll tell you when to turn."

Seattle, Washington, USA
The Magic Dragon
1827 15<sup>th</sup> Avenue West
March 22, 2017, 1015 PST

"Are you sure? This looks like a strip mall. Where's the storage building?" Tom asked, as they pulled up in the parking lot outside the Magic Dragon.

Lihwa studied the 3D view on Google Maps, and said, "Go back to 15<sup>th</sup> Avenue, the way we came. When you get past these buildings turn right. There should be a driveway."

When Tom pulled into the driveway he stopped. They both turned and stared at each other. Fifty yards ahead was a small brick building.

"You know, we never talked about what we would do if we found another bomb," Lihwa said.

"I've got that covered," Tom said, as he pulled out his wallet.

"That DHS asshole gave me his card in case I remembered anything else," Tom said, as he removed the card from his wallet and handed it to Lihwa.

"Dimitri Atkins? Sounds like a Russian. He could be a plant," Lihwa said.

"Says the lady whose father kept a nuke in her backyard," Tom said, and winced, as he was hit in the arm.

"Let's check the building," Lihwa said, as she tucked the business card into her IPad.

Tom pulled up in front of the small building and said, "Look at the sign on the door. Property of the Magic Dragon Restaurant, LLC and a phone number. I wonder if it's locked?" Tom said, as he shut off the engine, and put the car in park.

"One way to find out," Lihwa said, as she hopped out of the car.

"It's locked," she said, as she jiggled the door knob, and turned back towards Tom.

"Not for long," Tom said, as he got out of the Camaro and popped the trunk.

"What is that thing?" Lihwa asked, as Tom walked up with a strange looking tool.

"It's called a Hooligan Tool. Very handy for opening locked doors," Tom said, as he turned around, and checked the area for security cameras.

"Now put these on," Tom said, as he handed Lihwa a pair of gloves and donned another pair.

"Can't leave fingerprints, and wipe off the door knob," Tom said, after Lihwa stared at him with a questioning look.

"Now all you have to do is place the curved claw like this and . . . push," Tom said, as the door lock was torn from the frame.

"Of course this is breaking and entering," Lihwa said, as they stepped into the building.

"Don't go all lawyer on me now. We're trying to save the country," Tom said, as he stepped past her, and began checking out the interior of the building.

"All I see is old equipment, some restaurant flyers, a few boxes of plates and such. The walls look the same size inside and out," Tom said, as he leaned out the door to check the length of the building outside compared with the inside.

"I agree. This one's a bust. Let's get out of here before someone sees us," Lihwa said.

"My father's a terrorist and now I'm a burglar," Lihwa said, as they got back in the car and drove away.

"Hey, you can be Lucy Liu. You know, Joan Watson on Elementary. I'll be Sherlock Holmes," Tom said, as they hurried away from the scene of the crime.

"You . . . are a very strange man," Lihwa said, as she opened up her IPad.

"All right, Joan, where to next?" Tom said, as he headed back down 15th Avenue West.

"Enough with the Joan, unless you want another bruise. Turn right on Magnolia Bridge," Lihwa said.

"What if this next place is a bust?" Tom asked.

"Then I win the bet. Then I open up the military base file and we keep going. The only way to find out why my father was involved in this is to bust it wide open. We have to find another bomb," Lihwa said.

"Okay, turning right on Magnolia. Now where?" Tom asked.

"In about a mile this turns into Clise Plaza West. Then in a block it turns into 32$^{nd}$ Avenue. In a couple of blocks you turn right onto West McGraw," Lihwa said.

"The road changes names three times in three blocks?" Tom asked.

Lihwa just shrugged, as she worked on her IPad. Tom burst out laughing as 'Puff the Magic Dragon' began playing on Lihwa's IPad. Lihwa just smiled over at him and said nothing.

"Three blocks up on the right. When you get past it, take the next right," Lihwa said, as Puff faded into the background.

"Yeah, there it is," Tom said, as they drove past the Gim Wah Restaurant.

Tom turned right on 35$^{th}$, then slowed as they came to a road leading behind the restaurant.

"Take the right onto West Wheeler and slow down," Lihwa said, as she switched to the satellite view.

"Stop! Right there . . . look at that building. It looks just like the shed behind our restaurant," Lihwa said, as she pointed at the concrete block building behind the restaurant.

"Look at the padlock on the rollup door and on the main entrance. They're huge. I can see them from here, " Tom said, as he stared at the building and then at Lihwa.

"Crap, I might win this bet yet," Tom said, as they drove past.

"This is tricky. There's a house right across the street. I think we're going to have to come back after it's dark and everything quiets down," Lihwa said.

"The fence is eight feet tall. Let's chance it . . . or not," Tom said, then stepped on the gas as someone came out of the back of the restaurant.

"We'll come back about 2AM," Tom said, as they sped down the street.

.   .   .   .

The Camaro slowly turned from 35th Avenue onto West Wheeler Street. The lights were off. Both front windows were rolled down as the occupants checked for motion, lights, or noise. The night was still and cool. Only the street light at the corner betrayed their presence. Dumpsters from the restaurant lined the small building on both open sides.

"I'm parking on the street beside the building. If we have to bolt, I don't want anything in the way," Tom said, as he coasted to a stop and turned off the engine.

"Now we wait and listen," Tom said, as he turned off the interior light so it wouldn't come on when they left the car.

"Let's get this over with. I'm so nervous I'm shaking," Lihwa said, as she turned and stared at Tom in the near darkness.

Tom nodded, and after a couple of minutes he opened his door. He had oiled all the hinges in the car earlier in the day, and tested to make sure they wouldn't squeak when opened or closed. He pulled a satchel filled with tools from the back seat and slung it over his right shoulder.

The access door on the street side was fronted with a decorative metal grate. The padlock was large, but exposed. Tom placed the jaws of the bolt cutters on the shackle of the padlock and nodded. Lihwa wrapped a heavy towel around the bolt cutters and the padlock, and nodded back.

With a quiet snip the lock was cut, and Lihwa removed the towel and removed the severed padlock. Tom sprayed the hinges of the gate with WD40, and swung the gate open. After a few more sprays the gate swung back and forth without making a sound.

"This door is tougher. It's a Master Pro-Series padlock. I can't get the bolt cutters on the shackle. Fortunately the hasp it's attached to isn't the same quality," Tom whispered into Lihwa's ear, as he reached inside the satchel, and removed the same Hooligan Tool that he had used to get into the storage building behind the Magic Dragon.

"Watch this. I'll use the spur this time," Tom said, as he slipped the heavy spur behind the hasp.

"Wrap the towel around the tool; then back off," Tom said, as he braced his feet.

As Lihwa backed away Tom increased the pressure on the hasp. When it began to squeal, Tom stopped, removed the towel, and handed it to Lihwa. He removed the Hooligan, and saturated the padlock area with WD40. After replacing the tool and the towel, he motioned for Lihwa to back up and began to pull against the hasp again. It began to squeal, but then popped open with a slight crack.

"Listen!" Tom said, as Lihwa stepped towards the door.

After two more minutes, Tom placed the Hooligan claw against the door jamb beside the lock. He jammed the tool in and slowly wedged the door open.

Lihwa patted him on the shoulder as they slipped into the building, and shut the door and gate behind them.

"Same kind of stuff we stored behind our restaurant," Lihwa said, as they both turned on their flashlights and began inspecting the inside of the building.

"Look at this! Won-Ton wrappers stored out here. They're going to poison someone. They should be in a fridge," Lihwa said, as she bent over a box in one corner.

Tom shook his head and said nothing, but made a mental note to bring up the Won-Ton wrappers at a later date.

"Does the length of the floor going that way look short to you?" Tom asked, as he pointed at the far wall.

"I'm not sure," Lihwa said.

"Slip outside and pace off the length of the building on this wall. Then come back in here . . . and be quiet," Tom said, as he pointed at the wall to the right of the door entrance.

Lihwa nodded and stepped outside. She waited for a minute at the entrance as a car passed by on 35th Avenue. After pacing off the distance twice she quietly reentered the building, and shut the gate and door.

"Eighteen paces," Lihwa said, as Tom gestured for an answer.

"Pace it off in here," Tom said, as he motioned for her to back up to the wall.

She stepped off the distance while being careful to use the same gait as she had used outside.

"Fourteen!" Lihwa said, as she turned toward Tom, and placed her hand over her mouth.

"Are you sure?" Tom said, as he rushed up to her.

"Yes, I'm sure! Fourteen . . . four less steps than the outside," Lihwa said, in a loud whisper.

"Hooleee crap!" Tom said, as he slumped to the floor, and began playing the light across the far wall.

Lihwa sat down beside him and said, "I think I lost the bet," and stuck out her gloved hand.

Tom took her hand and shook it.

"Now what?" Lihwa asked, as she turned her head, and began staring at the block wall in front of them.

"We have to find a way to see what's on the other side. Until we see 'it' we don't know for sure that 'it' is there," Tom said, as he stood up while helping Lihwa to her feet.

"We may have to knock the wall down," Lihwa said, as she began to inspect the wall.

"No, all we need is a half inch hole. I can drill one, but that will be noisy," Tom said, as he joined Lihwa in inspecting the wall.

"What good does half an inch do?" Lihwa asked, as she began inspecting the top of the wall.

"Sherlock has more toys, Watson . . . always more toys," Tom said, as he removed a bound coil of half inch diameter tubing.

"This has a fisheye camera on the end. It's infrared, so I can see in the dark. I connect it to this monitor, and we can see what's on the other side. Fire fighters use this during search and rescue operations. You can run it into rubble and search for trapped people," Tom said, as he threaded the cable into the front of the handheld monitor.

"Sherlock Holmes? More like James Bond. I'm impressed," Lihwa said, as she stared at the blank monitor.

"You start looking. We have to find a way in," Tom said.

"Look up there, at the top of the wall. That looks like a gap," Lihwa said, as Tom began testing the piece of equipment.

"Looks like loose mortar. That's at least nine feet. I can't reach it," Tom said, as he began looking around for something to stand on.

"Let me get on your shoulders. Give me a screwdriver or something, and I can enlarge the hole," Lihwa said, as she gestured for Tom to kneel down.

"How much do you weigh?" Tom asked, as he knelt down.

"None of your damn business! Just kneel down and lift me up," Lihwa said.

Tom smiled and knelt down. After Lihwa climbed on his shoulders he stood up and groaned.

"I don't want to hear it! Now hand me a screwdriver," Lihwa said, as she balanced herself by placing one hand against the top of the ceiling.

"Move one foot to the left," Lihwa said, as she began digging at the hole with the flat tipped screwdriver.

"It goes all the way through. I just need to enlarge the hole," Lihwa said, as she continued to dig at the edges.

"How much longer? You're getting heavy," Tom said, then yelped after Lihwa rapped him on top of the head with the screwdriver handle.

"Hand me the camera thing," Lihwa said, as she scraped dust out of the hole and blew it clean.

"Here you go," Tom said, with a groan.

"It fits! How far do you want me to insert it?" Lihwa asked.

"Just past the end of the inner wall. Then let me check," Tom said, as he adjusted the aperture on the lens.

"What do you see?" Lihwa asked, as she began to squirm.

"Nothing! Quit squirming! Push it in six more inches," Tom said.

"I'm getting uncomfortable," Lihwa said.

"Tell me about it! Push it in!" Tom said.

"What do you see?" Lihwa asked, after inserting the cable in six more inches.

Tom didn't say anything as he adjusted the focus.

"Damn it, Tom! What do you see?" Lihwa asked, as she began to squirm again.

When Tom didn't answer, she put both hands on top of his head, and rested her forehead against the wall.

"Do you see a damn crate?" Lihwa asked.

"Yeah, I see a damn crate," Tom replied, as he began to kneel against the wall.

Lihwa slid off his back, and they both sat against the cinderblock wall.

"Now what?" Lihwa asked.

"Now we cover our tracks, and get the hell out of here," Tom said, as he struggled to his feet.

He shined his flashlight up at the hole Lihwa had made at the top of the wall.

"That hole has to go," Tom said.

"Wait, I'll be right back, Lihwa said, as she rushed out the door.

When she came back in she had a tube of toothpaste.

"It was in my backpack. We'll use this to plug the hole. Squat down," Lihwa said, as she pulled Tom down, and walked around to his back.

"Good idea," Tom said, as he grunted, and stood up with Lihwa sitting on his shoulders again.

"I'm going to need a back rub after this," Tom said.

"I'll buy you breakfast . . . double stack of pancakes instead," Lihwa said, as she squirted the toothpaste into the hole, and blended it in with her fingertip.

"We're good. No one will ever see the hole," Lihwa said, as she patted Tom on the head.

After she hopped off Tom's shoulders, Lihwa began looking around with her flashlight.

"I dropped the top to the toothpaste. Do you see it?" Lihwa asked.

"No, but we can't leave anything behind. Find it," Tom said, as he began packing up his tools, and checking the area for signs that someone had been in the room.

"Why are we doing this? The busted locks are kind of a clue that someone's been in here," Lihwa said, as she picked up the top that had rolled under a table.

"Good point, but we don't want anything to lead them to the wall," Tom said, as he took one last look around the room.

"Here, it was in the corner. It must have bounced off my boot," Tom said, as he handed the top to Lihwa.

They shut the door, and gate, and hung the broken padlock from one side of the shackle. After loading up, they got in, and drove down West Wheeler Street. Tom turned on the headlights as they turned right on 34th and headed south.

"Now what? Who do we contact first?" Lihwa said, as she removed her gloves.

"You get on your IPad and find a pancake house that's open. You promised pancakes. That's what we do first. I'm starving," Tom said.

"Are you out of your mind? We are not going to a pancake house after finding a nuclear bomb. We need to start calling people," Lihwa said, as she stared at him as if he had lost his mind.

"That bomb has probably been sitting there as long as the bomb that sat behind your restaurant. Did it go anywhere? No! So first we eat. Then we'll make some calls," Tom said, as he stared back at Lihwa.

"There's an IHOP over on East Madison Street. They're open 24 hours," Lihwa said a minute later, as she took a deep breath.

"You okay?" Tom asked, as they continued down 34th.

"Now I'm trying to decide if the breaking and entering we just committed was a misdemeanor or a felony," Lihwa said, as she stared out the window.

"Hey, if so, then you're my all-time favorite B&E pancake girl. Intersection up here, which way do I turn?" Tom said, as he stopped at a red light.

"You have no sense of direction. Turn left . . . and why do I like being with you?" Lihwa said, and then realized that she had said it out loud.

"Action and adventure, witty banter, fine dining and music, what's not to like?" Tom said, as he smiled.

"Seriously, Tom, what do we do next?" Lihwa asked.

"We call our pal up at DHS and tell him what we found. Then we go see if your idea was right too," Tom said, as once again the Beatles 'Hard Days Night' played out over the speakers.

"What? Military bases? You still want to do that?" Lihwa asked.

"Hey, Burglars R Us . . . you got something else you'd rather be doing?" Tom said.

"And which way do I turn?" Tom asked, as they came up to another stoplight.

"Straight! And we're buying you a Garmin today," Lihwa said, as she opened her file of Chinese restaurants near military bases in the Northwest.

Chapter 29

"The cost of freedom has always been high, but Americans have always paid it. One path that we shall never choose is the path of surrender or submission."

John F. Kennedy

San Francisco, California, USA
Department of Homeland Security
450 Golden Gate Avenue
Office of Senior Investigator Dimitri Atkins
March 23, 2017 0630 hours PST

"Holy shit!" Senior Investigator Dimitri Atkins said, as he played the messages on his office phone for the third time.

He took out his cell and called the number listed on the message.

"Damn it! No answer! You leave a message like this at my office and you turn off your damn cell phone?" Dimitri said, as he tossed his cell phone onto his desk.

"If this is a spoof, and I move it upstairs, then I look like an ass. If it's real, and I don't move it up, then I'm an idiot and fired," Dimitri said, as he called another number.

"Akeem, go get Louise and get in my office now. Screw breakfast! I mean now!" Dimitri said, as he hung up, and threw the phone on the desk again.

"More than one . . . holy crap . . . more than one! I can't believe this," Dimitri said, as the door opened.

"What the hell's your problem?" Akeem asked, as he and Louise entered the office.

"Listen to this message," Dimitri said.

*"Hey, Tom Jackson here. You said that if I ever had any more information about the item behind the Chinese restaurant that I should*

*give you a call. Well, it's not about that device, it's about a second one that we found . . ."* the message began.

"What? Another damn bomb? Akeem said.

"Shut up and listen," Dimitri said.

*". . . in Seattle. And no I'm not bullshitting you. There's a shed behind the Gim Wah restaurant at 3418 West McGraw Street. It has a false wall inside just like the place in San Francisco. We saw a crate behind . . ."* the message continued.

"Who's we? Is this serious?" Louise asked.

"Will you both just listen!" Dimitri yelled.

*". . . the wall. Someone will figure out that we were there so you might want to move on this pretty quick. What? No I'm not telling them what to do, but . . . Lihwa, just let me finish the damn message before it times out,"* the message continued, then stopped.

"Here's the second part," Dimitri said, as he played a second message.

*"Sorry about that. My partner interrupted. Anyway, it looks like the same size crate from what I could see, same cinder block wall inside the building. We figured out what to look for on Google Maps. We'll be checking places near military bases up here next. Have a nice day,"* and the second message ended.

The three agents just stared at each other.

"Is this legit?" Akeem asked.

"That's why I called you both in here. What do you think," Dimitri said.

"When did the message come in?" Louise asked.

"0620, ten minutes before I walked through the damn door," Dimitri said.

"Was the call from Seattle?" Louise asked.

"Yeah," Dimitri said.

"Then I think it's legit, and he mentioned 'Lihwa'. She's the daughter of our restaurant owner in San Francisco. It looks like they're conducting their own damn investigation. We haven't found shit, and they found a second device," Louise said.

"How did they do it? What are they looking for on satellite pics?" Akeem asked.

"Okay, it's 0645. Louise, contact our office in Seattle. Get them up to speed. Tell them to prep a team to hit this restaurant, and have them come up with a cover story for evacuating a 10 block area," Dimitri said.

"Akeem, here's Jackson's cell number. You keep trying to get the asshole to answer. Get someone to track their movements over the last few days; credit cards, cell phone usage, the usual. I'm going to talk to the Director personally. This shit is on the way to the White House," Dimitri said, as he downloaded the cell message onto his phone and left the room.

# Chapter 30

"The time is near at hand when Americans must determine if they are to be free men or slaves."

George Washington

Washington DC, USA
The White House
Outside the Oval Office
March 23, 2017, 0935 hours EST

"I don't care if he's meeting with the Queen of England. I have to talk to him now, and I mean right now," National Security Advisor Clarisse Beaumont said to the secret service agent at the door to the Oval Office.

"Ms. Beaumont, the President is in there with 14 members of the Cleveland Cavaliers. They are live on multiple networks. Do you want me to run them all out?" the agent asked, while still barring the doorway.

"Oh, crap! How much longer?" Ms. Beaumont said.

"It's scheduled for another 10 minutes. You know the President is a big hoops fan. It might be longer," the agent said.

"I'll be back in 10. If he isn't done by then, I'm going in," Ms. Beaumont said, as she turned and rushed down the hall.

Turning left, she ran down to the office of the White House Chief of Staff.

"Good morning Ms. Beaumont. Can I help you?" Julia Bark, the executive assistant for the White House Chief of Staff said.

"I have to talk to Roger now," Clarisse said, as she walked past Julia's desk and headed for the office door.

"I'm sorry, but he's taking a call," Julia said.

"He'll get over it," Julia said, as she barged into the office.

"I don't care who it is, but hang it up now," Clarisse said, as she stood in front of his desk with her hands on both hips.

"Senator, I'm sorry, but I'll have to call you right back," Lance said.

"More than a little rude, Clarisse, even for you," Roger said, as he hung up the phone, and stared at the National Security Advisor.

"I'll cut to the chase. A second nuke has been found in Seattle. I need to talk to the President now, and I mean right now. Either you get him out of there, or I will, TV be damned," Clarissa said.

Roger glanced at his watch and down at the President's daily schedule that was lying on his desk.

"I'll hand him a message and let him untangle himself. He's better at that than any politician I've ever seen. He'll exit the room, and they won't be the wiser," Roger said, as he stood up and headed for the door.

.   .   .   .

Washington DC, USA
The White House
Office of the White House Chief of Staff
March 23, 2017, 0955 hours EST


"Julia, hold all the calls and no visitors. I don't care if the building's on fire," Roger said, as he, the President, and the National Security Advisor entered his office and shut the door.

The president said nothing as he walked over to the pair of windows, and stared out on the manicured lawn of the White House.

He took a deep breath, slowly let it out, and then turned before saying, "Give me everything you've got, Clarisse."

"Mr. President, at 0930 I received a call from the Director of DHS. They received a call from the Regional Director in San Francisco. They received a call from a citizen, that another nuclear device was located in a shed behind the . . . " Clarisse began, then paused as she referred to her notes.

". . . Gim Wah restaurant in Seattle, Washington," Clarisse said.

"How do they know it's real? What citizen would know about this? This is all Sensitive Compartmented Information Top Secret. Please tell me we don't have a leak," the President said.

"Mr. President, the information came from a pair of citizens who were involved with the incident in San Francisco. One, was the fire fighter who was the first one to identify that the crate contained a nuclear weapon. The second, and this is more interesting, is the daughter of the owner of the Chinese restaurant who was killed in the fire," Ms. Beaumont said.

"What? A fire fighter and the daughter of a traitor? What the hell is going on?" Roger asked.

"Roger, let her finish," the President said, with a wave of his hand.

"Go on, Clarisse," the President said.

"Evidently, the senior agent in charge of the incident in San Francisco, came into his office this morning, and found two messages on his phone from the pair I mentioned. I downloaded a copy onto my cell, Mr. President," Clarisse said, as she pulled her cell phone from her jacket pocket.

After listening to the messages twice, the President walked behind Lance's desk and sat down. Lance and Clarisse just stared at each other, and then at the President.

"Okay, so how have we responded?' the President asked.

"Mr. President, our San Francisco DHS office contacted the office in Seattle. Seattle has formed a joint response team with the FBI and Seattle PD. Our people have also contacted the National Nuclear Security Administration. They're sending the same team that disarmed the bomb in San Francisco," Clarisse said.

The President said nothing. He leaned over in the chair, and began slowly rubbing his hands together as he thought.

"Has anything leaked to the press?" the President asked.

"Not that we know of, Mr. President. We're using the same protocol we used in San Francisco. After we verify that the device is actually in the building, the Seattle police will evacuate people from a 10-block area around the site. The media will be told it's a gas leak. The bomb team will be flown out of the desert will all their trucks and equipment on a C5A. They'll be on site in less than five hours," Clarisse said, as she read from her notes.

"How about the restaurant owners? They can't be allowed to contact anyone," the President said.

"The family has been identified and located. Teams will be sent to pick up each individual and isolate them for further questioning. Before the strike starts, we'll isolate their hard wire comms, and jam any cell calls in a five block radius," Clarisse said.

"Roger, can you think of anything else?" the President asked.

"Where are the individuals that found this device? Assuming this is real," Roger asked.

"Good question!" the President said, as he stared at Clarisse.

"We don't know at this time. We're actively looking for them. It's been less than two weeks since the first incident, and these two may have found a second device. If so, how did they know a device was located there? Are they working with someone else? If the Chinese government actually planted the first device are we dealing with a rogue department within the government that knows about these insertions? DHS, the CIA, and the FBI are working on a number of possibilities. Collectively, we're still sorting through the weeds, Mr. President," Clarisse said, while giving the President a wane smile.

"So . . . our intelligence agencies, with thousands of personnel, and billions of dollars in resources, are still sorting through the weeds. Meanwhile, two people using Google Maps have cut the weeds and found a second device. Would that be a correct summation of what you just told me, Ms. Beaumont?" the President asked, as he stood up and glared across the desk at the National Security Advisor.

Clarisse cleared her throat before saying, "Yes, Mr. President . . . that would be correct."

"Roger, I want a meeting today with the heads of CIA, NSA, FBI, DHS and the Joint Chiefs. I want this done discretely. The press better not get wind of this meeting. Let's do this at the Pentagon since I'm scheduled to pay them a visit this afternoon anyway," the President said.

"Clarisse, keep me up to speed on what's happening in Seattle. Roger, let me know when everything is arranged," the President said, as he headed for the door.

Chapter 31

"An investment in knowledge pays the best interest."

Ben Franklin

North of Groom Lake, Nevada, USA
1500 feet below Bald Mountain
March 23, 2017, 0730 PST

"Okay, sit down and shut up," Kate Williams said, to her assembled crew of nuclear weapon specialists.

"I know you all have had a good time dissecting our Chinese antique. Especially you, Karl; I know you love add-ons," Kate said, as other team members laughed, and Karl stood up and curtsied.

"Well, guess what, break time is over. Another device of unknown design has been found in Seattle, Washington. The MO looks the same. It's behind another Chinese restaurant. But until we lay eyes on the device, we'll have no idea what we're dealing with. Our friends in the United States Air Force are providing first class accommodations on a C5A. Load everything on our vehicles. That means leave nothing behind that we might possibly need on site. I want to be out of this facility by 0800. So move it," Kate said, as her team bolted from their chairs.

"All right Kate, the rah-rah speech for the troops is over. Now what do you think is really going on?" Jim asked, as the room rapidly emptied.

Kate looked around before saying, "I think the country's in deep, dark, shit. Two weapons found on the West Coast in less than a month? I'll make a bet with you right now that it's the same age as the other device. I'll even bet that it's almost identical to the first one. All our analysis says that these weapons are Chinese in origin, and that they've been modified by the Chinese. I just wonder how many more of these things are going to be found? If one of these devices goes off, it'll start World War III."

"Well, if you're right, then it sounds like we're going to be busy for a while. I hope you activated the 'rush clause' in our contract with the government," Jim said.

Absolutely! $3 million per job, plus expenses. We're officially on double time," Kate said, as they fist bumped and walked from the briefing room.

Chapter 32

"Believe you can and you're halfway there."

Theodore Roosevelt

Manassas, Virginia, USA
Mission Center for Weapons and Counterproliferation
Central Intelligence Agency
Office of Assistant Director Janet Davidson
March 23, 2017, 1030 hours EST

"What do you mean, he's not in? He wasn't in yesterday
either. Where the hell is he?" Janet asked on her cell, while talking
to the admin assistant of Director Caleb McElroy.

"As far as I can tell it's like yesterday. He didn't make it in
this morning, and he didn't leave me any messages, which is
strange. If he's going to be late or if he isn't coming in, he always
leaves me a message, and I mean always," Krissy Baldwin said.

"Did you call his home?" Janet asked.

"Yes, I called his cell 10 minutes ago and his home phone.
All I got was voice mail. Maybe he's been in a wreck?" Krissy
said.

"Well, something is going on. He lives in McLean. Call the
local police and the highway patrol. See if he's been involved in an
accident. Let me know what you find," Janet said.

"I'll get right on it. I'm sorry, I should have told you
yesterday," Krissy said, and hung up.

"That man's nothing if not consistent, almost compulsive.
It's not like him to just not show up, and not let someone know
where he is. Now what? I can't sit around and wait for him to show
up, not with this happening," Janet said, as she read the report
from Seattle for the fourth time.

"Another nuke . . . our little girl was right," Janet said, as
she picked up her cell and called Agent Amanda Langford.

"Yes . . . good morning, Amanda. Get down here with all the info you've got, and hopefully you've found something new in the last three days," Janet said, and hung up.

Her cell chimed three minutes later.

"Davidson here. What did you find, Krissy?" Janet asked.

"There's no record of him being involved in an accident. I called the McLean District Police and the Highway Patrol. I even tried three local hospitals . . . nothing there either. I even called his ex. I won't repeat what she said, but she hasn't seen him. I don't know where to try next," Krissy said.

"Keep trying his cell every 15 minutes. I'll make some calls within the agency. Maybe he has some meeting we don't know about, but that's a stretch. Thanks, Krissy," Janet said, as Amanda appeared in her doorway.

"Young lady, you better have something fresh, because I have a feeling you're going to be presenting your analysis to the Director of the CIA tomorrow. Now come in and close the door," Janet said, as she turned around and refilled her Marine Corps coffee mug.

"Yes ma'am . . . damn it! Yes, Ms. Davidson, I do have new information," Amanda said, as she presented a folder to the Assistant Director.

"As you can see, the first item is the analysis of the first device found in San Francisco. This was obtained from the Department of Homeland Security. They have a department called the National Nuclear Security Administration, and the NNSA has a contract with some company that specializes in disarming nuclear weapons . . ." Amanda began.

"Get to the point, Agent," Janet said.

"The point is . . . and I found this very strange; this company doesn't officially exist. They're off the books. I couldn't find any record of them: where they're located, personnel, contact numbers . . . nothing . . . anywhere," Amanda said.

"Amanda, welcome to the world of black budgets and secrets. Everything is compartmentalized. Everything is 'need to know'. After 9/11 all that was supposed to stop, but it hasn't. The intelligence organizations within this country are still keeping things from each other. I seriously doubt if that will ever change.

It's better than it used to be, but not much. Now, what did this organization, that doesn't exist, find?" Janet said.

"They go into great detail about the pedigree and design of this device, and how it was modified. The interesting part is the nuclear spectroscopy, the analysis of the isotopes in the High Enriched Uranium, the HEU, and the exact percentage of each isotope of uranium. Like I said months ago, every facility produces a slightly different mix in their HEU. It's like a fingerprint, and it identifies where the material for each weapon was made. Their analysis of the HEU matches the material produced by the Heping gaseous diffusion plant in the late 1980's," Amanda said, as she stood and began pacing back and forth across Assistant Director Davidson's office.

"Amanda, sit! You're wearing out my carpet," Janet said, as she began wondering about where the Director of the CIA was scheduled to be that day.

Amanda forced herself to sit, then began again, "Combine their analysis with the amount of missing HEU from Heping, and you have evidence that the Chinese have made an additional number of devices that we didn't know about. Now if we found another weapon on American . . ."

"We have found a second device . . . in Seattle," Janet said.

Amanda shot straight out of her chair and began pacing again.

"And from what I understand, it wasn't found by any government agency. It was found by two of the civilians involved in the San Francisco incident," Janet said.

"Oh, I'd like to talk to them," Amanda said.

"I imagine that a lot of people would like to talk to them. Right now they're still on the loose. Continue on with your findings," Janet said.

"Next item! On the 20th I went and talked to Detective Angelo Morehead at Alexandria PD. He has the lead on the hospital murders. They have a video of the murders in the Emergency Room," Amanda said, and paused hoping for an excited reaction from her boss.

She didn't get the reaction that she expected.

"Agent Langford, you've had a video of the murders and you didn't bother to tell me. Did you forget the instructions I gave you to keep me up to date?" Janet asked, as she stood, her voice increasing in volume.

"It was being reprocessed by our people. The quality was pretty crappy. I wanted to present you with the finished product. They just finished it this morning," Amanda said, as she dug a thumb drive out of her shoulder purse, and handed it over to the Assistant Director.

Janet inserted the drive into her PC and opened up the video file. Amanda pulled her chair around the desk and sat beside Assistant Director Davidson.

"The tech guys are still working on the sound file. It sucks, but they're hoping to get us a transcript later today," Amanda said, as the video began.

"Based on the timeline in the video, and our information of nurse Thompson's calls to her husband, she must have become suspicious about the tattoo and called her husband. He told her that she was correct. The tattoo was for a Siberian Tiger Special Forces operator. They don't have a camera in the treatment bay, but you can see when security shows up in the ER for the first time. That must have been when they secured him to the gurney. Then it skips to the end, when he woke up," Amanda said, then grew silent.

"Damn!" Janet said, as the feet of the first nurse could be seen sticking out from under the curtains in Bay 2.

A few seconds later the second nurse flew out of the bay and fell to the floor, obviously unconscious. The security guard then approached with his pistol drawn. When the gurney was used as a weapon to knock over the guard, and he was rendered unconscious with two punches, Janet paused the tape.

"Somehow he loosened one restraint in the treatment bay. When the nurses came in he must have kicked them or punched them with his free hand. The move with the gurney looked like something out of a Kung Fu movie. This guy has been well trained," Janet said, as she looked over at Amanda.

"The next part is where it gets brutal," Amanda said, as she pointed at the monitor.

When the video continued the man picked up the guard's pistol and shot him in the head. Then he proceeded to calmly kill both of the unconscious nurses in the same manner.

"The pregnant nurse at the end of the hall, standing beside the doctor, was Major Thompson's wife," Amanda said.

They both fell after being shot in the chest.

"Those shots were probably from 40 feet at least. He's an expert marksman as well," Janet said, as the killer calmly walked up the hall and pulled something from the doctor's pockets.

"What is that?" Janet asked.

"Car keys, the doctor owned a Lexus. The police have been looking for it for the last three days with no luck. This guy went into hiding somewhere close or they would have found the vehicle by now," Amanda said.

"That's very nice work, Agent Langford," Janet said.

"But I've got more, Ms. Davidson. The second item in the folder is the transcript of the interview with Major Thompson. He was in rough shape when I talked to him, but the information he provided was valuable. He told me something that he had forgotten to mention to the police. His wife and one other nurse were the ones initially treating the murderer when he was delivered to the ER. She told her husband that he was mumbling something about a torpedo. I haven't followed up on that yet," Amanda said.

"A torpedo? There aren't any sub bases on the East Coast except in New London, Connecticut and Kings Bay, Georgia. The only place around here . . . that can't be right," Janet said, as she began a search on her cell phone.

"No, that doesn't make any sense. It has to be something else," Janet said, as she stared at Amanda.

"What? What did you find?" Amanda asked.

"Have you ever been to the Torpedo Factory in Alexandria?" Janet asked.

"They make torpedoes there? That could be the link. Maybe they're planning to sabotage the factory," Amanda excitedly asked.

"Relax, agent. The last time torpedoes were made there was during World War II. Now it's filled with crafts people. You can walk around and watch them work. Some of them sell their work out of their studios. There are some nice restaurants in the area. It's right beside the Potomac. I've been shopping there a few times. It's a nice place to visit," Janet said, as she turned off her phone.

"But, he definitely said something about torpedoes. I've got the Major's cell number. I'll call him today and see if he remembers anything else his wife said about what this guy was saying while he was unconscious. At least he'll be sober this time. At least I hope so," Amanda said.

"He was drunk when you talked to him?" Janet asked and sighed.

"Very! About two pitchers worth. He wasn't very cooperative at first, but I got some coffee in him and he started to talk," Amanda said.

"Well, see if you can get something else out of him. I don't think our Siberian Tiger was in town shopping before he went on a killing spree," Janet said.

"Here's another strange item. We have no idea how this guy got into the area. The Alexandria police checked incoming flights for the past month, car rentals, even trains, and found nothing. Detective Morehead said the FBI had no interest in the case. I found that kind of odd," Amanda said.

"A man, supposedly from Taiwan, murders five people in a hospital and the FBI has no interest? I'll follow up on that one," Janet said, as she made herself a note.

"Are you going to arrange a meeting with Director McElroy? This has to be enough data to push this forward," Amanda said.

"I would, but he didn't show up for work this morning and no one seems to be able to find him. I don't know what's going on with that. As far as your new information goes, I agree, it has to be presented to the Director of the CIA. Polish what you've shown me so far. It would be nice to have the voice data complete and some facial recognition information. It needs to have been run through the data bases of the CIA, FBI and the DHS before the meeting. I'll take care of the link with the FBI and DHS, and get you points of contact. You take care of our end. We need a complete package to present and don't spare on the details. I know from experience that the Director is a detail man. If he looks like he isn't listening, don't panic. Just continue on with your presentation," Janet said.

"When do you think this will happen?" Amanda asked.

"Probably within two days, maybe three. Unfortunately these things don't always happen as quickly as you think they should," Janet said.

Chapter 33

"The general who is skilled in defense hides in the most
secret recesses of the earth."

Sun Tzu (~520 BC)

McLean, Virginia, USA
2000 Rockingham Street
Home of Director Caleb McElroy
March 23, 2017, 1045 hours EST

"Have you lost your damn mind? This is the last place you
want to be. You have other safe houses. I didn't even know that I
was on your list," Director Caleb McElroy said, as he winced at
the pain of having his hands bound behind him to a wooden chair.

"Now I see how the rich in America live," Aiguo said, as
he pulled the ropes even tighter, secured them with a cross
constrictor knot around Caleb's wrists, and then pushed him
against a wall in the kitchen.

"Too many windows in this house, it feels like a fish tank,
but this place will do for now," Aiguo said, as he walked over to
the refrigerator, and pulled out a bottle of Voss Artesian Water.

"This fancy little bottle of water . . . 500 ml . . . how much
did this cost?" Aiguo said, as he turned around and pointed the
bottle at Caleb.

"I don't know . . . three or four dollars, so what?" Caleb
said, as he felt his hands start to go numb.

Aiguo said nothing as he walked up to Caleb, and placed
the pistol he had taken from the security guard at the hospital
under Caleb's left ear.

"When I was a boy, the Chinese equivalent of four dollars
would have fed our family for week. You Americans are pathetic.
You waste the world's resources while millions die of starvation,"

he said, as he pushed the gun barrel even tighter against Caleb's head.

"Why are you doing this? I'm on your side," Caleb asked, as he stared at the time on the antique clock hanging to the right of his refrigerator.

"You're not on our side. You are a whore that goes to the highest bidder. You are a traitor to your own people," Aiguo said, as he bent over and spit in Caleb's face.

"You need to think this through. You've made a mistake. You've killed people. It's on the news. The police will be looking for you everywhere. If you let me go now, I can help you escape," Caleb said, as Aiguo began to pace back and forth in the kitchen while sipping on the water.

"The reason I'm here is that I'm already a dead man. My first contact tried to kill me. He wasn't successful, so I contacted another source of mine. He told me about you and where to find you. He said to stay here until I was contacted by him," Aiguo said.

"It won't work. I'm supposed to be at the office. I work for the CIA. When I don't show up it's noticed. And if I don't contact someone soon they'll suspect that something has happened to me. This is the first place they'll look. Didn't you hear the phone ringing earlier? They were trying to find me," Caleb said, while racking his mind to find a way to reason with this killer.

"Then you will have to call them. You will have to make up some reason why you didn't go to work. If they come here you will be the first to die," Aiguo said, as he walked up and placed the barrel of the pistol against Caleb's forehead.

"Get me the phone. I'll make the call. I'll tell them that I've come down with the flu and won't be in for a few days," Caleb said, as the smell of gun oil irritated his nostrils.

"Where's your phone?" Aiguo asked, as he began looking around in the kitchen.

"Second floor in my bedroom on the nightstand . . . a table beside the bed," Caleb said, as Aiguo turned and began heading for the open stairwell to the second floor.

"Jesus, it wasn't supposed to go this way. Four hours and I would have been gone. They would never have tracked me down," Caleb mumbled, as he struggled against the ropes.

"What the hell is he . . . a boy scout?" Caleb said; as the ropes seemed to get tighter the more he struggled.

"Here's the phone. What's the passcode?" Aiguo said, as he returned, and turned on the IPhone.

"1945"

"What am I looking for? Aiguo asked, as he opened the phone number file.

"It's just called work. It's 703-762 . . . something."

"5549?"

"Yes, that will get my admin assistant."

"Do something stupid and you're dead," Aiguo said, as he entered the phone number, heard the ring, and pressed the phone against Caleb's ear.

"Director McElroy. It's good to hear from you. People were starting to get worried. Is everything all right?" Krissy Baldwin asked, as she recognized McElroy's number.

"Everything's fine Ms. Baldwin, but I think I've come down with the flu. I didn't want anyone else to get it. You know how contagious these things can be," Caleb said, as he coughed for good effect.

"I'm so sorry. Do you want me to drop by after work and bring you some medicine or food or something?" Krissy asked.

"No, I'm fine. Please let Janet know that I'll probably be out for three or four days. Yes, thank you, Krissy. I'm going to try and get some sleep now, goodbye," Caleb said, as Aiguo nodded, hung up the phone, and removed the gun from Caleb's temple.

"Very good, Director McElroy. You might live to see tomorrow," Aiguo said, as he stepped back, spun in place, and kicked Caleb on the side of the head, knocking him to the floor.

"I'm in trouble because my resolve weakened. That won't happen again. He'll be out for at least 15 minutes. Time to move him somewhere away from all the windows," Aiguo said, as he knelt and began untying McElroy's bonds.

# Chapter 34

"Facts are stubborn things; and whatever may be our wishes, our inclinations, or the dictates of our passions, they cannot alter the state of facts and evidence."

John Adams

Kent, Washington, USA
Starbucks
23325 Pacific Highway South
March 23, 2017, 0715 PST

"Starbucks?" Tom said, as he and Lihwa left the store holding steaming cups of coffee.

"I had to have Starbucks coffee. That stuff at IHOP was as old as your car. And what's with the black coffee? Starbucks isn't a truck stop. I live off their coffee," Lihwa said, as she sipped her tall Cinnamon Dolce Latte.

"I prefer not to contaminate my coffee. A true connoisseur drinks his coffee black," Tom said, as he stuck his nose up in the air and laughed as Lihwa smacked him in the arm.

*"Why do I find myself attracted to this strange, strange man?"* Lihwa asked herself, as they approached the car.

"You sure the highway is the best way? The ferry would have been quicker," Lihwa said, as they both got into the old Camaro.

"One, ferries have security cameras, and two, we would have had to pay with a credit card. If the boys and girls at DHS got in early they're looking for us as we speak," Tom said, as he shut the door, handed Lihwa his coffee, and began rummaging through his cassette tape collection.

"Tom, I think we made our point. Why don't we quit now and let the government handle this?' Lihwa said, as she turned and stared at Tom.

"Yeah, I thought about that, but the dipsticks in the government will think that the Reds are just going for population centers. I want to check your idea about military bases being the primary targets. So, if it's okay with you, we'll take the scenic tour home, and check around the military bases. So what does your Google Map research tell us about Chinese restaurants near military bases around here?" Tom said, as he turned on the engine and placed a Seals and Crofts tape in the cassette player.

Lihwa stared at him and said nothing. Then she placed her coffee in the holder and pulled her IPad out of her backpack.

"Summer Breeze . . . 1972! I love this album. By the way, which way do we go?" Tom said, as he pulled out of the Starbucks parking lot, and headed back to Interstate Highway 5.

"Head south on 5 to Tacoma. We pick up Highway 16 there. Head north, and if you see a Best Buy along the way, pull over. We are buying a Garmin today," Lihwa said.

"Waste of money . . . plus, Sweetness might balk at new technology," Tom said, as he turned up the volume.

"So, military bases . . . there are two major naval bases west of Seattle. The first one that we would reach is the Kitsap Naval Base at Bremerton. This satellite pic is awesome. Look at this! It shows three big nuclear aircraft carriers docked there," Lihwa said, as she ignored Tom's comment about the Garmin.

"Three! That's definitely a likely target," Tom said, as he pulled onto the on ramp and accelerated.

"Then we pick up Highway 3 and . . . we drive north to the Trident Submarine Base at Bangor," Lihwa said, then placed her IPad in her lap and grew silent.

Tom was happily singing to the music when he glanced over at Lihwa. She wasn't sipping her coffee. She wasn't on her IPad. She was just staring out the window.

Tom turned down the volume and said, "What's up? I get worried when you get quiet. That means you're thinking or you're pissed at me," Tom said.

"Tom, I'm getting scared . . . I mean really scared. Two nuclear bombs . . . let that sink in for a minute. Now we're heading for a base with nuclear carriers and a base with Trident submarines. This whole area is one big nuclear weapons stockpile," Lihwa said, as she picked up her coffee, and turned to face Tom.

"Yeah, and the Peoples Republic of China wants to blow everything up and destroy our country. If these crates are all over the country . . . let that thought sink in for a minute . . . then they could completely destroy us. The fallout alone would poison the entire country for decades. This could be the biggest case of blackmail in history. They could order us to do anything, and we wouldn't have a choice. The only chance the US has is to find and disarm these things as quickly as possible. Guess what? We're the tip of the spear . . . we're the First Team . . . we're Gandalf at the bridge telling the balrog, 'You shall not pass'," Tom yelled, as he turned the volume back up and began singing to 'Diamond Girl'.

Her logical self told Lihwa that they had already done enough. Her emotional self told her that she still had a debt to pay, that she was still the daughter of a traitor. She fought back her tears and began nodding her head.

*"Whether I like it or not I'm in this to the end with this crazy man,"* Lihwa thought.

"Okay, Ensign Sulu, Klingons be damned, take us into the nebula," she shouted, while blinking back tears, and thrust her fist into the air.

"So . . . you do know some sci-fi. Ensign Sulu, huh? I should be Captain Kirk. You're Asian, you should be Ensign Sulu," Tom said.

"That . . . is racial stereotyping! Okay then, if I'm Sulu, then I get to drive Sweetness," Lihwa said, as she turned and smiled.

"Aye, Captain! Warp 5 it is," Tom yelled, and floored the car.

. . . .

Highway 16
8 Miles South of Naval Base Kitsap
March 23, 2017, 1005 PST

"In about a mile and a half there's a split. You take Highway 3 off to the right," Lihwa said, as she stared at her IPad.

"Got it. Have you picked out a Chinese restaurant yet?

"So far only one fits our specs. This one has an attached room with a gated door just like the last place. It's called the Emperor's Palace. The only other place is the China Wok and the layout isn't right. If we had a Garmin I'd plug in the address," Lihwa said.

"If I had a Garmin I wouldn't need you. I already have female companionship," Tom said, as he patted the steering wheel.

"You know I'm starting to get a little creeped out," Lihwa said.

"Was it the nuclear bombs or the vintage music?" Tom said, and began laughing at his own joke.

"Hey, pay attention, the right's up here," Lihwa said, as Tom cut across two lanes without signaling.

"No problem, Sweetness has the right-of-way," Tom said, as cars on both side started blowing their horns.

"Ni shi bai chi (you are an idiot)," Lihwa said, as braced her hands against the dash.

"What was that?" Tom asked.

"Nice move, that's all," Lihwa said, and smiled.

"In three miles, get off on exit WA-3. Then take a right at the bottom of the hill," Lihwa said, as Tom switched tapes in the cassette player.

"Affirmative, Captain!" Tom said, as 'Born to be Wild' blared out on the speakers.

"Get your motor running, get out on the highway, searching for adventure, and whatever comes our way," Tom sang, as he tapped his fingers on the steering wheel, and they headed for the Emperor's Palace.

.   .   .   .

Bremerton, Washington, USA
The Emperor's Palace
3509 Kitsap Way
March 23, 2017, 1205 hours PST

"Cruise around the block one more time," Lihwa said, as she took pictures of the restaurant on all sides with her phone.

"Good idea. Now we can study how we'll get in there tonight," Tom said, as he cut through the Burger King parking lot, and turned right on 11th Street.

"Stop!" Lihwa said, as they passed the back of the restaurant and halted behind a Jiffy Lube.

"Look at the doors," she said, as she took a series of pictures of the back of the restaurant.

"Two doors. The gated one probably leads back into the restaurant. The solid door goes to an attached shed. That's probably the spot," Tom said.

"I don't know, that room looks really small," Lihwa said, as she stared out the window.

"Based on what I'm seeing, I agree with you. How about the other place?" Tom said, as he kept looking at the attached shed.

"It's no good. It's worse than this place. Let me expand out a bit," Lihwa said, as she focused on her IPad.

"I'm going to start cruising for lunch. You keep looking," Tom said, as he drove off down 11th Street.

"Here's a place and it's perfect. But we'll have to back track a bit. It's on the other side of the bay. From this place you can look across the water, and see all the navy ships," Lihwa said.

"What am I thinking? We just drove through the Burger King parking lot. Two whoppers and I'm good-to-go," Tom said, as he spun the car around.

"Do they have salads?" Lihwa asked, as she continued her work.

.   .   .   .

Port Orchard, Washington, USA
Golden Grill on the Bay
1014 Bay Street
March 23, 2017, 1415 hours PST

"Damn, you weren't kidding. The land is pretty steep here. You can see all of the ships lined up in a row on the other side of the bay," Tom said, as they stopped on a street beside the restaurant.

"Look to your left, at the end of the parking lot. That's what I saw on Street View. That's a large out building with a roll up door. That could be a home for another bomb," Lihwa said, as she took her cell phone out of her back pack and began taking photos.

"We need to go rent a room," Tom said, as he slowly drove back down the hill and turned right onto Bay Street.

Lihwa just turned and stared at him. She had been around him long enough to know that you only took about half of what he said seriously. The only problem was she still didn't know which half.

"What I mean is, I'm beat and need some rest. Then we can plan when, and how, we want to pull this one off.

"I'll find a motel," Lihwa said, as she turned back to her IPad.

. . . .

Golden Grill on the Bay
1014 Bay Street
March 24, 2017, 0315 hours PST

"I never thought they'd close. It was after 1AM when the last patron left and the staff was there drinking until 2:30," Lihwa said, as she and Tom sat in a darkened car up the street from the Golden Grill on the Bay.

"It's Friday night, what did you expect? Most of the customers were sailors. I'm surprised they closed that early," Tom said, as he raised his seat from a reclined position.

"That was a good nap, but now my back's stiff," he said, as he stretched and twisted in his seat.

"It's been quiet for half an hour. I say we get this over with," Lihwa said, as she drank from a bottle of water.

"No traffic, no people, let's do it," Tom said, as he turned off the ceiling light in the car.

They got out of the car and gently shut the doors. Tom popped the trunk and they removed their equipment. They were both dressed in dark clothing as they shouldered their gear, walked down the street and turned left into the parking lot. Tom walked beside the tall retaining wall at the back of the small parking lot above the restaurant, careful to stay in the shadows. The only sound was the rustle of bushes and trees stirred by the stiff evening breeze.

As they approached the end of the parking lot, a dog outside one of the homes on the hillside above them began barking. Tom paused, and they both knelt in the shadows at the base of the retaining wall. They could hear the owner yelling at the dog, and the sound of a door slamming. They knelt in the darkness for five more minutes until Tom turned, and motioned them forward.

"Can you cut the lock?" Lihwa asked, as they stood before the rollup door.

"No, I didn't see this in your pics. The padlock shackle is completely covered by the guard. The whole thing is interlocked so you have to unlock the padlock to slide the guard out of the way. I can't cut this without making a whole lot of noise. We're going to have to try something else," Tom whispered in her ear.

Lihwa pulled her IPad out of her backpack as they retreated back into the shadows.

"Damn, that things bright," Tom said as they knelt against the retaining wall.

Huddle around it," Lihwa said, as she opened Google Maps, and called up an overhead view of the area around the restaurant.

"Here, look, there's a road . . . Coles Lane, about a hundred feet back up the hill. At the end of the road there's a small path that goes down behind our building. If there's another secret room in the building it would be at the end. This path gets us to that end of the building. Maybe there's a door or a window or someway to look inside," Lihwa whispered.

"That's where the dog was barking. I don't like it. But it doesn't look like we have another choice," Tom said, as Lihwa nodded and turned off the IPad.

They stayed on the side of the road as they left the parking lot, turned right, and began walking uphill towards Coles Lane. The only light was from a street light another hundred yards up the road.

As they turned onto Coles Lane, the dog began barking again inside a house on their left. Lihwa looked up, and saw the dog standing in a large plate glass window on the second floor, staring down at them while he barked. She grabbed Tom's hand, and pulled him against the side of the house just as a light inside came on. Their dark world was lit up by light shining down on them from the large window above.

They both froze against the side of the house as the dog continued to bark. A man's voice silenced the dog. They looked down at the street, and could see the shadows of the man and the dog standing at the window directly above their heads. After another bark, the man yelled, and the dog grew silent. A minute later the light inside the house was extinguished. They both stood against the side of the house, still holding hands. Both were afraid to move. After a few minutes, Tom tugged Lihwa's hand, and motioned with his head to the left, further down Coles Lane. She nodded and they began to walk down the road, staying against the side of the house until they could blend into some bushes of the left of the road.

There were homes on both sides, above and below them on the sloped hillside, as they reached the end of Coles Lane. They crouched in the darkness against a retaining wall on their left. They were still holding hands. Tom shook his head and rolled his eyes as he looked at Lihwa; she smiled, and nodded in return as she slipped her hand from his.

"It's time to do this," she whispered into his ear.

He turned his head. They were face to face, inches apart.

"This is where they start making out in the movies, right before the shooting starts," Tom whispered.

"I don't see any cameras, let's go," Lihwa said, as she resisted the urge to kiss this strange man who had yanked her out of her predictable life.

They stood, looked around, then turned right, and began walking down the path that led to the back of their target. The path ended at a sloped hillside. Below, and to their right, stood the building. They crouched in the shadows as they studied the end of the structure.

"No door, no windows, and it has metal siding. This isn't looking good," Tom whispered.

"Look at the roof," Lihwa said, as grabbed Tom's arm, and pointed with her other hand at a square structure on the end of the roof that stuck up a foot from the surface.

"Is it for ventilation? What is that?" Lihwa asked.

"I don't know, but it might be a way in," Tom said, as he grabbed her hand, and they began sliding down the steep hill toward the edge of the roof.

Tom pointed at a tree branch overhanging the roof as he stood up, grabbed the branch, and hopped over onto the roof with a quiet thud. He then motioned for her to follow, but she was too short to reach the branch.

"Toss me your back pack and jump," Tom said, in a loud whisper as he crouched on the rooftop.

"No, I'll wait here. You have all the tools with you," Lihwa said, as she slid back into the darkest shadows of the bushes on the hillside.

Tom nodded, turned, and scuttled over to the hatch. It was solid, so he couldn't look below into the room. It had a padlock, but it was a simple hardware store padlock, not the high end security type like the rollup door.

Tom slid his satchel off his shoulder and removed the bolt cutters. With a quiet snip, he cut the padlock, and set it aside. When he tried to lift the hatch, it squealed in protest. A little WD-40 and the hinges quieted down. After he gently dropped the hatch against the roof, he placed the bolt cutters back in his pack and removed a flashlight. The access was two feet on a side. He stuck the flashlight an arm's length into the room before turning on the light.

"Good, rafters and no ceiling, Tom said, as he dipped his head and one shoulder into the opening for a closer look.

The room was far larger than any room they had inspected before, but he could see a metal frame wall on three sides and a cinder block wall on the other. He swept the narrow beam of the flashlight left and right, and then stopped when he reached the corner below him.

"Damn, another crate . . . and it's a lot bigger than the others," he said, as he hung upside down in the opening.

He played the flashlight across the surface of the box looking for any markings. It was as plain as the others had been. He pulled himself out of the opening and looked over at Lihwa, barely visible in the bushes. She slid out as he approached the edge of the roof.

"There's a big crate in there. Give me your phone and I'll take a picture," Tom said, as he reached out his right hand.

Lihwa nodded, took off her backpack, and handed Tom the phone. She slid back into the shadows as Tom went back to the opening.

She could hear a helicopter in the distance, and it sounded as if it was coming closer.

"Come on, Tom, come on, let's get out of here," she told herself, as the sound grew closer.

She heard a slight rustle in the bushes behind her and turned her head. She almost screamed as she saw the outline of a large man with green glowing eyes. What she noticed most was the barrel of the automatic weapon that was six inches from her face.

The searchlight erupted from the helicopter as it hovered 50 feet above the roof. Tom jerked his body out of the opening, sat down, and raised his hands in the air. Three men dressed in black, wearing night vision goggles and carrying short barreled automatic weapons, were on the roof. All the weapons were pointed at him.

He looked desperately for Lihwa, and saw her kneeling on the path they had used to get down to the building. She had her hands on her head, and another man in black had a gun to the back of her head.

"Don't hurt her. She had nothing to do with this. It was all my idea," Tom screamed, and tried to get to his feet, but was shoved back to his knees.

"Mr. Jackson, it would be a damn shame to have to shoot you after all the trouble we've gone to. So why don't you just have a seat on the roof. No one is going to hurt your partner. We just have a whole lot of questions," the agent said, as she climbed onto the roof.

She waved the armed men away, knelt beside Tom, and said, "Why don't you come with me. You and Lihwa are now under the 'protection' of the Department of Homeland Security."

"Yeah, I know what that means. Separate us, put us in a room with cameras that record every time we fart, and ask us the same questions over and over for the next 24 hours. Been there, done that, no comment . . . Agent?" Tom said, as he stood up while keeping his hands in the air.

"Jamila Stone, and it's very nice to meet you, Mr. Jackson," the tall, slim black woman said, as she motioned for him to lower his arms.

"Well, Agent Stone, would you like to know what you're standing on?" Tom asked, as he lowered his arms.

"And what would that be? Mr. Jackson?" Agent Stone asked.

Tom leaned closer and said, "A nuclear . . . fucking . . . bomb; and it's bigger than the one we found in Seattle."

Agent Stone blinked, and couldn't help glancing down at her feet, as Tom smiled at her and said, "Welcome to the club, Agent Stone. Now the good news is  . . . if the wrong people see us up here and set it off . . . we'll never feel it."

# Chapter 35

"Patriotism is supporting your country all the time, and your government when it deserves it."

Mark Twain

Tukwila, Washington, USA
Department of Homeland Security
12500 Tukwila International Boulevard
March 24, 2017, 0915 PST

The caravan of black Chevy suburbans pulled into the parking garage below the Department of Homeland Security building and parked. Tom and Lihwa were hustled into an elevator, and taken to a third floor meeting room. Coffee, water and snacks were laid out on one corner of the large table. They were left alone.

"Not exactly how I thought the night would go," Lihwa said, as she reached for a bottle of water.

"I can't believe I had to leave Sweetness behind. Someone's going to steal her for sure," Tom said, as he stood up and walked over to the wall of windows.

"Maybe they'll let 'Sweetness' visit you in Federal Prison," Lihwa said, with more than a little sarcasm in her voice.

"They won't send us to jail. We know too much," Tom said, as he stared out the window.

"Legally they only have two options. They have to charge us or let us go. They can hold us for 48 hours, just like before, but that's it," Lihwa said, as she began spreading cream cheese on a bagel with a plastic knife.

"I'm starving. I can't believe you aren't hungry," she added.

"I think we found a much bigger device. The crate was three times the size of the other two. Fission weapons can only be made so big. If you put too much high enriched uranium in one pile then it can start to go critical all by itself. It wouldn't blow up, but the radiation would damn sure kill anyone around it. I bet they find a hydrogen bomb in that crate," Tom said, as he turned around and stared at Lihwa.

"How big would that be?" Lihwa said, almost choking as she gulped down her first bite.

"Well, it could be a hundred times more powerful than the other two, maybe bigger," Tom said, as he walked over to the plastic coffee carafe.

"It was probably a mile across the bay to those aircraft carriers. It would take a large bomb to take them out from that distance, at least one megaton," he said, as he poured the coffee into an insulated paper cup and sat down beside Lihwa.

"I'm sorry I got you into this. That was pretty bad last night," Tom said.

"You didn't get me into anything. It was my choice to come along. I'm a big girl, Tom. I make my own decisions," Lihwa said, as she turned and looked at him.

"At least we'll have a story to tell our kids one day," Tom said.

"You're impossible!" Lihwa said.

"So how are the bagels?" Tom asked, as he pulled the box towards him.

When the door opened, they both turned around and stared at the petite woman standing in the doorway.

"Here I was expecting the thumb screw brigade and in walks Mary Poppins. Is DHS going to try a different tactic during this session of grilling?" Tom asked, as he sipped his coffee.

"Don't mind him. It doesn't mean anything, it's just his way," Lihwa said.

"I don't work for DHS. My name is Agent Amanda Langford. I work for the Central Intelligence Agency at the Mission Center for Weapons and Counterproliferation," Amanda said, as she walked up and stuck out her hand.

"I didn't see that coming. Looks like we've moved up to the big leagues," Tom said, as he shook Amanda's hand.

"My name is Lihwa Yan, but I'm sure you know all about me already," Lihwa said, as she also stood and shook Amanda's hand.

"Please, have a seat. From what I've been told we've all had a long night. I just got off a federal redeye from the east coast," Amanda said, as she laid her satchel on the table and pulled out her laptop.

"So why the CIA and why you?" Tom asked.

"I hope the coffee's fresh. The crap on the plane was instant. Can you believe that, a hundred million dollar plane and instant coffee," Amanda said, as she reached for the carafe.

"Lady, we just met you, and I hate to be rude, but we don't have time to talk to some 'B' team bureaucrat. This country is getting ready to be royally screwed," Tom said, as he leaned over and stared into Amanda's face.

"Tom, sit down and quit being an ass. Let the woman talk. We'll find out why and what, if you give her a chance," Lihwa said, as he yanked on Tom's arm.

"His file said he was aggressive, sarcastic, with an extreme dislike for authority. It also said that he was brave, loyal to his friends, and a patriot," Amanda said, as Tom began to stand up again, before being yanked back into his chair.

"So what do your files say about me?" Lihwa asked.

"Well educated, hardworking, insightful, still suffering from PTSD after the loss of your father, but probably also suffering from guilt at what was found behind her family's restaurant," Amanda said, from memory.

"Interesting, a psyche analysis, and I bet it goes into a lot more detail than that. I've had more than a few prepared on clients of mine," Lihwa said.

"I'm going to be completely honest with you two. You have become a severe embarrassment to the intelligence agencies of this government. You have also become a major asset to those same agencies. The phone message that Tom left on Agent Dimitri Atkins' phone at DHS in San Francisco worked its way up the food chain until it stopped at the desk of the President of the United States. From what I've been told, he was not a happy man that two civilians were obtaining critical information faster than the thousands of people working for his multi-billion dollar intelligence agencies. That is why I'm here talking to you, and I'm not the 'B Team'," Amanda said.

"I need to know exactly what techniques you have been using to find these devices," Amanda said, as she opened a Word file on her laptop.

"We're not saying shit, until I get Sweetness back," Tom said, as he sat down a crossed his arms.

"Oh, for God's sake, Tom! Really?" Lihwa said.

"Who is Sweetness?" Amanda asked.

"His car! He calls his car 'Sweetness'. It's an old beater of a Camaro," Lihwa said.

"Beater? The marriage is off! If you don't respect Sweetness, then you don't respect me," Tom said, as he turned and glared at Lihwa.

"Is he for real?" Amanda asked.

"Yeah, I'm not sure if he's bipolar, schizophrenic, or just crazy, but he and the car have a long-term relationship. He takes some getting used to," Lihwa said.

"I imagine he does," Amanda said, as she glanced at Tom, and then began typing.

"Great! More stuff in my permanent record," Tom said, while reaching for a bagel.

"He's a throwback to the 60's and 70's. His music, his clothes, the car, and a general disdain for technology, are his thing. His cell phone, which he usually leaves off, is a $100 a year piece of junk. It's good for making phone calls, that's it," Lihwa said, as she squeezed Tom's arm.

"You know, I am able to hear all this," Tom said, while slathering cream cheese on another bagel.

"But it's taken the two of us to figure all this out. If I hadn't come along he would have started looking by himself. He probably wouldn't have found anything yet, but he was the force behind the start of the search," Lihwa said.

"What do you mean?" Amanda asked.

"It all started with this," Lihwa said, as she reached into her pants pocket, pulled out a Chinese coin, and handed it to Amanda.

"Damn, another ban liang, another reproduction . . . what's the connection?" Amanda asked herself aloud.

"Oh, it's not a reproduction. I had it appraised years ago. It's real and worth at least $30000," Lihwa replied.

Lihwa then led Amanda through her whole story, how she met Tom, and how they were able to locate two additional nuclear devices.

"*A childhood memory, a Chinese coin that can't possibly exist, that leads to Google Maps, Street View and nuclear weapons. This is starting to make sense . . . sort of,*" Amanda thought, as she remembered the coin she had seen in Detective Angelo Morehead's office.

"Google Maps, now that's funny. I had heard the message that Tom left, but I thought it was some kind of a joke. Most of that data is years old," Amanda said, as she laid the coin on the table, and photographed both sides.

"I know, but Tom is the one who figured out that this had been going on for decades. Once you put these things in place, he figured they weren't likely to move them again," Lihwa said.

"Agent Langford, these nukes are all over the country. There could be hundreds of them," Tom said.

"We don't think there are hundreds, but there could be quite a few. Now that we know for sure how you were able to find them, I suspect that we'll write an algorithm, and start looking at every Chinese restaurant, and probably every business owned by Chinese in the country," Amanda said, when her phone buzzed.

"They just loaded your car on a flatbed. It should be here in a couple of hours," Amanda said, as she read the text on her cell phone.

Tom looked up and glanced at the dome camera in the ceiling.

"They were listening to all this, weren't they," Lihwa asked.

"Of course they were. It was all recorded," Amanda said, as she closed her laptop, put up her phone, and loaded everything back into her satchel.

"So what are they going to do with us?" Lihwa asked.

"Well, there are at least half a dozen charges that I can think of. They could probably put you both away for five years, at least. I suspect they will offer you a deal. They will drop all charges if you agree to go home, keep quiet, and let the government handle this. It will be a legal document that you will have to sign, and if you break the terms of the agreement, like leave here and go talk to the press, then you will disappear for a lot longer than five years," Amanda said, as she stood up, shook both their hands, and turned for the door.

"What if we don't agree and won't sign?" Tom asked.

"You better talk some sense into him, and keep him under control," Amanda said, as she opened the door and glanced back at Lihwa.

"As if!" Tom said, as he grinned at Lihwa.

Lihwa just shook her head and sat back down.

Chapter 36

"Let your plans be dark and impenetrable as night, and when you move, fall like a thunderbolt."

Sun Tzu (~520 BC)

McLean, Virginia, USA
2000 Rockingham Street
Residence of Caleb McElroy
March 24, 2017, 1215 hours EST

"For God's sake, you haven't fed me for almost two days. I need more than water to keep going," Caleb said, as he tried to raise his head from the bed in the dimly lit bedroom in the basement.

There were no windows and the only light streamed in through the open doorway.

"I have lived for two weeks on water, beetles and roots. I think you will survive a bit longer," Aiguo said, as he checked the restraints on McElroy's ankles and wrists.

"What do you hope to accomplish? They'll be here soon. That ploy about the flu won't last forever," Caleb said, as he winced at the retightening of the restraints.

"It will last long enough. What do I hope to accomplish? Your death and my future; that is what I intend to accomplish," Aiguo said, as he sat on the side of the bed and looked into Caleb's face.

"You have betrayed your country and become rich. I have been loyal, and have been condemned by mine. I will have justice. During the last day I have found your financial records and where you have transferred all your wealth. I have all your passwords and account numbers. Against my better judgement I will give you a quick death. The same death I gave your dog. It's better than you deserve. At least the dog was loyal," Aiguo said, as he turned off the lights, left the room, and shut the door, leaving Caleb in a room more akin to a dungeon than a bedroom.

Aiguo climbed the stairs, and returned to his work in the upstairs study. He had already completed switching the passport ID photos, and had started on the more difficult task of switching photos on McElroy's CIA ID card.

"The CIA has a web of wiring built into the interior of the card. When I cut out the photo, the card will no longer work to get him into his office or other secure buildings, but after I insert my picture it should get me through airport security," Aiguo said, as he carefully cut through the CIA ID with an x-acto knife.

"The sheen on the surface of the card is different. His tickets indicate he's TSA-pre checked, but I still might get stopped. I will have to be forceful with the security guard at the airport," Aiguo said, as he completed the cut.

. . . .

Langley, Virginia, USA
1000 Colonial Farm Road
CIA Headquarters
Sub-room 506a
March 24, 2017, 1228 hours EST

Abe Moore had worked in anonymity for over 25 years buried within the underground maze that made up most of the CIA Headquarters. Today that would change.

"Strange . . . a card alarm . . . I can't remember the last time I had one of those," Abe said, as he answered the alarm sounding on his PC.

"Well, let's see whose dog or cat has chewed up their ID this time," Abe said, as he accessed the software for security card alarms.

Unknown to most people, including most CIA employees, their ID card contained a fine lattice of internal wiring that covered the entire surface of the card. Known to even fewer people was the fact that when the lattice was cut the card sent out a tampering alarm that lasted for 5 minutes.

"Director Caleb McElroy, Mission Center for Weapons and Counterproliferation . . . never heard of him," Abe said, as he picked up his phone, and called the office number on record.

"Director McElroy's office, can I help you?" Krissy Baldwin answered.

"Yes, I'm Abe Moore. I'm calling from CIA Security Division in Langley. I've had a tampering alarm on the ID card for Director Caleb McElroy. Is he in today?" Abe said.

"Actually, he hasn't been in for the last two days. He's out with the flu. Now you're saying that something's wrong with his ID?" Krissy said.

"Well, it's probably nothing. I'll try his cell number. Thanks for the help," Abe said, as he hung up.

"Okay, let's try the cell number," Abe said, while tapping in the numbers.

After the cell rang, and all he got was the message, Abe hung up tried again. After getting the same result, he hung up.

"Okay, one, the tampering alarm, two, he's been out sick for two days, and three, no answer on his personal cell . . . that's three strikes," Abe said, as he called his supervisor.

"Mike, yeah it's Abe. I've got indications of an active problem," Abe said, and relayed the information to his supervisor.

And so, through the glacial bureaucracy of the CIA, a minor alarm began to sound. By the end of the day it would reach the desk of the President of the United States.

Chapter 37

"Necessity is the mother of taking chances."

Mark Twain

Seattle, Washington, USA
Behind the Gim Wah Restaurant
3415 West Wheeler Street
March 24, 2017, 0915 PST

"Are you kidding me? We just got on site two hours ago. We're still setting up," Kate Williams said, as she stepped into the street behind the Gim Wah Restaurant in Seattle.

"Look, just tell them to not touch a damn thing. Those devices are a lot trickier than these old fission bombs. The safeties and traps are probably more advanced as well. Crap, I'm going to have to split my team. Text me the address and we'll be there in an hour or so," Kate said, as she shook her head, and walked back into the shed.

The roof on the old shed had already been removed. The debris from the cinderblock wall that had concealed the second device was still being cleared away.

"This one looks identical to the device down in San Francisco. We should be able to use the same technique. I bet the internal security wiring net is the same too," Jim Padenko said, as he stood up and stepped from behind the nuclear weapon.

"Yeah, well, we've got other problems. Our friends that found this device have found a third one. The new one sounds like a fusion device based on the description I just got on the phone," Kate said, as she began scrolling through a personnel list on her cell phone.

"We're going to have to split up. You stay here with our crew and finish this job. Don't rush. Take your time and do it right. I'll take our DHS compatriots and head over to Port Orchard. Holy crap, this place is right across the bay from the Kitsap Naval Base. That's where the Navy parks the big carriers," Kate said, as she studied the information she was getting on her phone.

"So much for just targeting the population centers. This is starting to look like a Pearl Harbor attack on a grand scale," Tom said.

"Just focus on your work. The big picture is someone else's problem. We just have to disarm these things as fast as they're found," Kate said, as she turned and left the shed.

"Alan, Nathan, pack up your stuff. We're taking a road trip," Kate said, as she called to the two DHS nuclear weapon specialists that had been loaned to her team.

"Road trip? We just got here. Don't tell me, they found another . . . holeee shit!" Nathan said, as Kate nodded her head, and began walking toward her truck.

.   .   .   .

Port Orchard, Washington, USA
Golden Grill on the Bay
1014 Bay Street
March 24, 2017, 1145 hours PST

Kate drove her truck through the flashing blue lights of the police road block at Bay Street and Kitsap. Boom trucks with elevated camera platforms were already on the scene. Live broadcasts were being telecast by two different local stations.

"Three blocks out from the site, three friggin' blocks. We need at least ten. This is a damn mess," Kate said, as she covered her face with her left hand as cameras flashed outside her window.

A block from the site they drove up to a second roadblock. This time the roadblock was staffed with DHS armed personnel.

"Kate Williams, National Nuclear Security Administration. These two are yours," Kate said, as the three presented their IDs to the DHS security personnel.

The operator checked his tablet while a second operator kept his automatic weapon aimed at the vehicle.

After checking each face, their IDs, and comparing it with the information on his tablet, the man said, "Agent Stone is expecting you. Go past the restaurant and take a right on Rockwell."

"Oh, I just bet she is," Kate said, as she rolled up her window and put the truck in gear.

"Well boys, this should be interesting. This will be my first fusion device too," Kate said, as she turned and smiled at Nathan and Alan.

"What? I thought you had seen everything," Alan said.

"I only know two men who have disarmed a fusion device and neither one of them works for us. One is an Israeli and the other a Russian. Now fission devices are pretty simple to build once you get the material. Fusion devices are a lot more complex. It's almost impossible for terrorists and wackos to find the material and expertise to build their own. Trying to steal one is like trying to break into Fort Knox. That leaves them with fission devices. If this is a fusion device, then we're dealing with major players, and the ante in the international game of high stakes poker has been upped . . . big time," Kate said, as she drove past the Golden Grill on the Bay and turned right.

"All right boys. It's fun time," Kate said, as her truck was directed into a parking space by another DHS operator armed with an automatic weapon.

Agent Jamila Stone was waiting at the rear of the truck when Kate got out of the truck.

"You must be Agent Stone," Kate said, as she shook the tall black woman's hand.

"And you're the bomb lady," Jamila said.

"Hah, I haven't heard that in a while, but yes, that would be me. So where's the device?" Kate asked, as she motioned for her two DHS partners to start unloading the truck.

"The building at the end of the parking lot. We made a hole through the wall large enough to get access to the room containing the crate. Then we drilled a hole in the side of the crate to get access for inspection, when we got word from you to leave it alone," Jamila said, as they began walking toward the far end of the restaurant parking lot.

"Did you take a peek inside?" Kate asked.

"Well, the technician with the optical scope might have inserted the camera in a little just to make sure this was for real," Jamila said.

208

"And?" Kate asked.

"And, you will have a very interesting day," Jamila said, as they stepped through the doorway into the storage building.

Supplemental lighting had been installed on either side of the entrance. The new opening that had been cut into the cinderblock wall on the far end was bathed in light.

"My, I feel like Indiana Jones after a big find," Kate said, as she peered into the dark interior of the adjacent room.

"I'm going to need lighting inside the room and additional power for our equipment," Kate said, as they approached the entrance.

"We've got everything you might need in a lot up the hill. Look around and just let me know what you want," Jamila said, as she gestured for Kate to duck through the opening.

"Agent Stone, one other thing . . . that perimeter has got to be expanded out at least 10 blocks. Otherwise the media will be looking over our shoulders when we pull this thing out," Kate said, as Jamila nodded in response, and pulled out her cell phone.

"Come on, boys, let's see what we're dealing with," Kate said, as she waved Nathan and Alan toward the opening.

"My, this crate is a lot bigger," Kate said, as she turned on her head mounted light and began to walk around the crate.

"I'm going to take a look inside. You two measure the box," Kate said, as she removed her own optical cable from her shoulder satchel and attached it to the heads up video display.

After securing the HUD around her head, she turned on the unit and verified that the unit was displaying a good feed and recording.

"All right baby, let's see what you got inside," Kate said, as she knelt before the hole previously drilled through the side of the crate, and carefully inserted the fisheye camera at the end of the cable.

"Hello . . . baby . . . you came off a Chinese DF-3A missile. We called you a CSS-2 . . . 3.3 megatons of nuclear death. Now how did they modify you?" Kate said, as she made the most of her limited view.

"Well, at least the inside of the crate is clean. We can open you up and have a better look," Kate said, as she slid the fisheye camera out and removed the HUD.

"Gentlemen, first I want cameras set up in all four corners of this room, up towards the ceiling. Run the cables outside the building through the walls. Get some help drilling the holes. You'll find the recorder and transmitter in the back of the truck. Set them up at the far end of the parking lot. I don't want the satellite link interfering with the signal this thing transmits to its owners. If anything's in the way, talk to Agent Stone. If you can't figure out how to hook everything up, then ask. When all that's done, come and get me. Don't touch the crate until I get back. I've got some calls to make," Kate said, as she turned and left the room.

"Just when you thought it couldn't get any worse," Kate thought, as she pulled her cell out of her pants pocket and stepped into the bright noon sun, a rarity in the Seattle area during March.

"Good morning, Clarisse, it's Kate. I'm calling from Port Orchard, Washington," Kate said, as she headed for the end of the parking lot.

"Kate! Good to hear from you. I see you didn't waste any time getting to work. Any good news?" the National Security Advisor asked.

"No, the news couldn't get much worse. The third one's a fusion device. Preliminary yield estimate, based on what little I've seen of it, is around 3 megatons," Kate said.

"Holy crap! This gets worse every day," Clarisse said.

"Yeah, I said that, and a few other choice things when I saw it," Kate said, as she reached the end of the parking lot and stepped into the street.

"I haven't gotten a detailed briefing on this one yet. Where is it located? What do you think the primary target is?" Clarisse asked.

"The location?" Kate said, and began laughing.

"Well . . . if I leave the parking lot, and head downhill about a hundred yards, I can look across this beautiful bay and see the ass end of three nuclear powered aircraft carriers parked over at Kitsap Naval Base . . . about a mile from here," Kate said.

"What? Damn, you're serious?" Clarisse asked.

"I'm dead serious. They're that close. A device this size would take out the whole base with the radiation and the shock wave. The fallout would cover Seattle to the east," Kate said.

"How long to remove the threat?" Clarisse asked.

"How long to disarm? I have no idea . . . days at least. I've had to split up my team; half are disarming the fission device in Seattle. I came up here with two DHS guys. I've got almost no equipment with me, but I'm reluctant to move my east coast equipment out here. We may need it there in a week. I'll probably have all our training equipment flown out from Missouri, but I'm out of personnel. I need some logistical help moving equipment and more people you trust with this information. I need people with an EOD background that I can train to do the simple stuff while I focus on the stuff that would leave a big crater if it's screwed up," Kate said.

"Use the same contact that flew your bunch out of the desert. If he balks, call me back and I'll rearrange his priorities. As far as personnel, let me talk to the Joint Chiefs," Clarisse said.

"Clarisse, one more thing, it may be time to talk to our Israeli friends. They have a man with experience disarming fusion devices. His name is Doctor David Barza. For god sakes don't call him Mister Barza. He's one of these touchy PhDs," Kate said, with a laugh.

"Israel? I don't know if the President will buy in on that one. He'll authorize all the internal help you need, but he may balk at letting outsiders in on our problem. If this whole situation goes public, the stock market won't just tank; it will disappear, and the world's economy along with it," Clarisse said.

"Yes, I know, but I need someone I don't have to babysit. Hell, he knows more about these things than I do. When this whole thing started in San Francisco, you and the President told me to be completely honest, and not hesitate to ask for help. Clarisse . . . everything I've asked for I need as soon as possible. You know me. I like my nice, tightly knit team. That way I can control every detail and not get anyone killed. We need this guy," Kate said.

"Okay, Kate, I believe you. I'll talk to the President and get back to you as quickly as possible. Be careful out there," Clarisse said, and disconnected the call.

Chapter 38

"A friend is one who has the same enemies as you have."

Abraham Lincoln

Washington, DC, USA
The White House
The Oval Office
March 24, 2017, 1300 EST

"Kate wants to bring in an Israeli? Is she kidding? If we do that, then we lose complete control of this situation," the President said, as he sat with National Security Advisor Clarisse Beaumont in the Oval Office.

"I know, Mr. President, but she was very adamant about needing this individual. She's normally unflappable, but I think she's stretched so thin that even she's getting worried about her ability to handle this many nuclear devices," Ms. Beaumont said.

"That means we'd have to brief Israeli intelligence, the Prime Minister . . . I don't like this. If news of this gets out . . . the panic, the markets . . . this could get very ugly, very fast. I don't think I can go along with this," the President said, as he rose from his chair, and stood facing out towards the Rose Garden.

"Clarisse, millions of Americans are out there, going about their daily lives, oblivious to the fact that everything that they take for granted could disappear overnight," the President said.

"Yes, Mr. President, and it's our job to make sure that doesn't happen. We promised her that we'd provide any resource she needed, and she has asked for this man," Ms. Beaumont said, rising from her chair and standing beside the President.

"Damn, I really don't like this, but I'll call the Prime Minister. I won't tell him everything, just that we need the immediate expertise of one of his citizens. He'll be curious, but I'll ask for his word that they won't probe into the matter. You arrange for a flight out of wherever it is that this gentleman is located," the President said.

"Dr. David Barza teaches physics at the Technion Israel Institute for Technology in Haifa. He's a Professor Emeritus there, and has a reputation for being quite the prima donna, and a ladies man. I don't know all the details, but he and Kate have a long history," Ms. Beaumont said, smiling as she looked down at her feet.

"Great, romantic entanglement, let me know when you finish the novel. It sounds like a good read. In the meantime, I'll call the Prime Minister," the President said, as he turned back to his desk.

Chapter 39

"So in war, the way is to avoid what is strong and to strike at
what is weak."

Sun Tzu (~520 BC)

Beijing, China
Central Military Commission Headquarters
August 1st Building
March 25, 2017, 1000 hours


This was not the meeting that Lieutenant General Kung was
expecting. He had anticipated a presentation before the entire Central
Military Commission along with the General Secretary of the People's
Republic of China. Instead he was standing in a mission briefing room
deep in the sub-basement system beneath the Chinese equivalent of the
Pentagon.

Kung had been marched into the room under armed guard. He
had been standing at attention before a panel of 10 of the most
powerful officers in the PLA for over five minutes. Each one was
examining a copy of his detailed presentation of his grand plan. The
Chairman of the CMC, also the General Secretary of the People's
Republic of China, was not present in the room . . . nor was Kung's
uncle, General Fan Shibo, one of the two Vice Chairmen of the CMC.

"Lieutenant General Kung Yusheng, out of respect for your
uncle, General Fan Shibo, we have decided to conduct this . . .
hearing, to allow you to present your reasoning behind your, some
would say, traitorous actions over the last 30 years. I will be blunt.
Half of us want you taken out and hung . . . immediately. The other
half are strangely impressed at what you have managed to accomplish
without any of us finding out," said General Xu Yang, the second Vice
Chairman of the CMC.

"Personally, I find the rope the proper response to your actions,
but the General Secretary has ordered an objective investigation. So,

Lieutenant General Kung, what do you have to say for yourself?" General Xu asked, as he glared down at Kung.

"Generals, Admiral, I am deeply honored that you would find the time to listen to me . . . "Kung began.

"Cut the crap, Kung! Three of your . . . our weapons, have been discovered on the West Coast of the United States. One of them is a thermonuclear weapon. You may be responsible for the start of the Third World War! How long do you think it will be before the General Secretary gets a personal call from the American President?" General Xu asked, as he slammed his fist on the table.

"As you say, General Xu, I will cut the crap. We will never dominate this planet as long as the Americans can dominate us militarily. On the surface they are a factious and divided people, seemingly ready to fall apart at any moment. The Soviet Union thought that all they had to do was wait, and the Americans would disintegrate before their eyes. We all know how that ended. They are the village neighbors that are always fighting amongst themselves . . . until they have an external threat to focus on," Kung said.

"Kung, you are a fool! Your own words condemn you. You have given them something to focus on. According to your documents, you have planted . . . 50 nuclear devices on their soil. They will focus their anger on one place, and that place is the People's Republic of China!" General Xu said, as he slammed the table once again.

"General Xu, if you don't mind, I will make the assumption that Lieutenant General Kung was aware of the military disparity between us and the United States when he started his bizarre plot decades ago. It was a time when we were far weaker than at present. You had to have an end game in mind when you started this, Kung. I, for one, want to hear it," Admiral Wu Yaoyan said.

Kung bowed to the admiral in respect, while still standing at attention.

"The Americans have a great deal of power: militarily, financially and culturally. They don't mind occupying or bombing someone else's country, if it suits them, but they have lived in peace within their own borders since 1865. Neither world war touched them while the rest of the civilized planet burned and tens of millions died. They lost a few hundred thousand men combined in both world wars, and have the audacity to consider themselves the saviors of all humanity. In actuality they are a plague of corruption. Their culture is like strong drink. Initially, it makes you happy, but in the end you find yourself nauseous and on your knees," Kung said, as the collective scowls before him began to soften, and show interest in his words.

"But remember this . . . above all else, Americans love their peaceful and prosperous existence. They no longer have the stomach for a true war. Look at the results of Korea, Vietnam and the Gulf Wars. Even as their military power has become more potent, they have become less willing to use it effectively. They always stop when victory appears on the horizon. As Sun Tzu said, 'In war, then, let your great object be victory, not lengthy campaigns.' The Americans are bankrupt. They are the rich man with fine clothes whose chests contain only dust. They have squandered the wealth bequeathed to them by previous generations," Kung said, as his honeyed words continued.

"Sun Tzu also said, 'All warfare is based on deception.' In their arrogance they have left their borders relatively open for decades. Their civil war was over slavery, but they leave their borders open, and import the modern equivalent of slaves from Mexico, Central and South America. They are like ancient Rome, grown fat and arrogant. We are the Visigoths ready to expand into new territory," Kung said, as he relaxed from his rigid posture, and began pacing like a caged lion in front of the assembled leaders of China's military.

"So you think that the Americans won't fight if we threaten them with these weapons you have planted in their territory?" Admiral Wu said, as he placed his right hand on the forearm of General Xu, and restrained him from rising.

"Admiral, I fully understand what I have done. As the American's would say, 'I have them by the balls'. All we have to do is squeeze, and they will drop to their knees in agony," General Kung said, as he gestured with a clawed hand.

"Kung, if you detonated every device that you still control, and that number is decreasing as we speak, then the American military would turn China into a nation-sized Hiroshima. Your plan is just another version of MAD. This is the same game that they played with the Russians for decades. It bankrupted the Russians and led to their downfall. No one wants to start a war like this. It is suicide for both sides," said General Ma Haiyang, Commander of the PLA Air Force.

"General Ma, I am not insane. I don't want a nuclear war any more than you do. What we want from the Americans is three things: one, the South China Sea, and everything that it touches, is in our sphere of influence. They have no business having bases or troops or ships in the western pacific. World War II and the Japanese threat are long gone. They need to go home, and leave this area of the world to us. Two, our civil war has never ended, and won't until the province of Taiwan is brought back under our control. Three, the Americans must leave Japan and South Korea and allow both countries to find their own way in the world instead of being protectorates of the US. Again, to quote the venerable Sun Tzu, 'To fight and conquer in all your battles is not supreme excellence; supreme excellence consists in breaking the enemy's resistance without fighting,'" Kung replied.

"I told you General Xu, he isn't insane, just incredibly bold, and perhaps even brilliant," Admiral Wu said, as he released General Xu's arm.

"Brilliant, my ass! The Americans will stall while they hunt down and disable every device inside their country. Then will come the time of retribution," General Xu said.

"Admiral, generals, I ask you this question. What would happen if we threatened to leak this to the global media?" General Kung asked, as he stopped pacing and faced the assembled tribunal.

"Leak our own aggressiveness? Are you insane? We would be condemned across the globe," General Xu said.

"So what?" General Kung replied.

"Don't you dare be impertinent with me. I'll overrule this entire group and have you shot in this room," General Xu yelled.

"My apologies General Xu. I did not mean to be rude," General Kung said, with a slight bow.

"What I meant was . . . who would suffer the greater harm from such a disclosure? Would the people of China panic and riot in the streets? Would our stock market drop by 80 percent? No, of course not. Our people would be calmed by the words of our media. Our markets would be shut by the government until the turmoil had subsided. The West, on the other hand, and the Americans in particular, would be devastated. Their people would be inflamed into a manic state by their freewheeling media, and their stock market would fall off a cliff. They would be hard pressed to maintain civil order, let alone conduct a war against China. They would show proof of the supposed invasion, and we would simply claim that it was a fabrication worthy of Hollywood. We would play the part of the wronged suitor who has found that his intended is not as chaste as he had thought. We would plead our innocence to the world, and show the greatness and generosity of the Chinese people. Half of their press would take our side just to make the existing President look bad," General Kung said, as he continued to pace.

The generals all began talking at once, half to him, and half with each other. Kung knew that he was close.

"*Xu is the key. If I can get him to agree then I've won*," Kung told himself.

"General Xu, you are senior here, and I bow to your superior wisdom and experience. Do you see the possible benefit of this path?" General Kung asked, as he faced General Xu, stood at attention and bowed.

General Xu said nothing for a moment, as the two men stared at each other.

"I'll admit only that I have set the rope aside . . . for the moment. Continue, General Kung," General Xu said.

"General Xu, their stock market is controlled by emotions that their government can't control. That freedom is their weakness. If we leak this information to the press in Europe, say from some credible source within their intelligence agencies that we control, then it will flow westward across the Atlantic like a great tidal wave. Their markets will crack and their inner cities will burn. Chinese Americans all across the country will be attacked. Video of such overt racism will lose them the moral high ground overnight. If given the choice they will not resist us. They will make some appropriate story about lowering their budget deficits or respecting the wishes of other sovereign nations that they still have occupation forces in. Without their interference we will be left in control of our half of the world," General Kung said, and knew that it was over, one way or the other.

"General Kung, my instincts still tell me to have you shot or hung . . . but part of me actually thinks that this crazy plan might actually work. It is classic Sun Tzu. Place your enemy in a box where he knows that if he fights, he will lose. But, give him a way out of the box if he surrenders," General Xu said.

"Remember, General, initially we do not release the information, we only threaten to release it. We give the Americans 48 hours to analyze their position. They will come to the same conclusion that we have. Their own survival is far more important to them than the fate of some countries on the other side of the world. After all, we aren't invading anyone," General Kung said.

"Admiral Wu, my fellow generals, raise your hand if you wish to pursue General Kung's plan to Chinese dominance," General Xu said, as he raised his right hand.

"I have said nothing as this tribunal progressed. I will have my say before we take this final vote," General Zhang Xibin, of the General Political Department, said, as he rose to his feet, and turned to stare at each officer in turn, before staring at General Kung.

"Personally, I think this is insanity of the highest order. I'm shocked that most of you have fallen into this spider's trap. Kung, you can't guarantee how the Americans will react. You have a reputation as an Anglophile. You admire their, what is the word . . . grit. You admire their grit and style, their music and art, the way they conduct war . . . and yet, you who knows them best, think that they will just fall over, and let us displace them from half the world? How can you be so sure?" General Zhang asked.

"Yes, General, I have studied their history extensively. I collect their artifacts and literature. I have read the writings of all their presidents and great generals. I also have an extensive collection of the writings of their most famous media celebrities, athletes and movie stars. Their movies, in particular, give great insight into how each generation thinks. This study has given me an insight into the slow decline of their nation over the last 50 years. They are almost ready for a second civil war. That is how divided they are. The elite and many of the young are only a few steps away from calling us 'Comrade'. You will say, 'Why not step back and let them crumble?' My answer would be that I believe they will emerge from their present difficulties as an even stronger nation. This lean to the left will not last. They love their individual freedom too much. Eventually, we will have to fight them or limit our influence around the world. If we strike now, and by now I mean within a few weeks at the most, then we have an opportunity that would make Sun Tzu smile with approval. They are at their weakest right now! Is there a chance of failure? Of course there is. If I said there wasn't, then General Xu would know that I was a fool, and have me hung, and then shot just to make sure," General Kung said, then smiled at the mild laughter from most of the generals.

General Zhang sat down and crossed his arms, still far from convinced.

"Admiral, Generals, I know that this risks far more than my meager life. I know that this is a great risk for the Motherland, and all her children. But in the end, all we are doing is continuing the revolution that Chairman Mao started. Without him, we would still bear the yoke of the Nationalists or the cursed Japanese. I humbly await your decision," General Kung said, then snapped to attention, saluted, and remained silent, while the senior officers began talking amongst themselves.

The armed guards reappeared, and Lieutenant General Kung Yusheng, was escorted from the room to await his fate . . .

.　.　.　.

August 1st Building
March 25, 2017, 1330 hours

General Kung was escorted back through the entrance doors of the tribunal briefing room. He had been left waiting in a locked cell for over three hours. When the guards finally came to get him he was prepared to be taken to another location for execution. He was not expecting to be left alone outside the room where he had presented his case for completing his grand plan.

He stood for a few seconds, as the quartet of armed guards disappeared around a corner. A few seconds later, he reached out, and opened the right-hand door leading back into the tribunal room. He was shocked by who was waiting for him alone, behind the long table previously occupied by the ten most senior officers in the PRC.

"General Secretary," General Kung said, bowing deeply, and staying in that position while just inside the entrance.

"Please come in, General Kung. It is difficult to have a meaningful conversation if one of the participants is 20 feet away and staring at the floor," General Secretary Li Xibin said, motioning for Kung to come forward.

General Kung stood erect, then straightened his uniform as he made his way to the long table. A chair had been positioned directly across from where the General Secretary was sitting.

"Please, be seated. I want you to be comfortable. If you are thirsty, I can have some tea brought in," the General Secretary said, in a calm, yet lethal voice.

"I am quite comfortable, General Secretary, thank you," General Kung replied, bowing once more, and then taking a seat facing the most powerful man in China.

"I have had a long and interesting discussion with the members of the Central Military Commission, even your uncle," General Secretary Li said, adjusting his glasses, and looking up from what Kung knew was a copy of his presentation.

Other copies were strewn across the surface of the table. One copy had been ripped in half, pages scattered across one end of the long table.

"The majority of them recommend that I approve your plan, this passive- aggressive position that you have put us in. It's quite amazing actually," General Secretary Li said, as he looked down, while turning a page on the document.

Kung could see that it was the map showing the general locations of all the devices positioned within the United States. His instincts told him to stay silent until a question was asked.

"General Kung, are you a member of the Communist Party?" General Secretary asked, as he slid a second copy of the document towards him, and opened it to the key that described all the devices listed on the map of the United States.

"Yes, General Secretary, the Youth League when I was 18, and the Party on my 21st birthday," General Kung said, wondering where this line of questioning would lead.

"You and I are close to the same age. We were both boys during the Cultural Revolution. My father was jailed, beaten and starved, primarily for his liberal views. I was removed from school, and sent to a farm for a better education in what mattered to the real people of China. I was large for my age, and soon learned how to defend myself. I believe that by then you were a Second Lieutenant in the PLA. You have always been a soldier. I have always been a politician," General Secretary Li said, closing both documents, and sliding them aside.

"I think, perhaps, that you have forgotten the purpose of the War of Liberation, General Kung. The West spent a hundred years carving up China like they carved up the rest of the world. A people, with a culture that had existed for over five thousand years, were no more than another resource to be consumed by the capitalists of the West. To achieve freedom, millions of Chinese died during our civil wars, and war against the Japanese, so that we could determine our own place in the world, and you would throw it all away on a wild gamble," General Secretary Li said, in a calm voice that sent shivers through Kung's spine.

"Permission to speak frankly, General Secretary," General Kung asked.

"Please . . . as I said, we are here to have a . . . conversation," General Secretary Li said, in a voice that was calm, but with a look in his eyes that told Kung, that his death was imminent.

*"Now is the moment. Everything lives or dies in the next few minutes,"* Kung thought, steeling himself, and seeing the opportunity that he had waited for, for all of his adult life.

"General Secretary, my father was a peasant. He followed Mao during the Long March, gradually rising through the ranks until he became a Major in the PLA. He never attended an academy like our young officers do now. His academy was in the mountains, and in the snows of Manchuria. His nickname was 'clubfoot'. He lost all the toes on his right foot to frostbite while fighting the Nationalists during the Gongzhutun Campaign in 1947. He stayed in the army despite the loss of his toes. He died fighting the Americans in Korea in 1953. My mother was pregnant with me when he died. All I heard as I grew up was what a hero my father had been to the people of China. All I ever wanted as a boy was to live up to his example . . . to also be a hero to the people of China," General Kung said, staring across the table at the taciturn face of the General Secretary.

"When General Fan assigned me to the position of Commander of 22 Base, I felt blessed by the memory of my father. It was a position of great responsibility. I felt that I had an opportunity to finally live up to the example that my father had set. What I saw were the fruits of China's great labors sitting useless deep underground. The older fission bombs were obsolete, and would never see service in defense of the Motherland. It was then that I conceived of a plan to give them a second life, a way in which they could still be of use to the people of China," General Kung said, and felt as if he was sitting before a statue of Buddha, sitting in silence, while passing judgement as he bared his soul.

"As a young officer I studied everything I could find about the American military. They seemed to stumble about the world like drunken oafs, never effectively using their power to change things. Troops would invade, bombs would fall, tens of thousands of civilians would die, and then they would go back to their comfortable lives, and grow fat from the riches they took from others. As I grew older, and rose through the ranks, I saw China grow stronger, our military more advanced, but the Americans were always far ahead of us. Their technology allowed them to do things we only dreamed of. Then Sun Tzu showed me the way forward. He said, 'To fight and conquer in all your battles is not supreme excellence; supreme excellence consists in breaking the enemy's resistance without fighting.' General Secretary, in all humility I bow to you and the will of the Chinese people, but I have presented us with a solution to a great problem. How do we remove the constant interference of these arrogant capitalists, and their decadent culture, without causing irreparable harm to ourselves? These devices that I have planted give us an advantage that the Americans can't overcome. If they attack us, they are destroyed. If they do nothing, we can still destroy them by destabilizing their economy, and creating chaos amongst their population," General Kung said, pausing when the General Secretary abruptly stood.

"General Kung, I will be honest. As I told you, I am a politician. I learned the lessons of my childhood, and have risen to my present position by staying within the strictures of the Party, and being better at my job than anyone else. I have ridden the flow of the great Yangtze, not fought against it. You, on the other hand, have not followed the flow of the river, nor have you fought against it. You have simply dug a small tributary down which you have sailed alone. It is conceivable that your path has some merit. Come, I think more clearly when I walk. So we will walk the halls of this great edifice together, and continue our conversation," General Secretary Li said, gesturing for Kung to follow him out of the room.

Chapter 40

"For it is the soldier's disposition to offer an obstinate resistance when surrounded, to fight hard when he cannot help himself, and to act promptly when he has fallen into danger."

Sun Tzu (~520 BC)

McLean, Virginia, USA
2000 Rockingham Street
Residence of Caleb McElroy
March 24, 2017, 1415 hours EST


"This suit will do. The man is slim for an American," Aiguo said, pacing back and forth, while stretching his arms.

Both hand guns sat on the bed. He knew that he would have to leave them in the car once he reached Reagan International Airport. In his mind he went over his checklist one more time.

"Flight leaves at 1900. I need to leave here by 1630 to arrive at the airport by 1730. His credentials should get me straight through security. I have his wallet with cash and credit cards, his passport, and his CIA ID with my image inserted. The suitcase is packed and sitting outside the bedroom door. Immediately before leaving, I say a final goodbye to Mr. McElroy," Aiguo said, while checking his image in the full length mirror in the walk in closet.

Aiguo was feeling quite pleased with himself until the front door bell rang. The bedroom overlooked the driveway that led to the front door. A slight parting of the blinds revealed a dark blue sedan.

*It's not the police, and it's not some delivery service,*" Aiguo thought, as he walked over to the bed, picked up the Kel-Tec .22 Magnum, and checked the clip.

"Only six rounds left," Aiguo said, while inserting the clip, and chambering a round.

He tucked the 9mm in the waist band at the small of his back, and started back down stairs. The Kel-Tec was lightly gripped in his right hand. He approached the front door, and slid the Kel-Tec behind his back. When he opened the front door a man and a woman in dark suits were standing on the front porch.

"We're looking for Caleb . . ." the woman began to say.

The silenced Kel-Tec made very little noise as Aiguo shot them both in the forehead. Aiguo dragged the woman inside with one hand while glancing around the street below the front of the house. No one was visible. The man was tall and heavy. Aiguo set the pistol on the entry floor when he went back outside. He waved as two cyclists rode by. A woman waved back, not noticing the large man who had tumbled backwards down the hill and into the azaleas. Aiguo walked down a short stone path that led to the rear of the bushes. After looking around, he threw the man over his shoulder with a grunt, and trudged back up the hill.

"Something triggered this visit. Either they didn't believe his flu story, or by cutting the card I set off an alarm," Aiguo said, while dumping the man onto the antique carpet beside his partner.

After retrieving the Kel-Tec, he checked the IDs of both dead people.

"CIA . . . I have to leave now. It looks like Mr. McElroy's time is up," Aiguo said, while shutting and locking the front door.

He dragged both bodies into the dining room, and left them beside the dog. Tucked neatly against the back wall, none of them would be visible from outside the house. After checking hands and clothes for blood, he headed for the stairwell leading to the downstairs bedroom.

"It would seem that my departure time has arrived, Director McElroy. I must thank you for the loan of your suit and your identity," Aiguo said, as he walked up to the side of the bed while holding the Kel-Tec in his right hand.

"You won't get away . . . they'll stop you . . . you're dead and don't even know it," McElroy croaked through parched lips.

Caleb McElroy hadn't eaten in three days, and had been given nothing to drink in over 24 hours. He lay in his own filth, and his wrists were raw and bleeding from struggling against his bonds.

"Perhaps, but you will die before I do. All your wealth and your power, a fine car, fine suits, and you will go down in American history as nothing more than a traitor. You will be found lying in your own shit. I'm half tempted to leave you here and let you starve to death. That would be fitting, but that would make you a loose end, and I was trained to never leave behind a loose end," Aiguo said, while showing the Kel-Tec to McElroy.

"This is the weapon that will end your life. It belonged to a man who was sent by my government to kill me. At first I thought it was too delicate a weapon for me. It feels like a plastic toy. But I was wrong. The .22 magnum round is quite deadly, and it doesn't make a mess. If I used a 9mm, it would blow out the back of your head and I might get splattered with your blood, but this weapon . . . no kick, no mess, it's almost silent, and all you have is a small hole in your forehead," Aiguo said, while placing the muzzle against McElroy's forehead.

"Oh, just in case. I can't afford a splatter," Aiguo said, while picking up a pillow from the floor and placing it over McElroy's face.

"Please, I beg you . . ." McElroy said.

The Kel-Tec made little noise with the silenced muzzle pushed against the pillow. The body of Director Caleb McElroy was still twitching as Aiguo turned off the lights, and shut the bedroom door.

After retrieving the luggage, and pulling on an overcoat from a hall closet upstairs, Aiguo walked back down the stairs to the basement bedroom, passed the closed door, and opened the door to the garage. He had hidden the assassin's Toyota Camry beside McElroy's Mercedes AMG S65. He caressed the smooth lines of the Mercedes as he walked past it.

"What a beautiful machine. It is so tempting, but if they sent a pair to look here, they will also be looking for his car," Aiguo said, as he turned towards the Camry.

"It seems I have some time to kill before the flight. It's only 1440, and I don't think I'll be waiting here," Aiguo said, glancing at his new Rolex watch.

He threw the luggage into the passenger seat of the Camry, opened the garage doors, and sped down the street, leaving another location filled with the dead behind him.

"I know right where to go, just to thumb my nose at America," Aiguo said, while turning left onto Williamsburg Boulevard.

Chapter 41

"It is far better to be alone than to be in bad company."

George Washington

Manassas, Virginia, USA
Mission Center for Weapons and Counterproliferation
Amanda Langford's Office
March 24, 2017, 1515 hours EST


Amanda couldn't believe that in less than 24 hours she had flown to Seattle, interviewed two witnesses, and then flown back to Virginia. She wasn't sure if she was jet lagged, exhausted, or just numb from so much flying time. All she knew for sure was that the coffee wasn't helping.

"I've got so much to do. I have to finish this presentation for the Director of the CIA, and things are changing so fast that the data is out of date in less than a day. Three nukes so far, and they were going to head up to another restaurant near a sub base before they were apprehended. If that pans out then I was probably right. These things are all over the country," Amanda said, then drained her mug.

"I think I'll switch to tea . . . with lots of sugar," she said, then jumped as her cell phone started vibrating across her desk.

Amanda sighed, as she picked up her phone, then sat up straight when she saw who was calling.

"Major Thompson, good morning, what can I do for you?" Amanda said.

"Well, you told me to call if I remembered something else, and . . . I have. We need to talk face to face. It's really something you need to see. I'm not sure what it means, but I think it's connected to the Chinese operative. Can you meet me in Old Town Alexandria, at a place called the Torpedo Factory? Please, I think it's important."

Amanda glanced at the time on her laptop, and then said, "Sure, I hear there are some decent restaurants near there, and I haven't eaten all day. I can be there in 45 minutes."

"I'll wait for you behind the building, on the river side. There's a stone plaza with benches. I'll be back there," Anthony said.

"Okay, I'll meet you there," Amanda said and disconnected the call.

"*Why wouldn't he say what he remembered? He sounded excited, almost . . . no, his type doesn't get scared . . . but something had him agitated. Damn, I'm not even sure if he's mentally stable,*" Amanda thought, as she resisted the urge to call him back.

"Well, I need some fresh air anyway. I'll just bring the laptop with me," Amanda said, while packing up and leaving the office.

Chapter 42

"Revenge is a powerful motivator."

Marcus Luttrell

Alexandria, Virginia, USA
The Torpedo Factory Art Center
105 North Union Street
March 24, 2017, 1600 hours EST


The sun was low in the cold, clear sky. In a few hours it would be dark. Aiguo had enjoyed his leisurely ride through the bustling streets of this city across the river from America's soul.

Aiguo slowly walked around the old diesel engine that he had escorted into the United States all the way from Shanghai, China. It was a monstrous thing in more ways than one, and he loved the powerful rush that he was having as he contemplated what he had accomplished.

"*They will come around when it dawns on them how important the completion of this mission has been. They will stop hunting me. I will be brought back to China as a hero. This is the dagger at America's throat. This will enable our final victory, and it was placed here by First Lieutenant Gong Aiguo of the Siberian Tigers,*" Aiguo thought, as he smiled and glanced around at the few people enjoying what remained of the bright sun on such a cool day.

He barely noticed the large man sitting alone on the other side of the plaza. The snow had been cleared, and lay in tall mounds on the river side. The great diesel engine had the appearance of a mountain top peaked with snow on its slopes and terraces.

"The American was right. You do have a beauty all you own. I didn't see it before, but I do now," Aiguo said, while checking the time on his Rolex.

"Still more time, perhaps some food," Aiguo said, as he glanced up at the diesel, and felt the 9mm shift in the pocket of his overcoat.

He left the plaza and walked down the street to the south. A brisk breeze blew in from the river causing him to pull up the collar on the overcoat. His fingers and toes still ached from frostbite, but it was a pain that he easily ignored. Turning right on King Street, he saw a restaurant on the corner.

"Vola's, I like the bright red lettering. It reminds me of home," Aiguo said, as he turned, and approached the entrance.

Amanda Langford was hurrying. Parking had been tight, and she had to walk half a mile to get to the Torpedo Factory. Her head was turned down into the stiff wind, and she never noticed the man crossing the street until she bumped into him.

"I'm so sorry, I wasn't looking where I was going," Amanda said, looking up into the eyes of a young man who was Asian, and oddly familiar.

The man said nothing, nodded in acknowledgement, then walked up the three steps to the restaurant, opened the door, and entered.

"Well that was rude. It was as much his fault as mine," Amanda said, as she hurried across the street, and headed for the plaza behind the Torpedo Factory.

She replayed the incident in her mind as she walked, careful to watch where she was going.

"Why was he familiar?" Amanda asked herself, stopping on the side walk, and glancing back over her shoulder.

She shook her head and hurried on, hoping that Major Thompson had remembered something significant. As she entered the plaza, the first thing she noticed was the enormous diesel engine sitting in the middle of the area It had been welded onto a lattice work support structure that looked far too fragile to hold up such and enormous machine. Then she noticed Major Thompson sitting on a bench, studying his cell phone, as she hurried in his direction.

"Major Thompson, I'm sorry I'm late. The traffic was bad and parking down here is terrible," Amanda said, while extending her hand.

"Oh, Ms. Langford, that's okay, I'm glad you came," Anthony said, while turning off his phone and placing in his coat pocket.

"Please, call me Amanda," she said, as he stood and shook her hand, then gestured for her to sit beside him.

Amanda couldn't help but recognize a picture of his wife before he turned off the cell phone.

"So what did you remember that you didn't want to discuss over the phone?" Amanda asked.

"This thing," Anthony said, as he nodded towards the diesel engine.

"I told you that my wife had mentioned something about torpedoes. I remembered that she also mentioned the killer talking about a train," Anthony said.

"What does that have to do with this . . . whatever it is . . . this big machine," Amanda said.

"When the weather's warm my wife and I used to come to Old Towne Alexandria. She really liked the architecture, and there are quite a few good restaurants in the area. We used to sit back here after eating and look out at the river. I proposed to her sitting on this bench. But this thing . . . it's an industrial diesel engine . . . this thing is new. I was curious about it, so I went into the Torpedo Factory yesterday, and talked to the manager. He introduced me to the Art Curator, a man named Markus Candee. This . . . piece of art . . . was donated by a company located in Taiwan. Mr. Candee says it will become a continuous art project. Anyone who wants to will be able to paint on it. Sounds pretty weird to me, but here's the interesting part. The diesel engine was trucked in on an extended flat bed trailer, and was escorted by a young Chinese man. He said the man told him that he had escorted the diesel all the way from Shanghai. I asked him what happened to the man, and he said that he walked off into the night after the delivery was complete. Mr. Candee thought that was odd because the man had told him that some friends were coming to pick him up, and the snow was starting to come down. It was the same night that the massacre at Inova Alexandria Hospital happened," Anthony said.

Amanda said nothing, just staring up at his face while her mind whirled with information.

"You think this man's the killer?" Amanda asked.

"I think he's the killer, and I think you know more than you've told me. If this is just a murder then the CIA wouldn't be interested. At most, the FBI, and maybe DHS because he's a foreigner, but not the

CIA. You never did tell me what department in the CIA you worked for," Anthony said, while leaning toward Amanda.

"No . . . it can't be. It's just a coincidence. The trainers in the academy would tell me that it's racial profiling," Amanda said, without realizing that she was talking out loud.

"What's racial profiling? And why aren't you answering my questions?" Anthony said.

"Do you know if Mr. Candee is still working?" Amanda asked, as she grabbed Anthony by the arm.

"Yeah, I think he works until 5PM. Why?" Anthony said.

"Come on, we have to find him. Now!" Amanda said, as she stood up, glanced around, and began heading for the back entrance to the Torpedo Factory Art Center.

"Ms. Langford, what's going on? What did I say to get you so excited?" Anthony said, walking in the wake of the diminutive woman.

"Enough with the 'Ms. Langford'. My name is Amanda, and we've got to find Mr. Candee ASAP. You lead," Amanda said, as she flung open the back door and stepped aside for Anthony.

"We turn left at the main intersection. Down at the end there's a set of stairs that lead up to the admin offices. He's in there," Anthony said, as Amanda ran past him and headed for the stairs.

"Damn girl, you move pretty quick for your size," Anthony joked, while he jogged after Amanda.

"I move fast when I'm scared," Amanda said, while taking the stairs two at a time.

The stony look on her face told him that this was no longer a casual conversation. Whatever he had said had flipped a switch in the CIA agent.

Amanda stopped at the receptionist's desk on the second floor and asked, "Where can I find Mr. Candee. It's very important."

"Good afternoon, my name is Lisa. What is the nature of . . ." the receptionist began.

"Which office?" Amanda repeated, while leaning over the woman's desk.

"I don't know who you think . . ." the receptionist started to say.

"Which fucking office?" Anthony shouted, appearing at Amanda's right shoulder.

"End of the hall . . . the big office," Lisa said, frightened, as both Amanda and Anthony glared down at her.

The pair rushed down the hall. Anthony slammed the door closed after they entered. Marcus Candee was reviewing a large portfolio from an artist from Cary, North Carolina, who specialized in pears and other fruit.

"I really love his style. I'm inviting him up for a showing in July. What do you think?" Marcus asked, while reversing the portfolio for them to view.

"Mr. Candee, my name is Amanda Langford. I'm an agent for the Central Intelligence Agency, and I need some information from you . . . right . . . now," Amanda said, while removing her CIA ID from her satchel.

"Are you for real? Why would the CIA want to talk to me? Is this a joke?" Marcus said, as he examined her ID and handed it back.

"Do you remember the Chinese gentleman that delivered the diesel engine you have on display out back?" Amanda asked, ignoring his question.

"Well yes, he was a very handsome young man. We talked at length while the art object in question was being unloaded and installed on its display stand. I invited him out for drinks afterwards, but he wasn't interested. I was quite disappointed. Why? Did he do something wrong?" Marcus asked.

"Would you recognize him, if you saw him again?" Amanda asked.

"Yes, I think so. He was quite handsome, like I said," Marcus said.

"Get your coat, you're coming with me," Amanda said, while gesturing for Anthony to open the door.

"Now? Are you crazy? I'm ready to go home. I've got a date tonight," Marcus said.

"Now!" Amanda and Anthony said, at the same time.

"All right! Don't yell, I'm coming peacefully," Marcus said, as he removed a scarf and coat from an ornate hook mounted on the wall.

Amanda led the way as they left the Art Center and turned left onto King Street. Anthony followed behind Marcus to make sure that he didn't wander away.

Twenty feet down the sidewalk Amanda stopped, and turning to Marcus said, "Marcus, do you see the restaurant on the corner?"

"Vola's? Of course, I go there all the time. They have great drink specials on Friday night," Marcus said.

"I want you to walk slowly past the restaurant, and see if you can identify the Chinese gentleman who escorted the 'art object'. I saw him go into the restaurant ten minutes ago. Don't stop and stare, and don't go in the restaurant. Just walk past and glance in. When you get past the restaurant, turn around and look at me. Give me a thumbs up if you saw him, a thumbs down, if you didn't see him. Repeat back what I just told you to do," Amanda said, while holding both of Marcus' hands.

"Walk past, look in, don't be obvious, thumbs up if I see him, and thumbs down if I don't," Marcus said.

"Marcus . . . if it's a thumbs up, you turn around and leave this area. Do you understand me?" Amanda asked, still holding both of Marcus' hands.

"Yes . . . and now you're scaring me. What is going on?" Marcus asked.

"Just do what the lady said, Marcus, and everything will be fine," Anthony said, as he stepped up beside Marcus.

"No big deal, Marcus. You know what to do, now go on," Amanda said, as she released his hands, and stepped to the side.

"Okay, no big deal," Marcus said, as he began to walk down the street.

When Marcus reached Vola's, he crossed over to the window, and began studying the menu posted near the base of the entrance stairs, while glancing inside the restaurant. With a casual wave he walked past the restaurant, and turned left down an alley that led to the back entrance of the Torpedo Factory. As he passed the last window on his left, he glanced up and saw Aiguo sitting alone in the back corner of the restaurant. His back was to a wall, and he was facing outward while studying his cell phone. Marcus turned and ran back down the alley and past the front of the restaurant. He was gasping for breath as he stopped in front of Amanda and Anthony.

"What happened to the thumbs up?" Anthony asked.

"Oh screw that! He's in there, bold as can be. He's wearing a very nice suit based on the cut. Definitely British, they have such good taste," Marcus said, as he loosened his scarf.

"Where's he sitting?" Amanda asked.

"If you go in the front door, turn right, then left at the end of the bar. He's all the way in the back facing outwards," Marcus said, as he began wiping his face with his scarf.

"Marcus, thank you very much for your help. Now go home!" Amanda said.

Marcus smiled at them both, hugged Anthony, then turned and walked north up North Union Street.

"Enough with the games, Amanda. Who is this guy? How is he connected to the . . ." Anthony asked, stopping mid-sentence as the truth hit him.

"Anthony! First, we need him alive. That is crucial. He's a critical part of an ongoing case of national importance. We have to be able to question him. Do you understand me?" Amanda said, as she grabbed Anthony's coat.

"You know you have a thing about grabbing men when you talk to them," Anthony said, while staring down at Amanda.

"It's like grabbing a big dog by the collar. They know you mean business," Amanda said, as she released Anthony.

"So why's this guy so important?" Anthony asked, as his breathing deepened, and the familiar rush of adrenalin filled his body.

"Promise you won't do anything stupid. Promise me!" Amanda said.

"Okay, I promise," Anthony said.

"He's probably the guy from the hospital. I'm calling for backup and the police. All we need to do is make sure he doesn't leave," Amanda said, as she stepped in front of Anthony.

She knew she had made a mistake when his eyes glazed over.

"That's what I thought. I just need to hear it from you," Anthony said, while brushing her aside with a sweep of his arm.

The Colt Model 1911 .45 cleared his shoulder holster, and hung from his right hand as he walked down the street.

"Damn it, Anthony! You promised," Amanda yelled.

"I lied . . ." Anthony said, as he approached the main entrance of Vola's Dockside Grill.

Chapter 43

"A good plan violently executed now is better than a perfect
plan executed next week."

George S Patton

Alexandria, Virginia, USA
Vola's Dockside Bar & Grill
101 North Union Street
March 24, 2017, 1530 hours EST

At 3:30 in the afternoon Vola's Dockside Bar & Grill had very
few patrons. The lunch time crowd was long gone, and the post-work
crowd was still toiling away at work. Most of the restaurant staff was
in the kitchen talking, and having something to eat, before the rush
started at 4:30.

Anthony stepped into the restaurant while keeping the .45
tucked against his right leg. He walked to the end of the bar, glanced
down the long side of the inside of the restaurant, and counted eight
people.

"*Two couples on the right, the bartender on the left, two at the
far end of the bar, and there's my friend, 60 feet away. One of us isn't
leaving here alive,*" Anthony said to himself, while slowly walking
down the length of the restaurant.

"*That's right, pal, keep looking at your cell phone. That's the
last thing you're ever going to see,*" Anthony thought, while passing
the two couples seated on his right.

"Bill . . . Bill, that man has a gun!" the older woman said, as
Anthony passed by them.

Anthony turned and shushed them both with a finger at his lips,
jerked his thumb towards the exit, and kept walking.

"*40 feet . . .*" Anthony thought, while flipping off the safety on
the .45 with his thumb.

He heard the two couples leave their tables, and head for the main entrance behind him. The target hadn't moved, still absorbed in whatever he was looking at on his cell phone. In his peripheral vision he saw the bartender rush up to the two patrons at the far end of the bar and whisper something to them. They both disappeared to the left with the bartender.

"30 feet . . . just you and me, pal . . . just you and me," Anthony said, as he raised the .45 to eye level.

Aiguo moved so quickly that all Anthony saw was a blur. Anthony instinctively ducked to his left and that saved his life. The .22 Magnum round clipped his right ear, rather than pulping his brain.

Anthony crouched and fired two rounds as Aiguo flipped up the heavy table and ducked behind it for cover. The .45 hollow point rounds blew holes though the heavy wooden table, but Aiguo wasn't hit.

Aiguo dove to his right and fired another round. He saw the big American flinch as the round hit him in the left arm.

Anthony yelled as he was driven to his knees by the impact of the bullet.

"What's he shooting? I can't even hear anything . . . silencer," he said, as he raised the .45 and shot at the prone figure 30 feet away.

Aiguo grimaced as the .45 creased him in the left hip. The American staggered, and fell to a sitting position, as Aiguo's third shot struck him in the left shoulder.

Anthony fell against a table leg. His left shoulder and side were burning in agony.

Aiguo stood up, clutching his left hip to stop the bleeding. He smiled at the American as he limped towards him while pointing the Kel-Tec at the American's head.

Stopping 20 feet away, Aiguo smiled down at Anthony.

"You lose, American, just as your country will lose to China. You had your time. It's our world now," Aiguo said, while pulling the trigger.

The click of an empty weapon was audible to both men. Aiguo swore and reached for the 9 mm tucked into the back of his waist band. Anthony raised the .45 and fired two shots. The first round hit Aiguo in the left thigh, spinning him around. The second struck him in the right side of his chest, and threw him backwards onto the floor.

The smell of burnt gun powder filled the restaurant as silence returned. Anthony rested the .45 in his lap, as he stared at the fallen man across from him. Aiguo groaned, and then screamed as he tried to get to his feet. His left thigh was shattered.

"Good . . . the fucker's not dead," Anthony said, as he staggered to his feet, the .45 in his right hand.

His left arm hung loosely at his side. He could hear the slow drip of blood splattering on the wooden floor, and knew that an artery had been nicked in his arm.

"I may bleed out, pal, but you're going first," Anthony said, while walking over to Aiguo's prone body.

Aiguo lay in a pool of his own blood. His eyes were wide with shock as he desperately reached for the cell phone that had fallen behind him.

"No, I don't think you'll be making any more calls today," Anthony said, as he stepped over Aiguo and glanced down at the blood splattered cell phone.

"Your girlfriend?" Anthony said, as he stood over Aiguo, and pointed the .45 at his head.

Aiguo nodded, unable to speak. Blood bubbled up between his lips as he began to choke.

"Remember the hospital? Remember all the people you murdered there? One of them was my wife. She was standing beside the doctor. She was pregnant with our first child. You took everything that mattered to me in this world," Anthony said, as searing hatred filled his mind.

"The only thing I have left to live for is revenge. We have a saying that revenge is a dish best served cold. They're wrong! I like mine burning hot and it tastes great," Anthony said, while pulling the slack out of the trigger.

"Anthony! Stop!" Amanda yelled from behind him.

"Go away, Amanda. I'm going to finish this now while I can still see the look in his eyes," Anthony said.

"Don't do it. He has to live. We have to question him," Amanda pleaded, as the sound of sirens could be heard approaching.

"I don't care about some bullshit case of yours. This bastard murdered my wife, and his time is up," Anthony said.

"Anthony, the Chinese have been placing nuclear weapons inside the United States. I think this man is part of that plot. I think a bomb is inside that diesel behind the art center. We have to able to question him. The safety of the United States is at stake. Please don't kill him," Amanda said, while approaching Anthony from behind.

"Sorry, he has to go," Anthony said, but relaxed his trigger finger.

"Anthony, put down the gun. The ambulance is here. The police are here," Amanda said, as she stood beside him, and placed her hand on his gun hand, slowly pushing it away from Aiguo's head.

Anthony glanced to his left and saw several police officers. All had their weapons aimed at him.

"They'll save him. You'll question him, and then the government will exchange him for one of ours. He'll go home a hero and marry the woman on his phone. How do I live with that?" Anthony said, as he resisted Amanda's attempt to move his weapon.

"Major Thompson, listen to me. China may have dozens of nuclear bombs planted all over the country. You have a sworn duty to the United States of America to protect her and her people. This man has to live whether you like it or not. Now put down the damn weapon," Amanda ordered, appealing to what she knew was his strong sense of duty.

Anthony stared into Amanda's eyes, then nodded, and placed the .45 in his shoulder holster.

He then knelt beside Aiguo and said, "I hope they save you and set you free. Remember my face because we'll be meeting again some time, some where," Anthony said, as he stood up, turned and walked toward the waiting police with his one good arm in the air.

Chapter 44

"When you reach the end of your rope, tie a knot in it and hang on."

Franklin D. Roosevelt

Washington, DC, USA
The White House
The Oval Office
March 24, 2017, 1700 hours EST

"Across the damn river? You're kidding me," the President said, while secret service agents swarmed in, and began ferrying him out of the Oval Office.

"Yes, Mr. President . . . in Old Town Alexandria, right on the river front," Clarisse Beaumont said, while jogging beside the President.

"How big?" the President asked.

"They aren't sure. This just happened. There was some kind of a shootout with a Chinese national and a Pentagon officer. He was with a CIA agent. The area is being contained as a crime scene," Clarisse said, as the President was rushed into an elevator leading to an underground bunker.

"Stop right here! Son, you touch that down button, and I'll have you transferred to the Antarctic," the President said, as he shook off the hands of a Secret Service agent.

"Clarisse, this is starting to look like the panic button has been pushed. Before we take another step, I want all the facts, and I mean right now," the President said.

"Mr. President, 30 minutes ago I received an Urgent from CIA. They've has been pursuing a theory that the Chinese have been systematically planting nuclear devices inside the United States for decades. Now we have confirmation that a Chinese Special Forces operator escorted a diesel engine from Shanghai through Port New Orleans, and then by train up to Alexandria. It was supposedly donated by some company in Taiwan, but the company is a front. The Taiwanese government says they have been watching this company for years, but haven't been able to find anything conclusive. To me, that means that somebody has been paid to look the other way. It seems that this Chinese operative has been involved in a string of murders in the area, including one of the CIA Mission directors. The CIA tracked him down and there was a shootout in Old Towne. The man was captured, but he was badly wounded. The CIA checked the outside of the diesel engine and found small amounts of radiation near the bottom. Mr. President, you really need to go into the bunker until this is resolved. This device is only six or seven miles away from here. Please, Mr. President, go to the bunker," Clarisse pleaded.

"All right, let's go, but I want to be kept abreast of this as it progresses, and find out if that damn Israeli bomb expert is on the way yet, and make sure he's coming directly here," the President told his National Security Advisor, as the elevator doors began to shut.

Chapter 45

"Only those are fit to live who do not fear to die; and none are
fit to die who have shrunk from the joy of life and the duty of life."

Theodore Roosevelt

Haifa, Israel
Beit Oren Kibbutz
Home 346
March 25, 2017, 0830 hours IST

The view of the eastern Mediterranean was stunning in the
early morning. Dr. David Barza sat on his balcony dressed only in
socks, sweats and wrapped in a blanket. A steaming cup of kafe botz
sat on a table to his right.

"British idiot . . . 100 years to get off the planet? I think his
disease has finally affected his mind," Dr. Barza said, as he rolled up
the magazine and threw it over the railing of his balcony.

He was reaching for his cup of mud coffee when he heard a
loud knocking on his front door.

"The door's open," he yelled, then sipped from the hot cup.

A mild breeze blew in from the sea, rustling the drapes as the
front door opened. He heard the footsteps of several men, and
wondered who would be coming to pay him a visit so early in the
morning.

"Well, whoever it is grab a chair. I'm not leaving the balcony
on a fine morning like this," Dr. Barza said, while burying his nose in
the cup, and enjoying the scent of cardamom.

"You always were a rude bastard," the Prime Minister of Israel
said, as he followed a bodyguard carrying a chair onto the balcony.

"Leave us," the Prime minister said, while positioning the chair
on Barza's left side.

"If I had to pick the 10 most unlikely visitors to walk in my
front door you would be very near the top of the list, Prime Minister

Herzbach. For what reason do you darken my home on such a beautiful day?" Dr. Barza asked, not bothering to formally greet the Prime Minister of the State of Israel.

"David, we have not talked for over five years. We don't like each other. If the Shield of David had not called me personally I wouldn't be here," the Prime Minister said.

"Ahh, things become clearer. Your leash has been yanked, and you wish to obey your master," Dr. Barza said, finally turning to acknowledge the presence of Israel's elected leader.

"Israel has no master but Yahweh, but Israel does have a few friends that we listen to. Your assistance has been requested by the American President. It seems that they need your specific skills," the Prime Minister said.

"Jacob . . . I'm an old man. I don't have that many years left. Why would the Americans need an old man cursed with Parkinson's?" Dr. Barza asked, while holding up a shaking hand.

"She asked for you personally. The President was relaying her message," the Prime Minister said, as he laid his hand on the shaking hand of Dr. Barza.

"She? By she you mean . . . Kate Williams. Is this a joke? Are you here just to torment me?" Dr. Barza asked.

"No, old friend, she has really asked for your assistance. The President made me swear . . . what is the American term . . . on a stack of bibles, that I wouldn't have the Mossad investigate his request," the Prime Minister said.

"What would make the Americans so desperate?" Dr. Barza asked, as he pulled his hand away from the Prime Minister, and began massaging his temples.

"I suspect that it has something to do with nuclear weapons. The Mossad has informed me of several odd occurrences in the US within the past week or so. They keep having chemical leaks that require the evacuation of thousands of people. It seems a bit coincidental for my liking. I think they have a very serious problem, and they are asking their friends for help. So, David . . . what is your answer?" the Prime Minister asked.

"You always did have good instincts. When we were young you told me that Kate would not make a good wife. She was too independent, too American, too focused on her career. I should have listened to you. It would have saved me a lot of heartache," Dr. Barza said, while reaching out and grasping the Prime Minister's hand.

"David, I'm sorry if I have caused you pain over the years. We aren't here for perfection. We are here to learn from our mistakes. So what is your answer?" the Prime Minister asked.

"So, where am I going in America? I hate cold weather," Dr. Barza said, and knew that he would miss the morning view of the Mediterranean from his balcony.

Chapter 46

"We should not look back unless it is to derive useful lessons
from past errors, and for the purpose of profiting by dearly bought
experience."

George Washington

Port Orchard, Washington, USA
Golden Grill on the Bay
1014 Bay Street
March 25, 2017, 1415 hours PST

"Okay, so what do we know so far," Kate asked, as she,
Nathan, and Alan, sat at a battered metal table outside the storage area
for the first thermonuclear device found on US soil.

"Well, it's an old Teller-Ulam two-stage design with a boosted
fission primary and a fusion secondary. The fusion fuel is probably Li-
6, but the design isn't our problem, it's all the crap they added to keep
people like us from messing with the device," Nathan said.

"Right . . . so far we've identified three anti-tampering add-ons.
I thought the mesh they placed on the inside of the fission devices, at
the other two locations, was pretty sophisticated for the time period,
but these three are much worse, and they seem to be interconnected,
meaning they're in series. We can't take them individually. We have to
take them all out at exactly the same time or . . . you know what
happens," Alan said, while mimicking the shape of a mushroom cloud
with his hands.

"This may take days or longer," Nathan said.

"Actually, it's simple. Since they put them in series, we just
treat the whole thing as one anti-tampering device," Kate said, and sat
back and waited.

"No, you can't do that . . . or . . . maybe you could, if you . . ."
Nathan began.

"The first anti-tampering device doesn't have any visible link. It's just a box with one line out. You'd have to . . . yeah, that would work," Alan said, talking at the same time as Nathan, as both men were thinking out loud.

"You boys hash out the details. I want a written plan, and don't touch anything until I approve the whole plan," Kate said, as she stood up, stretched and walked out of the building.

"Crap, I'm getting too old for this. I'm 51, and today I feel more like 71. It seems like yesterday when I could go for days on two hours sleep and lots of caffeine. Now, if I don't get eight hours, I feel sluggish all day," Kate said, as her phone rang.

"This is Kate, and you better not have found another one," Kate answered, when she saw the National Security Advisor's smiling face ID'd on her cell phone.

"Kate, things have gone from bad to worse. We just found one in Alexandria, Virginia, and it's not behind a Chinese restaurant," Clarisse said.

"Damn . . . did the President ever ask for Dr. Barza?" Kate asked.

"He's in the air as we speak. We're diverting the plane to DC," Clarisse said.

"Have you studied his file?" Kate asked.

"Well, not in detail, just his degrees and accomplishments," Clarisse said.

"He has Stage 2 Parkinson's. He has an enormous amount of knowledge and experience with nuclear devices, but he can't do the hands on work anymore. He can also be very hard to handle," Kate said.

"Listen, Kate, you were the one who recommended him. We need somebody reliable here . . . right now, who can disarm this thing. If it's as big as the one you're working on, it could take out the whole damn government," Clarisse said.

"Where did they find this one?" Kate asked.

"Inside an enormous diesel engine that was supposedly donated by a Taiwanese company. It's set up as an art object, if you can believe that one," Clarisse said.

"Are you sure it's a nuke? That MO is completely different. Why would they change?" Kate asked.

"The energy spectrum matches, and I have no idea why this one is different. How soon can you get out here?" Clarisse asked.

"At least three days, if . . . they don't find anymore devices out here. Look, I'll send my East Coast team up to Alexandria. They'll have everything Dr. Barza will need. They're based in Columbia, South Carolina, so they can be on site in 12 hours. Also, he's going to need a handler. He'll piss off everyone he deals with, so they will have to be diplomatic, with a thick skin . . . and he would prefer an attractive female. I know it's not PC, but that's the way he is," Kate said.

"Kate, we don't have the time to deal with . . ."

"I'm sorry Clarisse, but he's the best there is. He's better than me, and I'm the best we've got. He taught me everything I know about these devices. He wrote the book that the US uses to train all our EOD and nuke handlers. I'll try to be there in three days, but I have to take care of business here, unless you want a big round hole in the middle of the state of Washington," Kate said.

"All right . . . I'll deal with Dr. 'Pain-in–the-Ass'. He better be as good as you say . . . and don't blow yourself up," Clarisse said, as she hung up.

"More frigging calls . . ." Kate mumbled, while she sent a text message to South Carolina.

Chapter 47

"War can only be abolished through war, and in order to get rid
of the gun it is necessary to take up the gun."

Mao Zedong

Beijing, China
The Great Hall of the People
Liaoning Hall
A Special Meeting of the Politburo Standing Committee
March 25, 2017 2130 hours CT

Lieutenant General Kung Yusheng stood at attention just inside
the entry doors to the Liaoning Hall within the Great Hall of the
People on the west side of Tiananmen Square. The historic edifice,
over two-and-a-half times the size of the US Capitol, represented the
pride and dignity of the Chinese people. An armed escort stood beside
and behind him.

Kung stood before a great screen 30 feet long and 15 feet high.
It was built of bronze, wood, and a mottled gray stone carved to depict
a massive Siberian tiger perched on rocks. The fearsome beast seemed
to be roaring at the sun in seeming defiance of the sun's existence.
Some said that the sun represented Japan, and the tiger the defiant and
long suffering people of Northeast China. The Japanese atrocities in
the region during World War II may have been downplayed by Japan,
but the Chinese people had very long memories.

The choice of this room was not lost on Kung. He was from the
region of Liaoning. His connections within the Siberian Tigers,
stationed in that military region, had no doubt been found out. On the
other side of the screen, he could hear the voices of the seven most
powerful politicians in the PRC. Several of them were shouting at
once.

"Are you telling us that this traitor has planted numerous
nuclear weapons in the United States, and . . . that you support his

actions? General Secretary, please tell me that I didn't hear you correctly," said Zhang Gaoli, the number 3 man in the PSC, Head of Legislative Affairs.

"Yes, Gaoli, you heard me correctly. At first I reacted as you and several of the others have. You can imagine how the generals reacted when they first found out, but the majority of them are now in support of General Kung's actions," said General Secretary Li Xibin, in a calm and measured voice.

"The Generals? Are you trying to tell me that General Zhang supported this insanity?" Zhang asked.

"No, General Zhang was most vehement in his opposition. I thought he was going to have a heart attack," Li said, while chuckling.

"Comrade General Secretary, this is no laughing matter. This man has placed the nation on the brink of destruction," said Liu Zhengsheng, the number 5 man in the PSC, and Head of Party Bureaucracy and Ideology.

"Yes . . . we are either on the brink of destruction, or, on the brink of global domination. That is why I called you all out this late in the evening, on such short notice. Lieutenant General Kung has followed his chain of command . . . for once. As the American presidents are fond of saying, 'the buck stops here'. We decide the path of China, not the people, not the PLA, not the Central Committee, nor the Party Congress. The seven of us will decide our path going forward . . . and we will do it tonight. I have made a personal decision, and am in favor of supporting the position that General Kung has placed us in . . . and yes, it was against our will. No, actually it was without our knowledge at all," Li said, while waving for three of the other members to stay seated.

"General Secretary . . . Xibin . . . my friend of many years, you know I support you in all things, but this . . . this threatens . . . everything we have built . . . everything. Perhaps in 20 years or so, we would be able to face the Americans down, but now is not the time. Our military is not strong enough. You need to discretely contact the American President and be honest. Tell him . . . that this man has gone rogue, that no one within the political power structure knew anything about this. We give him all the locations of the weapons in the United States, and ask his . . . forgiveness," said Guo Quishan, No. 2 man in the PSC.

"Quishan, I'm disappointed. Of all the members, I thought you would stand with me," Li said.

"General Secretary, this is too important for friendship to play a part. You will have to be more convincing than this or my vote will stay 'No'," Guo said, as he held the hard gaze of his friend and leader.

"So . . . if Guo feels this way, then for the moment I stand alone. Raise your hand if you feel as Guo does," Li said.

All six hands were raised in opposition to Kung's plan.

"Well, I've always thought that I was a persuasive man. It seems that I was mistaken . . . for now. Before we vote officially, and conclude this meeting, I would ask that you listen to one more person. I have invited Lieutenant General Kung Yusheng to speak before our gathering," Li said, then smiled at the uproar that his announcement had caused.

"Quiet! You sound like American college students offended by the presence of one of differing opinion. As long as I am Party General Secretary, my voice will be heard. I cannot order you how to vote, but I can order you to listen," General Secretary Li yelled, while rising to his feet, and pointing at each member of the PSC in turn.

"Guards, bring in General Kung!" Li ordered.

General Kung was escorted around the stone screen by his guards. The guards turned and left, at a signal from the General Secretary.

The Liaoning Hall, 100 by 60 feet, had four polished marble pillars, each three feet in diameter, each carved to look as if it had come from the old Imperial Palace. The floor was completely covered by thick, bright red carpeting. The walls were 20 feet tall. Three were veined yellow marble with a satin finish. The fourth wall on his right was glass from ceiling to floor, covered in translucent white silk drapes. Kung knew that the glass wall faced to the east, and the morning sun light shimmering through the silken drapes must have been an exquisite sight. But, at night, the drapes had the sinister appearance of ghostly shades lined up like dead comrades awaiting his arrival. Seven politicians were seated facing him in the middle of the room arranged in a semicircle. Their rosewood chairs were large and solid, but the lines were still Chinese. The yellow fabric of the chair cushions matched the color and grain of the stone pillars. Kung could tell from the look on their faces that six of the men wanted him dead . . . immediately.

*"I despise politicians. They have no sense of loyalty to anything other than their own survival. How has China come to the point where we are ruled by such as these?"* Kung asked himself, while walking up to the entrance of the semicircle of chairs, snapping to attention, and bowing.

"Gentleman, I am General . . ." Kung began.

"Traitor! We know who the hell you are!" Liu yelled, while jumping to his feet and pointing at General Kung.

"Comrades, we are here to have an objective discussion with this man. If you are no longer able to control your emotions, you may leave this room," the General Secretary said.

Every politician knew that if he left the room he was resigning from his position in the PSC, and from the Communist Party itself.

The room grew silent, but Kung could not fail to see the glares of distrust.

*"They feel threatened by me, and they are correct. I am a threat to their very existence,"* Kung thought, while carefully maintaining a neutral face.

"Gentlemen . . . our beloved Chairman Mao Zedong is oft quoted by politicians, intellectuals, and students when they wish to curry political favor. If he was here, he would have most of you shot," Kung said, staring at each politician in turn, including the General Secretary.

"How dare you evoke . . ." Liu Zhengsheng, said while rising to his feet.

"Be quiet and listen for five minutes," the General Secretary ordered.

Kung began again.

"The mausoleum of the Great Helmsman is less than half a mile from here. I'm surprised that the crystal glass that covers him hasn't shattered from the rage that must seep from his remains," Kung said, while walking into the central core of China's ruling political class.

"Many of you are considered princelings, as if you were responsible for the founding of this great nation. You are nothing more than caretakers, and poor ones at that," Kung said, as he folded his hands behind his back.

"You dare to sneer at the Americans, when all you have become are money grubbing Americans standing under a different flag. The spirit of the revolution means nothing to you now. Look at you, preening in your 50,000¥ suits made in London, wearing Rolex watches made of gold and platinum. Some of you consider Mao a pariah. You find his corpse a constant reminder of China's bloody rise to independence, a past that you now find distasteful. The foolish Americans now purge statues of the losing side of their civil war, not understanding that by denying their past they may be condemning themselves to repeat it. We had two civil wars to gain our freedom from the West and from ourselves. Millions died in those wars. Millions more died during the Great Leap Forward and the Cultural Revolution. But what Mao accomplished in one lifetime was nothing short of divine. He took a loosely knit nation of peasants, merchants and warlords, and united them, removed the yoke of imperialism, and forged what will become the most powerful nation ever seen on this planet. Guo Quishan, you would have us kowtow to the Americans because you are afraid of their power," Kung said, while turning, and pointing directly at Guo Quishan, number 2 man in the PSC.

"Your specialty is economic matters, and yet you fail to see how vulnerable the Americans are. Their society is in a state of barely contained chaos. They are almost ready to start their own second civil war, yet you fear them. The eagle still has claws, but he has been placed into a cage of my making," Kung said, as he pivoted once again.

"Yu Yunshan, the expert on other countries and cultures. How would the Americans react, not to a threat, but to the rumor of Chinese nuclear weapons placed all across their country?" Kung asked, as he pointed at number 4.

Yu sat erect, looking around at his peers, afraid to give an opinion in such a volatile setting. He sensed that China's future would be determined in the next 10 minutes. He was nicknamed "the turtle" by his peers. He survived and prospered by staying neutral until the winning side in a debate had emerged.

"That is a difficult question. I would have to think about it," Yu said, and flinched at the sneers and sighs that he received at his indecision.

"Yunshan, we seven lead this country. That means that we have to make critical decisions. Now is not the time for hesitation. The General asked you a question. Give him your best answer," the General Secretary said.

"We could never make such an announcement. It would be the equivalent of a declaration of war. Americans can be like a family of lunatics, but when threatened or attacked by outsiders, they unite and fight fiercely, at least for a while. This would have to be subtle . . . a whisper in just the right ear. It would have to be in Europe . . . perhaps a reporter at some British tabloid. The article would be scoffed at, but it would be heard. Websites would then pick it up. It would become like a malignant tumor, eating at their psyche," Yu said, his mind whirling down paths of various possibilities.

"But how would the American government react? What about the media? What about their financial markets?" asked Wang Keqiang, No. 6, the Secretary of the Central Disciplinary Inspection Commission.

"As the rumor spread it would eventually land on the desks of the major networks. They don't like this President, but they would probably see the danger in spreading such a story. They would restrain themselves, for a while, until one of them broke ranks. Then it would flood across America like a great wave. The government would be indecisive. The political parties would point fingers at each other. This would panic the financial markets. At a minimum it would start a global recession, possibly a depression. Millions of Americans would have their savings wiped out. Holders of America's great debt would start demanding payment. They would want a currency other than the dollar. Foreign investors would pull out of the country, and turn to precious metals or other tangible assets. The people . . . the American people, would be driven into a rage. They are very unhappy with the indecisiveness of their politicians already. Their population is so heavily armed that they might turn on each other and the government. Their large cities . . . New York, Detroit, Atlanta, Los Angeles, and others, all would turn into battlegrounds. There would be a hundred Beirut's all across the country. The government wouldn't be able to control it unless they turned the military on their own people. If that happened . . . the United States of America would disappear," Yu said, as he shuddered at his own conclusions.

Kung smiled as silence reigned in the room. His spark had now turned into a smoldering fire. There was much smoke, but as yet, there was no real heat, but that would come. As he glanced from face to face he still saw hesitation and disbelief, but the hatred had disappeared. His plan was now under serious consideration.

At a nod from the General Secretary, General Kung began again; this time in a more conciliatory tone.

"Gentlemen, as I told my fellow officers in the Central Military Commission, we are only following the guidance of the two most famous and glorious military leaders in Chinese history: Sun Tzu and Mao Zedong. Sun Tzu said, 'The skillful leader subdues the enemy's troops without any fighting; he captures their cities without laying siege to them; he overthrows their kingdom without lengthy operations in the field. With his forces intact he will dispute the mastery of the Empire, and thus, without losing a man, his triumph will be complete. This is the method of attacking by stratagem.' It was 2500 years ago and his brilliance still shines like a polished steel blade," Kung said, while smiling and nodding at his audience.

"*Three, perhaps four are prone to say yes, but I want them all to agree,*" Kung thought, while pausing for effect.

"The Great Helmsman was flawed, as are all humans, but his flaws were insignificant compared to his brilliance and determination. The Great Chairman said, 'Classes struggle, some classes triumph, others are eliminated. Such is history; such is the history of civilization for thousands of years.' Gentlemen, it is time for the Imperialists to disappear into the pages of history. When they fall apart, like the Soviet Union, there will be chaos across the globe. China will stand alone as the bulwark between civilization and another Dark Age. The United Nations will be desperate for a solution to wide spread turmoil in the land formerly known as the United States of America. After a time, China will express its willingness to send a force suitable to protect the people of North America. We will restore stability and peace. Eventually the People's Republic of North America will emerge. After that . . . China will become . . . truly, for the first time in our long and noble history . . . the Center Country. China will be the center of the first global empire," Kung said, while slowly walking back to his position in front of the semicircle.

"As Yu Yunshan has said, it will have to be initiated with subtlety. When the boulder is finely balanced, it will only take the gentle touch of one chop stick to send it rolling down the hill. Once this starts there will be no stopping it," General Kung said, and bowed in the direction of the General Secretary.

"Remember, gentlemen, the intention of these devices is not to start the Third World War. The intention is to force the Americans out of our sphere of influence: the Pacific and all of Asia. If they are stubborn, then we have the option of releasing the information of their existence to destabilize the American economy. As China continues to expand into Asia, Africa and South America, we don't want American interference. We would only release the information if the Americans become . . . intransigent," the General Secretary said, as he nodded to General Kung.

General Kung snapped to attention, bowed to the assembled leaders, and left the room.

"General Secretary, what are you getting us into? I am intrigued and terrified all at the same time. This man despises us. You can see it in his eyes," Guo Quishan said, while sighing and shaking his head.

"I started out wanting him dead. Now I wonder if we won't wind up placing a statue of him outside with all the other heroes of the people," Wang Keqiang said.

"Zhang Dejiang, you are 7 amongst us, but you still have the right to express your opinion. What are your thoughts?" the General Secretary asked.

"General Secretary, we have made so much progress. As a nation we are rich and strong. Our people are healthier than they have ever been. We are expanding across Asia and the globe. Our military will equal the US in less than 20 years. Everything they develop we procure, and reproduce, without all the R&D cost. They are falling apart before our eyes. Why should we take this risk?" Yu Yunshan asked.

"Yu Yunshan, eventually we will come to the point where confrontation with the Americans will be inevitable. I don't believe they will tear themselves apart despite their internal political differences. They always seem to find one leader who will rise from the masses, and lead them from the brink of disaster. Their system spurs greed, but it also spurs enormous creativity. While we have been able to procure many of their technological secrets, there are many more that we have failed to find. The Americans bury their greatest secrets behind layers of secrecy so deep, that sometimes I wonder if they don't allow us to find old secrets just to protect the ones that really matter to them," the General Secretary replied.

"Gentlemen, as I said before, I can't tell you how to vote. All I have to say is this: we have been presented with an opportunity to resolve a long standing problem. I believe this can be resolved in our favor by presenting the facts to the American President discretely. I will request that he remove his bases and forces from the Western Pacific. This would include Japan, the Philippines, Australia, Malaysia, South Korea and the Indian Ocean. Their navy would be prohibited from sailing past the end of the Hawaiian Island chain. This would leave their presence in the Middle East and Afghanistan, Africa and South America. Those are problems for another time. This would be our initial position. If they agree, we would, after enough time had passed for them to remove all their forces from the agreed locations, provide all the locations of the devices within the continental United States," the General Secretary said.

"And if the President resists?" Guo Quishan asked.

"Then we present them with the 'Slow Leak of Information' plan. I would give him 48 hours to think it over. To say no under these circumstances would be suicidal. The Americans are not suicidal by nature. They would retract their forces and plan for the future. In the mean time we will have control of all Asia and the western Pacific. Over time, in another generation, we will turn the United States into another impotent Europe," the General Secretary said.

"Now, we have to vote. I would prefer a unanimous decision, but a mere majority will do," Li Xibin, leader of the People's Republic of China said, as he raised his right hand.

"Come, gentlemen, it is getting late, and my wife will be waiting for my return," Li said, his hand still in the air.

The other six leaders all glanced at each other as one hand after another was raised until only two remained undecided.

"I still think this is a mistake," Guo Quishan said, while slowly raising his right hand.

"I beg the forgiveness of all of you, but I can't go along with this. It is a grave mistake that we will all come to regret," said number 7, Zhang Dejiang, as he stood, bowed to the General Secretary, and left the room.

"Excellent, 6 is a luckier number than 7," said Zhang Gaoli, as he stood and began shaking the hands of the remaining six members of the PSC.

# Chapter 48

"Fatigue is the best pillow."

Benjamin Franklin

Alexandria, Virginia, USA
Vola's Dockside Bar & Grill
101 North Union Street
March 25, 2017, 0930 hours EST


Amanda sat at the bar inside Vola's Dockside Bar & Grill staring at her cup. She needed the caffeine, but her stomach was getting sour from too much coffee, too little food, and no sleep. When the adrenalin rush of the shootout had worn off, the only thing she wanted to do was go home and take a nap. Now, after being up for almost thirty hours, caffeine was the only option.

"Here, I made us sandwiches in the back. I think we both need something to eat. With the whole downtown area evacuated, I figured it was 'help yourself'," Janet Davidson said, while sitting on the bar stool beside Amanda.

"Have they started cutting their way inside yet?" Amanda asked, while pushing the coffee aside, and picking up the ham and cheese sandwich.

"EOD finally got set up when they got a call from some expert on the West Coast. The quote I heard from the EOD team lead was, 'Don't touch a fucking thing,'" Janet said, while adding a sugar substitute to her hot tea.

"Guy sounds a little blunt," Amanda said, while chewing her first bite.

"It was a woman . . . supposed to be the US expert on disarming nuclear devices," Janet said.

"Now that sounds like a fun job," Amanda said, and then picked up her cell phone.

"I already checked. Major Thompson's out of surgery. I called while I was waiting for the water to boil. They had to do reconstructive surgery on his arm, and had to dig some bullet fragments out of his chest, but it looks like he'll be fine," Janet said, while blowing on her mug of tea.

"How about our mystery man, the Chinese agent?" Amanda asked.

"Not so good . . . the .45 is an old school weapon. It was designed to knock a man down with one shot. Thompson hit him twice, and from what the police told me, you talked the good Major out of putting a bullet between the agent's eyes. You saved two lives with that one. The police would have dropped the Major like a stone," Janet said, while waiting for her sandwich to cool off.

"We had to notify the Chinese Embassy about the shooting. They were very upset about a citizen being shot until they were told he was the suspect in several murders. The last I heard he was still in surgery. They were trying to save his left leg. The femur was shattered and the femoral artery was nicked in several places. The chest wound wasn't much better, shattered rib, punctured lung. They had two surgical teams working on him at the same time. I was told the odds are 60/40 that he won't make it," Janet said, then took a bite out of her sandwich.

"So what do we do now? The media will have this place covered like it was election night," Amanda asked.

"As far as they know, this is just a crime scene. Local PD told them about the connection to the hospital shootings. One other tidbit, we're to expect a nuclear weapons expert on scene sometime tonight. He's being flown in from Israel," Janet said.

"Israel? We don't have someone capable of handling this? What about the woman on the West Coast?" Amanda asked.

"It seems she's a little busy. She's got two devices of her own to disarm. I guess people who specialize in this are pretty rare. Our orders are to maintain the cover of a murder investigation until the Israeli gets here," Janet said, between mouthfuls of sandwich.

"One thing the Corps taught me was to take advantage of down time. When you get into a combat situation, eating, and especially sleeping, become precious commodities. Why don't you go home, get cleaned up, and get some rest. Just be back here by 1800," Janet said, while taking the last bite of her sandwich.

"I'm okay. I need to get my laptop and start updating some files. One of these days we're going to have to give a formal brief to the Director," Amanda said, while looking around for her satchel.

"First of all, with Caleb's death, I'm the acting Director of the Mission Center. Second, when we give the briefing, it will likely be to more than just the Director of the CIA. Third, go home! That's an order," Janet said.

"Have we figured out what happened? How did this guy wind up at the Director's house? Could they have known each other?" Amanda asked, as she slid off the stool.

"Unknown, but it doesn't look good. Evidently, our guy was trying to impersonate Caleb, and get out of the country. We also found out that Caleb had plane reservations for Bogata, and he had cleaned out his bank account. The whole business about having the flu was a lie. Some of our analysts think he was in bed with the Chinese, but the evidence isn't conclusive . . . yet. God, I hope that's not true. I worked with the man for over ten years, and I didn't see it," Janet said, while sighing and sipping on her tea.

"Caleb was found tied to a bed in the basement and shot in the head. Two dead agents, a dead Director, even a dead dog; everywhere this guy goes he leaves behind bodies. Arlington PD is even trying to link two dead Asians found in an apartment to our guy. We aren't going to be able to maintain this cover for much longer," Janet said, as Amanda loaded up her satchel and slung it over her shoulder.

"Are you sure you want me to leave?" Amanda asked.

"Do I have to repeat a direct order to you, Agent Langford?" Janet asked.

No . . . Director Davidson. I'll be back by 1800," Amanda said, smiling as she headed for the exit.

"*I almost let the ma'am slip out*," Amanda thought, as she stepped into the chill morning air and smiled again.

Chapter 49

"Violence, even well intentioned, always rebounds upon oneself."

Lao Tzu

Beijing, China
22 Base Headquarters
100 meters below the Beijing Botanical Gardens
March 26, 2017, 0710 hours CT

"Come, Peng, we should be celebrating. After all these years we have won. The Party has accepted our grand plan. The General Secretary is ready to confront the American President, and tell him that Asia belongs to us. They will have to remove their influence from the entire western Pacific, and all without firing a shot," General Kung said, while pacing across his office.

"I do not claim to know or understand the Americans, but I remember a quote from one of their movies that I saw with you several years ago: 'It ain't over 'til it's over.' How can you be so sure that the Americans will just bow to China, and walk away?" Colonel Peng asked.

"Because, Peng, I know the Americans, and I know Sun Tzu. We have them trapped in a box valley with no exit. We have archers in the hills that surround them. Our invincible forces sit behind an impenetrable wall that crosses the mouth of the valley. We are a magnanimous people. We will allow them to live as long as they leave our territory and swear to never return. The end game is certain. Within a few hours from now the General Secretary will call the American President, and tell him what he is going to do. The American President will balk, and then be informed that we will destabilize his country, and wreck his economy, with one article, on one online site. He will laugh and hang up the phone. When his advisors tell him the truth of the matter, he will call back and concede defeat. After all these years the game we have played with the Americans will be over, and we will have won," Kung said, while smiling and slapping his hands together.

"After the call is complete the General Secretary is having a celebration at his residence at Zhongnanhai. The members of the Central Military Commission and the Politburo Standing Committee will be there. Peng, you have been at my side through all of this. How would you like to attend such a feast? It would be the greatest honor," General Kung asked.

"As you say, General, after all these years it will be over. It has been your plan. All of the honor should go to you. I would rather spend the evening in contemplation at my home," Colonel Peng said, as he stood, bowed deeply to General Kung, and left the room.

Chapter 50

"I believe it is universally understood and acknowledged that
all men will ever act correctly, unless they have a motive to do
otherwise."

Abraham Lincoln

Washington, DC, USA
The White House
The Situation Room
March 25, 2017, 2115 hours EST

"Why now on such short notice? Why all of a sudden, right out
of the blue? What the hell does he want to talk about?" the President
of the United States of America asked the assembled group of advisors
sitting in front him.

Konrad Miller sat at the head of a large mahogany table that
almost filled the Situation Room located below the West Wing of the
White House.

"Mr. President, everyone in this room knows about the ongoing
situation with the nuclear devices found on the West Coast, and the
suspected device found in Alexandria. Subtle, mid-level inquiries by
the State Department, directed at their counterparts in China, have
gone nowhere. We have detected unusual movement of key
individuals within the Chinese military and government; specifically,
high level members of the Central Military Commission and the
Politburo Standing Committee. They meet routinely, but it's usually on
a predictable schedule. Both groups have been gathered together for
meetings in Beijing, first the CMC, and the following day, the PSC.
Both the CIA and NSA agree that this is highly unusual," Clarisse
Beaumont, National Security Advisor, said.

The room grew silent as the President leaned back in his chair,
crossed his hands behind his head, and stared at the ceiling, as was his
habit while thinking.

"Ladies and gentlemen, I think we've been snookered. While we have played the game of globalization and inclusion with the Chinese, they have been reading Plato, specifically the Iliad. If I was a betting man, and I occasionally am, I would bet that this conversation will consist of a subtlety phrased ultimatum. They think they have us between a rock and a hard place," the President said.

"Mr. President, they do have us between a rock and a hard place. Our problem is, what do they hope to accomplish? If they set off how many ever nukes they have on our soil, our ballistic submarines would respond in kind. We'd both lose," the Secretary of Defense said.

"I agree Aaron, that wouldn't make any sense. That's what I meant by 'subtle'. They're up to something else, and we have . . ." the President said, while pausing to look at the clock on the wall.

". . .12 minutes to figure this out. What are they up to? Assuming they aren't suicidal, what do they want?" the President asked.

"Mr. President, the CIA has been working on a lead related to this situation for months. We have a theory that there is a rogue element within the Chinese military that has developed this plot over the past few decades. I have the acting Director of the Mission Center for Weapons and Counterproliferation, Janet Davidson, and an agent of hers, Amanda Langford, who have vital information, reference this situation," Director Perez said, while gesturing to the tall woman who sat beside him, and the petite young woman who sat beside her.

"Well, ladies, you've got 11 minutes until my teleconference with General Secretary Li begins," the President said, while leaning on the table and staring at the two women.

"Mr. President, these are primarily Ms. Langford's findings, so for the sake of brevity, you'll be hearing from her," Janet said, and nodded to Amanda.

"Mr. President, I had a one hour presentation prepared, but I'll cut to the critical points," Amanda said, as a chart of the People's Liberation Army Command Structure appeared on the various wall monitors around the briefing room.

"The Chinese have very strict control of their nuclear devices, just as we do. Their missile warheads and other devices are stored deep below the Quinling Mountain Range about a 100 miles west of Xian. They are controlled by an organization known as 22 Base. This organization has had the same leader since 1990, Lieutenant General Kung Yusheng. He is the nephew of General Fan Shibo, one of two Vice Chairmen of the Central Military Commission. In my opinion, we are looking at the rogue actions of Lieutenant General Kung. The CIA and the NSA both have extensive data bases on all personnel in the command structure of the PLA and the PRC government. General Kung has extensive holdings in multiple companies dealing with transportation and export of goods to the United States. I believe that he has developed an extensive infrastructure of agents and caretakers within the United States whose mission is to import and store nuclear weapons within the continental United States," Amanda said, as Janet leaned over and whispered 'six minutes'.

"Mr. President, there are many other links that connect General Kung to this plot. The latest is the Chinese Special Forces agent that has been responsible for several murders in the local area, and for escorting the Alexandria device from Shanghai to here. He has been identified as First Lieutenant Gong Aiguo of the Siberian Tigers Special Forces unit. He is the grandson of Colonel Peng Zihao, General Kung's adjutant. For the sake of brevity I'll now skip to the conclusion. General Kung has held a series of meetings with his superiors over the last week, starting with his commanding officer, and culminating with the Politburo Standing Committee, the seven men who control the People's Republic of China. Your scheduled meeting with General Secretary Li Xibin will be for one of two purposes: One, he will apologize deeply for the insertion of nuclear weapons within the United States, or two, he will demand the removal of American influence from all of Asia," Amanda said, pausing when several voices around the table began talking at once.

"Quiet! Let the young lady finish," the President said, then nodded at Amanda to continue.

"This isn't a declaration of war. They would never set off these devices. They know that we would destroy China. They are going to use these devices as leverage to force us to cooperate with their geopolitical objectives. Exactly how they're going to do this or what the threat will be . . . I don't know," Amanda said, as she looked the President in the eyes as if to apologize for the lack of a definite answer.

"Two minutes, Mr. President, you need to move to the secure teleconference room," an aide standing behind the President whispered.

"Thank you, Ms. Langford. Well . . . it seems we'll know what their plan is within the next few minutes. This conversation will be private between me and General Secretary Li, but it will be recorded. After we're through talking, we'll meet back here, review the conversation, and discuss our options," the President said, while standing and walking toward an adjacent communications room.

.   .   .   .

Beijing, China
The Great Hall of the People
Beijing Hall
March 26, 2017 0929 hours CT

"It is time, General Secretary. The American president in online," the aide said, while bowing deeply.

General Secretary Li Xibin sat comfortably in the upholstered yellow chair. Behind him in an arc were seated 6 of the members of the Politburo Standing Committee. Number 7, Zhang Dejiang, was under house arrest for his no vote during the previous day's meeting. Behind the members of the PSC sat the 10 senior PLA officers of the Central Military Commission. General Secretary Li had decided that the golden walls and blood red carpet of the Beijing Hall had been the perfect backdrop for the meeting.

General Kung had been allowed to attend the meeting, but off screen, seated along a side wall. As he watched the aide depart, Kung checked his pocket watch.

He lingered over the outer cover, his finger tip lightly tracing the engraving, while he read, "Babe Ruth . . . Yankees . . . World's Champions 1923. Soon your entire country will be a collectible."

He checked the time . . . 0930.

The face and upper torso of the American President appeared on the 70-inch monitor that had been set up in the room. He was alone, and seemed to be in a non-descript office. The glass wall behind him gave a momentary glance of another room filled with suited and uniformed men and women, before the glass wall turned an opaque white.

"General Secretary Li, I am always ready to exchange views with you. Precisely what do you wish to discuss tonight?" the President asked.

"*Interesting, he has isolated himself from his supporters, as if he didn't want them to hear this conversation first hand,*" General Secretary Li thought.

"Mister President, a pleasure as always. I apologize for the late time of this meeting, but we have important matters to discuss. I will get right to the point. I believe the time has come for the United States to remove its military presence from the western Pacific. After all, World War II is long past, and the nations of Asia no longer require your presence in the area to ensure their peace and tranquility," General Secretary Li said, in a calm voice as he stared at the American President.

"*All his toadies draped around him. This meeting is staged Chinese theater, a public demonstration of his power. That young lady was right. But what is the threat?*" the President thought, as he studied the setting and the individuals behind the General Secretary.

The President said nothing for a moment, and then replied, "General Secretary Li, why would the United States withdraw from international waters, and nations that have requested our assistance in maintaining the stability of the region and the security of their nations? I have received no such request from any nation in the region."

"Mr. President, it has come to my attention that you have recently had some . . . unusual occurrences within your country. Occurrences that, if they became known nationally and internationally, would create a sense of . . . discomfort in the global community. Pardon, my English is lacking . . . would create a loss of faith . . . in the stability of the United States. Such a loss of faith would be truly unfortunate. I fear that your financial markets would react in a panicked manner. Following that, your citizens would express their displeasure. That could lead to destabilization. Nuclear powers, such as ourselves, and others, can't allow such instability. The international community might feel the need to . . . intervene . . . in such a case, to restore order," the General Secretary said, his voice as hard as stone.

"General Secretary Li, this almost sounds like a declaration of war. Is that where the People's Republic of China wishes to head?" the

President asked, upping the ante, and stalling for time while he thought.

*"It's the bombs . . . he'll leak information about their presence while denying any responsibility. He's right, the news will destabilize the markets, and they're already overextended. If people think they're sitting near nuclear bombs ready to explode, there will be panic. This conversation needs to end, and I need some time,"* the President thought.

"General Secretary Li, I truly regret that relations between the United States and the People's Republic of China have deteriorated to this point. You are, in effect, trying to blackmail the United States," the President said.

"Mr. President, in no way am I trying to blackmail your country. I am only informing you that certain information may be leaked within 48 hours if the United States does not announce a decision to withdraw from the western Pacific, and close all of its military bases in Asia. This . . . advice . . . is intended to benefit the US, and allow it to preserve its financial and territorial stability. China cherishes its friendly relations with the world's only other superpower. We only wish global security and prosperity for all. If the unfortunate happens, and I do not hear from you within the next 48 hours, then I wish you well in your endeavors to maintain stability within your country," General Secretary Li said.

"General Secretary Li, you've given me a lot to consider. You will hear from me in less than 48 hours. I hope you have a pleasant day," the President said, and cut the connection.

When the screen went blank, General Secretary Li stood, and turned to face the power structure of the People's Republic of China.

"Well, Comrades, what do you think?" he asked, as a broad smile crossed his face.

One after the other they stood and applauded.

.   .   .   .

Washington, DC, USA
The White House
The Situation Room
March 25, 2017, 2200 hours EST

The Situation Room was silent after the second playing of the conversation between the President of the United States and the General Secretary of the PRC.

"Well, ladies . . . gentlemen, let's hear it," the President said.

"It's outrageous. First the bastards sneak nuclear weapons onto our soil over a couple of decades, and during multiple administrations, I might add, and then they threaten to tell the world that America is no longer a stable place," Vice President Matt Parker said.

"Actually, it's supremely clever. They don't attack us. They don't even threaten to attack us. He never admitted to placing the weapons on our soil, or even saying they knew about the weapons. If you broadcast that tape on CNN, FOX, and every other network on the planet, you couldn't prove a damn thing. But between the lines, we know exactly what they're saying. Give us what we want or we'll release this information, then sit back and watch your country self-destruct," Secretary of State Raymond Taggert said.

"Sam, what do you think? If they leaked information to the press that there were nuclear weapons stashed all across the country, how bad would it be?" President Tremont asked Sam Murkowski, the Secretary of the Treasury.

"It would 1929 on steroids. The only reason that our markets have kept increasing in value is our stability. As the rest of the world slowly slides into anarchy, the US looks better and better. The world feels like they can invest in America and their money will be safe. The Chinese must think they could ride this out, close their markets for a time, and emerge the winners after the dust has settled. As much as I hate to admit it, they might be right. They would become the point of stability on the globe, despite their restrictive policies and dictatorial form of government," Sam said.

"John, any ideas on how to respond to this, or can we respond militarily at all?" the President asked John Masters, the Secretary of Defense.

"We can't attack them conventionally or with nuclear weapons. They could just trigger these devices, where ever the hell they are, and we have an old fashioned MAD situation. There is one other option though . . ." John said, as he stared at Miller Perez, Director of the CIA.

"Secretary Masters, I know what you're talking about, but that program is a very, very compartmentalized Special Access Program. The President doesn't even know about this. Sorry, Mr. President, it's a very closed, very need-to-know program. I would not advise talking about it, even in this group," the CIA Director said.

"Well Miller, then why don't the three of us just go somewhere private for a few minutes, and have a little talk. I'd like to know what you boys have been hiding from your boss. The rest of you take a short break, we'll be back soon," the President said, and stared at the Director of the Situation Room.

"This way Mr. President, gentleman," Lieutenant Colonel Tiana Xavier said, as she led the three men to a small, secluded, briefing room down the hall from the main briefing room.

"Lieutenant Colonel Xavier, if this room has any audio or video recording devices, they have to be secured before we start this briefing. Is that understood?" the CIA Director ordered.

After the President nodded his approval, she said, "Give me five minutes, Director Perez. I'll secure the comms and data recorders myself, and guard them until you gentlemen are done."

The three men sat quietly in the room, each lost in their own thoughts, when the Assistant Director of the Situation Room appeared at the door.

"Mr. President, the room is secure. Lieutenant Colonel Xavier is guarding the circuits and I'll be guarding her," the Major said.

"Thank you, Major. We'll let you know when we're finished," the President said, while standing up and closing the door.

"Okay, gentlemen, you've got your damn privacy. This better be good," the President said, as he sat back down.

Chapter 51

"If you want something said, ask a man; if you want something
done, ask a woman."

Margaret Thatcher

Port Orchard, Washington, USA
Golden Grill on the Bay
1014 Bay Street
March 25, 2017, 1900 hours PST

"All right guys, let's see your plan for disarming this thing,"
Kate said, as she opened the written plan presented by Nathan and
Alan.

"Okay, you took my suggestion, and treated this like one
device rather than three. I like that. Now, let's see what you missed,"
Kate said, as she began studying the electrical plans for the bypass.

"Hmm . . . one question, what if the devices are different
voltages?" Kate asked, while looking at both of her DHS trainees.

"Shit! We didn't think about that. Why would you build series
devices with different voltage requirements?" Nathan asked.

Kate didn't respond. She just waited, and looked at both of
them.

"Because that's what they would expect us to think. I would
assume that the voltages would all be the same in a series setup," Alan
said, as he turned his head and stared at Nathan.

"We would have to place a voltage regulator in line to maintain
the same voltage. Otherwise it would trigger a signal, or . . ." Nathan
said.

"Detonate the device," Kate said, and gave both of her trainees
a thumbs up.

"So, assuming that neither one of you wishes to be atomized on
this job, I would suggest that you come up with an in-line voltage

regulator to defeat the anti-tampering devices," Kate said, as she stood up, and walked out of the building and into the cool night air.

"Once they complete that, I'll review the plan one more time. We'll get some sleep, and start removing the boosted fission primary tomorrow morning. We should be finished by noon," Kate said, when her cell phone start to buzz.

"Ahh, my favorite National Security Advisor. Yes, Clarisse, what can I do for you?" Kate asked.

"First, you can hurry the hell up and get here. The good Doctor has arrived, and he is a royal pain in the ass. Second, using the technique provided by our helpful citizens from San Francisco, we found another device near the Bangor Trident Base, so it looks like I have to handle the good doctor without your help," Clarisse said, and laughed.

"We'll have this device safe by noon our time. Send me the address of the new one and we'll start moving up there tonight," Kate said.

"How are you holding up, Kate? This may go on for a while," Clarisse asked.

"It's getting rough. I always thought that we had more than enough people and equipment to handle anything, but I was wrong. We're starting to have maintenance issues with some of our more delicate instruments. I'm also starting to see fatigue mistakes, and tempers are getting a little short," Kate said.

"Kate, the President just had a teleconference with the Secretary General of the PRC. It didn't go well. There were other meetings with a few members of the cabinet after that, but I wasn't privy to the content. The only way we can defend ourselves is to find and disarm as many of these devices as quickly as we possibly can. If we can find them, your people have to disarm them. It's the only chance we've got," Clarisse said.

"Wow . . . the situation is that bad?" Kate asked.

"Yeah, it's that bad. Just keep going as long as you can. When I hear anything else, I'll let you know. Sorry, Kate, but that's the best I've got," Clarisse said.

Kate terminated the call, and sat down at a table her crew had set up outside the work area in the open air. She looked at her hands as they began to shake.

"David, I'm beginning to understand why you got out of this business," Kate said, as a chill breeze blew in off the bay.

Chapter 52

"People ask the difference between a leader and a boss. The
leader leads, and the boss drives."

Theodore Roosevelt

Alexandria, Virginia, USA
The Torpedo Factory Art Center Plaza
105 North Union Street
March 25, 2017, 2130 hours EST

"Why isn't the equipment here? I've been ready to start for over
an hour," Dr. David Barza asked, while pacing beneath the elevated
mass of the diesel engine.

"Doc, the team from South Carolina should be here in less than
an hour. Based on the guidance I got from their boss on the West
Coast, they should be ready to start work within an hour after arrival,"
said Colonel Malcomb Douglas, commanding officer of the 184th
Ordinance Battalion EOD Response Team.

He stood watching technicians complete the elevated work
surface beneath the diesel, install additional lighting, and electrical
connections requested by Dr. Barza.

"Colonel, I have two PhDs: one in Physics and a second in
Mechanical Engineering, so I'm not some quack 'Doc' from 'littletown
USA'. You will address me as Doctor or Doctor Barza. Is that
understood?" Dr. Barza said.

"Whatever you want . . . Doctor Barza. Whatever you want,"
Colonel Douglas said, with a smile.

"Good, and I'm going to need some relaxing music, and I don't
mean some American Boom Box. I work better with music. It helps
me think, and I don't want digital, vinyl only, the classics if you
please: Handel, Beethoven, Pachelbel . . . for starters. I'll need that set
up before we start actual work," Dr. Barza said.

"Like I said . . . Doctor Barza, whatever you want," Colonel Douglas said, while he turned, and walked out of the huge scaffold tent that had been erected around the diesel engine.

"What a fucking prick!" said Captain Barry Watkins, second in command of the 20-soldier EOD response team.

"Can that shit, Captain, unless you know how to disarm a booby-trapped hydrogen bomb. Find out which one of your boys or girls is an audiophile. Every unit I've ever been in has at least one. You heard what the man wants. Make it happen, and get it set up within the next two hours. One other thing, remind your people that we're here as civilians, not as soldiers from Fort Campbell, Kentucky. So no more saluting, understood?" Colonel Douglas said.

"Understood, Mr. Douglas," Captain Watkins said, while grinning at Colonel Douglas.


David Barza stood beneath the diesel engine and lowered himself onto the cold metal floor of the new platform. After removing his tablet from his backpack, he opened the files that Kate had sent him on all the nuclear devices found in the United States so far. The constant tremor in his hands made accessing files increasingly difficult.

"Three fission devices and an old Teller-Ulam fusion weapon . . . someone is using left overs. This stuff is all repurposed scrap. This whole thing strikes me as unsanctioned or they would have more advanced weapon designs. The anti-tampering and control electronics are more clever. That's where they spent their effort," Dr. Barza said, as he looked up at the welded underside of the huge diesel engine.

"They would have had to remove the crankshaft and crankcase, at a minimum. That would leave enough room in and above the oil pan to insert a weapon of substantial size. They probably had to weld in internal supports for the weight. What yield weapon would they want here, right beside the capitol of the United States? I'll bet it's massive. They haven't told me anything. Are these terrorists or a foreign government? I'll know who made it when I get a look inside," Dr. Barza said, as he lay on his back, and studied the underside of the diesel.

"You can see the new weld lines. They unbolted the oil pan, crawled in and took out all the components they needed for room. Then they inserted the device, and welded the oil pan back on so it couldn't be easily removed. Then they repainted everything to cover their modifications. Kate said the other thermonuclear device had a lattice installed inside the storage crate to prevent tampering. I can't see how they would have done that here. So what did they do, or . . . did they do nothing. Is the diesel enough by itself? An art object . . . hidden out in the open . . . brilliant. Whoever is behind this is laughing at America. They're laughing at me, and I find that insulting," Dr. Barza said, while imagining how he would have inserted the device into the shell of the machine above his head.

"I need an inspection port, actually multiple ports," Dr. Barza said, as he struggled back to his feet.

"Damn disease . . . I hate you Parky, I really do," he said, as he stood and rested against the scaffolding rail.

"Stress and a lack of sleep all make you stronger, Parky. I know your game, but you're not beating me," Dr. Barza said, as his balance stabilized.

"Of course, all the normal maintenance ports are welded shut. So, where do I want holes drilled?" he asked, as his cell phone began playing Beethoven's 'Night Music'.

"Ahh, dear Kate, what have you gotten me into? It's cold here, and you know how much I love cold weather," Dr. Barza said, after accepting the call.

"Well, it's cool and rainy here, and I've had 8 hours sleep in the last 4 days, so I feel your pain. So, David, how are you doing? We haven't talked in a few years," Kate said.

"Your choice, not mine, my dear, and I was doing fine until you had me kidnapped, and flown to this ice box," David replied, while cherishing the sound of her voice.

"I believe that you volunteered at the request of your good friend, the Prime Minister," Kate said, as she couldn't help but notice the mild shaking in his voice.

"More like I volunteered at gun point. Then I arrive to find no equipment, a condescending American Colonel, and the most fascinating problem I've ever faced in this line of work. Just when you think you've seen it all, somebody hides a nuke inside a diesel engine," David said, while regretting ever letting Kate escape from him.

"David, I'm in the middle of my own entanglement. A series of three anti-tampering devices set to respond to three different voltages, but I think I have it figured out," Kate said.

"You always were overconfident. The most obvious solution isn't always the correct one. It reminds me of our relationship. You always were the one for the easiest, short-term solution," David said, as he ended the connection.

"*Oh, she'll figure out the trap. She always was the smart one,*" Dr. Barza thought, while sighing, and contemplating the trap that he had accepted to resolve.

"Now where is her damn team? I'm ready to start," David said, as the sound of rain disrupted his train of thought.

"Great! No doubt the tent will leak and I'll be cold and wet," David said.

Chapter 53

"Love is a smoke made with the fume of sighs."

William Shakespeare

Port Orchard, Washington, USA
Golden Grill on the Bay
1014 Bay Street
March 25, 2017, 1940 hours PST


"He never will understand why I broke it off," Kate said, while staring at the dated image of David Barza that she had on her phone.

"David, I would have been standing in your shadow forever. I had to find out if I could make it on my own. You just couldn't see it from my point of view, and you were so angry, that I had to walk away," Kate said, as she tucked the phone into her jeans, and began thinking about what David had said.

She turned and walked back into the storage building. Nathan and Alan were huddled over a laptop making changes to the plan that she had requested.

"Before you finish that plan, check and make sure they didn't install an internal pulse width modulator in any of the anti-tampering devices. If they did, compare the signals. This may be a little more complex than I thought," Kate said, as she walked up behind the two bomb techs.

"Where'd that idea come from?" Nathan asked.

"My guardian angel," Kate said, as she patted him on the shoulder.

"The legendary Dr. Barza? Rumor has it that you two were once an item. Any truth to that?" Alan asked.

"I was one of his grad students back in the day. There were only a few of us that were able to work with him. He had very little tolerance for stupid, and to him, all grad students were stupid. In the end we became . . . friends, but that ran its course like many things in life. Professionally, I still have a great deal of respect for him," Kate said.

"You still didn't answer if you two ever . . . " Alan began.

"Shut up, Alan, and focus on the work," Nathan said, as he glanced back at Kate.

"Okay . . . pulse width modulator . . . easy enough to find, but might be tough to develop a work-around," Alan said.

Chapter 54

"You don't lead by hitting people over the head - that's assault, not leadership."

Dwight D. Eisenhower

Alexandria, Virginia, USA
The Torpedo Factory Art Center Plaza
105 North Union Street
March 25, 2017, 2200 hours EST

"So, that's all you're going to tell me? Some mysterious individual delivered this huge machine here, and it just happens to have a nuclear device inside. Agent Langford, do I look like an idiot? As soon as I see the device I'll know who made it. That will tell me who's behind this, because I have my own connections within the intelligence world. If someone had lost a large nuclear weapon, I would have heard about it. Since I haven't, that means one of the major players is behind this, and that leaves only two choices: Russia or China. So which is it?" Dr. Barza said, as Kate's team from South Carolina finished setting up equipment inside and outside the massive tent built over the diesel engine.

"I'm sorry, Dr. Barza, but that's all I'm authorized to tell you at this point. You have been brought in to neutralize whatever device is located within the diesel. What assumptions you wish to make after seeing the device are up to you," Amanda said.

"CIA, MI-5, SVR or Mossad, you're all the same. Close minded little people, puffed up with your own self-importance," Dr. Barza said, while looking down his nose at the young agent.

'We do have a restaurant available. Would you like something to eat while they continue to set up?" Amanda asked, dodging the questions and the insult.

"Is it kosher?" Dr. Barza asked.

"No, and we should have thought of that in advance," Amanda admitted, as she pulled out her cell phone.

"Don't bother, young lady. I'm only kosher when I'm in Israel or among Jews. When I'm working with gentiles I'm more flexible. It's allowed," Dr. Barza said, with a wink.

*"Oh Lord, why did I agree to babysit this man? There are so many other things I need to be doing,"* Amanda thought, while trying to control her anger.

"Well, in that case, how about a pork barbecue sandwich, Eastern North Carolina style: chopped pork basted with a vinegar and red pepper sauce?" Amanda replied, knowing that she would hear about this exchange later.

"Are you familiar with how Jews feel about eating pork?" Dr. Barza asked.

"Well, if you work with 'gentiles', I guess you'll just have to eat like one," Amanda said, while turning and walking away.

The laughter from nearby soldiers and technicians told David that he'd lost the exchange.

"So where do you want the first inspection hole drilled, Dr. Barza? Oh, and by the way, don't mind her; those people from North Carolina are strange. I'm Jackson. I'm from South Carolina. We do pork barbecue right. We use a mustard sauce," the burly technician said, with a grin on his face.

"I've marked 11 spots with a red 'X'. I placed a number under each 'X'. Drill them in numerical order. Use a ¼ inch bit, and don't leave any burrs. The first hole is on the next level to the left of the ladder. Any questions?" Dr. Barza asked, as he stared at the back of the departing CIA analyst.

"No sir! It should take me about eight minutes per hole using diamond coated bits," the technician said, as he walked off with a portable magnetic drilling machine resting on one shoulder.

"Dr. Barza, my name's Tarshon. I'm your optical specialist. This is Sholonda, IT is her game. Her sister, Casandra, is out at Best Buy looking for your tunes and equipment," Tarshon said, while extending his hand.

"Do any of you have last names?" Dr. Barza asked.

"We're family, Dr. Barza. Black, White, Latino, Asian, whatever. We live or die as family. Family don't use last names when they're together. Some people in this country try to split us all up, like you're not supposed to hang with people that aren't the same color as you. Kate hired each one of us, and she won't put up with that kind of crap. So all you're going to hear from our team is first names . . . like family," Tarshon said.

"That . . . big man . . . he'll be drilling a series of ¼ inch inspection holes. I'll need optical equipment that will fit through to perform my visual inspection of the device . . . and I'll need to record everything that I see. Multi-spectrum would be a bonus," Dr. Barza said, not quite sure how to take these Americans.

"No problem, the equipment is portable. We'll be able to go with you from place to place. I'll set up by Hole No. 1 after Bubba gets through drilling the hole," Tarshon said.

"Bubba?" Dr. Barza asked.

"Oh, I mean, Jackson. We call him Bubba because he's a big country boy from South Carolina. And just because he grins a lot, don't make the mistake of thinking that Jackson is stupid. He spent eight years in the Navy and came out as a Master Chief Equipmentman. Then he went to Georgia Tech and got a degree in Mechanical Engineering. He grins a lot because he's friendly. That's just the way he is. Not a mean bone in his body, unless you piss him off. He's also just about the strongest human I've ever met. That drill he was carrying weighs over 80 pounds. He carries it like it was a shovel. He's here because he likes working with his hands, and Kate pays really, really well," Tarshon said.

"Thank you, Tarshon. I've always thought that Americans were different . . . like a litter of puppies, some black, some white, some tan or a mix of everything, but all from the same litter . . . all Americans," Dr. Barza said.

"Well, let me go get ready, Dr. Barza. We should be rolling in a few minutes," Tarshon said.

. . . .

Diesel Engine Inspection Port No. 1
March 25, 2017, 2330 hours EST

The sounds of Handel's Water Music, Suite No. 1, in F major, filled the tent as Dr. Barza was finally ready to start his internal inspection of the diesel engine.

"*How appropriate, Suite No. 1 for inspection number one. It begins with a beautiful French-style Overture, continues through a cheerful Bouree, a splendid Minuet, and ends with the magnificent Alla Hornpipe.*" David thought, while closing his eyes, and losing himself in the music for a few seconds.

"All right, Tarshon, I'm familiar with the controls for this type of inspection unit. Insert the camera through No. 1, and I'll start recording," Dr. Barza said, while studying the screen on the small hand-held control unit.

"LED lights on . . . I have an image. Lower the camera slowly. Stop every foot unless I tell you to stop sooner," Dr. Barza said.

Fifteen minutes later they had their answer.


.   .   .   .


"So what do you think Dr. Barza? Can you disarm it?" Colonel Douglas asked, while he stood beside Dr. Barza inside Vola's Dockside Grill.

"To be honest . . . I'm not sure. This is a device of Chinese construction. It was probably made in the late 90's. The design is an old Teller-Ulam warhead for an ICBM. It doesn't have a permissive action link to prevent accidental detonation. Based on the size, I'd say it's in the 10-megaton range. I've never worked on a device with a yield like this. All nations quit making these because they're an inefficient use of a missile. Ten one-megaton warheads are far more useful than one 10-megaton warhead. But our real problem is the three safeties installed on the device. I believe that only one is still active. If we lose that, then the boosted fission primary detonates. Milliseconds later the fusion secondary ignites and a small sun appears in Northern Virginia," Dr. Barza said, as he sipped on strong black coffee.

"So where do we go from here?" Tarshon asked.

"It has an external transmitter. There weren't any anti-tampering devices that I could see. We checked various electromagnetic spectrums and found nothing else. I think it's just a device that's old, and was jostled too much while travelling half way around the world. I need one end of the oil reservoir cut out. You can't use a cutting torch. It will have to be a grinder. We can't have sparks flying around inside, so the grinding has to stop a few millimeters short of penetration and then . . ." Dr. Barza was saying.

"Listen, Dr. Barza, let me get Jackson. You tell him exactly what you want. He's the master mechanic. He'll figure out how to do it," Tarshon said.

"Dr. Barza! One other thing, your chef just got here," Colonel Douglas said, as he pointed at an elderly woman walking into the restaurant.

"Michelle Greenbaum, meet Dr. David Barza. He's flown over from Israel to help us with a problem," the Colonel said.

"Dr. Barza, my pleasure," Michelle said, in a heavy New York accent.

"I hope these people haven't talked you into eating non-kosher. I throw up at the thought," Michelle said, as she pumped his hand in a vigorous handshake.

"No, but they were getting close," Dr. Barza said, and couldn't help but smile at the cheerful woman.

"Give us thirty minutes to clean this dump and I'll start cooking. You'll be stuffed in less than an hour. I promise," she said, as she gestured for her crew of four to follow her into the kitchen.

"David, I hear you have some work for me," Jackson said, as he followed the cooks through the restaurant.

"I told you that I wish to be addressed . . ." Dr. Barza began.

"If Kate has you here, you're one of us now. First names only, remember?" Jackson said, as he sat at the bar beside Dr. Barza.

"So what do I need to do?" Jackson asked.

Chapter 55

"We must accept finite disappointment, but never lose infinite hope."

Martin Luther King, Jr.

Port Orchard, Washington, USA
Golden Grill on the Bay
1014 Bay Street
March 25, 2017, 2030 hours PST

"Damn, that was pretty simple once we figured out the trick," Nathan said, as he, Nathan, and Kate walked out into the cool evening air blowing in from the Sinclair Inlet.

"One down, one to go, now we pack up and move up to Bangor," Kate said, while thumbing through her cell's phone list.

"David, how are things going in Alexandria?" Kate said, as David's tired face popped onto her screen.

"Oh, just brilliant . . . your crew almost had me eating barbecue from some damn place . . . North or South Carolina. I don't remember which. The EOD commander has taken pity on me and found a delightful Jewish woman who will cook for me. I don't think that pork is on the menu. So at least I won't starve to death while I'm here," David said.

"That's good. How has the inspection gone? And by the way, thanks, your suggestion about looking closer paid out. We were able to get past the anti-tampering devices and stabilize the nuke," Kate said.

"Well, that's good news. Things are a bit tougher here. This weapon's older, in the 10-megaton range, and two of the three safeties are already off. This is really going to be dicey. I haven't made up my mind yet on how I'm going to approach this one," Dr. Barza said.

"Is it stable enough to move?" Kate asked.

"I don't think so. That was the first thing I considered. I just ran a simulation on NukeMap. If this device goes off the Capitol of the

United States is gone. With the present wind conditions the entire Northeast of the US will be uninhabitable from the fallout and millions will die. If that happens, the United States will incinerate China and the rest of the world will go with it," Dr. Barza said.

"Then remove the transmitter and leave it in place," Kate suggested.

"Leave a 10-megaton Chinese nuclear warhead in place across the river from Washington, DC? Somehow I don't think that's what your government had in mind when they brought me here," David said.

"David, you told me once that sometimes we have to choose between the lesser of two evils. At the time I thought that was trite and condescending, but now I understand the truth. Don't over reach. All you can do is the best you can. Stabilize and isolate the weapon. We can figure out what to do with it later," Kate said.

"Kate, when I stared at that simulation, and the estimated deaths and radiation levels from Baltimore to Portland, Maine, I was devastated. Why did we ever build such things?" David asked, whispering into his phone.

"We used to talk about this while drinking wine and looking at the Mediterranean. Do you still live in that little kibbutz?" Kate asked.

"Yes, and the view is still beautiful, Kate. Please promise that you'll come back there when this is over," David said.

"When this is over, and all the devices planted in the US are gone . . . I'll come and stay with you, David. We'll talk about our lives, and the things that we've seen and done. I promise," Kate said, as the cold air blew in from the bay and made her long for a warm Mediterranean breeze.

Chapter 56

"Any sufficiently advanced technology is indistinguishable
from magic."

Arthur C. Clarke

Papoose Lake, Nevada
Defense Advanced Research Center (DARC)
Hanger 1
March 28, 2017 0300 hours PST

The base of the hill seemed to split open as the camouflaged
hanger doors retracted into the hillside. The rectangular opening, 60
feet long and 20 feet high, emitted no light, only a sense of
anticipation.

The first craft appeared like a beast leaving its lair. Its matt
black surface reflected little light as three thrusters ignited, and lifted
the vehicle silently into the air. It drifted out of the hanger and across
the dry surface of Papoose Lake. A second vehicle appeared at the
opening of Hanger No. 1, following its twin until both triangular craft
hovered side-by-side. When the third craft appeared, and joined the
other two, the hanger doors slid shut. The three craft floated above the
lake bed in a triangular formation, and then drifted upward until they
were above the peak of nearby Papoose Mountain.

.  .  .  .

"I don't believe it. We've got them on video . . . three of them,"
Johnny Barr said, as he and his wife, Celise, lay on Millers Ridge, two
miles west of Papoose Lake.

They had been in their camouflaged pit for over two days.
They had walked in, moving only at night, carrying only water and dry
rations. It was their third foray into the Groom Lake security area. The

first two attempts had resulted in a warning, followed by 30 days in jail for each of them.

"These infrared shielding cloaks are awesome. That's how they got us before, the body heat that we gave off at night. Now we're invisible," Celise said, as she and Johnny shared a fist bump.

"Look, they're still hovering above the mountain. Each one has a glowing ball at the corners of the triangle. That's how they move around. Wait! Now the center is glowing," Johnny said, as the central bulge in each craft began to grow brighter and brighter.

Suddenly, each ship was surrounded by a ball of golden light. As quickly as the golden light had appeared, it disappeared, and so had the three triangular craft.

"Damn! They're gone. I didn't hear a thing, but they're gone. Please tell me you got that," Celise said.

Johnny just turned toward her, lowered the camera, and grinned.

"We're gonna be famous . . . we're gonna be famous," Celise said, while dancing around in a circle.

"Let's review the video!" Johnny said, as he and his wife settled down into the bottom of their observation pit.

They never saw the drone that had been hovering 10 feet behind their concealed position for the last 20 minutes. It drifted away, mission complete, having scrambled the data on the camera's video card.

.    .    .    .

"Dory Leader to Dory Flight, setting AI pilot for destination coordinates 39.905003, 116.3917536 . . . flight altitude 100,000 feet . . . standard combat stealth modes active. Final destination altitude 5000 feet above target. Total flight distance 6178 miles. Estimated flight time 41.18 minutes. Local Chinese Time will be approximately 0920. Transferring data now. Linking AI pilots now. Ladies and gentlemen secure your tray tops in the upright position," Colonel Walt 'Buzzard' Allen said, as the Mercury Plasma Field Engine in his TR-4 'Dory' Fighter-Bomber cycled up to speed.

Lt. Colonel Marsha 'Brady' Bunch and Lt. Colonel Jake 'The Snake' Morris both laughed in reply as they verified receipt of data and interlocking of the AI pilots.

The Aurora program had started as a 'black' CIA program back in the '80s and had never surfaced. Like the B-2 and F117 stealth planes of Gulf War fame, the Tactical/Reconnaissance planes had been born in the Lockheed Skunk Works, and had evolved steadily over the decades since. The TR-4a 'Dory' was the single seat fighter version of the old top secret TR-3 Black Manta.

The 'Dory' didn't have a joy stick. It was directly linked to the pilot's brain. In flight, the pilot and the AI became one organism that controlled the craft. All the pilot had to do was think an action and the AI would perform all actions needed to complete the request.

"Buzzard, I still don't like flying in there with all the offensive systems deactivated. I feel like I'm buck-ass naked," Lt. Colonel Bunch said, from Dory 2.

"They don't have anything that can touch us, Brady, and we're not flying there to start World War III. This is an intimidation flight. Our visible presence, and the message that will be sent by Kraken 1 should be sufficient," Colonel Allen said.

"He's right, Brady. When the Kraken lets loose, they'll shit themselves," Lt. Colonel Morris said, from Dory 3.

"Damn, Buzzard, any chance we could stick around to see the impact?' Lt. Colonel Bunch asked.

"Not unless you've got a rear view mirror on that thing. Our mission is to deliver the message up close and personal, and then leave in an expedited manner. But we'll see how this plays out," Colonel Allen replied.

"If we pop out at full power from ground level, their fillings will fall out," Lt. Colonel Morris said, and smiled, as he heard the others laugh.

The flight of TR-4a's shot straight up from Papoose Lake until they reached an elevation of 90,000 feet. They had reached that altitude in less than 10 seconds.

Chapter 57

"Any soldier worth his salt should be antiwar. And still, there are things worth fighting for."

Norman Schwarzkopf

Beijing, China
The Great Hall of the People
The Great Auditorium
March 28, 2017 0900 hours CT

"Thirty minutes, Comrades, and then the next step in the Great Struggle against the imperialists will end. When America leaves Asia, China will finally be the Center. No ruler, no nation, no empire, has ever ruled all of Asia, not even the Great Khan. My comrades, my friends, we, the People's Republic of China, shall be the first in all of human history," Party General Secretary Li Xi bin said, to the 3000 members of the National People's Congress seated in the Great Auditorium of the Great Hall of the People.

En masse, the assembled members stood in thunderous ovation as they collectively basked in what was promised as the greatest accomplishment in all of Chinese history. They weren't sure what they were applauding, but the General Secretary had the support of the NPC Standing Committee and the Central Military Commission.

They had been shocked to be summoned to an unannounced assembly of the NPC. The 19th Congress had been scheduled to assemble late in the Fall, but the mysterious call to come to Beijing had been delivered less than 24 hours ago. Now they all stood, and applauded at the most wondrous news of their lives. How such an amazing thing was possible, they didn't know. But if the Party Secretary said it was so, then it was so.

His speech continued, and talked of China's wondrous future . .

.

Beijing, China
5000 feet above
The Great Hall of the People
March 28, 2017 0920 hours CT


    Colonel Allen was always amazed at the maneuverability of the MFD powered craft. Fifteen seconds ago he was travelling in excess of 9000 mph. Now he and his wing mates were hovering above the Great Hall of the People in Beijing. There had been no indication that they had been detected as they approached.

    "Verify activation of video countermeasures. Activate 'Live Fly'. Dory 2 and 3 proceed to specified locations," Colonel Allen ordered.

    "Confirmed!" came both answers, as the pilots eased the AI auto-pilot into the background, and took over active control of the craft.

    The southern end of the Great Hall contained an immense open courtyard. It was used for private shows and dinner parties for the Communist Party elite, away from the prying eyes of the citizens of Beijing. At over 200 feet on a side there was more than enough room for Dory 1 to fit inside. Colonel Allen guided the Dory over the upper edge of the building, and allowed the vehicle to settle, until it stopped 50 feet above the stone courtyard. With his cockpit facing the balconies that lined the central portion of the building, he waited until the other two craft were in place.

    Dory 2 slid into position 1000 feet above the Mausoleum of Mao Zedong. Dory 3 hovered at 1000 feet above the north end of Tiananmen Square. The panic on the great courtyard below, at the sudden appearance of the two strange craft, was immediate.

    The hull of the Dory was a layer of aluminum, carbon nanotubes, and diamond. The melting point of the diamond outer skin limited the atmospheric speed of the Dory to 9000 mph. The diamond coating also allowed the hull of the Dory to take on any pattern that was humanly conceivable. The carbon nanotubes were affixed in a lattice of programmable mirrors capable of projecting over 1,000,000 colors. The Dory could visually disappear in almost any environment.

His orders from the President had been specific. Colonel Allen grinned as he told the AI to initiate 'Old Glory'. The matt black surface of the Dory instantly changed into a red, white and blue, fluttering American flag.

"Oh hell no, they won't like that," Colonel Allen said, as he saw personnel running on the various levels of the balcony and pointing at his craft.

Dory 2 and 3 descended until they were both facing each other only 500 feet above Tiananmen Square. Both craft duplicated the coloring of Dory 1.

"Now we wait," Colonel Allen told his wing mates.

. . . .

A single officer marched onto the stage of the Great Hall as the General Secretary's speech continued. He stopped 10 feet away, and snapped to attention, saying nothing. As the speech continued, he stepped three steps closer.

Party General Secretary Li Xibin stopped his speech, turned, and glared at the young PLA Air Force Captain.

"Has the Third World War started, Captain? If so, that is the only thing saving you from a labor camp," the General Secretary said.

"Comrade Chairman . . . the Americans are here . . . in the southern courtyard," the Captain said, the shock in his voice apparent.

"What are you talking about? Have you lost your mind? Get off this stage!" the General Secretary ordered, as he turned back towards the confused audience.

General Ma Wanquan, Commanding General of the PLA Air Force, rose from his seat on the stage, and approached the terrified Captain.

"What is the meaning of this indignity, Captain?" General Ma asked.

"General, an American craft of unknown design is hovering in the courtyard at the south end of the building," the Captain said, while standing rigidly at attention.

"That's impossible! How could they get a helicopter here?" the General asked.

"It's . . . not a helicopter, General. I don't know what it is? And, General Ma, it looks like an American flag. It . . . waves," the Captain said.

The General Secretary stepped away from the podium, and approached the trembling Captain until they were almost touching.

"If this is a lie, I will have you shot," the General Secretary said, as General Ma stepped up beside the young officer.

"What did you see, Captain Wu?" the General asked.

"I was walking by the doors leading onto the fourth level of the balcony when a matt gray triangular plane settled into the courtyard, and just stopped in midair. I opened the door, and ran onto the balcony to see what it was. It just hung there, not moving. There were no rotors, and the only sound was a deep hum . . . I don't know how to describe it, Comrade General.

General Ma looked at the General Secretary before saying, "He is a reliable officer. His father is a Colonel who works on my staff. We need to go see . . . whatever this is, General Secretary," General Ma said, and bowed.

The other five members of the PSC had stood, and were approaching the General Secretary as he turned, and began following the Captain and General off the stage. The audience of elected and appointed officials all began talking at once.

"I will have to see this with my own eyes to believe it," the General Secretary said, as the three men were soon joined by a mix of politicians, armed soldiers, and bureaucrats.

The outside balcony was filled with people, all pointing, snapping pictures, and yelling at the same time.

The General Secretary halted as he reached the doors. He glanced down at his watch. It was 0930, 48 hours after he had talked to the American President.

"*It seems I have his answer, but I still have the leverage. What can one little plane do to all of China? He plays poker, so I will call his bluff,*" General Secretary Li thought, then jerked open the door to the balcony.

"Get all of these people off these balconies . . . now!' he yelled, as soldiers began herding people back through the doors.

After all the balconies had been emptied, Party General Secretary Li Xibin, ruler of the People's Republic of China, tightened his tie, and smoothed his suit before stepping out onto the balcony. He stepped up to the stone railing, calmly folded his hands, and placed them on the railing.

"You are trespassing in the air space of the People's Republic of China. I am ordering that you leave now, or I will have you shot out of the sky," Li said, and waited.

The vessel did not move.

General Ma entered the balcony, stepped up beside the General Secretary and said, "There are two more identical craft hovering above Tiananmen Square."

"General Ma, what are these things?" Li asked.

"They are just a rumor. We have no real intelligence information on these craft. The internet has been filled with bad photos and unsubstantiated details for decades. They may be anti-gravity craft. The Germans were reported to have been working on this technology back in the 40's. It seems that the Americans may have perfected the technology," General Ma replied.

"What can it do? How powerful is it?" Li asked.

"Comrade General Secretary . . . this is reported to be alien technology. We are flying biplanes in comparison. If they have been developing this technology in secret for decades there is no telling how advanced these craft have become. It is probable that they are flight capable outside the Earth's atmosphere. I have no idea what weapon systems they may have developed for these . . . marvelous craft," General Ma said, the awe, mixed with envy, obvious in his voice.

"You sound as if you are ready to surrender, Comrade General. Please tell me that I am mistaken. Otherwise it seems that the PLA Air Force is in need of another commander," Li said, while glancing at the fluttering American flag so brazenly on display in front of him.

Li jumped, as his cell phone rang, and began playing the American National Anthem. He jerked the phone out of his coat pocket, and was going to throw it at the American craft, when he noticed the face of the American President on his phone.

He stared at the picture, and then accepted the call.

"Mr. President, it seems that one of your aircraft has become . . . lost. It would be unfortunate if such a . . . theatrical vehicle . . . was lost to you," General Secretary Li said, in as calm, and sarcastic a voice as he could muster.

"Mr. Chairman, it is highly unlikely that you could put a scratch on that vehicle. I like to think of it as a business card, an introduction if you will. You have been operating under a misconception. You Chinese are fond of quoting Sun Tzu. Americans are also fond of quoting great leaders from our past. Ben Franklin is one of my favorites. He once said, 'Tricks and treachery are the practice of fools that don't have enough brains to be honest.' Have your people monitor the areas within your country at the following coordinates," the President said, as four sets of coordinates were transferred to the General Secretary's cell phone.

.  .  .  .

"Well Colonel, it's about time for Archie to unleash the Kraken," Lt. Colonel Bunch said.

"Brady, Snake, go vertical to 50000. Stay on station, but transmit what you see to me, understood?" Colonel Allen said.

"Snake . . . we go vertical to 50K on 3 . . . 2 . . . 1 . . . punch it," Lt. Colonel Bunch said, as both Dory 2 and 3 lit up, and disappeared from their waiting areas above Tiananmen Square.

.  .  .  .

The SB-7 Kraken stood in geosynchronous low earth orbit, 100 miles above the Peoples Republic of China. Despite its massive size, 600 feet on a side, the SB-7 was invisible to all known detection devices. Even the light from stars, blocked by the craft, was visible due to the image projected on the craft's outer hull. Like the Dory, it was capable of disappearing in any environment.

"Colonel Crowley, permission to proceed has been received and verified. Coordinates have been verified. Mass Drivers 1, 2, 3 and 4 are loaded, charged, and target coordinates verified," Captain Barstom, weapons officer on the Kraken said.

"Commence firing sequence, Captain Barstom. I hope they get the message," Colonel Crowley said, while sitting back in his chair, and studying the weapon monitors.

*"I'm in command of the most advanced spacecraft ever built. The places we've gone . . . the things we've seen that the public doesn't know anything about. Sometimes I feel like an alien living on another planet. Now we're getting ready to launch ceramic coated steel rods with a mass of over 10000 kg at another country. Well, the Chinese wanted to play hardball. Let's see if they know what a brushback pitch is,"* Colonel Crowley thought, as he felt his massive vessel shudder as the first magnetic railgun fired.

At 60,000 miles per hour, the impactor looked like a bolt of lightning as it reached the surface of Lower Mongolia in less than six seconds. It was coated in multiple layers of the same diamond impregnated graphite nanotubes as the outer hulls of the Dory and the Kraken. The coating lasted for 5.95 seconds.

.    .    .    .

"Buzzard, I'm relaying video of the Kraken strike," Lt. Colonel Bunch said, as Dory 2 and Dory 3 hovered 50,000 feet above Beijing.

Colonel Allen smiled as four bolts of lightning seared through the atmosphere, one after the other.

"Damn, so that's what a kinetic strike from space looks like. I wonder what that looks like from the ground?" Colonel Allen said, as he glanced up at the man standing on the balcony in front of him.

"I hope you make the right call, Party Secretary," Colonel Allen said, as he slowly pulled Dory 1 out of the courtyard, and then shot straight up to 50,000 feet.

"Dory 2, Dory 3, form up on me. We're going home," Colonel Allen said.

"Roger that, Buzzard!" came the reply, as both craft appeared on either side.

.    .    .    .

Mandakh, Mongolia
10 kilometers northwest of Impact No. 1
March 28, 2017, 0932 CT

The Naadam festival was in less than four months, and Jurgakhan knew that his horse, Sanale, needed more training. The morning climb over the hills south of Mandakh had started at sunrise. It was a cold, clear day, and Jurgakhan paused at the peak of the highest ridge to allow Sanale to rest. The high desert to the south opened up below him. He had never seen the ocean, but imagined it must look like this only wet.

When the lightning came from the open sky, and struck the desert 5 miles from where he sat, he could only stare in disbelief. Jurgakhan struggled to control Sanale as the ground trembled, and bright fire erupted from the sand. A few seconds later, the sound of the detonation slapped him, and Sanale threw him from her back. She screamed as horses do, and fled away from the horror.

Jurgakhan rose to his feet as his heart pounded in his chest. He gaped as the growing cloud, shaped like a blossoming flower, rose into the sky. He wondered if some god from Mongolia's ancient past had come back to the land to punish his people.

Chapter 58

"Now, when your weapons are dulled, your ardor damped, your strength exhausted and your treasure spent, then no man, however wise, will be able to avert the consequences that must ensue."

Sun Tzu (~520 BC)

Beijing, China
Central Military Commission Headquarters
August 1st Building
March 28, 2017, 1830 hours CT

The 16 men that formed the power base of the People's Republic of China sat at a long rectangular table deep below the August 1st Building, headquarters of the Central Military Commission. Ten senior officers sat opposite five politicians. Each group talked quietly amongst themselves. Party General Secretary Li Xibin, the man to whom all had sworn their allegiance, sat at the head of the table.

"General Fan, what is the latest information?" General Secretary Li asked, the Vice-Chairman of the CMC.

"As you know, after the three American craft departed the Great Hall, we attempted to follow them to exact our revenge, but were unable to keep up with them. Our radar never saw them, and our fighter interceptors never had any visual contact after they left. At the same time, there were reports of seismic events in Mongolia and Inner Mongolia. General Ma has further information," General Fan said.

"Comrades, we have received scattered reports of explosions in the area of the Gobi desert. Also, there were reports of bolts of lightning coming from a clear sky and . . . mushroom shaped clouds. Aircraft and search teams were dispatched to verify the reports. We also used the Yaogan-4 satellite to obtain a visual analysis of the area from orbit," General Ma said.

"General Ma, has the PLA Air Force confirmed whether or not these were nuclear explosions?" General Secretary Li asked.

"Comrade Secretary, four huge plumes were detected stretching from southeast Mongolia into Lower Mongolia. There was no indication of any radioactive material in the plumes. Upon further investigation, aircraft found four huge craters that were spaced precisely 16 kilometers apart. If you would please observe the screen on the wall at the far end of the table, I will display an image obtained from Yaogan-4. The image is somewhat blurred due to the amount of dust remaining in the atmosphere above the impact areas. As you can see, the craters are in a straight line from northwest to southeast," General Ma said.

"What is the size of the craters, Comrade General? And if the explosions were not nuclear, what made the craters?" General Secretary Li asked.

The craters were immense, almost 300 meters in diameter and 70 meters deep. A nuclear detonation at ground level would have to be in the 300 to 500 kiloton range to produce such a crater," General Ma said.

"Comrades, General Ma and I have discussed the likely cause of these craters at length, outside this room. We have come to the conclusion that the Americans have developed some type of orbiting platform capable of launching kinetic weapons from space. There have been rumors and stories about such a weapons system for decades. Their science fiction writers even named such a weapon system. They called it 'Thor', after the Norse god of war," said General Wei Yaoyan, Commander of the PLA Rocket Force.

"Comrades, American children have a game called 'Connect-the-Dots'. When you draw a line from dot to dot it makes a picture. Am I the only one that sees that when you connect these four dots, as shown on the satellite image, that the line points directly at Beijing?" asked Yu Yunshan, No. 4 in the Politburo Standing Committee.

"Comrades, four craters that point at Beijing, at the heart of our nation, possibly launched from a weapon system that we didn't know existed. Combine that with the audacious invasion of our air space by three American craft of another unknown design. General Secretary, you confronted the American president, with the support of all of us, I will admit, but I think that you and General Kung have, as the old saying goes, 'tried to strike a stone with an egg'. By doing so you have weakened our position in the world at a time when more patience would have allowed us to grow stronger. Comrade, time was on our side. We no longer have that benefit," Guo Quishan, No. 2 in the PSC said.

"Then we may have to initiate the plan to release the information about the devices on America's soil. We still have the better hand in this game," General Secretary Li said, feeling nervous as he felt his position of dominance over these men begin to weaken.

"Gentlemen, you politicians seem to be missing the point. The Americans have demonstrated that they have the high ground and the will to use it. They may well be able to destroy us without using nuclear weapons, and without setting foot on our soil. Your plan may wreck their economy, and much of the world's, but we won't be around to see it. They will not target our population centers. They will target out military capability. The People's Liberation Army, and Navy, and Air Force, will all cease to exist. Without the military to maintain order, the People's Republic of China . . . will cease to exist. That is a gamble we should not take. Comrade General Secretary, with all due respect, we need to vote on this, and see where everyone stands," General Ma said.

The vote was far from unanimous, but in the end, 12 voted to pull back from General Kung's plan. Of the four that still supported General Kung, two were politicians, and two were military. One was General Fen, General Kung's uncle. He notified his nephew by phone, and Kung's reaction was immediate.

# Chapter 59

"For it is precisely when a man has fallen into harm's way, that he is capable of striking a blow for victory."

Sun Tzu (~520 BC)

Beijing, China
22 Base Headquarters
100 meters below the Beijing Botanical Gardens
March 28, 2017, 2000 hours CT

Lieutenant General Kung sat in his office behind Douglas MacArthur's old desk. He had been staring at his cell phone in absolute shock for several minutes when Colonel Peng knocked on his door and entered.

"I beg your pardon General, but it is my last day, and I wished to say goodbye," Colonel Peng said, while snapping to attention and saluting.

Kung said nothing, still staring at his cell phone, and then said, "They have betrayed me, Peng. I have handed them everything, the entire world. All they had to do was start a rumor, but they became terrified by the American show of power."

Kung pushed away from the desk and stood up.

"Every one of them should be shot for cowardice and treason," Kung yelled, as he opened a drawer, pulled a gun case out, and laid it on his desk.

He open the case and removed one of the ivory handled Colt .45 revolvers.

"This is one of Patton's sets. He was a man who wasn't afraid to act. Even the American's were afraid of him. Did you know that they had him killed right after the war? Then they disgraced MacArthur a few years later, lucky for us. Our supposed leaders are no different. Now they are betraying me!" Kung said, as he began waving the loaded .45 revolver in the air.

"General, please, if the General Secretary has made his decision then we are duty bound to obey," Colonel Peng said, while shutting the door behind him.

"If they told you to march a division off a cliff would you do it? Don't be an idiot. Men at our level of responsibility are trained to think, not simply obey," Kung yelled, while walking over to a stylized portrait of Sun Tzu that hung on the wall opposite Kung's Andy Warhol portrait of Mao Zedong.

Kung swung back the portrait of Sun Tzu, and revealed a control panel locked behind bulletproof glass. After entering a code into a small panel built into the glass, he flipped out a small handle, and pulled the glass aside.

Kung stood before the panel and the power it possessed. The panel was black until Kung entered a four digit code into a small device built into the base. The panel lit up revealing five rows of square buttons. The buttons were numbered 1-50. Kung didn't notice as Colonel Peng walked behind him, and approached the general's desk.

"This . . . is power, Peng . . . the power of life and death. When I begin pushing these buttons a countdown will begin. Three minutes later . . . the world will change forever," Kung said, as he reached for button number 2.

"General Kung, please lower your hand and turn around. I can't allow you to destroy us all," Colonel Peng said, as he pointed the second of Patton's revolvers at Kung's back.

"Peng, Peng, Peng . . . once again you disappoint me. First, you went against my orders, and tried to save your nephew. Then, I allow you to live, and retire in honor with all your benefits, and this is how you repay me," Kung said, while lowering his left hand and slowly turning around.

"General, please drop the pistol . . . please, I beg you," Peng said, as Kung began to slowly raise the revolver in Peng's direction.

"You will have to shoot me, Peng. I don't think you are . . ." Kung began.

The shot rang out and struck General Kung in the right arm. His pistol went flying, as the impact of the bullet spun him around. As he fell towards the floor he reached out with his left hand, and pressed one of the buttons . . . No. 50.

## Chapter 60

"The courage of life is often a less dramatic spectacle than the courage of a final moment; but it is no less a magnificent mixture of triumph and tragedy."

John F. Kennedy

Alexandria, Virginia, USA
The Torpedo Factory Art Center
105 North Union Street
The Diesel Engine
March 28, 2017, 0758 hours EST

"I'm glad you flew here, Kate. This one is tricky, and I need someone to bounce ideas off," David said, while sipping a mug of hot tea.

"We just finished disarming our third device on the West Coast in the last 48 hours. Luckily, it was identical to the second one. We had it finished in less than eight hours. I got five hours sleep on the plane, otherwise I'd be drooling," Kate said, as she blew on her mug of coffee.

The two greatest nuclear weapon disarming experts in the western world stood side by side on scaffolding erected below the diesel engine containing the 10-megaton thermonuclear warhead.

"You look good, David. I'm so sorry about the Parkinson's. You should have called," Kate said, while glancing in David's direction.

"And said what? We haven't talked in . . . almost 10 years. I don't want anyone's pity, certainly not from you," David replied, instantly regretting how that sounded.

"Kate, I didn't mean it that way. I've always been a little abrupt with people, but now . . ." David began.

"David, you are what you are. I didn't walk away because of that. I walked away because I wanted my freedom. To you, I would have always been your grad student. I had to get out from under that. Leaving you was the best professional decision that I ever made . . . but it also left me empty and alone. We used to have a mental link, a connection that made me feel . . . I don't know how to describe it," Kate said, while trying not to stare at his shaking hand.

"Complete is the word you're searching for. Complete! It sounds so old fashioned, so 20th century doesn't it. I've thought about you every single day for the last 10 years. I tried to hate you for a while, but it never lasted. You just became a dull ache that never went away. Then my friend 'Parky' came along, and I had something else to focus on. That's what I call my disease. It's my way of trivializing the thing that's going to destroy me," David said, as he rested the cup on top of a scaffold rail to keep it from shaking.

"So where do we stand . . . with the device?" Kate asked, desperate to change the subject.

"Well . . . 'Bubba', took his sweet time removing the end of the oil pan, but at least we have access to the device. Unfortunately, the way it's oriented, all the instrumentation is at the other end. It's tight but you can squeeze past all the supports to get there from here," David said, grateful that Kate had moved on to the real purpose for her being in Virginia.

Kate took her flashlight, and began studying the device from the opening in the oil pan. She had to bend over, and insert her torso to get a good look.

"First thing we need to do is disconnect the transmitter. I don't think that the Chinese are in any hurry to blow up DC, but I'd feel more comfortable if that thing was inert," Kate said, her voice echoed, while focusing her light on the transmitter mounted on the side of the warhead.

"That was always the first thing I removed on the other two devices. This warhead is bigger, but the configuration of the electronics looks the same. These things were probably constructed by the same people in China at about the same time," Kate said, as she pulled herself back out of the oil pan.

"Good, that simplifies things. How long did it take to remove the transmitter?" David asked.

"About an hour, more or less," Kate said, but then turned back toward the device when she heard an audible click.

"Oh, God . . . the transmitter just went active," Kate said, as she scrambled back into the oil pan.

David heard cursing, as she pulled herself back out.

"David . . . three minutes. It's going to detonate in less than three minutes. It's counting down," Kate said, as she fought back the waves of adrenalin fueled panic that were rushing through her.

Instinctively, she wanted to turn and run as fast as she could, for as long as she could, but she knew that was pointless.

"Kate, what do you need to disconnect the transmitter? If we stop the signal then it won't tell the weapon to detonate," David said, as he grabbed Kate's shoulders with both hands and shook her.

"It's bolted to the housing . . . four bolts. I need a nut driver set, metric not Imperial. I can't just stop the signal. That would cause detonation. Then I have to bypass the signal from the wiring leading to the conventional high explosives that trigger the fission device," Kate said, while taking several deep breaths to calm down.

Then she jumped back into the oil pan.

"Everything's here, Kate. Tarshon and Shalonda have already staged their tools for the work," David said, while dragging two heavy tool boxes over to the opening.

"Two minutes and 45 seconds," Kate said, as she jumped back out and grabbed a battery powered nut driver and two sockets.

"Hand me everything I ask for," Kate said, as she went back in.

"I need more light!" Kate yelled, while test fitting the two socket heads that she had brought with her.

"Good, 10mm," she said, while carefully snapping the 10mm socket onto the nut driver.

"*2:30*"

The area inside the oil pan lit up as David dragged over a tripod mounted light set and turned it on.

"Come on Kate, you can do this," she told herself, as she began spinning off the four bolts that held the transmitter to the weapon housing.

"*2:15*"

David opened up both tool boxes, and removed the trays to give him instant access to anything Kate needed.

"How are you going to bypass the signal?" David asked.

"I don't know. I'm thinking while I work," Kate said, as the first bolt spun out and fell to the bottom of the oil pan.

"*2:00*"

"How much time?" David asked.

"Shut up and let me work. If we run out of time you'll never know it," Kate said, as the second bolt fell into the oil pan.

"*1:46*"

David looked down at his hands. They had stopped shaking. He heard the third bolt rattle into the oil pan.

"One left!"

"*1:35*"

"*Why now . . . is it the adrenalin or is Parky running away?*" David asked himself, and smiled at the stupidity of the question.

"I need a small Philips head screwdriver . . . real small," Kate said, as she dropped the fourth bolt, flipped the transmitter over, and stared at the four small screws that held the back plate on.

David grabbed a set of instrumentation Phillips screw drivers in a plastic case, and slapped it into Kate's waiting hand.

"Perfect," Kate said, as she lifted the smallest screwdriver out of the case.

"1-2-3-4-5," Kate said, as she spun each screw out of the plate.

"*1:12*"

"I need a short jumper wire with alligator clips," she said, as she dropped the plate into the oil pan.

"*1:00*"

"Dammit, David, hurry!"

"*0:45*"

David ran over to a third tool box and flipped open the lid.

"Oh, thank God!"

Kate's hand was sticking out of the opening, and snatched the jumper when he laid it into her hand.

"*0:30*"

Kate attached one of the clips to the lead going from the transmitter to the inside of the warhead. She jammed the other alligator clip into one of the bolt holes that had held the transmitter in place on the housing.

"*0:10*"

"Bypassed, now I have to cut the wire . . . David! Cutters!" she said, and felt a pair of wire cutters lay in her palm.

"*0:05*"

She cut the wire, and watched the timer count down, and held her breath.

*"0:04"*

*"0:03"*

*"0:02"*

*"0:01"*

*"0:00"*

She heard an audible click and winced. The timer stayed at 0:00. She stared at the red numbers, praying that they wouldn't disappear in a flash of searing light.

Kate took a deep breath, shuddered, and looked at the work she had done, afraid to move least she disturb something.

"Kate, we're not dead!" David yelled.

"David, this is still delicate. I bypassed the signal to the explosives, but is it a constant signal or just on single transmission? I can't remember," Kate said, as tears began to stream from her eyes.

"It's a single transmission, grad student! Don't you know anything?" David laughed, as Kate slowly backed out of the oil pan feet first.

David grabbed her legs, and pulled her to her feet. They just stood there staring into each other's eyes. Both were sobbing and shaking with relief.

"As the Brit's would say, 'that was bloody brilliant!'" David said, as he gently kissed her.

"I think I'm going to throw up," Kate said, as she staggered away, and leaned over the handrail on the scaffolding.

"The kiss couldn't have been that bad," David said, as Kate waved him away, as she began to get sick.

# Epilogue

"I am in politics because of the conflict between good and evil, and I believe that in the end good will triumph."

Margaret Thatcher

Beijing, China
Central Military Commission Headquarters
August 1st Building
The Courtyard
March 31, 2017, 0759 hours CT

Lieutenant General Kung Yusheng stood with his back against a stone wall on one end of the courtyard behind the CMC Headquarters. He still wore the same uniform pants that he had been wearing two days previously. His right arm was in a sling. They had patched up his wound, but hadn't bothered with pain killers.

"Another beautiful day . . . I will miss my walks in the garden," Kung said, as he watched an officer and 10 soldiers march in, halt, and turn to face him.

With his left hand he reached into his pants pocket, removed his Babe Ruth pocket watch, and flipped open the cover.

"After all these years, it still keeps perfect time . . . 0800," Kung said, as he saw the second hand reach 12.

Kung Yusheng felt nothing as 10 bullets tore into his chest, and ended his life.

.  .  .  .

Beijing, China
The hills above the Xiangshan Residential District
Residence of Colonel Peng
March 31, 2017, 0800 CT

Colonel Peng Zihao sat on his back porch and sipped his tea. He knew that PLA security forces would be coming for him soon. Despite his actions in stopping General Kung from starting a war with the Americans, he was still complicit in the general's plot. He knew from experience where this story would end.

"*It will be a beautiful Spring*," he thought, while breathing in the heady pine scent of the forest that surrounded his home.

Setting the tea cup aside, he stood and removed the Type 77 pistol from the holster at his waist. He was in full dress uniform, and glanced down at all the medals that hung from his chest.

The last sounds he heard were the morning songs of Chinese Bulbul, come to eat the seed from his feeders.

.   .   .   .

San Francisco, California, USA
Fire Station 31
April 1, 2017, 0730 hours PST

"I didn't think lawyers got up this early. I thought you were like vampires, shunning the daylight," Tom said, as he and Lihwa walked down 12th Avenue away from Fire Station 31.

"You're the one who was up all night on shift. Did you get any calls?" Lihwa said.

"Yeah, it was pretty exciting. We had a dumpster fire over behind the Thai Time Restaurant on 8th Avenue. No nukes around though, just some kid causing trouble," Tom said, as he slid his hand into Lihwa's.

"You up for breakfast?" Lihwa asked.

"Am I still breathing?"

"The usual?"

"The Saturday Special is buy one, get one omelets, and they make huge omelets," Tom said, as he emphasized huge with his right hand, but didn't let go of Lihwa's hand with his left.

"Then IHOP it is," Lihwa said, as they reached Tom's old Camaro.

. . . .

Alexandria, Virginia, USA
Inova Alexandria Hospital
Room 1001
April 10, 2017, 1145 hours EST


Aiguo awoke and stared up at the white ceiling tiles filled with little holes. He tried to move his limbs, but found that all four were tightly secured. His body ached, and it hurt to breathe, but it dawned on him that at least he was still alive. He smiled, and then heard a tapping sound to his right.

He jumped when he saw the face staring through the glass window. It was the last face that he thought he would ever see, as he was laying on the floor in the restaurant.

Anthony stared through the glass, as his wife's killer awoke. He came to the hospital every day hoping that he would be there when the man awoke. He could see that the man named Aiguo could see him.

"Listen friend, don't cause any trouble. Our orders are to leave you alone unless you try to get at this guy. The Feds want him alive, and we plan on keeping him that way," the policeman said, while gesturing at his partner.

"Don't worry about me, Officer. I want him alive. As soon as the Feds are through with him, we have some unfinished business," Anthony said, as he smiled, and nodded at Aiguo.

Aiguo nodded back, took a deep breath, and fell back to sleep.

. . . .

Raleigh, North Carolina, USA
106 East Whitaker Mill Road
August2, 2017, 2330 hours EST

"Daddy, I still can't believe you sold the farm and moved into the city," Amanda said, as she sat on the front porch of her father's new home in Raleigh.

She and her father sat on the porch swing. The sun had set hours ago. The stifling heat and humidity of the day had finally departed.

"Well, your brothers had no interest in farming, and you certainly weren't moving back in, so your mother and I decided it was time for a change. I'll admit it was getting to be too much. We're both getting too old for that much work. The only problem is she still feeds me like I was still working from sun up to sun down. I've already put on 10 pounds, and now I can smell fresh apple pie," Will said, as he began sniffing the cool, fall air.

"I do love the house," Amanda said, as she ignored her cell phone buzzing in her back pocket.

"We got an offer we couldn't refuse for the farm. You know, developers are always looking to expand. The county population has more than tripled since 1970, and it doesn't look like it's going to slowdown anytime soon," Will said, as Amanda's phone buzzed again.

"You going to answer that thing?" Will asked.

"I'll check it in a while, Daddy. What do you know about the house?" Amanda asked.

"Evidently it used to belong to a printer, if you can believe that. There's a nice basement, and I've already started moving some of my woodworking equipment down there. By Thanksgiving I'll be making toys for your kids," Will said, as Amanda's phone buzzed for the third time.

"Daddy . . . I don't have any children," Amanda said, wondering if her father's mind was starting to get old along with the rest of him.

"Exactly! Work's important, but you need someone to help you through the hard times, and I'm not talking about a dog. Girl, somebody's trying to get hold of you real bad. You might as well answer that thing," Will said.

Amanda sighed as she removed her work phone from her back pocket and opened it up.

"Crap, it's my boss," Amanda said.

"Watch your language, child. Your momma still knows how to use a switch," Will said, and laughed as he remembered how his wife would tie a switch to her apron as a warning when the kids were misbehaving.

"Yes, Ms. Davidson," Amanda said, as she accepted the call.

"Agent Langford, the CIA gives you a cell phone for a reason, and it's not so you can ignore calls. Am I understood?" Director Janet Davidson said.

"Yes ma'am . . . Ms. Davidson, what can I do for you?" Amanda asked, as her father chuckled.

"Go turn on the TV and find out what's happening. Where are you, out in the woods, or in the middle of a field picking berries?" Janet asked.

"Yes, Ms. Davidson, checking right now," Amanda said, while running into the house.

"Amanda, if something is going on around here, it will be on WRAL. Put it on Channel 3. Selma, you better come in here. Something is going on," Will said, as Amanda picked up the remote.

"There, it's on WRAL," Amanda said, as she sat down between her parents on the sofa.

.   .   .   .

"This is Gilbert Baez with Breaking News. I'm broadcasting live from the intersection of New Hill Holloman Road and SR 1135. This is as close as the Highway Patrol will let anyone get to the Shearon Harris Nuclear Power Plant. We have it from numerous reliable sources, including from a worker located inside the plant, that the nuclear plant has been taken over by suspected terrorists. You can hear the sound of sirens as first responders of all types are converging on the area around the plant. I have been told that there are no indications of a radioactive release at this time. No evacuation sirens have been sounded, but police are going door to door in this sparsely populated area of the county, and are requesting that people leave the area immediately. We will be staying live with this story for the foreseeable future. This is Gilbert Baez, WRAL Breaking News."

.   .   .   .

"Holy crap!" Amanda said, as she jumped off the sofa.

"Young lady, I did not raise you to use such language," Selma said, as Amanda ran outside to the porch.

"Director, this looks bad. What do you want me to do?" Amanda asked, while pacing on the porch.

"The State of North Carolina will be activating their EOC in downtown Raleigh. Get down there and find out what they know. I'm sending a team down there, but I need information right now. Stay in touch and answer your damn phone," Janet said, and hung up.

"Momma, Daddy . . . I have to go. You two need to pack some bags and get ready to leave the area. Harris is the biggest nuclear waste repository in the Southeast. They've been storing spent fuel there from four different plants for decades. This could get really bad," Amanda said, as she ran inside, grabbed her backpack, car keys, and ran out the door.


# THE END

To be continued in 'HARRIS'

Made in the USA
Middletown, DE
11 June 2018